e. marie robertson

nothing larger
than these
stars

iona duology, book 1

NEW MOON MEDIA

design ✦ publishing ✦ promotion

For my wonderful husband John, who is always exactly what I need and doesn't mind me spending all this time in outer space with people who don't exist.

and the back door opens onto a porch or patio of some kind. In the distance, I can see another collection of sand-colored buildings squatting at the base of the ridge.

I'm barely in the door when a cheerful voice calls out, "You must be Faith. Welcome to Iona!"

The owner of the voice is about my age, mid-twenties, with pepper-dark skin and a kind expression. "I'm Wenda," she says, leaving her terminal and coming forward. I have a horrifying moment of realization that I'm about to be hugged. I try not to be too stiff when she wraps her arms around me; apparently sensitive to my discomfort, she makes it a brief squeeze instead of a full body embrace and pats my arm approvingly.

"We got your data," she says. "Fanny's running up your stat chip row."

"That I am," says a gravelly voice from the other side of the room, and for the first time I notice the hefty forty-something woman behind the second terminal. A holo display floats in front of her, casting a sparkling green reflection across her short fuchsia hair and pale face. She's scrolling through the results with one hand and occasionally taking a pull off a silver flask held tight in the other. "General maintenance and repair, are you? That'll make Pauly a happy man indeed."

"Uh, yes," I say. "Who's Pauly?"

"He's our general coordinator and a gigantic asshole," the woman replies, not taking her eyes off the display.

"Fanny!" Wenda admonishes playfully.

"WHO'S AN ASSHOLE?" The loudest speaking voice I've ever heard booms out of the side room. A few seconds later, a short, wide man with buzz-cut hair and an enormous smile fills the doorway.

"You are, Pauly," Fanny says without missing a beat.

Pauly beams at her and is on the verge of a reply when he notices me.

"YOU'RE THE NEW RESIDENT!" he shouts, striding forward. "It's a PLEASURE to MEET you. What's your NAME?"

"Faith," I say. "Faith Feathergrass."

"I'm Pauly MacFarland. Have you met everyone?" he asks, reducing the volume of his voice to a few decibels below air traffic as he comes closer. "I see you're acquainted with Wenda, since she's still latched onto you. The drunk in the corner is my sister Fanny."

Wenda self-consciously drops her hand from my arm, where it had remained since my sort-of hug. Fanny sticks out her tongue at Pauly and pulls a face that suddenly makes the family resemblance obvious. I laugh despite myself.

"Be fair. I'm not drunk *yet*," Fanny clarifies. She takes another swig from the flask, then holds it out in my direction. "Here, have some 'welcome' hooch. We don't throw parties for new arrivals or any kind of crap like that, so this is gonna be it for celebrations."

I'm a breath away from declining. All the weird compulsions and terrors I've felt every moment since the accident are still hovering in the back of my mind. I don't know these people yet, much less trust them. But if I really want to fly under the radar, I should at least try to fit in.

One little gesture. I can do this. And hell, maybe it will help calm me down a little.

I take a quick look at Pauly and Wenda, then cross to Fanny's terminal, take the flask, and throw back a mouthful of the burning, stinging alcohol. It's like being punched in the throat. I finally recover from the resulting coughing fit and wipe away the tears occluding my vision to find all three of them grinning at me. Fanny in particular looks delighted.

"Looks like we got a natural," she rasps, reclaiming her flask. "Wenda will take you on a tour and show you to your pod. And dear gods of light, make sure to stop by General Supply and pick up some normal clothes so you don't look quite so much like a space tourist."

"Come on," Wenda says, tugging at the sleeve of my slick brown Company-issued jacket. "Let's get you settled."

After a run through General Supply for more Iona-appropriate clothing and other basics, Wenda gives me what passes for the grand tour. It takes less than ten minutes for her to point out Clinical Aid, Security, the Machining Shop, and Storage. Finally, she shows me the fancy structure I noticed from the landing pads.

"This is the Preservation Theater," she says in a credible official tour guide voice. "It was the first building constructed on Iona, almost fifty years ago. It originally held residences and important services for the team that founded this community. It's been repurposed and is now the center of recreation and learning on Iona. Any time there's an all-hands meeting, it will be in the theater's main auditorium."

"It's beautiful." I run my hand over an elaborate carving on the door. "Where did the wood come from? Clearly not here."

Wenda laughs. "Definitely not here. Each of the founders contributed a bit from their worlds of origin, so as to represent everyone. They knew there weren't really any raw materials here, and they wanted to make a statement—maybe about doing the impossible with teamwork, or something like that. But only the decorative carving above the archways and inside is organic wood. Most of the building was 3D-printed after they got here. The material holds up to the elements a bit better than the real thing."

I'm finally ready to ask the question I really want answered.

"So there's no Company money supporting Iona?"

Wenda shrugs.

"It depends on what you mean by 'Company money'. They're customers, like every other Enterprise that sends mining and supply ships out this way. There are only a couple of service planets in this sector, so if you need something out here, Iona's where you have to land no matter who sponsors the mission. But if you're asking if the Company owns any of what you see here, or directly pays for any of our citizens' support or has anybody here on their payroll, the answer is no."

You need to go somewhere the Company doesn't own everything you see. I hear my friend Von's voice in my head, the night I decided to leave. It feels so distant, yet that was less than two months ago. The accident itself was almost two years ago, and somehow feels like it happened yesterday.

My spatial awareness quivers as memories threaten to swallow me. I physically shake myself to bring myself fully back to the present.

"Are you okay?" Wenda asks. I've already figured out that she notices everything. I won't be able to keep this from her for long.

"Yeah, just a headache. Too much activity, not enough food. And even one swallow of that hooch was brutal." I attempt a wan smile in her direction.

"Understandable," she says, although I can't tell if she believes me or not. "A snack and a nap are in order. Let's get you to your new home. You're assigned to Charis' residential pod. That's my pod too; in fact, it looks like Fanny made us roommates. You must have impressed her."

She pauses. "I hope that's okay."

She looks genuinely worried that I might object. Am I already off on a bad foot with these people?

I make a concerted effort to smile and look ... well, normal.

"That's absolutely okay," I say. "Let's go. Food and a nap sound good."

The first flashback happens a week later.

Wenda asks the simple question of what it was like to grow up on Home World, and I suddenly go from sitting comfortably in my hammock with a mug of tea in my hands to sprawled on the floor sobbing and gasping and unable to breathe. In that smallest of moments, I hear the roar of the transpo bearing down on me and Arden, feel the impact shake my bones, then topple as the world swings out from under me. I relive the terror and trauma of coming to in Clinical Aid without any sign of him, the agony of months of rehab, and the gut-wrenching shock of walking into our home after my long convalescence and finding literally no sign of him, as though our two years together hadn't even happened. The rage and hurt and confusion I so successfully shoved to the deepest part of my consciousness explode to the surface like an erupting geyser.

I hear myself, far outside myself, cry out "I can't do this!" I feel Wenda near me but carefully not touching me, attempting to soothe me with her voice and her presence. Slowly, I come back to where I am: on Iona, in my pod, on the floor covered in tea. I've crab-walked across our small room and have huddled against the wall, my arms crossed in front of my face in a defensive posture. My worried roommate hovers a few feet away. She's on the floor with me, holding her hands out to me and chanting "you're here, you're here" over and over, as if trying to bring me back to reality through sheer force of will.

"I'm okay," I lie, struggling to control my shivering body. Wenda, who still looks a little traumatized, helps me stand and get back into the hammock.

"I think we should take you to Clinical Aid," she says. My back stiffens and a rush of cold comes over my body. I clench my hands together in my lap, hoping Wenda can't see how much they're shaking.

"No, I ... I don't need that. I just need a minute. I'm fine."

Wenda studies me, her expression shifting from concerned to adamant. "You are not fine. You have two choices. You can come with me to Clinical Aid, or you can tell me the whole story. And really, you only have one choice, because after you tell me the story, I'm taking you to Clinical Aid anyway."

I was so determined not to let anyone here into my past. But Wenda's my roommate and could one day become a friend. At least one person on Iona should know what they've gotten into by letting me come here.

I take a deep breath.

"I used to work for the Company," I say, "but then they tried to kill me."

7

Want to stay connected?

USE THIS QR CODE for all my links in one place: website, newsletter subscription, FREE Patreon, social media, ongoing promos, events and more!

*Find clickable links to all
my socials in one place!*

tomorrow. The Company will likely be glad to have a scapegoat for all these problems and will be delighted to be rid of me, so I'll be leaving Home World."

I absorbed this quietly.

"Where will you go?" I finally asked.

"Wherever the Council sends me. But what's important is that the malfunctioning code has been deleted. Some innovations will be lost, but no more people will die because of me."

I followed a thread in my mind as he spoke, bright dots connecting to one another as things I knew and had heard and seen twisted around each other and formed patterns. When all the pieces finally aligned and became obvious, I was so shocked I gasped aloud and clenched Arden's hand in a grip that nearly broke his fingers.

"It won't matter," I said.

"Of course it won't matter to the families of the people who have already died, but it's the only thing I can ..."

"It won't matter," I interrupted, more emphatically, "because your code isn't the problem. None of this is your fault, but someone wants you to believe it is. *I can prove it.*"

3

Before: Home World ™

It wasn't enough to simply tell him the story, he needed to see this with his own eyes. And I needed to do something to set things right. So I made him come with me to the Resident Services building, running through the city in the middle of the night. The streets were oddly quiet. Abandoned vehicles were everywhere, some left sitting at intersections, others bent and twisted around each other like putty. The occasional empty public transpo rattled past on its journey toward the maintenance yard, its 24-hour circuit disrupted. We encountered one Security Team patrolling on foot but ducked behind a personal conveyance that had lurched across the sidewalk, and they walked past without seeing us.

When we reached the building, I led Arden to a little-used side door. It purred quietly as it processed my credentials and swung open. The floor tiles radiated a soft light and provided a ghostly illumination of our progress through the dim hallways to my office. The streetlamps cast their soft glow into the room through a wide picture window. I didn't bother to turn on the lights.

"I appreciate your conviction, but I've already made up my mind," Arden began as I sat behind my desk and pulled up my computational screens.

"Hush," I interrupted, not taking my eyes off the lines of code that scrolled across my virtual display. "You're not the only master programmer here. And this isn't even complicated. If you had just told me everything, I would have made the connection sooner."

"I don't know what you're talking about. If you're planning to ..."

"*Shut up*, Arden. Sit down. Let me focus. I'll have something to show you in a minute."

Startled into acquiescence, he sat down. My fingers flew over the virtual keyboard in front of me until I found what I was looking for. One glance told me I'd guessed right, inspiring a mix of heady elation and freezing dread. A few quick keystrokes later and the most important project of my career was disabled. A long stream of data poured out in front of me, sparkling golden lines of code against the darkness. I quickly copied the data and keyed in the information to print to a chip. A few seconds later, the small white plexi piece popped up through a slot in my desk.

"Hold onto that," I said, handing it over. Arden absently tucked it into his pocket.

I turned back to the display and called up our version tracking, narrating as I searched for the detailed records I wanted.

"Our department controls everything associated with individual residents, and we take safeguarding privacy very seriously. I completed this project just before my promotion. I didn't really understand its importance then. It's obvious now. I can't believe how stupid I've been."

"What are you talking about?" Arden asked.

"Look," I said, expanding the display and pointing to my now-disabled files. "Tell me what you see here."

Arden got out of his chair and moved behind me to get a closer view. He studied the code intently for a moment, then gasped. His eyes narrowed, the muscles in his jaw tightened and flexed.

"This program disables any code targeting individual ID signatures," he murmured.

I nodded. "That's exactly what it does. I know because I wrote this program. Look at the activation date."

"It was deployed a few weeks before I completed the code for the Governing Council."

"And it runs on every piece of software that's pushed out to the public space—our own surveillance, incident tracking, medical, environmental control ..."

"... and transport," he finished grimly, his mouth drawing into a taut line. "I'm guessing if we looked at the updates pushed out across Home World, we'd find all of my snippets were removed by your program ..."

"... and something else causing these malfunctions was inserted, by some other piece of programming we can't access. Whatever it is, it's behind a firewall that requires the highest level of security clearance."

I turned toward Arden, feeling the desperation mount inside me. "You're being had, Arden. The Company knew what you were doing. You're not the cause of what's happened, but they clearly wanted you to think you were. And you were just about to fall on the sword they handed you."

I became increasingly angry as I spoke. I couldn't stop the torrent of furious words coming out of my mouth, even though my world crumbled just a little bit more with each one. This project, my project ... my home ... my employer ... my lover ... nothing was what I believed it to be, all this time ...

"There are two horrible truths here," I continued, steadying myself with a deep breath. "One: The Company is willing to murder its citizens to protect its leadership from scrutiny. Two: your cover is blown and has *always* been blown. I don't know how, but it's obvious they saw this coming well before you got started."

Arden glowered at the screen, his hands balled into fists. "People died because of this," he growled. "I want to go into Master Control with a sledgehammer and bust the place up."

"No sledgehammers," I interrupted. "That chip in your pocket should have the data you were after—the movements of the top tier Company Officials across the last month. We need to get you out of here on the next ship to anywhere, because if these people are as nefarious as you say they are, your life is in danger."

Arden looked stricken. "And yours," he said. "They'll know *you* figured this out. You're the only person who could have put these pieces together. They'll be coming after you, too."

It was the last thing he said before the room was flooded with the brilliance of headlights and the roar of a renegade public transpo, too loud to ignore. We both stared, transfixed, out the wide window that faced the plaza and watched as the hulking machine left the road and lurched at full speed the short distance across the manicured lawn, directly toward us. As it slammed into the building just to the right of the now-shattering picture window, I felt Arden's hands on my shoulders, trying to pull me out of the way. There was a thunderous roar as building materials exploded around us. I smelled pungent vehicle fumes and something burning, felt horrific pain throughout my body, then everything disappeared into a thick blanket of nothingness.

I awoke, unsure of how much time had passed, in a cold white room filled with soft light and the hushed whispers of attendants in pale green. The scent of antiseptic tickled my nose. I was weak and groggy and wrapped in some kind of body restraint—I couldn't shift my weight at all. At least I could wiggle my fingers and toes.

One of the aides noticed and came to my bedside. "Hello, Faith," he said in that practiced reassuring voice that all clinicians seemed to have. "Do you know where you are?"

"Clinical Aid?" My voice was thin and raspy, barely a whisper.

"That's right," he said. "You were in an accident. Do you remember? You were seriously injured, but you're going to be all right. I'm Von, I'm your recovery aide. I'll be helping you get better. Let me get the Med Lead. She'll want to look you over."

The green-robed figure moved out of my field of view.

Clinical Aid. I'm not dead.

A well of panic erupted inside my chest. *Arden. Where is Arden?*

The health drone floating above me recorded the increase in my heart rate and breathing and made an anxious chirping sound. Von and another person I presumed to be the Med Lead came running.

"What's causing this distress?" the Med Lead barked. The clinician responded with an exaggerated shrug.

"I don't know, I was just here and her stats were fine," Von said. "She might be remembering the accident. It was horrific."

He looked down at me and said in his professional voice, "Faith, are you in pain? What's upsetting you? Can you tell us?"

My brain was spinning. I fully believed the Company was the reason I was in Clinical Aid in the first place, and not being dead was a plus I wanted to maintain. If I mentioned Arden by name, would that send the Company after me again? My instinctive urge to be cautious battled against my need to know what had happened to him.

In a split second, I decided to feign confusion.

"My friend," I managed to rasp out. "Is my friend all right?"

Von's brows knitted together for a moment, and he frowned, looking over to the Med Lead. "She's asking about someone. I don't know who she's talking about."

"Let me look it up," sighed the Med Lead, the exhaustion in her voice clear. After consulting her holo for a minute she offered the screen to him. He took a moment to read the display, then turned back to me.

"We're a little confused, Faith. Who are you asking about?"

The Med Lead gave me a side-eye. I didn't like her expression. I gestured for Von to come closer. Understanding, he bent down low enough to hear me.

"My friend, with me at Residential," I gasped. "He was right behind me."

"Oh." The aide's mouth held the crisp firm circle of the vowel, as he turned to consult the Med Lead again. I held my breath, preparing for the answer I'm certain is coming, but the Med Lead instead leaned over the bed, studying me. Her eyebrows drew together, and her lips pulled into a thin taut line.

"She's confused," she said over her shoulder to him. "She's only just come to, after all."

She turned her attention to me.

"Faith," she said, louder than necessary. "I'm Dr. Wren. You seem to be concerned about a friend of yours, is that right? Someone who was with you at the time of the accident?"

I couldn't speak any more. I felt my eyes stinging with tears as I braced myself. Arden couldn't have survived.

"I can't give you an answer," she continued, "because there wasn't anyone. You were found in the rubble by yourself. You were brought to Clinical Aid alone."

Shock and surprise hit me, a punch to my chest. Then the world spun out from under me again, and I collapsed into unconsciousness.

Wenda's face is twisted with emotion when I finish, and she doesn't say anything for a moment. I can't tell if she wants to hug me or burst into tears or both; my own reaction to it varies day to day. At the moment, it feels good to have gotten some of it out, good that at least one other person knows. When she does speak, she agrees that maybe I don't need to go to Clinical Aid this instant, and she lets me off the hook completely when I promise to check in with a counselor tomorrow, which of course I won't. She settles into her own hammock, yawning, and we turn off the lights.

Wenda thinks she knows my story now. She doesn't.

I told her about the accident, the long months of recovery and the physical pain I endured as my body healed. But I didn't tell her about the day I finally walked into my pod again, only to find every scrap and trace of Arden utterly gone, as if he had never existed. I described how Von helped me recover physically, and how he and his husband Orrin became dear friends, but I omitted how he had to pull me out of the depths of despair over and over again as anxiety, depression, panic, and paranoia became my constant companions. I didn't tell her how I became obsessive, scouring every record of every morgue in every city, looking for Arden's name, hoping simultaneously to find it and not find it, or how I alternated mourning him and hating him every single day.

And I didn't tell her about the flowers.

A few days before my departure from Home World, Von came to my door with an armload of stunning flowers, too beautiful to be leftovers from one of Orrin's events. The huge fragrant white blossoms featured oblong crisply-pointed petals clustered around bright purple centers, with the tip of each petal stained pink and lavender. The effect was spectacular.

"I knew you'd love these," he said, taking in the expression on my face.

"What are they?" I asked, placing them in the center of the table. "They're amazing. I've never seen flowers like this before."

"It says on the card." Von handed me a small envelope. "Daggerflower, I think? They don't grow here naturally. Orrin says he gets a few shipped in from Thane now and again."

I froze.

"Thane?"

"Mmm-hmm. Special order and very expensive." Von pressed his face into the blooms and inhaled deeply. "Someone is out to impress you. And with a real paper card too! Open it, I'm dying."

"These aren't from you?"

"No, doof. Have you even been listening to me? They were ordered specially for you by some anonymous admirer. Insanely expensive Thanish flowers paid for in cash, so I'd say a fervent admirer. And they kicked down extra for paper instead of sending them with holotext. Open the damn card."

My hands shook as I tore open the beige envelope and tugged out the small card. The front bore the word "Congratulations" scrawled in a celebratory font—nothing special there. But the back was printed with a Thanish proverb that even Home Worlders knew by heart: *There is nothing larger than these stars but love.*

Across the bottom of the card, the words *I love you* were written in Arden's hand.

That card is in my jacket pocket now. It bolstered me down the jetway when I left the only home I'd ever known, it drove me forward every time I became unsure of myself or wondered if I was overreacting. I reach for this little scrap of paper again and again, like a magic talisman. Sometimes touching it warms my soul. Other times it sets it on fire or shreds it like cobwebs caught in the wind.

I didn't tell Wenda about the flowers because she'd have questions I'm not sure I want to answer. I can only say that the instant I held that card in my hand, the mourning/hating cycle I had trapped myself in was replaced by an indefinable *something else*. He lied to me. He left me. But Arden is out there somewhere, and we are, improbably, still connected.

And I can't quite work out how I feel about that.

4

Now: Iona

"Faith, what are you DOING? I can't HEAR you!"

Pauly's voice comes loud and sharp through my headset, so startling that I almost drop my tools. It's been eight years, and I'm still often taken aback by Pauly's sheer volume; down here in the dark silent belly of the pit, the sound is like being punched in the head. I think *now I can't hear you either because you just blew out my eardrum*, but I don't say it aloud. Pauly is my friend, but even so, I'm never that flippant with him when we're on duty. He's our Task Coordinator and is as close to a boss as I have on Iona.

"I'm finishing up the work on this fuel coupling," I say instead, giving the coupling a pat for good measure. "I'm almost done." In reality, that job has been finished for a while. I'm down here scavenging parts now, pulling together scraps to use for my personal projects.

"NEW PRIORITY," Pauly booms again, and I wince. "Drop it and come to Resident Services right away. We need everybody to help with arrivals."

"Will do," I say. Inwardly, I cringe a little. I don't love working arrivals. It's a lot of detail stuff, done standing in front of a terminal: scanning stat chips, plotting work teams, and making residential assignments for new people just landing on Iona, and making horrible small talk. It's not stressful—in fact so few people transfer here that arrivals is usually pretty sedate—it's just that I'd rather be down here where it's less people-y and I can do whatever I want.

I look at the scraggly collection of parts in my cart and sigh. At this rate, my little side project is going to take a while to finish.

I punch in the coordinates and watch as the cart floats off toward my build space, then jog up the ramp leading out of the pit. Even in the dull flat light of Iona, it takes a moment for my eyes to adjust. When they do, I gasp in surprise: our usually sparsely populated square is crawling with people. Groups of five and ten and twenty-five snake from the landing pads toward the Resident Services center. Transport vehicles stream overhead, as thick as a cloud of Ionian sand gnats; the instant a vehicle takes off, another one lands in its place. Ionians run to and fro, trying to help, to lead, to organize. I'm still trying to make sense of the scene when I spot my podsister Wenda in the distance, hurtling toward the Resident Services Building with an intense expression on her face. She waves at me frantically.

"Hurry!" she shouts. "Looks like everybody from Bardazel is moving over!"

We learned a few weeks ago that the Company was shutting down its entire operation on Bardazel, a small service planet like our own. We'd been worried when the Company settled the small moon-sized planet to begin with, since we figured they'd be taking over maintenance of all of the Company's mining ships and eating into our income, but apparently things hadn't gone according to plan and business was slow. Bardazel's closure was good news for us on Iona, because it made us the only service planet in the sector once again, and while we were excited to get Bardazel's customers, no one anticipated getting the settlement's population as well.

"Everybody?" I shout back, quickening my pace. "Where are we going to put them all?" Bardazel had an active population of around 600. Finding space among thirty pods for 600 new people, some of them families—no wonder Pauly called me in a panic.

Wenda throws her hands into the air in a gesture that I know means we'll figure it out because we have to. We'll be resourceful. It's what we do here.

Arrivals is wall-to-wall by the time we reach the building. The former residents of Bardazel are everywhere, sitting on every available surface—desks, railings, tables, even the floor. They look tired, bedraggled, and dazed. Some are carrying fat, heavy packs while others have only a kit bag or nothing at all. They range from very young to very old, and some of them are sick. No one looks like they had much time to prepare for a move. I can't help but wonder when *they* found out their base of operations was closing.

But then Pauly is in my face, shouting at me to hurry up. I run to my terminal, and he begins herding people into line in front of me. I take a deep breath, look into the drawn, sad face of the first former resident of Bardazel, put on my most comforting smile, and say, "I'm Faith. Welcome to Iona."

It takes the rest of the day to sort out the new residents, but like all things on Iona, it does finally get done. The total number of transferees is listed at 408 rather than the 600-plus residents officially documented on that planet. There's no word about the remaining 200.

"Pauly!" I shout, as he hurries past. "Is this everybody?"

Pauly checks his holo quickly. "Looks like," he says. "No more transport vehicles scheduled to land, everything on the pad is clear."

That means the dozen people still in the Resident Center are the last of the transferees. It's a massive discrepancy, and I'm profoundly curious. The Company doesn't make mistakes counting assets, and people are assets as much as spaceships and drones.

The last person to step up to my terminal is a man I've noticed over the past hour or two. He's devoted most of his energy to looking after his planet-mates—comforting the concerned, fielding questions, fetching water, helping with forms, and gently shepherding people along. He has the bearing of someone used to being in charge and it's clear the others hold him in high regard.

"Looks like you're the last one in," I say as I swipe his stat chip through the reader. "Number 408."

I smile in a way I hope is charming. He smiles back, but it's only a brief tilt of his mouth, with no feeling or sense of engagement behind it.

"The numbers we have say there were more than 600 people in residence on Bardazel. Is that wrong? What happened to that last 200?" I ask, attempting to sound casual. "I'd hate for us not to be prepared for them to arrive."

He's distracted, watching the handful of Bardazelians milling around the center, and takes a long time to respond. When he does, it's with a noncommittal lift of his shoulders.

"I don't think you have to worry about that."

His eyes are a strange luminous gray, and the way he keeps averting them says he knows more, but he won't be sharing it with me. I let it drop, welcome him to Iona, hand him his freshly printed credentials and direct him to Pauly's pod.

In the end, we establish ten new pods—lucky we never tore down the old visiting flight crew quarters—and add people to existing pods wherever there was room and a fit. Pods of fourteen or fifteen are booted up to twenty. It will be tight at first, but we'll get used to it. Everything is going to be a lot more crowded now. In a single afternoon, Iona's population has nearly doubled.

After the last person leaves the Resident Center and all the terminals go dark, I walk out to the portico to find Pauly, Wenda, and Fanny, sprawled out on the steps smoking and drinking brew. "Well that was fun," Fanny is saying in her gravelly voice, shifting her ample form on the stones. She looks at me and hands me her flask. Half the time, Fanny's flask is just water, but tonight it's a pungent bitter brew. I take a long swig and sigh as it courses down my throat and into my stomach. The effect is instant relaxation.

"I can't believe we just processed all those people," Wenda says. She reaches for the flask. "We might actually have enough people to fill up our work teams now. We haven't had that in a long time."

"That would be something," I say. "They seem like good people. I think they'll fit in well here, after a while."

Pauly snorts. "A long while," he says. "Why did you put the governor in my pod?"

"The what?"

"The governor of Bardazel. Regal fellow, forty-ish, dark hair, about so tall?" Pauly gestures well over his own head. He's talking about Mr. Gray Eyes.

"He was the governor? It didn't say that on his stat chip."

"It wouldn't," Pauly smirks, pleased to know something I don't. "That position was chosen by the people, not by the Company."

"I put him in your pod because the program said he fit best there. Do you think he needs to be leading his own pod?"

Pauly thinks for a minute. "I don't think he wants to lead his own pod," he says.

Fanny, who has taken the flask from Wenda and indulged in several more pulls, suddenly perks up. "I'm glad he's in our pod," she says. "He's handsome. I fancy him."

Pauly scowls at his older sister. "Don't go getting any ideas," he says. "He's probably fifteen years younger than you. And you don't even know him."

Fanny takes another drink and raises an eyebrow at her brother. "Age doesn't matter," she says. "And I know everyone else here and I don't fancy any of them. I say it's worth a shot."

We all know Fanny is kidding, trying to get a rise out of her brother, and as always, it's working beautifully. Pauly looks utterly exasperated. Wenda hides a laugh behind her hand and casts a sideways look at me.

Fanny catches Wenda's expression and laughs good-naturedly.

"Wenda, little Wenda," she says, waving her smoke in Wenda's general direction. "You're how old, twenty-five? You're still a baby. On Hokka, where we were raised, you'd need the permission of two Elders before you could Pair with someone."

Wenda and I have heard this story before. "I'm thirty-two, but you and Pauly are ancient," Wenda says. "We know Hokkans would insist you got the approval of two Youngers before either of you could Pair. What are you now? 200?"

The joke is an old one. We've seen their intake data; Pauly is fifty-two and Fanny is fifty-five. Middle-aged on Hokka, maybe, but not elderly by any planet's definition.

I pick up the jibe. "This could be a good time for you, Fanny," I say. "The new arrivals skewed the median age of our population upward. More choice for you old farts."

Fanny chuckles and looks pleased with herself. "I believe I've made my choice. But how about you, Wenda? Maybe you would like an older lover, they have more talents than younger ones." Wenda laughs but a powerful blush burns through her dark brown cheeks. Fanny takes a drag from the smoke, followed by a long drink from her flask. "Let me know, I can fix you up," she says with a wink. Pauly rolls his eyes.

Now we're all laughing. "What about me?" I say in mock indignation. "You're not going to offer to fix me up with one of these special older lovers?"

"Hmmm. The governor might suit you, too bad I've already claimed him," Fanny says, waving her smoke in the air. "Just as well. You could probably only be suitably Paired with some magical being we've never seen before. Nobody on Iona can handle you, and probably nobody from Bardazel either. But if you like it that way, who am I to judge?"

Fanny winks at me; I smile ruefully in return. The people surrounding me, my de facto family, my planetmates, give me looks ranging from pity to curiosity. They all know I had someone once. They all understand the end of that relationship is somehow connected to why I chose to leave my life in a sparkling city on a Company planet to come to the dust and grease and daily hard work of a tiny independent service planet on the hind end of the mining sector. Some know more details than others, but after eight years, no one has the whole story—in part because I'm loathe to relive it through retelling, but also in case knowing more could one day put them at risk. At any rate, they all think it's tragic that I don't have someone here. But Fanny's right—I like my solitude. I've cultivated it carefully and it works for me.

A soft silence settles around us. Iona's two tiny moons creep up over the horizon as our weakling sun sinks below it. The plaza that was teeming with chaos and people a few hours ago is empty and still—a testament to how resourceful

31

we are. The new people are checked in and all have appropriate work team assignments and living quarters. Tomorrow they'll wake up to comforting routines that will help ease the transition. And Ionians will act as if these newcomers aren't newcomers at all, but instead have always been here—that's how we are. We get a lot of strays on this planet, but they don't stay strays for long.

Fanny holds her smoke up to Pauly; he accepts it and takes a drag. "Day's done," he says. "Let's go home, old woman."

Fanny smiles at her brother in a moment of pure unguarded fondness as she clambers to her feet. But then the moment is over, and she says, "Let's do that. Time for me to get to know the governor better."

"Oh, Fanny," Pauly huffs, before slipping his arm through hers. We descend the steps together and head for our pods.

Five of the new arrivals from Bardazel were added to my own pod: two women, a man, and a pair of teenage twins. By the time Wenda and I walk in, our podmates have made them welcome and spent the last few hours shuffling hammocks and personal zones to make room for them. I'm bone-tired, but as pod leader, one of my responsibilities is to see to the new arrivals. I make it a point to let them know they're welcome and ask if they need anything before I head to my quarters for the night. They're doing as well as one might expect; a bit shell-shocked, exhausted, and in no real mood for small talk, but grateful to have a roof over their heads. I also thank my podmates for doing what they had to do to make space for the former Bardazelians. We're now a pod of nineteen. It will be tight and I'll need to revise my food, water, and energy consumption plan, but I'll deal with that tomorrow.

I grab a bite to eat from the kitchen, then go to my room. A bonus of being pod leader is a private room, and I'm selfishly relieved to walk into the solitude of it, pleased that my podmates continued to respect this tradition despite the new hammocks hanging over one another in the larger sleeping spaces. One of our little ones has left a drawing of a vaguely daisy-like flower on my pillow. I smile as I pick it up and study it before pinning it up on my wall. They must be learning about Home World flora in school now. The only vegetation on Iona is scraggy and tough from constant exposure to wind and sand, and nothing even remotely like a daisy grows here. But everyone knows I was born on Home World, and I may have mentioned liking flowers at some point.

I miss flowers. The phrase echoes through my head and suddenly I'm swimming in visions of pink, lavender and white petals around a purple center from long ago. I feel tears roll down my face, carving tracks in the dust I've yet to wash off. I create a million excuses in the few seconds it takes to wipe them away with the back of my hand. I'm tired, it's been a long day, I'm empathizing with the worry and upset of Bardazel's former residents, I'm feeling a little feverish, I didn't eat enough, I'm dehydrated. Those things are true, but so is the simple statement that evoked my tears. I do miss flowers. I miss green. I miss the sound of waves rolling onto the shore, and bright and shining skylines, and rain, and things that are not covered in dust. *And you*, my brain adds. *I miss you.*

No. I won't think about that. Not after all this time.

I push myself through undressing and washing and preparing for bed. I extinguish the light and climb into my hammock. The last thing that catches my eye as I retreat into sleep is the flower on my wall, drawn sweetly and simply from a child's imagination. The sorrow returns and follows me into my dreams.

5

I WAKE UP WITH Iona's sunrise, just as Wenda sounds the rising chimes. I wonder how our new citizens are doing and when I step into our Common Room, I'm pleased to see them all present. But even though the rest of my podmates have taken their seats around our family-style breakfast, the transferees are still standing and almost snap to attention when I enter the room, even the sixteen-year-old twins. Apparently, Bardazel was much more regimented and formal than Iona has ever cared to be.

"Pod Leader Faith," says the oldest of the group, a forty-something woman with shoulder-length sand-colored hair. She straightens herself as if for inspection, and the four others follow suit. My podmates, in the middle of eating their breakfasts, stare open-mouthed. I look at the name on her newly issued beige service jacket. It reads *Karloa*.

"Good morning, Karloa. All of you, please sit down and eat some breakfast," I say. "That's what I'm going to do." I sit down and reach for the closest serving dish. For a moment, a look of pure confusion passes among the transferees, then Karloa slowly, almost suspiciously, takes her seat. She gives the others a glance and in response they throw themselves into their chairs. Still, no one is eating. Our usually boisterous gathering room has gone dead quiet.

"Please eat," I say again, softly. One of the twins takes me at my word this time and reaches for a piece of toast, despite the glares thrown at him by Karloa and his sister. He returns their scowls with a raised eyebrow and a shrug, then stuffs the toast into his mouth and begins to chew. His jacket identifies him as *Hinn*.

"Perfect, Hinn, thank you," I say, and he jumps a little before nodding toward me and resuming his chewing. "And everyone, please call me Faith. Not 'leader' or 'pod leader' or 'exalted poohbah Faith,' just Faith. You're making me way more special than I deserve to be." At this, the original members of my pod laugh heartily. The new transferees stare at the table and look uncomfortable, although they all slowly begin to eat breakfast.

Pauly might be right. It may be a while before they adapt.

After breakfast, my podmates scatter to take care of their work assignments for the day. Wenda takes the new Ionians out on a tour of the town and for an orientation session about what to expect living and working here. Within minutes, Pauly is barking instructions into my headset. This time the job is Materials Intake—a delivery of supplies has come in from Home World and needs to be unloaded, catalogued, and sent to the proper storehouses. It also means care packages and personal mail. Delivery day is a good day for Ionians.

The sweetly drawn daisy flashes into my mind and I start to choke up, but I push down my emotions and hurry to the cargo docks on the southwestern edge of the town.

The job takes Pauly and me four solid hours of unloading and categorizing the goods brought in by the latest skiff. While we work through the cargo, the skiff's pilots nap inside the launch pad control room or stroll into town for food and brew. Sometimes they chat with us, but not often. They tend to focus on getting in and out as quickly as possible. I'm sure this is some kind of Company directive, but no one shared those details with us. It marks a significant change from the way we used to do things, and it's a little hard to get used to.

It started with the equipment upgrades. These sleek new skiffs are formed from modular parts and are quick and easy to build. They hold almost as much as the old landers but require only half the crew and all their maintenance is done by robot. Not long ago, a Materials delivery would have meant a full-sized lander and an overnight stay for its crew of six to give Ionians time to perform the necessary hours of maintenance work before relaunch. When the Company switched to skiffs like these—and why wouldn't they, given the advantages—Iona suffered.

Although we always provided overnight quarters for the crews free of charge, they ate and drank and gambled at their own expense while they were here. But what I loved most were the stories. The crews filled us in on happenings on Home World, and shared tales of their travels through the sector and beyond. They were a point of connection to the places we left behind to come to Iona. One more connection, severed.

We're down to the last two crates of goods. Pauly scans one, laughs, and then scans it again. He says, "This one is yours."

"Mine?" I ask, puzzled. I wave my scanner over it and a holograph pops up with my name and picture. The notation is "personal durable goods," which means, well, anything. The sender is a generic Company address. The crate is large: maybe six feet by four feet, and approximately four feet high. Pauly looks at me with an arched eyebrow. I have no idea what might be in this crate. I shrug, punch in the coordinates of my personal storage, and send the flat scuttling on its way. "It's from the Company," I say to Pauly. "New bathmats or something?" He laughs and moves on to the last crate.

It has no named recipient; instead, the hologram reads "Warehousing Leader: Iona" and nothing more. Pauly shakes his head. "Idiots," he mutters. "We don't have a Warehousing Leader."

"You're getting one in about a month," says the skiff pilot, just emerging from the control room, stretching. "I heard them talking about it last week. Some hot-shot guy who's being taken out of deep space for personal reasons."

"Oh great," moans Pauly. "A fancy-pants with emotional issues."

The pilot laughs. "Isn't that always the way?" she says. "Somebody decides they're a Star God and then can't handle being out in the black."

"I wonder how much he'll like being in the dirt?" I mutter, and she smirks knowingly.

"My guess is he'll hate it just enough to be a huge pain in the ass," she says. "Maybe if you're lucky, you can patch him up and get him back into space before he drives you crazy."

"I'm sorry to interrupt this little tea party but speaking of getting back into space ... " Pauly looks at the pilot and gestures toward the now-empty skiff. The tough little articulated robots we call *fivefingers* have done a full systems check and performed any needed maintenance while we were unloading the cargo. Everything is ready to go.

"Ah, right. Can I have ten?" the pilot asks. Pauly nods. She drops the mic on her headset and begins delivering instructions to her crew.

"What now?" I ask Pauly. He consults his holotablet.

"No more arrivals scheduled, and Maintenance is all caught up," he says. "You can help with Orientation for the new residents over at the Preservation Theater. Fanny and Wenda are both scheduled for it, but they always need more hands for these things."

Inwardly, I sigh. No excuse to go down to the pit, then. But outwardly, I smile and acquiesce. "Good enough," I say. I turn to head back to town and wave to the pilot, who gives me a thumbs-up and mouths the words, "good luck." I'm puzzled for a few seconds before remembering our conversation about the soon-to-arrive Warehousing Leader. I had already forgotten about him.

Most of Iona's new residents are seated in the Preservation Theater by the time I arrive. Fanny, Wenda, and a handful of other Ionians are there too, in a cluster near the stage.

"What can I do?" I ask.

Wenda makes a face. "Pray. You will not believe what I've been through today."

"Oh no. Our new podmates?"

"Well, not all of them. I think the twins in particular will do fine."

"Karloa."

"Yes. She has some ... interesting preconceived notions."

37

"Everyone has ideas about other cultures they're just encountering, though," I begin. "It's a normal response."

Wenda cuts me off. "This is NOT normal. She thinks we're up to no good. There's so much resentment, yet it's almost as if she's afraid of everyone on Iona."

"What? Where would they pick up such a ..."

"We'll talk later," she interrupts, casting a meaningful glance over my head. I'm about to object when Mr. Gray Eyes appears at my shoulder. He is slightly less guarded than yesterday, and actually manages a smile.

"You're Faith," he says. "You checked me in."

"I did your intake, yes," I say. "I'm sorry, I don't remember your name." I do remember his eyes, though. Luminous and pale, like Iona's moons.

"Graham. Graham Thorn."

"Pleased to meet you again, Graham Thorn. Faith Feathergrass."

"Feathergrass? Like the plant?"

"Why yes, like the plant. Is there feather grass on Bardazel?"

His face darkens for a moment. "No, we didn't have much in the way of ornamental grasses on Bardazel," he responds. "Its terrain is much like Iona's. Sand, wind, and more sand."

"How did you come to learn about feather grass? Part of your schooling?"

Again, a small smile. "Something like that." He looks up and catches Fanny's eye, and she smiles at him in a way I imagine might be conspiratorial if I were given to those kinds of wild and reckless thoughts.

"Did you find my holo?" she asks him in a sweet sing-song voice. He produces a small holotablet from his pocket and hands it to her.

"Fanny forgot her notes," he explains. "She asked me to run back to the pod and get them."

"And it looks like all the seats are taken now, oh dear," Fanny sings in mock consternation, scanning the packed house. "You'll just have to sit on the edge of the stage here next to Faith."

Oh no, I think with a sigh. *Please tell me this isn't what I think it is.* As if in response, Fanny looks squarely at me and winks. Graham misses none of this and colors almost as intensely as I do. Wenda stifles an outright laugh. I look apologetically at Graham, who responds by gesturing toward the edge of the stage as though it's a gilded carriage. He waits for me to settle in before parking himself next to me.

The lights go down and Wenda begins the presentation. Sitting in the dark with our legs dangling like eight-year-olds, I begin to feel more comfortable with the situation. He seems pleasant and smart, and Fanny was right—he is handsome. The people of Bardazel found him trustworthy enough to make him their governor. Maybe it wouldn't be such a bad thing to get to know him a little better. I've been on Iona eight years, and sometimes it feels like I've had every conversation I can have with every person who lives here. It might be nice to have a new friend with some experiences, history, and opinions I don't already know by heart.

I take a quick look over at him, and sure enough, he's looking at me quizzically. I smile in a way that I hope is friendly. He returns the smile in equal measure this time, not like yesterday's perfunctory smile, then turns his attention back to Wenda's talk.

I scan the audience and spot Karloa sitting in the third row. She's not listening to the presentation. Instead, she's staring at me, with an expression that appears to be a mix of disgust and rage. Instead of meeting her eyes, I plaster a generic smile on my face and look past her. Her face does not change, and she glares at me for the next two hours.

Orientation ends, and I wave farewell to Graham as he and Fanny depart. Fanny coquettishly slips her arm through his and takes another moment to look over her shoulder and wink at me again. I help Wenda put away the equipment and close the theater. We walk together toward our pod on the opposite side of the residential section.

"Tell me about Karloa," I say, once I'm sure we're the only ones on the path.

Wenda sighs. "I don't even know where to start," she says. "I heard a commotion shortly after you left and found her trying to make our new residents puke up their breakfasts. She was literally sitting on Hinn, trying to pour something down his throat. When I asked her what the problem was, she said she was concerned that our diet was too rich for them, and it would be better for them if they didn't eat it."

I blink in shock. "How *interesting*," I say, choosing my words carefully.

Wenda continues.

"I told her everyone is free to use the kitchen any time, and they can make whatever they like to eat, but she didn't want to do that. She said she brought a store of special protein bars and medical supplements, and she wants the transferees to eat those things, to the exclusion of everything else."

"For how long?"

"That's the creepy part. I asked her that same question, and she said, 'until the end'."

"The end? What did she mean by that?"

"She wouldn't explain. She started talking at lightning speed, making bizarre statements about not trusting anyone and how 'we' weren't going to get away with this. No one seemed to have any idea what she was talking about. The other transferees were confused and scared. Hinn and Holly were terrorized. They asked if they could move their sleeping quarters to the other end of the hallway just to get away from her."

"What the hell?"

"I can only think that something is seriously wrong with her that goes beyond being in shock from losing her home and everything familiar to her," Wenda says. "All day she kept trying to herd the Bardazelians around like livestock. If I asked someone how they were doing, Karloa would appear at my shoulder, glaring at us both. If anyone smiled or laughed or made a vaguely contented sound, Karloa was down on them in an instant. I'm at a loss as to how to deal with her."

I know what that means. My least favorite part of pod leadership is rearing its ugly head.

"I'll talk to her," I say. "It sounds like she's determined not to fit in. I may not be able to change her mind, but maybe I can convince her to let the other transferees decide for themselves whether life here suits them."

We're a few hundred feet from our pod when we're met by Hinn, flying down the path toward us. His face is red and stained with tears, and his voice is cracking with panic.

"Come quick!" he shouts. "Hurry, hurry please!"

"Hinn, what's wrong? Are you all right?" I call as we quicken our pace.

"It's Karloa," he gasps. "I think she's dead."

Wenda and I trade wide-eyed looks and break into a run.

WE FIND HER LYING on her back on the floor in the common area, her eyes frozen open in an icy stare. Her lips, nose, and fingertips are an odd turquoise blue. Holly is pressed against the wall crying hysterically. Our podsister Shar is herding other members of the pod away from the scene. "I called for the medic," she tells us as we come in. "Darrow's working on her now."

Darrow, our pod emergency medical technician, is crouched over Karloa, scanning her for signs of a pulse, breath, heartbeat, anything that will ping the scanner's monitor. He looks up at me briefly. "She's still alive, but I can't say how long she'll stay that way," he says. "Everything is so faint, almost no pulse at all. And Holly found her like this about five minutes ago, so we have no way of knowing how long she's been in this condition."

At that moment, Iona's Chief Medic Macha comes in with her assistants and shoos everyone out to the courtyard except Darrow. Other members of our pod are beginning to trickle in for our weekly meeting. I intercept them one by one to tell them what's happening and direct them to the courtyard to wait. Everyone is visibly shaken.

Wenda huddles with the remaining Bardazelians, speaking to them in a low, steadying voice. Holly is sitting nearby, still crying. Hinn has his arms wrapped tight around his sister and is doing his best to comfort her. They may have been the last to see Karloa before her collapse, and Holly may have been witness to it. I'm sure Macha will want to question them both, as well as the Bardazelians who were sitting with Karloa at the presentation, and Wenda, who spent most of the day in her company. But right now, Macha has her hands full trying to stabilize the patient.

I hate this feeling of helplessness; I need to think of something to do. I walk a few feet away from the others and ping Pauly on my headset.

"WHAT?" he booms. "Aren't you supposed to be leading a meeting?"

"We've had a situation with one of the Bardazel transferees."

"Situation?"

"Medical. Is Graham around?"

"Graha ... oh. The governor. Yes, he's here."

"Could you pass the headset over to him? I want to ask a couple of questions that might help us sort this out."

"This better be important," Pauly growls. "Just a sec."

A few moments later Graham's voice pours into my ears, warm and amiable.

"Hello, Faith. What can I do for you?"

"We're having a medical issue with one of our new podmates. Was there any unusual sickness in the population of Bardazel? I noticed some of the transferees appeared ill when they came in."

Complete silence. Then Graham clears his throat. The pleasant friendly tone is gone, replaced by one of officiousness and condescension. Clearly, I'm now talking to The Governor.

"To what kind of *unusual sickness* might you be referring? Any medical conditions would have been documented on stat chips and should have been fully evaluated at Intake. I would anticipate there might be some reactions to the overall climate of Iona, as well as some social issues due to the transfer. Your own medical staff should be able to sort this out. Of course, if your capacity in this regard is suboptimal ..."

I mean to be diplomatic, but the tone of his voice sets me off and I can't stand it. I don't bother to let him finish his ridiculous, arrogant sentence.

"Karloa collapsed in my pod's common room. She's rigid and unresponsive and her face is blue," I snap. "Our medic is with her now. If you know anything, you need to tell me immediately. And if this is something contagious, you need to tell everyone, because this entire planet including all of your transferees may have been exposed."

Furious, I snap the mic away from my face. It's all I can do not to rip my headset off and fling it across the courtyard. Idiotic bureaucracy and obfuscation were part of the reason I left Home World and came to Iona. It makes me crazy to think that we may have all been put in danger through whatever hubris this might be.

Unsurprisingly, the next voice that comes through the headset is Pauly's.

"The Governor's on his way," he says.

In a testament to Graham's common sense, he doesn't walk to my pod but instead grabs one of the sand scooters we leave scattered across town. Within minutes, he's pulling up to the edge of our courtyard. I wave to him as he steps off the scooter and walk out to meet him.

I'm relieved to see the person standing in front of me has the demeanor of the man I sat next to earlier, rather than the one I spoke to over Pauly's headset. His gray eyes reflect concern, and his bearing is soft and considerate.

"How is she?" he asks. I sigh.

"No clue. They've been working on her for ten minutes. She was alive when Macha arrived, but it didn't look good. Her pulse had slowed down to almost nothing."

"I should talk to them. I think I have some insight into what's going on. If I'm right, she isn't contagious and is in no danger of dying, but there are other potential considerations."

"Good, they need your help," I say, ushering him to the Common Room. Before the door closes, I see Karloa, still lying on the floor, eyes wide open. The blue has spread to most of her face and down the length of one arm.

Half an hour passes before the medic and her team emerge, followed by Darrow and a hovergurney upon which Karloa is tightly strapped. She's wearing an oxygen mask and has a white sheet pulled up under her chin. The blue coloration has cascaded across her chest and down both arms and covers her face and scalp. Her eyes, at least, are closed now and her face is relaxed.

Graham is last to exit the room. His expression is drawn and serious.

Once clear of the doorway, Macha mounts the gurney's control seat. "Darrow will fill you in," she says to me. She then locks eyes with Graham and says, "Thank you," before she kicks the gurney into motion and speeds off across the sand toward Iona's medical facility.

I look at Darrow expectantly. His lips form a tight line, and he glances briefly at Graham before he speaks.

"She's alive and stable for now," he says. "She appears to be in some kind of stasis which is likely the result of a specific drug she ingested. We aren't sure how long she'll stay in stasis, or if she'll come out of it at all. There are still a lot of unknowns."

"A drug!" I exclaim. "Where would she have obtained this drug?"

Darrow looks again at Graham.

"We believe she brought it with her from Bardazel. The good news is we can be sure that this is not a threat to the rest of our residents, whether Ionian or Bardazelian." He then excuses himself and heads to Clinical to continue assisting Macha with the patient.

Graham crosses the pathway to me. "I have a lot to tell you," he says, almost apologetically. His tone suggests that may be an understatement.

"Let me update the pod and get them squared away, then we'll go for a walk," I say. His expression signals his agreement, and he stands aside while I bring my podmates together to fill them in.

The Ionians are concerned and murmur among themselves. The Bardazelians appear shocked and no more informed than the Ionians. Holly continues to sniffle into Hinn's shoulder as they pace around the common room. There is no other sign remaining of the turmoil we encountered an hour or so ago when we came up the path, as though the strange rigid blue figure of Karloa lying on the floor was merely a hallucination, banished by the pale beige light of the sunset filtering through the windows.

Graham and I walk away from town, toward Iona's western bluffs, and find a natural outcropping of rock that gives us a full view of Iona's moons with the town below. We sit, and I wait for him to start talking. When he does, he's deferential and unaffected.

"A little more than a year ago, we had a serious industrial accident on Bardazel, an explosion in one of the mines that released a massive cloud of toxic gas. It threatened our entire population," he begins. "I initially thought you were referring to that when you spoke to me earlier."

"Oh," I say. No wonder his initial response was so terse. "No, we weren't told anything about that."

"Bardazel was such a small outpost, we didn't really have anything at our disposal to help us deal with the cloud. We had no choice but to wait for off-world help, and that was going to take time to arrive. Our medical resources were also limited. If people were exposed, we had no way to combat the toxin. That's when we began tinkering with some synthetics we had on hand. Our team managed to create a concoction that we called Blue. The thought was to drop anyone exposed to the toxin into extended stasis, to arrest the process and preserve them until we managed to obtain the right medical help."

"That's a clever solution. Creepy, but clever."

"It might have been a little too clever. A group of conspiracy theorists emerged who decided this drug was going to be used by the Company to thin the ranks and save money. A worker in stasis doesn't have to be fed, housed, entertained, clothed, listened to. They began peddling the theory that people who took Blue would just go into stasis and never awaken—they would simply disappear. It became a serious threat to our social stability."

"Was Karloa one of these fringe extremists?"

"She wasn't at the beginning, although we thought she might be sympathetic from some of the conversations she was having."

"How did things get resolved?"

Graham's shoulders droop and his face becomes dark. "We got lucky. Less of the toxin was released into the atmosphere than we initially thought, and the prevailing winds shifted just in time, taking the bulk of it away from our populated area. That gave us enough time for the help we needed to arrive, and we never had to use Blue at all. But the extremists just considered that proof of their theory. They really started upping the noise, insisting that Blue was designed to be a tool to control the workforce. They constructed a huge complex away from town where all the faithful lived together. Anyone who didn't buy into their worldview was the enemy, especially anyone aligned with the Company. Of course, the Company couldn't have this going on. It was wrecking productivity and making Bardazel unsafe. They told local leadership we had to move on the complex. They made our job very clear: extract anyone we thought might be a victim rather than an instigator, and then take out the rest. But above all, do it quickly."

"Take out?"

Graham bows his head, and his voice becomes momentarily shaky.

"We were given authorization to use deadly force. We were determined not to use it. But the Company made it clear that we were supposed to do whatever it took to subdue these people."

A powerful sense of *deja vu* sweeps over me and I shudder. I'm personally acquainted with the notion of Company-sanctioned murder, after all. Even though it's been a long time, my memories remain vivid and painful and my paranoia still gets the better of me from time to time.

"I agree, it's reprehensible," Graham says, misunderstanding my reaction. "I could never have done that. We came up with an alternate strategy."

I let out my breath just a little.

"What did you do?" I ask.

"We began sending people into the compound to help pull out anyone who could be convinced to leave," he explains. "We'd only barely begun that process

47

when we learned the conspiracy theorists had somehow obtained an enormous quantity of Blue. We sped up the extractions as best we could, but we only managed to recover forty people before they performed a mass ritual and dosed themselves with it. The whole complex: men, women, children—everyone. All locked in stasis."

"The 200 Bardazelians who weren't on the transfer roster for Iona."

"Yes. More than 200 people who are now locked in a state of suspended animation. A third of Bardazel's population. That's the real reason the station was shut down."

"Why didn't the Company just revive them?"

Graham's mouth forms a thin flat line and his eyes focus somewhere far away.

"You've hit on the most difficult thing about this," he says. "There's no antidote to Blue."

I squeak in surprise. "How can there not be an antidote?"

"It was developed in a hurry, to try to get out in front of the spread of the toxin. As long as a substantial number of people were in danger of dying, an antidote to Blue wasn't the priority. The Company pledged to develop one quickly after the threat had subsided. But when the only people who needed an antidote were conspiracy theorists and extremists who were hampering the Company's operations, the priority dropped considerably."

I feel tremors in my chest and struggle to make my breathing normal. I want to scream *and you were okay with this?* but I keep reminding myself that Graham's not the Company, not the enemy, and not one of the shadowy figures from my past.

"Do you think Karloa somehow got her hands on some Blue and brought it with her to continue to carry on the protest?" I ask, composing myself quickly.

"I suppose it could have been something like that. I'm not sure why she would do it."

"I think she may have been trying to dose the other Bardazelians with it as well," I say. "Wenda caught her trying to pour something down Hinn's throat this morning."

Graham stares at his hands. "The twins were among the first people we got out of the complex," he says. "They were excited to leave. Their parents weren't so agreeable, or so lucky."

I shiver a little and look up at the darkening sky. Iona's little moons, not quite full, will not be up to the task of lighting our way home if we linger much longer, and frankly I'm not sure how much more I can stand to hear.

"We should head back," I say. Graham stands and extends his hand to help me up, a gesture I would have found charming had we not just been talking about Company-sanctioned mass murder and 200 people crazy enough to put themselves into stasis without knowing if they could be revived.

"How many of the extractions came to Iona? Do we need to worry about them carrying out a similar kind of protest?" I ask as we walk toward the softly glowing lights of Residential.

"They all came, but I don't think there will be any issues," Graham says. "Technically, Karloa wasn't an extraction. She'd been living at the complex a few weeks when the group performed their mass self-medication. For some reason she didn't go through with it. We found her after the fact, sitting in the middle of a room full of people lying where they fell after consuming the drug. She was holding a cup of Blue in her hand, but she was shaking like a leaf and she hadn't touched a drop."

I consider this, listening to the sound of sand scrunching under our feet. It makes no sense to me. It's obvious from Graham's expression that it makes no sense to him either. We walk in silence for a while, and as we approach the glowing lights of Residential, I decide to shift the subject.

"It sounds like you lived on Bardazel a long time, but when did you leave Home World?" I finally ask. I hadn't thought about his origin story until I heard in my memory his voice saying *Feathergrass, like the plant?* and I can't believe I missed it.

He winces. "Ah. You figured it out."

"Only just now. It wasn't obvious."

"But still, we stand out, don't we? My family transferred to Bardazel when I was fourteen. My parents went back to Home World five years later, and I had the option to stay on, and I did. I worked some temporary assignments in other sectors and put in some space time like most of us, but I've lived more of my life on Bardazel than Home World."

We're nearly back to the pod. The lights are on in the common room, and dinner is probably being served, but my guess is that the usual boisterous laughter we're known for will be missing tonight.

"I'll look in on Karloa and report back," Graham says as he mounts the sand scooter, kicks it in to motion, and glides away.

The smell of Wenda's stew is wafting through the open windows. I'm tired and I know I should eat, even though I have no appetite. I do want to try to normalize things at least a little for my pod members, so I attempt to shake off my deepest concerns and put on a confident face. The last two days have been incredibly difficult. I want to believe tomorrow will be better but the highest level of optimism I can reach at this point is to hope that tomorrow won't be insane.

7

MORNING ARRIVES AGAIN WITH Wenda ringing the rising chimes. I climb out of my hammock and throw some water on my face at my washbasin. My headset is already pulsating on its stand, and I pull it on as I sort out my clothes for the day.

"Faith ARE YOU THERE?" Pauly is roaring.

"I'm here, I'm here. What's up?"

"Oh, THERE YOU ARE. Just a minute."

I wait patiently while Pauly does ten other things, and continue to get myself dressed. When he comes back on, it's only to hand me off to Graham. At least Graham doesn't yell.

"Hi," I say. "We need to get Tech to put a rush on your headset, I think."

To my surprise, he chuckles a little. "Pauly clearly doesn't enjoy these little interludes without his. And he's gesturing at me right now to hurry up."

Now I smile a little, envisioning the scene.

"Okay, Pauly, okay, I'm getting on with it," Graham says over his shoulder, before he resumes talking to me. "I checked on Karloa last night, and again this morning. There's no change in her condition. She's in deep stasis, but her vital signs are stable and she's not deteriorating. That's a positive."

"Yes, so far so good."

"I also spoke to the pod leaders that have extractions in their pods to make them aware of the situation and what to tell their people about what happened."

"Also good. What should I tell the twins?"

"I'm going to come by to speak to them personally. But in the meantime, I'm sure you'll know what to say if they have concerns. You seem to be good at that."

My face heats up at the praise, but I immediately quash the warm rush of pleasure.

"All right, we'll be seeing you for breakfast then?"

"Yes, see you shortly."

Graham's warm tones are replaced by Pauly's ear-splitting roar.

"See you LATER," he shouts, and the connection closes.

Our common room this morning is a much more normal looking scene than the one that greeted me yesterday, which seems particularly odd given the events of the last twelve hours. The Ionians are chatting amiably and including in the conversation the other two adult Bardazelians, an unrelated man and woman both in their late twenties. The twins are seated together, and although they both look tired, Holly is at least no longer crying and responds occasionally to Hinn's entreaties to eat something. Another positive difference: no one is resisting the food. Despite yesterday's trauma, Hinn appears to have already plowed through several of Wenda's excellent breakfast muffins.

I'm sitting down with my plate and a large steaming cup of coffee when Graham arrives. Hinn and Holly perk up considerably when he comes through the door, and I remember that he is essentially the person who rescued them from certain doom. He greets everyone with a wave and a smile, Wenda brings him a cup of coffee and they talk for a few moments before he turns his attention to the twins. Holly and Hinn hang on his every word and beam at him, responding to his inquiries with a degree of animation I haven't seen from them before. After a few minutes he gestures toward the door. They respond enthusiastically. All three of them stand and the twins turn to face me.

"Faith, do we have any tasks to complete this morning?" asks Hinn. "Governor Thorn would like us to spend some time with him."

"You two only have school orientation this afternoon," I tell them. "I think you have plenty of time."

They shout, "thank you!" in unison and run to Graham, who waits for them by the door.

"We'll be back soon," he says. I lift my coffee to him in salute and he smiles warmly. It seems—although it might be my imagination—that he lets his gaze linger on me a little longer than necessary as the twins dart out the door ahead of him.

After breakfast, everyone scatters to take care of their work assignments for the day. Relishing the quiet, I take an extra cup of coffee back to my quarters and dive into my weekly administrative pod management duties, making sure everyone's schedule is set and pod tasks are divided up, food stores and water units are planned and ordered, and various podmember requests are dealt with—Wenda's recommending an additional toaster, Darrow's requesting more medical supplies, as well as basic first aid kits for all the new podmembers. The twins also need holotablets for their lessons, and all the new arrivals need headsets.

It's a lot of detail work, filling out the appropriate forms and sending the requests in the right formats to the right places, but the easy routine of it makes for a pleasant break from the intensity of the last couple of days.

The last issue on my list of tasks is personal storage. Our living and sleeping spaces are quite compact and very little in the way of personal possessions can be kept in-quarters—not much outside a few changes of clothing and a handful of small personal objects. Wenda will have already explained to the new arrivals that we aren't anti-personal property, so everyone on Iona gets their own personal storage space designed to accommodate whatever their needs might be. Assigning those spaces is my job. The additional personal items the transferees brought with them will have been directed automatically to our storage warren when they were added to our pod. I'll need to take a look at what each person brought along to make sure everyone gets adequate space.

I push my chair back from the desk and stand up, stretching my back and arms. I'm looking forward to doing something besides sitting for the next hour or so. I pop on my headset and grab my credentials, then pass through the common room to pick up one of our holotablets and another coffee to take along. Then I set out for the short walk to our storage warren, out on the western edge of Residential.

The walk is pleasant, as walks go on Iona. The best walking conditions are usually in the early evening after the planet's insistent wind has died down; at this hour, I still have to deal with blowing sand. But the thing that catches my attention this morning is the sky. The dense beige clouds that usually surround our world have thinned out a bit, and I can almost convince myself I see patches of blue behind them. Iona's atmosphere isn't blue, of course; a clear sky here would be pinkish tan, if we ever saw one. I'm letting my nostalgia for Home World fill in the gaps. It feels like that happens more and more often now.

Walking at a comfortable pace for ten minutes, I arrive at our storage warren to see two autoflats floating in its courtyard; Darrow's medical goods and Wenda's toaster have already arrived from General Supplies. I punch in the coordinates for our pod's common room and the flats move away, retracing the path I took to get here. I watch them float off, then use my credentials to pop open the main door and enter the warren.

"Lights, sixty percent," I say as I walk in, and the lighting comes on and adjusts as requested. I head down the straight wide hallway lined with small cubbies, most often assigned to our youngest podmates, along with personal lockers roughly the size of a decent walk-in closet back on Home World. The name of each unit's owner flickers in soft blue light above the doors.

At the far end of this hallway is our Share, a large open space designed to hold things potentially important to the pod as a whole. It's lined with stacks of most-used furniture like hammocks, chairs and desks, plus emergency supplies like generators, water purifiers and temporary rations. Along the far wall are open cubbies holding equipment and materials for small repairs to plumbing, windows, and walls.

From this room, five more hallways branch off in a fan pattern. While some of these are also lined with cubbies and lockers, others feature doors that open into much larger spaces positioned between the spokes. These bigger rooms are preferred by our builders and artisans.

I find the Bardazellians' belongings stacked neatly in the center of the Share. The largest bag is teal blue and decorated with fat white flowers. The tag on it reads *Holly Fortin*. It's full of something soft and squishy, bulky but lightweight, like pillows or stuffed animals. There is also a box with her name on it. By contrast, her brother Hinn brought only a single military-style backpack. The two will be able to share a single locker with ease.

I enter the new assignment into our schematic using my holotablet, then load their belongings onto a miniflat and punch in the locker assignment. The mini floats off toward the twins' new locker. Once there, the match between our schematic and the information encoded into the miniflat's controls opens the locker's door. The mini deposits its cargo inside, then returns. The door shuts once its sensors determine the mini has moved away.

A backpack, a heavy bag, two boxes of books on military history and a hefty box of electronic scraps are labeled with new podmember Maybree's name. I assign her one of the mid-sized rooms on the warren's interior. Quimby, the last new member of our pod, came with only a kit bag, so I mark out one of the cubbies for him. The process for each is the same: enter the assignment on our schematic, load a mini, and punch in the coordinates to send the goods on their way.

That leaves one backpack, conspicuously black and weighty, sitting in the middle of the room. I know the name tag will read *Karloa Arduval*. For a moment, I consider going through the pack, to see if there's anything dangerous in it. But even with the bag's owner unconscious in Clinical with a reawakening date possibly as far out into the future as *never*, it strikes me as an unsavory invasion of privacy. And if there's anything dangerous in the bag, I might not even recognize it as such. I decide to leave it for now, and perhaps ask Graham to examine its contents later for safety's sake. As I watch the last mini float down the hall, something pushes at my memory. There's something else I've been meaning to do here, but I can't quite pull it into my consciousness. I shrug and say aloud to no one in particular, "I guess I'll remember it later."

At that moment my headset goes off and Pauly shatters the silence in my head. "Faith, are you THERE? We've got Maintenance incoming in six minutes."

I shake my head with a smile. Pauly and his loud, crashing urgency. He's like a brother to me, elder or not, my pod or not.

I drop my mic to my mouth and say, "Keep your wig on, old man. I'll be right there."

Three weeks after the Bardazelians arrived, we start to find our rhythm again. Despite the dramatically rocky start, things have smoothed out and everyone seems to be happy. The transferees are getting the hang of their work teams or their schooling, and reports suggest the new arrivals are content with their assigned pods. Truthfully, the program we use for placement has never steered us wrong, using personality metrics and psychological data to create groups that are likely to be harmonious. I've seen it time and time again. podmates bond easily with one another and form strong family-like attachments. Transfers between pods only happen when individuals want to be with family members or romantic dalliances turn serious.

In my pod, the new Bardazelian residents are breaking out of their shells at amazing speed. The twins are doing well in school, and are adjusting nicely. I'm sure Graham is a substantial part of this. He visits often, spends time with them, takes them on outings, listens to their concerns. He's also on-call for the rest of the transferred population, and he frequently drops in on other pods and worksites just to check on his former planetmates. He apparently thinks of this as a delightful responsibility—he even visits Karloa regularly, although her condition hasn't changed and it's unclear whether she's aware of his presence. Perhaps I misunderstood what it meant to be the Governor of Bardazel.

At any rate, I feel good about the way things are going. And Graham has become part of my personal optimism as well.

He comes by most evenings after dinner and we walk together—along the ridges, up the dunes, through the scrub—anywhere, really. And we talk about everything from how things were done on Bardazel and could be done better on Iona to the funny things our podmates are doing. But especially, we talk about Home World—the beautiful part of Home World. When he describes the mountain laurel where he grew up, I can smell their sweet heady fragrance. When I tell him about the silky white sand on the beaches of my childhood, I can feel it between my toes. It is rare and delicious and a little painful to have someone who can understand how vastly different it is to live there.

On this walk, we wander out along the dunes to the edge of the landing pads and stop to look up at the stars.

"Which one is Home World?" I ask, although I already know. He smiles and points into the sky at a small blue dot amid a million other blue dots and says, "That one." And we stand there together quietly, looking up at it, lost in our thoughts and longings.

"Would you ever go back?" he asks suddenly. There is something else behind his question, but I cannot—or perhaps refuse to—read it.

Even for that, I answer him honestly.

"Part of me wants to see it again, because there's so much I miss about it. But I had some bad experiences there, and I'm not sure I could go back. After eight years, it's probably not the same anyway."

"Not being the same might be a good thing." His hands are stuffed into the pocket of his hoodie. He's still looking up at the stars with an expression on his face that I can't quite read.

He's right. That could be the key to everything—not being the same.

"What about you?" I ask.

"Well, I could be tempted. I'll leave it at that."

"By what?"

"The right ... situation. The right person. That sort of thing." A small smile curves his lips upward.

"Was there ever?"

"Ever what?"

"A right ... situation. Person."

"Oh." He laughs softly, and pauses before he answers, this time looking down at the sand beneath his feet instead of at me. "I thought there was," he says, "But no, not really. You?"

I hesitate. It's my turn to look anywhere but directly at him.

"I thought there was. But no, not really."

The silence that descends now is warm and unifying, like a blanket we are both wearing to protect ourselves. We understand that this is as far as we will go tonight, but also that this *might* be a start. We stand together quietly for a few minutes more, wrapped in the comfortable silence, until he says, "Let's head back to Residential."

We turn to make our way back down the path, as we've done many times before. But tonight, he reaches for my hand, and I reach for his, and we walk hand-in-hand until we are one step away from the lights at the edge of Residential. We say goodnight and he squeezes my hand gently before he lets it slip from his grasp, and we go our separate ways.

When I step into my quarters, I find another drawing on my pillow from my littlest podmate, this time of a stick girl and a stick boy standing close together under the moons and stars, large smiles on their faces. Like magic, I feel the crayon smile transfer itself to my face, and before I turn out the lights, I take one more long look out my window at the vast expanse of stars above the northern ridge, punctuated by Iona's hopeful little crescent moons, and I marvel at this planet's strange beauty and optimism.

THE MORNING RISING CHIMES wake me from a night's sleep that was peaceful, restful, and painted with pastel dreams. I climb out of my hammock with a stretch and smile. It's my rest day today, which means Pauly will be yelling at someone else through his headset. I have some fun planned: a picnic with Fanny, whom I've seen far too little of recently, and then some time to myself to read or explore or, more likely, creep off into the scrub to work on my personal projects. We've had some substantial Maintenance jobs come through in the past week, and I've been able to squirrel away an impressive and useful cache of parts and materials.

Most of my podmates have finished breakfast and departed for their work assignments before I step into the common room. Only Hinn and Holly are still in the kitchen, taking their turn cleaning up before they leave for school. Hinn sees me wander in and within seconds presents me with a large cup of fresh coffee. "It's good," he assures me. "Wenda taught us how to make it. She's showing us how to make her special muffins tomorrow. I'm going to take over as pod chef."

"He's lying, *I'm* going to be pod chef!" Holly chimes in. "But Wenda really did teach us how to make coffee right. And we made an extra pot for you to have during your rest day."

I hug them both in thanks. They hug me in return, and then laugh and snort and poke each other as they gather their tools and lunch bags and tumble out the door, shouting goodbyes and well wishes as they go. It's hard to believe they haven't always been members of our pod. The last month has transformed them in the best possible way. And whether it's just the influx of all the new people or a

testament to the positivity of the Bardazelians themselves, Iona has an unde-
niable new energy about it. It's as though our little settlement has been reborn.

This idea resurfaces when I meet Fanny later. Our picnic takes place inside
a brand new clear-domed room her pod has built on top of an outcropping of rock at the edge of their residential space. As we settle in with our
old-fashioned blankets and containers of food spread out in front of us, I'm
grateful for the space's added bonuses of soft, comfortable pillow seating and
a lovely outdoor view that we're able to enjoy without having to deal with
Iona's infamous blowing sand. The motto for a typical Ionian picnic is that
our planet literally puts the "sand" in "sandwich."

"Let me guess, a Bardazelian thought of this," I say, adjusting my pile of
pillows into a kind of chaise-lounge. "It's such a fanciful and optimistic idea."

"It was definitely a Bardazelian idea," Fanny confirms, tucking a few extra
pillows behind her back and breaking out her ever-present flask. "They're
calling it The Star Parlor. They said they wanted to be able to look at the
moons and stars at night without getting bug-bit, but I suspect ulterior
motives."

"I can't believe Pauly authorized it, it's totally impractical," I say.

"Oh, he was completely against the idea until Graham talked him into it,"
Fanny says. "That man could charm the pants off a statue."

I laugh and Fanny throws me an expectant look. "Well?"

"What?" I say. She scowls at me, takes a drink, and hands me the flask.

"I gave him up for you," she says in mock indignation. "The least you could
do is provide me with a detailed description of the goods."

I'm puzzled at first, but then it hits me. "Do you mean Graham?" I ask.
Fanny rolls her eyes and huffs.

"Of course, I mean Graham. Everyone knows you two are a thing. And
neither of you will say a damn word about it. It's driving us all nuts."

I'm a bit stunned and don't quite know what to say. "But we just ... we
aren't ... we're not really ..."

"Don't tell me you aren't. You've both transformed from the most serious people in the universe to cheery little vessels of happiness and light. Only two things can cause that kind of transformation: either lots of money, or lots of sex."

I splutter helplessly. "I mean, we're ... ah ... it ..."

Fanny shakes her head and stares at me. "I can't believe you two. You really *aren't*, are you? Why the hell not? He's hot, you're hot, you're both available and of age, you look at each other like dogs staring at ice cream. What's wrong with you?"

Even though Fanny means it as good natured ribbing, it's making me ache in a way I can't describe. I feel something akin to panic building up in my chest as I blurt out, "He's from Home World, he worked for the Company. I can't go through that again."

Fanny stares at me open-mouthed. She takes in my expression and her demeanor changes.

"Honey," she says, reaching out and placing her hand over mine. "I'm sorry. I get it now. But please just know I really want this for you. We all do. You deserve to be happy."

"I'm happy," I croak, tears welling up in my eyes. "I was already happy."

Fanny looks at me for a long moment, then squeezes my hand gently. "You haven't been happy in years. You've been safe. That's something else altogether."

She's right and I know it. I take a long drink from her flask, letting the bitter liquid burn its way down my throat into my stomach. Then I take another drink before passing the flask back to her. We sit in silence for a little while, nibbling on our picnic lunch, watching Iona going about its daily business below.

"We're just going slow," I finally say. "We're friends now, really good friends. But we both need to go slow."

"I get it," Fanny says, and takes a drink herself. "But please try to get around to fucking before I die of old age. That's a story I want read aloud."

After Fanny and I leave the Star Parlor, I drop by Clinical Aid to visit Karloa. We didn't get off to a good start and I'm not sure my presence is something that will benefit her, if she can even detect it, but she's still my podsister and a planetmate, and I do care how she's doing. Macha meets me in the lobby and gives me an update on her condition; no meaningful change, which is both negative and positive. The one thing that is different is her appearance. She's now completely blue from head to toe—hair, skin, nails, everything. Even the whites of her eyes have turned blue.

"I've been learning everything I can about this drug and its effects," Macha tells me as we walk upstairs to the intensive care unit. "The coloration is meant to work as a gauge of effectiveness. This level of intensity suggests full suspended animation. That's good; it means there should be no deterioration while she's in stasis, at least in the short term. But there's no information on what happens in the long-term. There's a chance that the drug might just wear off, but we don't know when that might happen or how. The body might clear it all at once, or it might progress in stages. An uneven decrease in efficacy across body systems could cause some serious problems."

I don't have to be a doctor to immediately understand. A complete clear would mean Karloa's body systems would simply "wake up" together and all begin functioning at a normal level again. A gradual clear would mean some systems might wake up while others would still be artificially slowed or suspended. Any organ or system that reached a normal metabolic rate before heart and lungs ramped up to provide adequate blood and oxygen would mean disaster. Too much blood or oxygen to "still sleeping" organs could be equally catastrophic.

"Clearly, some way to control the revival would be best," I say, thinking not only of Karloa but also the other 200 Bardazelians lying in stasis somewhere in a Company holding area.

"Yes," Macha agrees. "We'd like to work on that, but it appears some of the materials that go into this drug are fairly exotic and the equipment required for rigorous testing exceeds what we have here. We're hoping the Company will approve this as a formal project and provide support. Otherwise, it will all be seat-of-the-pants, but we're used to that here. We're prepared to try, with or without the Company on-board."

Even though Macha described Karloa's condition to me, I'm not really prepared for what I see when we step into the intensive care unit. It's as though Karloa has been turned into a finely made turquoise sculpture. Every inch of her is brightly, brilliantly blue, with darker blue veining visible along the insides of her arms, her neck, and chest. Her skin and hair glimmer like polished stone. The monitor drones hovering above her bed report pulse and respiration rates beyond human ability to perceive. I place my hand on her arm and feel a texture that is not stone but also not skin: something in between, cool and firm but not entirely rigid.

One of the drone monitors pings, and I look up to see it registering the heat of my hand on Karloa's arm. Macha scans her quickly and says, "It's best if we not touch her, just to keep variation at a minimum."

"Of course." I remove my hand, guiltily aware that I reached for her not out of concern or an urge to comfort, but out of curiosity.

"Does she know we're here?" I ask. Macha's forehead creases as she considers her answer.

"She's not completely unconscious, so technically there is always that possibility," she says. "We don't know what this drug does to perceptive abilities. Her brain, remember, has been metabolically slowed down just like her pulse and her breathing. If she's aware of what's going on around her, we don't see any evidence of it in her vitals. But it may be that we don't know what to look for."

I study Karloa, searching for ... what? I'm not certain. At last, I simply say, "I hope you're better soon, Karloa. I didn't get a chance to know you, and I think you might like Iona more than you imagined. The twins are doing well, Maybree and Quimby are doing well. You still have a place in our pod when you recover, if you want it."

I leave Clinical feeling even more trepidation than when I arrived. There is something about the whole situation that makes me uneasy. I can't put my finger on it. It must be the fact that I feel utterly useless in this situation. I like to be helpful, and there's nothing I can do for Karloa or for the others in stasis whom I've never met and can only imagine.

That evening, Graham appears at our pod for our evening walk, and I find myself visiting the Star Parlor for the second time. There are some logical reasons for the change in our evening habits; Iona is entering its colder season, and although our temperate location affords us none of the dramatic evidence of seasonal change that we see on Home World, it does result in sometimes exceptionally clear and chilly nights. The comfort of the pillow-piles and warm wraps, plus the guarantee of privacy, such a rare thing on Iona, make it an even more appealing choice.

Graham and I stack the pillows to create a large cozy nest and settle inside it, eyes turned to the stars above. He's brought brew in a real glass bottle instead of a metal flask, and the taste difference signals something rarer and more finely made than Fanny's preferred libation. The liquor is sweet on my lips and feels silky and warm going down.

"Fanny asked about us today," I say, feeling the alcohol melting away all my reservations and concerns. "Apparently all of Iona is anxious for us to become a couple."

I feel rather than see Graham smile. "I've taken my fair share of ribbing from Pauly and some of the others," he says. "I've just left them hanging. But if you want me to tell them definitively that we're not a couple, I will."

I pause, uncertain how I feel about what he's just said.

"What do you want to tell them?" I ask.

He doesn't hesitate. "I'd like to tell them that we're working on it."

"Oh. Well, then, you should tell them that." I sit up slightly, angle toward him, and look into his eyes. He reaches up and strokes my cheek gently, carefully. He's prepared to let me lead, and whether it's the alcohol or the moment I had with Fanny earlier, I realize I'm tired of caution, tired of waiting, tired of merely being safe. Fanny won't get her whole story tonight, but she might get the first paragraph.

I bend my head and brush my lips across his. He pulls me tight against him and we kiss: long, slow, and deep. It's a wonderful kiss, but I feel my anxiety level rise almost immediately. "This might take a little while for me to get used to," I say, apologetically. "I don't mean to put you off, but ..."

He waves away my explanation, then cups my cheek with his hand and looks into my eyes, his expression gentle.

"You do whatever you need to do," he says. "I'm in no rush, no one is going anywhere, and I have plenty of my own baggage to deal with. We'll just take our time. And it'll work out exactly the way it's supposed to."

I'm so grateful for his words that I kiss him again, but that's where we stop on this night. Instead, we easily resume our usual pattern of conversation and laughter, and slowly my comfort level returns. When we emerge from the Star Parlor hours later, I feel energized and hopeful.

But as usual, privacy on Iona is an utter illusion. As I'm walking to my assignment in Maintenance the next morning, Pauly starts ribbing me through my headset.

"SOMEONE kept my Maintenance Team Leader out PAST HIS BEDTIME LAST NIGHT," Pauly roars in my ear, and I laugh. Graham and I did stay in the Star Parlor quite late. But only minors have curfews on Iona, and I know Pauly is just needling me out of affection.

"You might want to speak to whoever did that, she might be compromising a valuable Ionian asset," I say. Pauly is on the verge of making a sarcastic response, but his attention is suddenly directed elsewhere. I hear some commotion in the background and Pauly shouting unintelligible instructions.

I feel the cause of the consternation even before I hear it, the bone-crunching vibration that seems to shake the very air, followed by a thunderclap shock wave and the scream of engines overhead. I look up in time to see the enormous white cylinder of a full-sized lander blasting through Iona's gritty sky, then slowly rotating to 90-degree vertical as it prepares to set down on our pad. The Company insignia is emblazoned on the lander's side.

I know this wasn't on the manifest and we're being caught somewhat unprepared. But Iona is resourceful—we'll make it work.

Pauly is shouting into my ear again. I can't hear him over the din of the lander, but I don't need to. I know what he's saying. I shout, "I'm coming!" and run for the pads.

By the time I reach them, there are twenty people working frantically to complete the preparations for the lander's unloading, maintenance, and provisioning. We haven't had a full lander come in for months, so it's a little bit scatter-shot, but no one is panicking, and the necessary jobs are getting done. Pauly sees me come onto the pad and waves me over. "Get over to Intake and see where we can put up the crew. Anywhere there's an overnight will be fine."

"On it," I say. "How many?"

Pauly checks his holotablet. "Five overnight, one staying permanently," he says. "Looks like our new Warehousing Leader has arrived."

"Do we have any data on the permanent?" I ask. Pauly shakes his head.

"Not yet. Just find six overnights for now. I'll send our new Whoop de Doo over with his stat chip and you can sort out a permanent assignment once everyone is on the ground. We'll deal with his orientation procedures tomorrow, after the flight crew is gone."

"Good enough." I turn and start jogging toward Intake. The lander will have to go through a shut-down process that lasts about an hour before the crew can disembark, and they'll also need to see to whatever cargo is onboard and complete the appropriate forms and certifications regarding its delivery. Then they'll probably want to get some food. That means I have a couple of hours to pin down those sleeping arrangements.

My brain is already working it through. I know I'll have to split the crew up, as our former crew quarters were repurposed into residential pods when the Bardazelians arrived. It's going to take finding an open hammock here and an extra bunk there, and the accommodations might be cramped and less than ideal. But they're likely to be "early to bed, early to rise" types anyway, and for most of them it's just a single night. Most lander crews, like most Ionians, can put up with almost anything for one night.

I use my credentials to open the Intake building and get the lights on and humming. I go to my terminal, access our residential plan, and start looking for any open spaces. It's harder than I anticipated. The influx of Bardazelians left us eyeball to elbow as far as sleeping space. Only four pods are listed as having provisional capacity, but at least that's four spaces. I send the affected pod leaders priority communications and hear back from them immediately; they'll make sure spaces are prepared for the visiting flight crew. I find a fifth space when I see a notation about an Ionian who is away on a field mission and not expected back for two days—fingers crossed that's accurate. The last space is giving me fits, until I remember my own pod. Karloa is still listed as a permanent resident, but she won't be leaving Clinical while she's in stasis. I change her status to "long-term relocation," and I have my sixth space. Excellent!

I hear the main door open and footsteps echo across the empty room. "I did it, Pauly, I've got everyone sorted!" I say, but instead of Pauly's thunderous voice, I hear something else—a quieter, warmer timbre that is so very familiar. A voice I used to hear every day, a voice that brought me the greatest pleasure and the most intense pain of my life. A voice I've only heard in dreams for the eight years.

"It can't be," he says, his tone incredulous. "Faith?"

I turn and look at him. I know now I'm not imagining it. My stomach rises into my throat, and I freeze, uncertain what to do. So many conflicting emotions. So many disrupted desires. So many memories, both beautiful and vile.

It takes me a moment to get my wits about me. My mouth is dry and my voice, when I finally find it, comes out as a brittle croak.

"Arden," I say. "It's you."

9

IT'S NOT MY IMAGINATION, I'm not trapped in a flashback loop or some kind of weird hallucination. Arden Wilson stands in front of me in the flesh, his stat chip dangling between his fingers. He's a little heavier and a little older and he looks tired, but the force of his personality still lights his face. His expression is a mix of shock and uncertainty, with maybe a hint of excitement. He's covered in dust, like all of us here. And he's still beautiful to me, whether I like it or not.

Suddenly I'm angry and I wish I could scream.

"I didn't know you were here," he says haltingly. "I thought you were ..."

"... dead?" I finish the sentence and immediately wish I hadn't.

He looks at the floor. "I thought maybe you'd gone back to Home World." He pauses, then lifts his gaze to mine. "I knew you weren't dead," he says quietly.

My breath catches in my throat one more time and I fight to control my facial expression, my voice, my behavior. Although what would be normal in a situation like this, I wonder? How *should* you act when you suddenly find yourself face-to-face with the person who was your world for two years, who then literally vanished without a trace during the worst crisis of your life—a sequence of events you've been struggling to make sense of ever since?

Oh dear god. Pretend he's someone else, pretend he's someone you've never met. Try small talk. Try official talk. Try anything but thinking about the past.

I take refuge in the mundane. "You're our new Warehousing Leader?" I ask, although I've already figured out the answer.

"Yes," he responds. "My glamorous career as a space pirate has ended." He offers a small smile, and I see a flash of long-ago Arden, the lightness, the ease. A voice in my head whispers *he'll fit in well here*, and I involuntarily wince. He sees the expression, misunderstands it, and looks away.

"Let's get you set up," I say. "Stat chip?" All business now. He hands over his chip and I plug it into the terminal, letting the program do its work. I don't even look at the display as it runs. The processing finishes in less than a minute and his credentials appear in the bin in front of him. He holds them up to examine them and is clearly taken aback.

"Is this right?" he asks, waving them at me.

"That's what the program generated," I say stiffly. "What's wrong with it?"

"Nothing's technically wrong, it's just ..." He lets out a short, anxious laugh.

"What?" I demand.

He reads aloud from his credentials. "Permanent residential assignment: Pod C-1419, pod leader Faith Feathergrass."

My mouth falls open, but nothing comes out. It's just as well. At that moment Pauly comes thundering into Intake with the five other crewmembers in tow.

"Your overnight arrangements are all set. Faith has seen to it," he booms. He catches sight of Arden and charges forward, shaking his hand energetically and slapping him on the back. "WELCOME to Iona," he says. "Looks like you're already settling in. I'm glad Faith's taking care of you."

Arden responds to Pauly with the genuine warmth and charisma that have historically made people like him instantly. It still works its magic, as the expression on Pauly's face is nothing short of charmed. "Thank you, Pauly, I'm looking forward to getting to know you and everyone here," Arden says.

"EXCELLENT," Pauly roars. "Make Faith your go-to. She's a fine guide and knows how to do everything around here. Faith, why don't you show him around? I'll take care of getting these folks squared away." He then turns his attention to the other crewmembers.

Arden can't help himself. "The grand tour, then," he says enthusiastically. He looks at me and smiles in a way that is simultaneously innocent and intimate, then makes a theatrical gesture toward the door. It's goofy and sweet with an undercurrent of significance. And he's painfully sincere. There's no way I can shield myself from these parts of him I loved so completely, and I smile back at him as I precede him out of Intake onto the square. I won't ever let myself love him again, but it would seem I can't make myself hate him either.

"It's good to see you, Faith," he says. I know he means it.

"Thank you," I say. I wish I could just return the sentiment, but my brain is jumping, and my emotions are a jumble. I have almost a decade of unanswered questions and part of me wants to ask him all of them right now, but I'm also unsure if I can trust any answer he might offer me.

After eight years, you might not even know him anymore, I tell myself. *Really, you might never have truly known him at all.*

"How long have you been on Iona?" Arden asks, interrupting my inner monologue.

"Almost eight years."

"You must like it, then."

"I'm used to it. It's Iona."

"I hope I get used to it. It's very different than ..." Arden reframes his response midsentence. "It's just very different."

"You'll have formal orientation tomorrow," I say. "It won't seem so different after that." I know that's not what he means, and he knows I know, but he lets it go without comment.

We walk toward the Preservation Theater, which sits in the middle of town. I plan on giving him a thorough tour, starting there and spiraling out to include Clinical, Maintenance, Security, Goods Distribution, Warehousing, Research & Engineering, and Construction, ending at Residential around sunset. Wenda will already have received an automated communication to let her know that there will be a new arrival for dinner tonight. I'll have to work on adjustments for his more permanent assignment to our pod tomorrow.

Another 100 feet to the Theater, and then I can start my basic New Resident spiel. *Can we just walk in silence for a hundred feet?*

"Things are going well here? It's a lot more populated than I expected," Arden says.

Apparently not.

"They seem to be. We're growing. We recently got a substantial influx of new residents."

"Really! No one mentioned that."

I'm not surprised.

"Yes, the Company closed down another station and most of the residents transferred over."

"Oh." His brow creases momentarily. "Bardazel?"

"Yes."

"Oh." Silence at last. I take a sidelong look at him. His face is an expressionless mask, but I'm surprised to see his lips twisting into a frown.

We reach the Theater and I launch into Iona 101. "This building is the Presentation Theatre, the first building constructed on Iona. It originally held residences and important services for the small determined team that founded our station. It's been repurposed and is now the center of recreation and learning on Iona. If you'll come this way, I'll show you how the founders approached the problem of multiuse requirements ..."

I'm doing my best "impersonal guide" routine. He's playing along, examining architectural details and listening intently, like a good new resident. I have no sense of whether he's thinking at all about the way our time on Home World ended. I've been filtering this in my head for eight years trying to recover and move past it. Even if he wants to talk about it, I'm not sure I do. At least I know I can't let it be about what *he* wants, this time.

We're halfway through the tour when my headset goes off; it's Wenda. As one of just a few people on Iona who knows any details of my past, she's aghast as she says without preliminaries, "Dear god, not *that* Arden Wilson."

"Actually, yes, the very one," I say. Arden has thoughtfully moved several yards away so I can respond to the hail with a certain degree of privacy.

"And you're with him now."

"Again, yes."

"Faith. I'm so sorry. Are you all right?"

"I *think* I am, but it's early yet." I attempt a laugh. Wenda snorts derisively.

"Does Pauly know?"

"No, he doesn't."

"He's truly been assigned to our pod?"

"I ran the program myself." Every time I think about it, it feels more unfair.

"We can make some kind of adjustment and move him into a different pod."

"No, it's okay."

"It's not okay. I don't want you to have to go through this."

Suddenly I'm excruciatingly tired. "We'll talk about it later," I say. "See you at dinner."

I turn back to Arden, who is pretending not to have listened to every word I just said.

"We'll finish this up then head home so you can meet your new podmates," I say. "They're anxious to get to know you."

Arden offers a wan smile and says, "Whatever you say."

We get to the pod just before sunset. Laughter and the buzz of convivial conversation float down the path to meet us, and as we walk into the common room Arden receives a boisterous greeting from all sixteen people gathered around the long serving table. Wenda meets us at the door and ushers Arden to a seat between Darrow and Hinn, both of whom start peppering him with questions. He flashes his breathtaking smile around the table. Even Wenda can't help but smile back. I catch her attention and nod toward the kitchen; the two of us leave the common room ostensibly to start serving dinner.

As soon as we're safely across the threshold, she looks at me and says, "Wow."

"Arden's still Arden," I say, reaching for serving platters, bowls, and utensils.

"You were not kidding about him," she says. "He's ... *different.*"

"That's one way to describe him."

"And attractive, too, in a really unusual fashion. I don't think you ever mentioned ..." Wenda catches herself in mid-sentence and looks at me guiltily.

"That's another way. Also true."

"Wow," she says again. "Has he said anything about ... then?"

"I haven't let him," I admit. "I suppose he might want to talk eventually. I don't know if I'm ready."

"How do you feel about him being here?"

I suddenly realize I've been struggling with this question for the last several hours.

"I don't know," I say. "I used to fantasize about what it would be like to see him again, what I would say, how I would feel. It doesn't seem to fit any of the scenarios I anticipated. It was a shock to see him without any warning, and I was angry at first—for everything in our past, for him invading my safe place and showing up here. But that only lasted a little while. I know he didn't choose this place; he didn't have any idea I was still here. And you see how charming he is—he's very good at diffusing negative emotions. I'm just kind of in the moment now and I don't really know how I feel about it."

"Is that because of your relationship with Graham?"

Graham. My stomach drops with the realization that I haven't thought about Graham once since Arden walked into Intake and spoke my name.

Wenda reads the look on my face.

"Uh oh," she says.

We spend a few minutes working in the kitchen in silence, slicing thick hunks of home baked bread and ladling steaming hot soup from a pot on the stove into a large serving tureen. At last, she asks, "Are you going to tell them?"

"Tell who what?"

"The two of them about each other."

I hesitate. "I'm not sure what there is to tell," I say. "Graham and I aren't really in any kind of formal relationship. I mean, we have a nice friendship, and it might have been heading toward being more, but realistically ..."

Wenda is scowling at me, her lips twisted in a way that suggests her bullshit meter is pinging on the high end. I sigh.

"I just don't think it's a big issue," I say. "They'll meet, obviously. All of you are so anxious for me to get it on with the governor that I'm sure Arden will pick up on that even without me spelling it out for him. But the fact is, I'm not in a relationship with Graham. We're *friends*. And my past isn't anyone else's business unless I elect to share it. Why should it matter? Arden and I have a history, but that's all it is. It's the past."

"The question isn't about what's in the past," Wenda says, lifting the soup tureen and casting me a meaningful look. "It's about what's in the future." With that, she turns and heads out into the common room to start dinner service. She's greeted by loud, energetic cheers. I pick up the tray of bread and follow her out, struck by the fact that I can clearly discern Arden's voice in the middle of all the noise, automatically and without any effort at all.

Through dinner and afterwards, everyone in the pod wants to talk to Arden. He's happy to entertain them with one energetically rendered story after another about his adventures in space. He's been to many places and interacted with many cultures over the last eight years. His stories almost always focus on breaking down stereotypes and finding a way to make even the most extreme-sounding practice relatable. I notice too that those experiences have taught him to listen more. Time has sanded down the rough edges of his youth and tempered his intense fiery nature into one that tends more toward gentleness and a spirit of kindness. I wonder what might have been if this version of Arden had been with me on Home World. Fighting back a burst of sentimentality, I excuse myself and head to my quarters for some quiet time.

I catch up on some pod management tasks first, adjusting our water and food requests to accommodate an additional podmate, then I extinguish the lights and stretch out on my hammock in the dark where I can look out the window at the stars. Replaying Wenda's comment in my head, I know she's right, but I still can't work out how I feel. Part of me has truly missed Arden and is happy to have him crashing into my life on Iona, no matter how much trepidation it might cause. Another part of me resents the complexity that his presence brings into my life, because it seems he might still care about me, and I can't yet sort out my emotions about him. But then there's the angry and hurt part of me that can't forget how he left me behind all those years ago and believes that for all the charm and sweetness he might be able to deliver now, nothing can make up for that transgression. I shift between all these feelings as rapidly as the dust clouds blow across the Ionian dunes. *It's only been a day*, I tell myself. I'm sure I'll have more clarity soon. I *have* to get more clarity soon.

10

IT'S AN ENORMOUS RELIEF to hear the rising chimes and awaken from my dark dreams of Home World to Iona's pale sunlight spilling in through my window. I feel distinctly unrested but drag myself through my morning routine to prepare for another day. I pull my headset on. Before I reach my own door, Pauly is booming into my ear.

"HOW'S THE NEW GUY DOING?" he yells.

I wince, partly from the volume and partly from the question.

"Fine," I say, steadying my voice. "He gets formal orientation this morning and will be ready to meet with the team this afternoon."

Pauly says something over his shoulder, and in the background, I hear Fanny peal with laughter. Pauly snorts derisively.

"Fanny saw you giving him the tour yesterday. She says he's DEFINITELY FINE."

Great. I attempt a fake laugh, which falls spectacularly short. I haven't even left my room yet and I'm already crabby and short-tempered.

"Anything else? I'm about to grab breakfast and head out. Do you need help with the lander launch?" I ask, trying to craft my tone into something businesslike rather than irked.

"Nah, that's sorted. We have two maintenance requests you can handle, but for today if you can keep shepherding the new guy along, that will be enough. What's his name again?"

"Arden. Arden Wilson."

Pauly speaks over his shoulder, and I hear Fanny's laugh again.

"Don't even tell me what she said," I say, before Pauly can speak again.

"Okay, okay. I'll see you and uh ...."

"Arden."

"ARDEN this afternoon, then."

The connection goes blessedly silent, and I pull off my headset for a moment. As I walk down the hallway toward the Common Room, Pauly's roar is replaced by the sound of Arden's voice curling through the chatter of my podmates, like a stream of cool water on this dry planet.

The scene in our Common Room is the usual level of cheerful commotion and laughter. The soft Ionian light makes the windows glow, and most of my podmates are seated at the long table with their breakfasts, listening eagerly to a story Arden is telling with great animation. Hinn and Holly are particularly mesmerized, and each twin takes turns interjecting a gasp or exclamation of delight.

Wenda meets me at the kitchen door with a large cup of hot coffee. "They've been like that for half an hour," she says, nodding toward the twins. "That might be the longest I've ever seen Hinn sit still."

"Maybe Arden should be Youth Education Leader instead of Warehousing Leader," I murmur, and Wenda stifles a small laugh.

Arden appears to reach a natural break in his story, and Wenda takes advantage. "You two are going to be late for school if you don't leave now," she says in her sternest mom-voice. Hinn and Holly wail objections but recognize the tone and hustle to gather up personal belongings and lunches then hurry out the door. Arden offers a lopsided smile to Wenda and mouths the word, "Sorry." In completely atypical fashion, Wenda giggles, colors, and waves her hand in the air, saying, "Oh no it's all right, I can see they're fascinated by you!" She stares at Arden and I stare at her until she remembers I'm standing next to her, at which point she hurries into the kitchen immediately for some unarticulated reason. Arden, staring into his coffee, seems to miss the whole exchange.

The rest of my podmates stir to life, muttering about time, and soon it's just me and Arden in the common room. Wenda clatters in to bring me some breakfast and hurries back into the kitchen before I can even say, "thank you."

He sits across from me, relaxed with a soft smile on his lips, and I decide I've got this under control. I smile at him.

"Is there a Part Two to the tour?" he asks, and I realize he's really asking how much time he'll get to spend with me today.

"No Part Two," I say, and he pouts charmingly. "After I drop you off for formal orientation this morning, I'll take care of a couple of maintenance projects down in the pit. This afternoon, we'll meet with Pauly and the rest of your team. You can set up your duty roster and assignments. We can sort out anything else you need as Warehousing Leader. Tomorrow, you get tossed into the deep end to see if you can swim."

He sighs. "Warehousing," he mutters. "What have I become?"

"Pragmatic?" I offer. He shoots me a mock scowl. "It's just how we operate out here," I explain. "We don't specialize much; that's the core difference in being on an independent world as opposed to a Company world. We all pitch in to do whatever jobs need to be done. It's team-based and may feel unstructured at first, but it works out quite nicely. You'll see."

"I hope you're right," he says. He leans toward me slightly; his hand barely touches mine. My pulse jumps and my heartbeat starts to ricochet. *So much for having things in hand.*

Hinn bursts in suddenly, having left his holotablet behind in the morning rush. He treats Arden to a stream of questions as he thunders around the room searching for the tablet. Arden sits back and as he does so, our hands break connection, but he keeps his eyes on me as he answers Hinn's inquiries. The teen finally locates his holotablet, grabs it, and runs back out, shouting, "Can we talk about that at dinner, Arden?" to which Arden calls out, "Sure thing." I stare down at the table, rattled by the intensity of my response to him, but when I look up at him again, his expression has reset to casual and light.

Did I imagine the whole episode?

"I guess it's time for us to go," he says, draining his coffee cup and setting it back on the table with a thump. We stand in unison, and he steps back to let me precede him out the door.

We make the walk in a comfortable silence. I start to feel more settled once I drop him off at the Preservation Theater and veer across the square toward Maintenance. I'm relieved for the assignments this morning; some quiet time in the pit is just what I need. It's been days since I've been able to collect any parts for my project, and the busted hover-flats and skiff controller waiting for me might have the exact components I'm looking for. It could still be a good day. It's Iona. Anything can happen if you're resourceful.

By the time I climb out of the pit into Iona's anemic afternoon light, I'm reinvigorated by the hours of solitude working with my hands, and don't even care that I have silver streaks of parts lubricant decorating my shirt, hands, and chin. It's time to pick up Arden for the Warehousing Team meeting.

Arden is sitting outside on the Theater steps and offers up his easy smile as I approach. I automatically smile back. This feels normal and acceptable, and not entirely uncomfortable as long as we stay focused on the business at hand. He stands and walks out to meet me.

"How was it?" I ask, and he nods his approval.

"I learned a lot," he admits, as we walk across the square together. "Your planet is very different than a Company planet, as you said. It's an interesting balancing act, maintaining your sovereignty when the Company is, in large part, your bread and butter."

I agree. "It can feel a bit tenuous sometimes, but the personal freedom is worth it."

"I can certainly appreciate that," he says, and I know he is thinking about what happened to us, living on a Company planet.

I wish I could tell him that the suffering we experienced on Home World at the hands of the Company can't happen here. But despite Iona's status as an independent planet, I'm always aware of the Company's reach and how much influence they can have if they want it. Iona has escaped the Company's interest because we're small and don't draw attention to ourselves, but the influx of Bardazel's population combined with the presence of people who know all too well the reality behind that station's closing may threaten to bring our history of anonymity to an end. I sincerely hope not, but I've been worried about this for a while. Even though I pretend it's simply a little diversion for my own amusement and a test of my expertise and ingenuity, my little pet project built out of scraps is evidence of my concern.

Arden makes chitchat as we climb the steps to Intake's door. The Conference Room lights are on and the multiple voices floating through the air means we're among the last to arrive. I enter first and find myself unexpectedly face to face with Graham. He gives me a smile and a slightly quizzical look; I try to smile back and not appear quite so much like I've just been punched in the chest, which is how I feel.

That feeling is nothing compared to the one that replaces it when he looks over my shoulder and I see his face flash in recognition, followed by the sound of Arden's laughter and voice saying in amazement, "Graham Thorn! How the hell are you? It's been years!"

I barely remember the rest of the meeting after seeing Graham and Arden back-slapping each other like old friends. Two hours later we depart Intake with Arden and Graham walking together deep in animated conversation, and a sour dusty taste in my mouth.

"Isn't that SOMETHING," Pauly thunders to me as we cross the Square. "Who would have GUESSED our two newest residents would be old pals?"

"Certainly not me," I say drily. Neither Arden nor Graham is offering any elaboration on how they know each other, just that they met 'years ago, out there' and that it's been a long time.

"What's this now? JEALOUSY? You can't be the man's center of attention all the time." Pauly attempts to whisper, which is impossible for him—his voice comes out more like a painfully loud hiss. I understand he's trying to tease me about my alleged relationship with Graham, but I'm not finding anything about this funny. I give Pauly a mock-angry frown to hide my irritation; he buys it and laughs heartily.

"We're going to tour the Warehousing set-up and grab some brew afterwards," Arden says, turning toward us and clearly speaking for himself and Graham. "Everyone coming?"

"Oh, not me," I say, taking the first opportunity at escape. "I have a few things I need to finish up. I'll see everyone later." Neither Arden nor Graham object, and I find myself jettisoned from the main group like junk from a skiff. Pauly, at least, turns and waves good-bye as they walk away from me, heading toward the warehouse.

I don't want to be in the tight quarters of my pod, though. I want to be somewhere empty where I can gather my thoughts, so I head over to the pit. I have a good stash of parts from this morning that I can haul over to my project space to play with. It'll only take an hour, it will be nice and quiet, and I'll stay on my headset in case anyone needs me.

I'm hoping the hands-on work will keep my brain occupied, but it's only a matter of minutes before it grabs on to the specter of Arden and Graham shaking hands like old friends and begins running wild. Who are these two men, to each other? To me? Do I really know anything about either of them?

I manage to avoid intimate conversations with or about Arden and Graham for next two weeks. Arden is absorbed in his work and getting the Warehousing system set up and running, and I'm increasingly able to relax in his presence. Our past stays in the past and invades my thoughts less and less. Other more mundane tasks take up my headspace: Wenda requests my help with planning a spring greenhouse garden, and I secretly order her some fancy Home World tomatoes as a surprise. Hinn talks me into being the test case for his new breakfast muffin recipe and I have to admit he's becoming an excellent chef. It seems that everyone on Iona is busy and content.

Graham and I get together a few times to share meals or take walks together, but there's no repeat of the intimacy we shared that night in the Star Parlor and I don't seem to miss it. I finally manage to wrangle some personal time with Fanny, whose company I do miss. We meet one evening in the Star Parlor for a late dinner. This time it's Fanny's turn to tell all—a Bardazelian gentleman named Tommas, blessed with an impressive stomach and an even more impressive mustache, has energetically begun courting her, and she's as giggly as Holly when she talks about him. We make it a very late night, and I creep back into the pod with a light heart, hours after everyone else has gone to bed.

The next day is a rest day for me, and by the time I rise, our common room has reached its peak morning chaos. Wenda and Hinn clatter around the kitchen enthusiastically, while Darrow and Arden sit by the fireplace deep in conversation. Some of my podmates are leaving the table while others are just sitting down. Our littlest ones play an energetic game of tag in the courtyard with their mother. Holly runs coffee from the kitchen to everyone in the common room.

Arden spots me and smiles broadly, waving me over. I smile in response and cross the room to join them.

"Darrow's been telling me about your medical mystery," he says.

"Oh, you mean Karloa? It is quite the mystery."

"Speaking of which, I'm due at Clinical now," Darrow interjects. "Her general case review is in a couple of hours. Faith, you'll be attending, won't you?"

"Yes," I say. "I believe Graham will be there as well, since he's the closest thing to family she has on Iona."

"Good. I'll see you both this afternoon." Darrow rises from his chair and makes a polite bow in my direction and excuses himself. Arden, beaming with excitement, gestures toward the now-vacant chair and I sit down.

"I have so many questions," he says, leaning forward. "She's in full-on stasis? Not just extended sleep?"

"Macha would be able to answer with more detail, but yes, apparently she's in full-on stasis. Her body systems and processes have slowed to nearly immeasurable levels, but there's no cellular degradation and she's stable. The tricky part, which makes it significantly different from extended sleep, is that we have no options for waking her up."

"Darrow mentioned that. No antidote. How did that come about?"

"That question's better suited for Graham. She was one of our Bardazel transferees and there's an elaborate back story. I'm not sure how much of it is supposed to be public knowledge."

I see then—or possibly imagine—a brief cloud pass over Arden's sunny expression, but it's dispelled almost instantly, and his monologue of questions continues.

"And the color effect is extraordinary. She's blue?"

"From head to toe. It's quite startling when you see her. There's no way you can be prepared for it."

"Blue," Arden murmurs, his focus shifting inward momentarily. I can almost hear the wheels of his mind turning; that part, at least, hasn't changed since I last knew him. *"Blue."*

He's yanked out of his thoughts by Pauly roaring into his headset. It's so loud that I can almost make out the words from where I sit. Wincing slightly, Arden swings the mic down and reassures Pauly that his Warehousing Leader has neither decided to sleep all day nor transferred to Night Services and will be there in short order.

"Clearly, I have to go," he says, and stands up. "One last question though."

"Yes?"

"Does he always yell like that? I'm nearly deaf now, and it's barely been a month."

"I'll just say you've caught him at a good time. Once you catch him at a bad one, you'll long for these days," I laugh. Arden makes a mock-terrified face over his shoulder as he hurries out.

I'm still sitting by the fire smiling when Wenda comes over, hands me a cup of coffee, and sits down across from me. Our podmates have dispersed for the day, and we have the Common Room to ourselves.

"You two seem to be getting on well," she says, tilting her head toward the door to clearly indicate who she's talking about. Her intonation also makes the statement less casual than its wording suggests.

"We're getting along," I say. "We live in the same pod; we work on the same team. We might as well, right?"

"Have you talked?"

"We talk all the time."

"Have you *talked*?" Wenda repeats, looking levelly at me. I can't pretend I don't know what she means.

"No," I say, looking pointedly into my coffee. "It hasn't come up."

To be fair, I haven't let it come up. There have been moments over the past two weeks when it felt like Arden might have been gathering himself, getting ready to broach the subject of us in the long ago, and I've made every imaginable effort to put him off: leaving the room, changing the subject, doing anything to avoid the conversation.

Wenda isn't fooled by my casual statement. She frowns and leans forward.

"You need to talk to Arden," she says.

"I will eventually. But we're doing fine right now, and I don't want to ..."

She interrupts me, her tone serious. "Maybe you're doing fine," she says, "but I'm not sure Arden's doing fine. When you didn't show up before lights-out last night, he was very anxious. I told him you were with Fanny and wouldn't be home for quite some time, but that didn't appease him. He was keeping watch out here after we all went to bed. He claimed it was insomnia, but I'm certain he was waiting for you. He could *not* let it go."

I blink back my surprise. A few of his comments might have suggested a lingering connection between us, but our interactions have felt balanced and rational, and I truly believed it was my imagination.

84

Wenda takes stock of my reaction, and her demeanor becomes gentler. "You always said he left you," she says quietly, reaching out and taking my hand in hers. "I'm just saying, maybe you had it wrong. You've always assumed you knew the truth, because that's what it looked like to you. Well, maybe he did what you said. But maybe he didn't. Maybe there's more to it. And you two should talk about it."

I don't know what to think, much less to say. Wenda's words have shattered nearly eight years of armor and torn to shreds a story I wove around myself for protection from the hurt that Arden's disappearance caused. I became guarded and careful because I learned that love gave people power over you. It never occurred to me that I'd had that same power, and that the manner of our separation might have damaged him as much as it did me.

"All right, I promise we'll talk," I breathe. Wenda smiles and squeezes my hand. She rises and heads back to the kitchen. I sit with my thoughts awhile longer, my fingers wrapped tightly around my coffee cup to still their sudden shaking, trying to understand the impact Wenda's revelation is having on me.

11

I ARRIVE FOR KARLOA'S review a few hours later and find Graham waiting in the reception area. His continued consideration and engagement with her, even as she lies in stasis, makes me think I'm not a very good pod leader. Pods are supposed to be a stand-in for family here, since no one is really "from" Iona. But I remind myself that I didn't even get a chance to know her, much less befriend her, and that Graham has known her since her arrival on Bardazel. They were at the very least colleagues, if not friends.

Graham looks up as I approach, greeting me with a tired smile. He pats the seat next to him, and I sit.

"How is she?" I ask. "Are you still visiting every few days?"

A vaguely guilty expression flashes across Graham's features and he looks down at the polished stone floor. "I've pared it down to once a week," he admits. "As far as I can tell, there aren't any changes in her from one visit to the next. I want to be supportive, but sometimes it's depressing. I feel completely powerless. Lying there like that, she's such a powerful reminder of everything I failed to do to protect the people of Bardazel."

"That wasn't your fault," I interrupt. "You did what you could, but your hands were tied. And those people who drank the Blue, Karloa included ... ultimately, *they* chose what they did. You can't take responsibility for that."

He passes me a grateful, slightly sad smile. "I take responsibility for it anyway," he says. "I know it wasn't my *fault*, but I can't help feeling that I should have done more."

I spontaneously take his hand and squeeze it tight but release it when I hear a powerful stride hurrying toward us across the marble-tiled lobby. I look up expecting to see Macha, but instead see the flushed and anxious face of one of her medical assistants.

"Macha sends her apologies, but the case review has to be rescheduled," the assistant says breathlessly. "There's an emergency and we're all needed on-scene immediately."

Before I can ask where "on-scene" might be, he spins on his heel and sprints across the lobby, joining a phalanx of medical personnel streaming down the stairs and out into the open air. Graham's headset goes off, followed by mine. We rise and rush outside after the medical team, toward the plaza.

Graham looks back at me with an expression of alarm as he says into his mic, "We'll be right there." We're already running by the time Wenda's voice, straining with emotion, says into my ear, "Get to the Warehouse as fast as you can, Security just reported an explosion. Pauly and Arden are in trouble."

The Warehouse is set back from the square, tucked into a space between Intake and Goods Distribution. Even from this distance we can see thick smoke roiling out of a shattered window toward the back of the building on the second floor. Dozens of Ionians are rushing toward the building, only to be held back by our Local Security personnel; not even the Medical Team is allowed inside the perimeter. I spot my Bardazelian podsister Maybree helping hold the line. I wave to get her attention and then approach the line as close as I can and call out, "What happened?"

"Not sure," she shouts back. "Based on witness accounts, some kind of explosion."

"Is everyone okay?"

"Unclear. Five reported in the building, two out now with non-life-threatening injuries. Rescue and Recovery will be going in shortly."

"Shortly? Why aren't they in there now?"

"Company assets appear to be involved, so that means we have to follow Company safety protocol. The team is suiting up and getting the structural integrity survey started." Maybree looks at me apologetically, and I remember that Arden is her podbrother as well. "They'll go in as soon as they possibly can," she says.

It's a logical answer, but it's not the one I need to hear. I turn away from Maybree and work my way back from the line, through the growing crush of anxious citizens surrounding the accident scene. Graham stands to one side, not too far from where I left him. He's alternately listening intently to his headset then shouting into his mic. His eyes are hard and his lips are drawn into a tight line of frustration. Finally, with a muttered expletive, he snaps the mic away from his mouth. I realize we're feeling the same way.

"Three people are still inside but Rescue won't go in until the building is evaluated," I say. "Company safety protocol."

Graham scowls, nodding.

"I was talking to Miley from Goods," he says. "She was on the first floor and got out with minor cuts and scrapes. Three still inside on the second floor."

"Pauly, Arden, and ...?"

"Bennid." He's one of the team members from Bardazel, barely eighteen years old. No wonder Graham is upset.

I look toward the smoke pouring unabated from the broken-out second-floor rear window. There's a line of Rescuers attaching sensors to the outside walls and donning protective clothing and breathing apparatuses in front of the building, while newly dispatched safety drones hum overhead. I catch Graham's eye.

"This won't do," I say. "We have to do something."

He understands immediately and responds, "Let's go."

Graham follows me as I make for Intake at a dead run, heading for a side courtyard door that will leave us a few feet from the rear of the Warehouse. In less than two minutes, we come into the courtyard. The view of the Warehouse seems even more dire up close than it did from the square, and I panic for a moment. The smoke is thick and noxious, and hangs just above our heads. But the thought of three people trapped up there, conditions unknown, makes me push through my tears. I hurry to the fire escape that stands along the rear right corner of the building. It's at a 90-degree angle from the blown-out window. Its distance from the source of the explosion is both a positive and a negative; this far away, it should be largely unaffected and intact. It does mean, however, that it will take us longer to reach our friends once we get to the second floor.

I put my hands on the railing and give it a shake. It's little more than a metal ladder affixed to the exterior of the building, an almost straight-up climb to small landings at egress windows on the second and third floors, then continuing up to the roof. It appears to be intact and still firmly attached, but the smoke wrapping the building now is strangely dense and low-lying. I can barely make out the landing for the second floor, even though it's no more than twenty feet above the ground. To further complicate things, the smoke appears to be getting thicker rather than dissipating.

"This smoke," I say to Graham. "What do you smell? Or, more to the point, what do you not smell?"

"Anything related to burning," he replies. "The smoke isn't being created by a typical fire. It's some kind of chemical reaction."

I agree. I don't know whether this is good news or bad.

My feet are on the first rung of the fire ladder when there's a commotion behind us and a voice calls out, "Wait!" I turn to see Darrow, Macha, and Wenda round the corner.

"We saw you run," says Darrow, panting with the exhaustion of trying to keep the pace that Graham and I set. "We knew you'd do something like this."

"Take these," says Macha. She holds out two respirator masks, and Darrow and Wenda each produce first-aid backpacks, which they hand to us. "We knew we wouldn't be able to stop you ..." her voice trails off. In her silence I hear all the logical issues and concerns cemented with a final vote of confidence.

"Thank you," I say, truly grateful. I pull on the mask she's offered me and slip on one of the packs, and Graham does the same. We take a last quick look at our friends and begin climbing up to the second floor as quickly as possible.

By the time we've gone half-way, the smoke is so thick I can hardly see the metal treads below my feet. Graham is only a few rungs below me, but he might as well be back on Bardazel; I can't see him at all. At least I can hear his voice, muffled by his respirator mask, reassuring me. He's repeating, "Keep going, I'm here, I'm right behind you," almost as a form of echo location. After what feels like a long time, the treads finally widen out into the small landing, and I feel my way along the wall to the large window intended to serve as the emergency exit. When I touch the plexi, it feels cool, further confirming that this is not an ordinary fire. Graham appears alongside me. I make eye contact with him, and he nods. Together we reach out and spring the window. It swings easily up from its casement and opens wide.

A torrent of dark gray smoke pours through the opening, and my spirits start to flag. I had hoped the effects of whatever happened had not reached this far corner of the Warehouse, that our friends might have had a chance to gain some respite if they could make it this far. Graham places his hand on my shoulder gently, recentering me. "Let's go in," he says. "Climb in, stay low."

Together we climb over the sill and, once inside, drop to our hands and knees and crawl along the wall in the direction of the blasted-out window, on the opposite side of the room. The smoke is thick but there's some relief here at floor level, and there is no heat whatsoever. I try to be grateful that at least we won't be evacuating victims with 3rd degree burns.

We find Bennid first, lying on his stomach on the floor. His slender frame is twisted in an unnatural way, as though he was thrown through the air like a rag doll. It's clear his left arm is broken just below the shoulder. But his eyes flutter open briefly when I touch him and call his name.

"You're going to be okay, Bennid, we're getting you out of here," I say as convincingly as possible. "Do you know where the others are?" No response. I try again. "Where are Pauly and Arden?"

He tries to roll over, disturbing his injured arm, and promptly wails in pain and collapses again, unconscious.

"Get him out," I say to Graham. "I'll keep going."

"We'll take him out together ..." Graham begins.

"Don't argue," I interrupt. "Get him to the egress, at least. I'm going to keep searching."

I carefully crawl past Bennid's prone form, and continue along the wall, leaving Graham behind. It's almost impossible to see through the smoke, so my other senses take over. Beneath my hands, I feel small fractured pieces of plexi and metal, likely parts of a crate that's been destroyed. It probably contained or was in proximity to whatever exploded. I'm also very conscious of what I hear. There's a low sizzling hiss coming from up ahead and to my right, toward the center of the floor. It might be the sound of a flare or smoke bomb, which would explain the strange behavior and quality of the smoke.

And then I hear coughing.

It's ahead of me, but it's moving, traveling from where I expect the center of the room to be, further away to the right. I lift myself up on my knees, up into the dense smoke and lift my mask and call out, "Who's there? Arden? Pauly?"

There's a pause, more coughing, and then the sound of someone moving nearer to my location. I finally hear Arden's voice say weakly, "Faith? Where are you?"

I find myself fighting back an almost overwhelming urge to weep with relief and instead manage to say with convincing calm, "I'm by the outside wall. Are you all right?"

There's a pause and I hear Arden exhale heavily. "I'm all right enough," he says. "Pauly is hurt bad."

"Do you know where he is?"

"He's here. We have to get him out."

"I'll come to you. Keep talking. Tell me what happened." I crawl toward the sound of Arden's voice as he speaks, navigating carefully around scattered boxes and collapsed shelving units.

"Uh ... okay. We were opening a crate and something ... blew up. I don't know what happened. It knocked me out. I came to and there was all this smoke, and I ... I ..." Arden's voice is fading. He stops his monologue and coughs hard.

"Take your time," I say. "I'm nearly to you."

"Okay. So ... smoke. And ... Bennid was here, oh my god ..."

"We found him," I say. "We got him out."

"I can't remember who was here. Was Graham here?" Arden's voice is weaker still, and his confusion is becoming evident.

"No, Graham's with me. He'll be in to help soon."

"Okay."

Arden's breathing has become loud and labored, punctuated by intense coughing fits. I worry that he's more seriously injured than he's letting on. I don't know what I'll do if he loses consciousness. I try to keep him engaged.

"Arden?"

"Mmm?"

"You okay? I'm almost there. Stay with me."

"I'm staying."

"Stay by Pauly."

"I'm staying."

"Keep talking to me if you can."

"I'm here. I'm staying."

"I'm glad."

"Yeah?" His voice is falters, but the spate of coughing that follows it is enough to direct me. I can see him now, a couple of feet in front of me, lying on his back on the floor. There are cuts and bruises on his face; more concerningly, bright spots of blood are expanding on the front of his shredded service jacket. But his chest is rising and falling in a reasonable rhythm. I reach out and grab his hand, squeezing it hard.

"It's going to be okay, Arden. I've got you."

Arden keeps his eyes closed, but he squeezes my hand weakly in return. I take exactly four seconds to appreciate without judgment my relief that he is alive, but then drag myself back on track.

"Where's Pauly?" I ask again.

Arden waves his hand in the air, indicating a point past his feet. I crawl forward until I find Pauly, lying unconscious in a large pool of blood. His face is battered, and his hands and arms appear to be shredded up past his elbows. There's a thick splinter of metal and plastic, about two inches in diameter and several inches long, protruding from the left side of his abdomen.

"Pauly, Pauly!" I shout but receive no response. He appears to be breathing; however, the movement of his chest is shallow and irregular.

Then blessedly I hear clattering and commotion behind us, and Graham calling my name.

"Follow my voice!" I call out. "I found them. They're both in pretty bad shape, but at least Arden is conscious."

"I'm ... fine ..." Arden protests feebly, which fires off another flurry of coughing.

In less than one minute, Graham joins us. The clattering turns out to be a lightweight emergency litter he's put together from the first aid kit and is dragging behind him. "Macha and Darrow have commandeered hovergurneys. Once we get these two outside, the rest is easy," he says. "Bennid is already on his way to Clinical."

I'm encouraged by my resourceful friends who have so much faith in us. I know we're a long way from being out of the woods, but I feel my energy returning. "Let's get Pauly on the litter," I say. "Arden, can you sit up? Can you crawl with us?"

"I'll try," Arden says, pushing himself slowly to a sitting position and peering through the smoke. "Where's Pauly?"

"We're putting him on a manual litter. We're going to be pulling him over to the window."

"Good," Arden says, losing the end of the word in violent coughing and a long low groan.

Graham gives Arden a look and says, "I'll manage Pauly. You keep an eye on that one."

It takes a bit of effort to get Pauly's large frame on the litter. Graham has to stand to effectively pull the litter to the window, so proximity to the wall is crucial, as that will be his only guide. Simultaneously, I keep encouraging Arden to crawl with me. He's clearly in pain and has lost a lot of blood and seems on the verge of losing consciousness. Slowly, we proceed toward the emergency egress, Graham pulling Pauly in the lead, Arden and I crawling behind them.

We manage to reach the corner where the outer and back walls meet about fifteen feet from the emergency exit, when the hissing sound in the middle of the room changes pitch and gets louder.

"Hurry up!" I shout to Graham. "Something's about to happen!"

We can't risk the slow speed of crawling any longer. "Stand up, Arden," I say. "We have to hurry." As Arden braces himself against the wall and struggles to rise, I hear Graham hesitate. "Get Pauly out NOW," I say, and breathe a quick sigh of relief when I hear them start moving again.

I turn my attention to Arden, who is in a half-crouch. I hook his arm across my shoulders and lift hard with my legs, pulling him awkwardly to a partially standing position. "Lean on me, and let the wall support your other side, then start putting one foot in front of the other," I tell him. He staggers forward a few steps, and then collapses to his knees, dragging me down with him. His breathing is labored, and his head droops. When he closes his eyes, I almost panic.

"Come on, Arden. Stay with me," I say. His head comes up with obvious effort, and he struggles to stand. I get him balanced between me and the wall, and this time we do better. Two steps, then three, then three more. The smoke is thicker now, and the hissing is louder. I'm 100 percent certain this is not a good sign. But it's clear Arden is doing the best he can, and I'm not going to bail on him now.

"Stay with me," I say again. He convulses slightly, then leans his head against mine. His voice is so faint I can scarcely hear him when he gasps out, "I will."

Suddenly Arden's weight is completely taken from me by someone else—I hear Darrow's voice encouraging him to hurry—and Graham is hustling me along the wall to the window so quickly my feet barely touch the floor. The sound of hovergurneys pours in from outside and I hear Macha's voice shout, "Clear!" Then Darrow and Graham lift me through the window and onto the landing. The smoke behind us now is black and significantly denser than before, and the hiss from inside has turned into a loud high-pitched whine.

Graham and I approach the last hovergurney together.

"Get on, lie flat," Darrow instructs and I do. Graham then positions his body over mine and grips both sides of the gurney hard. The autostraps draw tight around us, and all kinds of warning sensors go off, telling us the weight limit has been exceeded and the gurney may not be safe. But at this point, it's the fastest way down, and we have no choice but to take it.

"This will be tricky. Hang on," Darrow says, then shouts, "Clear!" and guns the engine, kicking the gurney into motion and over the edge of the landing. It's not designed to fly and should only carry one person plus the driver, so I'm guessing we'll first feel a gut-wrenching drop, followed by the hover mechanism kicking in to keep us from hitting the ground with a few feet to spare.

At least, that's what we would have felt if not for the monumental explosion inside the Warehouse just as we clear the landing, that blows us twenty feet out from the collapsing wall and flings us to the ground in a terrifying tumble.

12

I WAKE UP TO a wonderful sensation of warm sunlight on my face and the whispering sounds of the sea, the kind I remember from my childhood when my family went camping on the beach. It was my favorite thing to do, wake up on soft sand and listen to the world coming to all around me as the sun crept over the horizon. My mind half-expects to hear my father's low voice telling me it's time to get up, to hear the birds and bugs and other creatures begin their peaceful morning sounds.

But of course, I'm not a little girl out camping on the beach with my parents. It comes to me slowly that I'm lying in a bed, and more slowly still that I'm lying in a bed in Clinical. The light pouring over me isn't the sun, it's a medical drone tracking my vital signs, and the whisper of the ocean is really the whisper of Clinical's enviro system cycling on. I open my eyes and stare at the drone for a moment, feeling an irrational sense of hostility that it dared to impersonate the sun in my dream.

A voice says softly, "Oh there she is. Look who's back." A familiar pleasant face peers over the bedrail, looking into my eyes with a smile.

Wenda.

"How are you feeling?" she asks, patting my hand on top of the covers.

I attempt a faint smile. "I'm not sure," I say. "Okay, I guess?"

I start to sit up, but my head starts pounding like a lander short of its launch pad. I abandon the effort and lie back again. "Maybe not okay," I amend.

"You can go with okay," another voice interjects. This time it's Macha. She comes to Wenda's side and reviews some data from the drone. "You got a good whack on the head when the gurney hit the ground, so you suffered a concussion. You sustained a couple of broken ribs because Graham is a heavy bastard and landed on top of you, but we've already repaired those. So aside from lingering effects of the concussion and some bruising and residual soreness that you'll get to enjoy for a while, you *are* basically all right."

Apparently satisfied, she looks away from the drone and down at me. "You need more rest and some food, but you'll be ready to go home in a couple of days. Only light duty for you for the next few weeks, though, so no heavy lifting, no climbing, no operating heavy machinery, and definitely no more flying through the air and landing on your head."

I struggle to follow Macha's words and connect them to events. My brain's trying to pull up memories of whatever happened, but I only get pieces, like out-of-focus snapshots. Some seem meaningful while others are simply confusing.

"I don't remember everything," I say cautiously. This is an enormous understatement. I barely remember anything and trying to remember is making my head hurt again.

"That's not unusual," Macha responds patiently. "You might get it all back at some point, or you might not, but it's nothing to worry about. I'm going to order some food for you. You rest now and I'll check in on you later." She bustles out of the room.

Wenda leans over the bed again, so I don't have to try to sit up to see her. Her expression is a mix of exhaustion and relief. She looks like she could use some rest as well.

"How long have I been here?" I ask.

"The accident was three days ago. Do you remember?"

"It's all in bits and pieces," I say. "I remember going to rescue ... people. I remember smoke, and a big explosion. Oh ... is everybody okay?"

"Yes and no. Graham has a couple of bruised ribs, and he broke his wrist in the gurney crash—do you remember that? But he's in good shape otherwise. Darrow hit a piece of the gurney and wound up with a partially collapsed lung and a fractured collarbone, but he's going to be fine as well."

"We found someone inside ... Bennid ..." I say, and cringe as my mind delivers a snapshot of the horrific twist of his arm.

"Yes. His arm was badly mangled, and Macha had to amputate it. It will be replaced with a bioequivalent as soon as they can get one delivered, but once that's done, he'll be fine too. He asked me to thank you for getting him out of there."

Wenda keeps talking, but I hear her voice as though she's speaking through a layer of cotton. Fog is overtaking my brain now. Even the words I hear aren't really registering. I know there's more I want to ask, but I can't sort out what those things might be. That will have to do for now. My eyes are closing on their own.

"More sleep will help it all come clear," Wenda says. "I'll be here when you wake up." With that, consciousness slides out from under me, and I'm gone again almost before she finishes speaking.

The next time I come to, my mind is clearer and the memories more vivid—and all the more distressing for it. I wake up in tears, gasping in near panic.

Wenda is there as promised and comes to my side immediately.

"Are you feeling all right? Should I call Macha?" she asks, clearly concerned. I shake my head no and finally manage to gasp out the words, "I remember."

"Oh." The concern on Wenda's face increases. "Everything?"

I grab her hand and squeeze it hard. "Pauly and Arden. Don't leave anything out. Are they ... are they ..." I'm sobbing and can't finish. I stop to wipe my face with the back of my hand.

"I should get Macha," Wenda says and tries to disentangle herself from me. "She'll be able to tell you more."

I don't let her get away and grab her hand again, squeezing it hard.

"Tell me if they're alive," I say. I'm so terrified of the answer it's almost impossible to get the words out of my mouth. Wenda's expression doesn't change as she squeezes my hand again and then gently withdraws her own.

"They are," she says. "But you will still want to talk to Macha. I'll get her for you."

With that, she leaves the room and I'm alone with my miserable conjecture. They *are* alive. I'm glad. But for how long? What kind of condition are they in? How badly are they hurt? Were we able to reach them in time for it to make any difference at all?

The tears continue to flow down my face, although I try to compose myself so I can have a reasonable exchange with Macha. But by the time she enters the room, I'm no better. I'm just going to have to cry and talk at the same time.

"Wenda tells me you've regained your memory," Macha says, bending over me.

"I need to know what happened to everyone," I sob. She looks completely unphased and makes a quick check of the drone stats.

"Intense emotion is a symptom of concussion," she tells me. "This means you're still in the recovery process, so we'll limit the amount of detail we cover at this point. For now, know that your friends are alive and stable, but have substantial healing ahead of them, just as you do. And if it makes things any better at all, you should also know that if it wasn't for you, there would have been a much worse outcome for everyone involved."

I want to protest and ask more questions, but Macha's stern expression makes it clear I'll get no more information from her tonight. "Rest now, talk later," she says, firm but caring—the perfect medical professional. I hear her footsteps as she leaves the room, and Wenda replaces her in my field of view.

"Are you hungry?" Wenda asks. "Mealtime was a little while ago, but I can grab the food cart. You should eat."

"With you here, who's feeding our pod?" I ask, and finally get a smile out of her.

"I'm letting Hinn fly solo," she says, her fondness for the boy shining through. "He's actually ready to take over, but he's anxious about it. Having him jump in to help this way is boosting his confidence."

I smile too, hearing about Hinn's ongoing success.

"Thank you for being here," I say quietly. "I hope everything is all right."

"Of course," Wenda says in an even tone, but I see a shadow in her eyes that worries me. "I'll go track down your food."

With that, she leaves again. I let out an exhausted sigh. I don't feel hungry at all, just tired and frustrated. But it will make Wenda feel better if I eat, so I will.

I'm holding on tight to the two words Macha left with me: "alive" and "stable." Granted, this is not the same thing as "just fine," but it will have to do. At least it seems like a reasonable place to start. And it helps to know we made a difference, even if I don't yet know how significant that difference might be. I close my eyes and feel my mind starting to drift again when I hear the hum of an automated serving cart coming into the room. I'm about to wave it away and tell whichever clinical aide is guiding it that I'll eat later when a warm familiar voice says, "I believe the lady requested a meal?" and I find myself looking up into Graham's shining gray eyes.

There are some cuts and bruises on his face and his lower lip is split, but otherwise he seems normal and healthy and in good spirits.

"You're okay," I say, feeling relief warming the pit of my stomach.

"Just bruised ribs," he says. "Wasn't lucky enough to break them. Bruised is not bad enough to waste the resources on, so Macha tells me. I'll have to suck it up for a few weeks."

"Your wrist, though—they fixed that, right?"

Graham waves his left hand in the air like a flag, flexing his wrist this way and that. I see the small hospital admit chip flashing blue on the back of his hand, like my own. "Yep," he says. "Good as new. But they're still not ready to let me go. How is your head?"

"A little foggy," I admit. "I remember almost everything now, but apparently I'm still having concussion symptoms, so Macha is taking a hard line with me. So maybe you ..." I look up at him hopefully, but he shakes his head.

"So maybe I'll help you circumvent doctor's orders? I don't think so. Unless ..."

"... unless what?"

"Unless you eat. Then maybe." Graham activates the tray, and it spins out of his grasp and over my bed, slowly settling itself down over me. Little legs pop out to turn it into a standing bed tray, perched above my lap. In concert, the head of the bed begins to lift, raising me to the perfect angle for eating.

I look at the tray skeptically. The food doesn't look as appetizing as Wenda's. I pick up the fork and regard Graham with an arched eyebrow. "Is this a bite-for-byte transaction?" I ask. "One bite of food for one byte of information?"

"You're in no position to make the rules," Graham responds. "You eat and I'll think about it in the meantime."

"Authoritarian."

"Grump."

I laugh a little and scoop up a fork full of something that looks like scrambled eggs, put it in my mouth, and start chewing. It's not delicious but it's reasonable. Graham nods his approval, and I swallow and take a second bite. By the third bite, though, my eyelids are starting to feel unreasonably heavy. Graham helps me lift a cup of water to my lips and drink, then takes the fork out of my hand and places it on the tray. The little legs retract, and the tray lifts and floats gently out of the way. As it departs, the bed's angle of elevation becomes gentler until it is almost flat again.

My eyes are closed, but I can feel Graham fussing over me, pulling up covers and adjusting pillows.

"I'm sorry," I say. "I want to know everything." The words come out slow and thick.

As I slip back into sleep, I hear Graham say, "In time, Faith. If I'm not here when you wake up, I'll be just down the hall."

When I wake up again, daylight is shining through the windows, and I finally feel mostly normal. I have no idea how long I've slept, but at this point I'm truly sick of being in bed. I try to sit up, but the drone above me flashes red and informs me that a technician is being called. Despite promises by both Graham and Wenda, the room is empty except for the angry drone, which keeps repeating, "please lie down, a technician is coming to assist you" in a voice I can only interpret as vaguely hostile.

I lie back but keep my body raised on one elbow, in a modest show of defiance toward the drone.

The technician, a young curly-haired woman named Pepper, arrives within thirty seconds, and greets me with a large smile.

"Look at you!" she says cheerfully as she begins resetting the drone and checking its readout. "You must be feeling much better now."

"I am. When can I get out of here?"

"Oh, I can't say, that's up to Macha. But everything looks good, so probably soon. We can turn the drone off, so it will stop bugging you every time you sit up." A few taps and the drone powers down its surveillance functions and moves away from the bed, finally settling on a shelf on the other side of the room.

"Let's get Macha, then, because I'd really like to go home," I say.

The technician's face falters for a moment, although her voice retains its chirpy cheerful tone.

"Macha is in a meeting, but I'll make sure she comes in as soon as it's done. Can I do anything else for you?"

"Is one of my friends out there? Can you get one of them to come in?"

"Your friends?"

"Wenda? Graham? You know them both, right? They've been here a lot."

"Oh. Right." The technician's face blinks out of cheerbot mode briefly, but she recovers quickly and beams at me. "They are in the same meeting as Macha, I believe. But I'll see about getting word to them that you'd like to see them ASAP! Do you want something to eat or drink? The carts will be coming around shortly."

"Can you tell me how Arden and Pauly are doing?"

This time the crash is complete. Pepper's expression becomes full-on dour.

"Oh no," she says, shaking her head. "I can't discuss another patient's condition with you."

"Macha was going to, but I fell asleep before she could," I lie, smiling pleasantly. "I'm sure it would be all right."

The gambit doesn't work. Her smile this time is definitely forced, but she spreads it across her features anyway and says to me as charmingly as possible, "Oh, well, then it's best to let Macha finish what she started. I wouldn't want to speak for her!"

"Of course not." I surrender. Pepper's unquenchable cheerfulness has worn me down.

"I'll send the cart and you can grab a bite to eat. I'm glad you're feeling better!" Pepper almost shouts from the doorway. Her smile is more genuine now, no doubt at the prospect of getting away from me and my inconvenient questions. I throw myself back against the pillows in annoyance. It feels like I've been lying in bed forever, and I can almost taste my own frustration. But at least with the drone no longer tracking me, I can move around a bit more. I stare at the admit chip embedded in my left hand, glowing blue. If it wasn't for that little bugger, I'd be able to sneak right out of here and go back to the pod.

I remember the admit chip on the back of Graham's hand, his promise that he was just down the hall. It might stand to reason that since we all came into Clinical together, they would put us into rooms near one another. Maybe I won't have to leave the hospital to get the information I want. Maybe I won't even need to leave this floor.

I sit up cautiously and swing my legs over the side of the bed, checking the drone on its shelf to make sure it's not still tracking me somehow. *Silence.* I smile as my feet hit the cool tile floor and I stand, taking a deep breath.

I'm a little wobbly, to be sure, probably from lying down for so long. I hold on to the bed for a second until I'm stable on my feet, then carefully pad across the room. I look in the mirror over the washbasin, pretending to examine my own appearance while I get a cup of water from the faucet. I'm relieved to see that I don't look too horrifying—a bump on the left side of my head, a couple of fine scratches, and a little discoloration under my chin are all that looks vaguely out of the ordinary, aside from my wild unbrushed, uncontained hair. I make an attempt to pat it down a little—a futile effort—and take a long sip from the cup of water I just poured. It's cool and sweet against my tongue and I drink it down quickly. As I draw another cup from the tap, I take stock of what I'm wearing: a standard issue ugly green hospital nightie that comes to mid-calf, and a compression top, probably to help my newly fixed ribs stabilize. I convince myself I'll blend in—what could be more normal than a hospital patient walking around hospital corridors?

I drink the second cup of water and walk to the doorway of my room, where I pause to listen and look for any potentially interfering perky technicians.

The hallway is quiet. Diffuse light washes down its pale teal walls and floor. There are doorways to other rooms on the same side of the gently curving hallway as my own; along the opposite wall are supply lockers, a conference room, and windows looking out to the courtyard below. The patient rooms are easily discernable from other types of rooms, as their entryways are covered with holographic readouts hovering in open space rather than physical doors. I walk out of my room and to the nearest window in a show of bravado and conviction, entirely artificial, that what I'm doing is not breaking any rules whatsoever. I'm just going for a little stroll.

I look out the window onto the little desert garden staunchly resisting Iona's almost ceaseless wind and count the rows of windows to the ground.

I'm on the third floor.

I walk along the width of the window, staring out as though this courtyard is something I never noticed before. Sensing no one coming or monitoring me, I step back across the hall and begin checking the readouts hovering in each patient room doorway.

I know that for the most part the readouts will be far too clinical for me to absorb, but each begins with the patient's name and status, and that's what I'm after. The first two rooms beyond my own are vacant, although the readouts still contain the last name of the patient and the notation "discharged." This feels like it would be a terrible invasion of privacy if I were to read on, so I skip them. The next room is occupied by someone named Bock, who based on the coughing and sneezing I hear, must be dealing with some kind of respiratory infection.

I finally come to a room labeled *Thorn* with a status of *ready for discharge*. Bingo. Graham's room. But when I peek inside, he's nowhere to be seen.

I feel a rush of victory when I see the next room is labeled McFarland—Pauly's last name. I'm so excited that it doesn't quite registerer that his status is listed as "unknown." I don't see the red "quarantine" label until I step eagerly through the doorway and set off the alert.

Within seconds, technicians rush up to pull me away from the door. Macha scolds me and gives orders to her techs to take me back to my room and activate the tracking drone until further notice.

"I only took one step inside," I say, but Macha gives me a look that is simultaneously angry and dismissive. As Pepper tries to hustle me along, I crane my neck to look behind me and almost regret my impetuousness.

Across the room, lying in bed, I can see Pauly. Both of his arms have been amputated above the elbow. A pair of small discs lie over his closed eyes, a medical device is attached to his skull in the middle of his forehead. Two drones hover over him, tracking his vitals.

I can only see parts of his face, along with his neck, upper chest and shoulders, but it's enough.

Pauly has turned blue.

13

THE TECHNICIANS HUSTLE ME back to my room and put me in bed. Pepper gives me a pitying look as she reactivates the drone. She makes a show of tinkering with its settings until the other techs leave the room.

"I'm sorry," she says quietly, once we're alone. She gets me a cup of water and puts it into my shaking hands, then folds her hands over mine to help steady me as I lift it. "I wish I could have told you, but the staff's divided about what to do. Some wanted to involve you as soon as possible, given your previous experience with this ... phenomenon, but others didn't want to distract you from your own healing. I can see both sides, frankly."

I shake my head, partially to clear it, but also partially in disbelief.

"Who gave him Blue?" I ask. Pepper looks confused, so I clarify. "How did he get the drug that causes the stasis?"

"This wasn't caused by anything he ingested that we know of," Pepper says. "More likely, it was the result of something he was exposed to in the explosion. It took effect about an hour after everyone came in."

I gasp and look down at my own hands and arms in pure reflex, then gasp again in panic and whisper, "Arden?"

"He's all right," Pepper reassures me. "I mean, he was badly injured, so that's of concern, but he's not blue. And neither are Bennid, Darrow, Graham, or you. Pauly was trying to open the crate when it exploded, so he got the most exposure to whatever was in it, and a part of the crate pierced him in the explosion—you saw, you were the one who found him. Macha is confident that either something

106

in the crate or the explosion itself, maybe some residue on the crate piece that struck him, led to what you just saw."

"So Pauly is in stasis, like Karloa," I say.

Pepper's eyebrows knit together for a moment.

"I really don't know if it's the same," she finally replies. "Macha will have to explain what's going on with him medically. She'll be here soon."

I look down, contemplating my next visit from Macha. I can feel Pepper studying me. Her empathy makes me supremely uncomfortable.

After a few moments of silence, Pepper takes the cup from my hands and places it on the nightstand. "Macha should be here shortly." With that, she pats my hand and walks out of the room, leaving me with my shock, my questions, and my new nemesis, the VitaWatch 8000 Health Drone. On impulse, I swing my open hand at it, but it deftly lifts itself just out of my reach, before saying in its imperious mechanical voice: "Please lie down. If you require medical assistance, say 'help.' If you would like to order a meal, say 'meal.' Medical rounds will begin shortly."

Fortunately, Graham arrives before I can formulate a plan to damage the drone.

"Could you please stay out of trouble for five minutes?" he says, sitting on the edge of the bed, taking my hand in his. He's trying to sound relaxed and teasing, but there's an overlay of tension in his voice. His face is drawn and troubled, and his shoulders slump in uncharacteristic dejection. His funk puts me into a funk as well and I find myself suddenly agitated and petulant.

"Someone should have told me," I say.

"Someone would have. But Macha wanted to make sure you were strong enough to hear the news."

"That shouldn't matter. Someone should have told me as soon as I was awake."

Graham exhales in a way that belies his utter exhaustion and there's a long silence. When he speaks, all lightness has left his voice and his tone is flat, bordering on angry.

"This isn't about you," he says sharply. My mouth falls open in surprise, but he doesn't notice. "Two people who were almost killed, one of whom is now entering a physical condition we have no idea how to reverse. Others sustained major injuries that will limit their activity for quite some time. We've lost use of a physical facility and part of its contents due to the damage caused by a powerful explosion. And now the Company is coming here to investigate, because some of its assets have been destroyed or damaged. No one has had the time or bandwidth to make addressing your curiosity a top priority."

"What are you even saying to me?" I snap. "This is not about *curiosity,* and you know that. Those people are part of my family. I have a responsibility to them that I can't begin to fulfill if I don't know whether they're alive or dead."

Graham cuts me off. "You just spent the last five days lying in bed not knowing where you were most of the time. You weren't in any condition to fulfill any responsibility to anyone, not even to yourself, and you *knew* they were alive because Macha told you that much. Now, because you couldn't possibly wait half an hour to find out what was going on, you blew off recommendations from medical professionals and people who care about you to insert yourself into a potentially dangerous situation that could have repercussions we can't yet imagine. You broke a quarantine field. You disrupted care for others when medical technicians had to wrestle you back into your room. And now Macha has to file a report and figure out what to tell the Company about this stunt, which is fabulous because she only just figured out what to tell them about our little rescue mission."

He's dropped my hand. His expression is one of complete exasperation. I can see the struggle on his face as he fights to choose his words carefully. When he speaks again, his voice is low and tightly restrained.

"What you did for Arden, Pauly, and Bennid was wonderful," he says. "Truly a selfless act that was instinctive for you. And most likely the Company will see that, and it will mitigate any negative consequences as a result of those actions. But what you did out there in the hallway was stupid and irresponsible, and it puts us all under the Company's lens. And you don't want that, Faith. Believe me, you don't want that."

He stands and moves away from the bed. I want to ask him a thousand questions. I want to tell him I know far better than he does what it's like to be under the Company's lens. I want to blurt out *why are we fighting?* But I can't find any words to say at all.

He takes my silence to be acquiescence. "I have to wrap up my discharge with Macha," he says. "You should rest. They're unlikely to let you go home today after all." With that, he leaves the room.

I fling myself back against the pillows and screw my eyes shut in my own fit of pique, battling multiple emotions. I'm anguished and miserable about what's happened to Pauly. I'm frustrated by my inability to do anything about it, and by the idea of staying in Clinical even one more second. I'm confused and upset by Graham's speech. And I'm sad about ... well, about everything. Too much is happening that I don't understand. That was one of the things I loved about Iona compared to Home World—its flexibility, its looseness with routine. I'm afraid my rough-and-tumble indie planet may be changing in a way that makes sense for it, but not for me.

I rub my face and moan. "What the hell is happening here?" I ask aloud.

From the doorway, a familiar voice says, "Another day in the fabulous life of Faith Feathergrass?" I open my eyes to see Arden, battered and weary, but smiling all the same.

As he comes toward me, I notice he's in a hoverchair rather than walking. He glides to the bed and we reach for each other's hands instinctively. He's also wearing Clinical's signature ugly green nightie. The admit chip on the back of his hand glows yellow.

"How are you?" I ask, searching his face. He has a few bruises and scrapes that Macha will have deemed too small for Clinical intervention and he's definitely weak, but any other injuries are not immediately obvious.

"I'm not too bad off," he says, squeezing my hands. His voice is thin and raspy. "I have some throat issues that Macha has me in treatment for, but it's getting better every day. I had some serious lacerations on my chest and lost a lot of blood, and something I was exposed to made me hurt like hell all over. I hear it was touch and go there for a little while, but I'm here."

"You're *here*," I echo, looking into his face. A sudden rush of emotion threatens to overtake me, and I look down for a moment. "The chair ...?" I ask, focusing on it instead of Arden's face.

"A precaution. I'm expected to make a full recovery, but I'm still weak and sometimes not breathing as well as I should be. But it's good that I'm breathing at all. And that's because of you."

The tears make their way into my eyes despite my best efforts to blink them back.

"Not just me," I say, still looking down. "Graham, Macha, Wenda, Darrow ... "

"You, Faith. They helped, to be sure, but no one else would have done this if you hadn't started it."

"Oh, I don't know about that."

"I do. It's what I would expect of you. And I know you better than anyone on Iona, no matter how close you might have become to anyone else here."

A parade of faces runs through my mind, people I love and consider family, with whom I've shared so many experiences over the last eight years, and I see again how I have kept them all at a distance in one way or another with secrets and silence and my mysterious past. Arden is right. He's the only person on Iona who knows the deepest parts of me.

But there's more to me now that he hasn't experienced, a woman he's only now getting to know. For an instant I feel profoundly alone—no one on this entire planet has a full understanding of who I am—but I hear Graham saying sternly, *"this isn't about you,"* and I push those thoughts to the back of my mind.

"Graham told me the Company is coming," I say, shifting my gaze to Arden's face and gripping his hands hard.

"They are. But it's going to be all right," he responds, his voice soft and soothing. "You don't need to be afraid."

It's the first time I realize that I am.

"How do you know?" I ask. "When is it ever all right when they get involved?"

"I understand why you would feel that way," Arden says in a measured cadence, "but you have to believe me. There's nothing to worry about. It's going to be okay."

I examine his face for any sign that he's simply telling me what he thinks I want to hear or sugar-coating the truth in some way but find none. He lifts his hand and strokes my cheek, tucking my hair back behind my ear, in a gesture that is as old as our time together and still as comforting. I tilt my face into his hand and close my eyes, permitting myself to enjoy this moment of connection. The fullness of our past comes rushing back into my mind, but it doesn't spoil the moment. I open my eyes and look at him, finally seeing him clearly in this new landscape, this new context.

"We have some catching up to do that we've been avoiding," I say, feeling strangely calm and grounded. "Maybe that's something we should do before the Company arrives."

His face glows with pleasure as he says, "That's a good idea."

We're interrupted by Macha, who comes into the room loudly tut-tutting, taking Arden to task for tiring himself out. He successfully makes a case in his own defense by showing her the readout from the monitors built into his chair, empirically proving he's been careful. She approves but shoos him out of my room anyway.

"I'll come back in a little while," he says from the door, and simply laughs when Macha gives him her sternest look. I notice the sound of his laugh is thinner than normal, but it still has its enchanting musical quality. As he glides away, Macha smiles, despite herself. Arden's charm has clearly worked on her as well.

"That man," she mutters, shaking her head, but her face is lit with amusement.

She then turns her attention to me, and the stern expression reappears. Before she can speak, I interject.

"I am really, truly sorry," I say. "I know what I did was stupid and impatient, and caused all kinds of problems for you. I didn't mean to do that; I just didn't know ..."

She holds up her hand and stops me in mid-apology and I brace myself. But the censure I expect doesn't follow. Instead, her face softens, and she regards me with a kind expression.

"Don't apologize," she says. "You couldn't imagine what you were walking into. I wish perhaps you had been more trusting in our ability to judge what was best for you, but at the same time I also wish I had not been quite so circumspect with information you had a right to have. It's no secret that you're not the most consistent rule-follower on Iona. But this is probably why you have the friends you do."

At this, a conspiratorial smile creeps across her face, and I understand she includes herself in this group. I smile gratefully in return.

"What now?" I ask.

"You were scheduled for a four-day isolation because you breached a quarantined area, but that's just our automatic protocol. I've already filed the administrative notes to downgrade it to two days of observational status. Clinical staff have been working hands-on with Pauly from the instant he came in, and none of them have suffered any ill effects—the quarantine is more for his benefit, because we want to keep things around him as calm as possible. Our experience with Karloa also suggests this is noncontagious," Macha explains. "but we're puzzled about how Pauly was exposed when neither Arden nor Bennid were. So that mystery forces us to be careful."

"I hear the Company is coming for a little visit."

A small frown twists Macha's lips. "Yes, we're coordinating it now," she says. "Perhaps they can shed some light on this for us."

"How?"

Macha pauses for a moment, as if considering putting me off again, but then thinks better of it.

"The crate that exploded was sent here by the Company. Hopefully they will have further information to share."

"*The Company* sent the crate that exploded?" I echo, trying to still the tremor in my voice. I struggle to tamp down the flashing sirens in my brain, warning me of a repeat of my experience on Home World. "What was inside?"

"No one seems to know. The Security Team was able to piece together enough of its data file to see that it appeared on our intake manifest quite some time ago, but there was no additional data on the sender or what might have been inside. The final explosion obliterated both the crate and its contents ... and everything else in a 20-foot radius, for that matter."

I shudder, knowing how close we all were to being inside that radius when the blast occurred.

Macha looks at me philosophically for a moment. "You did a good thing, Faith," she says. "You're going to get tired of hearing this, but you must rest. Try to at least get some sleep before Mr. Personality glides back in here and gets you wound up again."

A faint cough echoes in the hallway, and Macha, looking toward the door, says in an elevated voice, "Don't think I don't know you're out there just waiting for me to leave. Go to your room and get back in bed or I'm taking that hoverchair away."

"Abuse of power," I hear Arden complain, followed by more coughing and the whisper of the hoverchair moving down the hall.

"I'll set your status to 'do not disturb' temporarily," she says to me, eyeing the doorway suspiciously. A few quick commands later, and a holographic barrier appears above the door. The admit chip in my hand also shifts color, from blue to the same pale-yellow hue as Arden's.

Satisfied, Macha adjusts the drone's settings and then pats me on the shoulder. "I made the drone less invasive but promise me you'll limit your movement. You should be able to sit up or walk to your sink or toilet without it going off, but if it senses you're out of bed for longer than a few minutes, it will make a most unpleasant scene. And I've had enough unpleasant scenes involving you for one day. Got it?"

"Got it," I say, and lie back against the pillows, resigned to the inconvenience I managed to bring on myself. Macha leaves the room and I stare up at the drone balefully. I'm determined to be the best patient possible so I can get the hell out of here and back to something that at least might pass for normal. But with two people in a mysterious irreversible stasis, a massive unexplained explosion, and an anxiety-inducing visit from the Company hanging over our heads, I worry "normal" may be slipping away from Iona forever.

14

THE NEXT TWO DAYS are long and dull. My new status means no outside visitors, although Pepper procures a holotablet for me so I can chat with Wenda. I ping Fanny also, to see how she's doing and to express my sympathy for what's happened to Pauly. Her eyes are red from crying, and she looks like she hasn't slept in days; she still seems to be in shock. I'm glad Tommas is with her to provide moral support. I take a brief call from Graham who is clearly distracted as he speaks with me. Our conversation is perfunctory and distant. It's obvious he called because his conscience insisted he should, not because he wanted to. He tells me he's been chosen pod leader in Pauly's absence, then asks basic questions about my recovery and whether Macha has adjusted my work schedule. He doesn't broach the terse exchange we had the last time we were together.

Macha also makes good on her threat and restricts Arden to his own room, so even that prospective diversion is removed, although he manages to send me a couple of encouraging messages through Pepper. I read, I listen to music, I play with my food, I sleep, and I count the hours down almost literally one by one, until Macha finally comes into my room on the evening of the second day to let me know my penance is over and I can go back to my pod. I am at last discharged.

Wenda is waiting in the hallway and darts into my room the instant the "do not disturb" hologram disappears from the doorway. "Do you feel like walking back, or should I get a scooter?" she asks. In truth I'm so excited to be free I feel like I could fly to the pod under my own power, but I reassure her a walk will be fine. But before we leave, I run down the hall to find Arden. He's sitting in his room looking out the window at Iona's pale little moons creeping over the horizon. The expression on his face is something that's not quite sadness, but clearly a longing for something, an ache. I'm a little concerned about interrupting what might be a private moment, but he hears me at his doorway and looks around with a warm, delighted expression.

"You're being set free?" he says, motioning me into the room. I look up quickly to verify he's able to have visitors. No colored barrier warns me away.

"I am," I confirm, stepping over the threshold. "Wenda is here to walk me home. Has Macha said when you'll join us again?"

"She says soon. She wants to see a little more improvement in my airway, but things are apparently progressing nicely. I'm almost there."

He stands and walks toward me steadily, his posture much more upright and stronger. I look into his face and notice his color is much better and his eyes have regained their light.

"No chair," I say.

"No chair," he repeats, and opens his arms wide. Without hesitation, I step into them, and we hold each other tight for a moment.

"I'll bring you home as soon as Macha says it's okay," I assure him, "and then we'll have that talk."

"Excellent plan," he says, as we move apart. I rejoin Wenda in the hallway. When I turn for one final look over my shoulder, he's still watching me, eyes dancing. He waves and calls to Wenda, "Don't let her overdo it." Wenda waves back with a reassuring smile.

"I take it you two are getting along so well because of your shared convalescence?" Wenda teases as we head for the exit. "Oh, or maybe it was that dramatic 'saving his life' thing. That can sure grab a guy's attention."

"Hush," I say. "Arden and I have known each other for a very long time and there's no point in pretending any differently. That's all there is to that, and I'm good with it. We've reached a new plateau."

Wenda considers this with a sly smile on her face. "Make sure you know where the edges of that plateau are," she says as we walk outside. "We wouldn't want you falling."

I shake my head and laugh. "Don't worry," I tell her. "You'll see."

I look up at Iona's little moons and the bright stars overhead, joyously breathing in the gritty air and relishing the crunch of sand under my feet. All I can think is how delighted I am to be out of that building and away from the constant scrutiny of drones, to be walking on my own, and to be heading back to my pod and my podmates. As heartbroken as I am about what has happened to Pauly, I cannot contain my own relief and appreciation. I throw my arm around Wenda's shoulders in a companionable walking hug.

She wraps her arm around me too, patting my ribs carefully. "Did they feed you in there at all?" she asks. "Arden looked thin too."

"I wouldn't call it food," I say, grimacing. "So many times, I would have killed for one of your breakfast muffins."

"Well, we can get you fed, but it won't be my muffins," she laughs. "Hinn has taken over. And he's so good no one will eat my cooking anymore. But that's all right. I'm happy to pass the torch."

The last thing I expect when I walk into the pod is a welcome home party, but there it is, with balloons and music and brew and food. My podmates excitedly cluster around me, from oldest to youngest, hugging me and cheering my arrival. Fanny is also here, with Tommas in tow. Bennid's present too, and is showing off his new bioequivalent arm. And sitting by the fire wearing a contemplative expression is Graham, looking more like the Graham who stormed the damaged warehouse with me than the Graham I last saw in Clinical. I catch his eye and we manage to smile at each other before I'm enveloped in a tag-team bear hug by Hinn and Holly.

"I baked you a cake!" announces Hinn proudly, gesturing toward an elaborate multilayered concoction on the table that must have required a week's worth of sugar and egg stores to create. But it's gorgeous and looks delicious. Wenda, reading my mind as usual, murmurs, "Can't be mad at that," and I chuckle as I gratefully accept a large slice of cake from Holly.

It's not long before the dancing starts. Tables and chairs are pushed aside and couples begin spinning each other in our common room as Shar and her partner Venus play lively tunes on dulcimer and drum. Tommas is going out of his way to make Fanny smile, succeeding more often than not. Holly is cheerfully accepting dancing lessons from Bennid, while Hinn explains the finer points of cake-making to Darrow. I'm about to comment on the scene to Wenda when Maybree glides up with a shy smile and asks her to dance. Wenda casts a quick concerned look at me, but the delight on her face is clear and I shoo them onto the floor with a wave.

In my estimation, that leaves exactly two people not dancing. Well then. I turn expectantly toward the fireplace and am surprised to see Graham is no longer there. I barely have time to register his absence before I'm pulled into a five-way reel with Holly, Bennid, Hinn, and Darrow. The rest of the evening goes by in a blur of music and laughter, and by the time the party comes to an end and I collapse into my hammock to sleep, I'm too exhausted to give any thought as to where—or why—he might have gone.

When the rising chimes sound in the morning, it takes me a moment to remember I'm finally at home in my own little hammock instead of on a stiff hard bed in Clinical. The light playing across my closed eyelids is, at last, sunlight, rather than the scan of a health drone, and the welcome clink of cutlery and crockery replaces the mechanical whir of autocarts. And the *smell* ... it's as if whatever Hinn is making is pulling me out of bed by my nose. I sit up and stretch, taking it all in. I'm so very happy to be back.

But on the heels of that good feeling, I can't help but think about Pauly, so seriously injured and trapped in stasis. Things will be different now. Someone else will be barking the orders over my headset. Someone else will be coordinating Iona's many moving parts. Who else can possibly do that job? Pauly and Fanny have been here the better part of fifteen years, and Pauly was already an old hand in his role by the time I arrived. I can't imagine how we'll fill those shoes. I can't imagine Iona without him.

I look over at my headset, lying on my bedside table. I'm still on medical leave for the next few days, with fairly specific restrictions on my activities, but surely it wouldn't hurt to monitor the chatter and find out what I missed while I was stuck in Clinical. After I complete my morning routine, I give in to the temptation. I pick up my headset and drop it on, tapping in before I walk toward our common room for breakfast.

The first voice I hear is Macha's, snarling, "Faith Feathergrass, take that headset off immediately. You are NOT available for duty today."

"I just want to listen," I complain, but Macha is unmoved.

"Log out or I'm readmitting you," she says. "Your discharge specifies you are to take it easy. If you can't make yourself adhere to that rule, I can."

I sigh. Very smart of her to threaten me with the one thing she knows I'm absolutely not willing to face.

"All right, all right," I mutter. Macha's threat has done its job. I fold up the little headset and put it away.

The common room is buzzing with energy, despite the late night most of us had. Holly is running coffee to everyone, and Hinn has just emerged from the kitchen carrying a platter loaded with amazing-looking muffins. My podmates start trying to grab them from the tray as he walks past, not even waiting for them to make it to the table.

"Hold on, hold on," Hinn admonishes, pulling the muffins away from the tangle of reaching hands. "Pod leader gets first choice." He grins at me as he presents the platter with a flourish, and my podmates, just now noticing I'm in the room, break out into cheers and applause. I can feel myself blushing as I fight the urge to tuck my head and run. Instead, I offer a wan smile and select a muffin from Hinn's tray.

The first bite is an utter revelation. Wenda wasn't wrong. Hinn is a natural at this.

"This is the best thing I've ever had," I say, when I can bear to stop chewing. This inspires another cheer from the room, and Hinn grins broadly. He sets the platter of remaining muffins down on the table, where they are instantly claimed.

"More coming in a few!" he promises the room, winking at me as he disappears back into the kitchen. I'm struck by his confident, mature demeanor. Hinn isn't just doing this job, he's owning it. Like a grown-up.

"Well?" Wenda appears at my elbow, beaming with pride. I think for a moment, savoring the bite of muffin in my mouth.

"How did you turn him into an adult in a week?" I ask. "That's almost more amazing than this muffin."

"I had very little to do with it," Wenda protests. "Hinn found something he's passionate about. I just got out of his way."

"That sounds like you had everything to do with it," I chide, but Wenda shakes her head.

"He was terrified when I asked him to take over so I could be with you in Clinical," she says, "but he was also inspired. Every day, he would talk to me about what he was going to make for you and Arden when you got back to the pod and how important food is in healing the body and the spirit. It was as much you as it was me. He regards you both as heroes. He had the talent, but you provided the inspiration. All I did was give him the keys to the pantry."

I feel another blush coming on and shake my head. "I'm no hero," I say around a mouthful of muffin.

"You are to them," Wenda says, gesturing at the rest of my podmates, who are bustling through the common room, sharing coffee and food and preparing for the day's work assignments. "You are to *me*."

This admission startles me and I'm about to disagree vehemently when I catch the expression on Wenda's face. It's not worshipful or aggrandizing in any way. She isn't gushing over me or being sentimental. She's serious and matter-of-fact. This is the Wenda I know better than to argue with. Really, it would seem a bit ungracious to.

My train of thought is interrupted by Holly, who throws her arms around me and says into my ear, "I'm so glad you're home. It didn't feel right without you." I return the hug and she's off again, gathering holotablets and personal items for her day at school and skipping toward the doorway, where Bennid stands waiting. He beams at Holly, then crosses the common room to me.

"Not another heroic declaration," I murmur under my breath, and feel Wenda's elbow dig into my side sharply.

Fortunately, Bennid has a more practical purpose. "I have a message for you, Faith," he says. "The Governor has been trying to reach you, but he says you're not on headset. He asked if I could let you know he needs your input on something important. He'll be working at the Intake building all morning if you could stop by? If you feel up to it, of course."

"Oh, of course," I say. "I'll head over after breakfast. Thank you for delivering the message."

"You're welcome." Bennid's gaze strays back to Holly. "I promised Holly I'd walk her over to Education this morning, so it was no trouble." With that, the slender young man joins Holly in the doorway. Without missing a beat, she shifts her belongings so she can link her right arm through Bennid's bioequivalent left one as they move out into the courtyard.

"I leave for a week and everything changes." I sigh, feigning consternation as well as I can with a smile on my face. Wenda makes an amused sound that shows she isn't fooled.

"So, the Governor requires your counsel," she teases instead. "I wonder if that's personal or professional?"

"I couldn't tell you," I say. "I saw him here last night, but he left before I even got a chance to say hello."

"We were only barely able to convince him to show up at all," Wenda explains. "He appears to be under a great deal of pressure. I get the impression pod leadership is not what he wants to be doing, and I hear now he's also been tapped as interim coordinator. With you and Arden and Bennid all on medical leave and Pauly injured, the Warehousing Team has been cut in half."

"He's definitely having issues of some kind." I sigh. "The fight we had in Clinical made that pretty clear."

Wenda scowls. "You had a fight in Clinical? That seems so unlike him."

"That's what I thought too. It was strange. He seems especially worried about the Company visit, to the point I'd almost characterize it as paranoid. He lectured me about how unwise it is to draw the Company's attention."

"He lectured *you* about that ..." Wenda's eyes widen in astonishment.

"To be fair, he doesn't know my history. But yes, he basically ripped into me the day I broke Pauly's quarantine field, and it was mostly about how I wouldn't want to be under the Company's lens."

Wenda lets out a short, sharp laugh. "He has no idea."

"I guess what it comes down to is I don't know his full history either. Maybe his dealings with the Company during his time on Bardazel were enough to fuel this kind of response. They were fairly horrific if what he's told me is true. Maybe he's had other interactions with them I'm not aware of. Either way, it felt like he was angry, and it wasn't because of me. I was just a convenient dumping point."

"Then ask him. Maybe you can get some private time to work out what's really going on, in addition to whatever official input he wants from you."

"That's exactly what I'm going to do," I say, "as soon as I have another muffin."

15

Once fortified with another muffin and a large mug of coffee, I head out to meet Graham. At the last minute, I grab my headset and gingerly place it onto my head. The general channel is alive with chatter and the life of Iona, proceeding with its day as if Iona's lead coordinator wasn't lying frozen in Clinical with an uncertain future, as if an 18-year-old Bardazelian wasn't now equipped with one almost-biological arm that he'll be learning to use for months.

My ten-minute walk to Intake takes closer to twenty minutes. Several of my fellow Ionians stop me along the way to ask about my health and comment on my apparently universally-admired "brave deeds." I have to hear the word "hero" repeated several times, which makes me cringe inside.

When I step into Intake, the lobby is quiet and dark. There's a light on in the conference room, but it's vacant. I'm not sure why Graham wouldn't activate the general lighting if he's working here today. The building feels spooky and strange.

Peering down one of the hallways, I see a splash of light coming from Pauly's office.

"Graham?" I call. I take a few steps down the hallway and feel all my senses tingling. Something just feels off about this situation. I'm so on-edge that when someone taps me on the shoulder from behind, I shriek aloud.

"Sorry, sorry! It's just me, I didn't mean to scare you!" says Tommas, who appears to be as startled by my response as I was by his touch. Sweat's beading at the edge of his brow and his eyes are wide.

"It's okay," I say, trying to will my heartrate back to normal. "It was just weird with the lights being off."

"Yeah, something's wrong with them. Graham's out back trying to figure it out."

"Oh, that explains it. Are you here for the meeting?"

"Meeting? No, I was helping Graham go through some of Pauly's records. This Coordinator job is a big one, there's a lot to figure out. But I'm due somewhere else now, so I gotta run. Enjoy your meeting."

Before I can reply, Tommas spins around and walks quickly away from me, across the lobby and out onto the square. As the door shuts behind him, there's a whir from deep inside the building and all the lights finally come on.

I head back to the lobby just as Graham comes in. He looks preoccupied, his eyes distant and his jaw tense. When he sees me, though, he allows himself a small smile.

"Ah, so Bennid delivered my message. How are you feeling?" he asks.

"Good," I say. "Good enough to be here anyway, as long as Macha doesn't find out I'm doing anything work-related."

He lets out a short laugh. "I heard that assault this morning. That was truly terrifying. I'll try to keep it brief."

He walks to the conference room and I follow. I take a seat at the table looking out onto the plaza, with a view of Clinical in the distance, and beyond it, a couple of skiffs on our landing pad. If this was a normal day, that's where I'd be, guiding ships in and out, gathering parts for my project, and laughing at Pauly's unfunny jokes.

If this was a normal day.

"You look upset," Graham says as he drops into the chair next to me.

"I was thinking about Pauly."

His mouth tightens into an expression that is almost a grimace and he sighs.

"I don't know how Pauly did all this," he says, gesturing at the whole of Iona. "I'm barely keeping up." His gaze drifts toward the window, and he too seems lost in Iona's blowing sands for a moment. The calm mask drops, and I see another Graham, one who is haggard and tired and on-edge.

"You wanted my input about something?" I prod.

"Ah, right. Yes." He rubs his eyes as if trying to dispel a vision. "You know we have a visitor from the Company coming soon. You worked for the Company, you were born on a Company planet, and you understand their protocol well."

"Yes, that's true," I say, making a conscious effort to sound relaxed. "What's up?" *Understanding their protocol* might be the understatement of the century, but I let him continue.

"Originally, a team of investigators was coming from Home World, and I was to coordinate their visit. But we just found out that the Company's Operations Security Chief is coming in person, and she intends to oversee an Ionian team to complete the investigation."

I wince. "That probably won't go well," I say. Graham continues to stare out at Iona's horizon, but his expression registers his agreement. A Company Officer won't have the first idea how to manage and direct residents of an independent planet and may not even understand our basic skill-sharing team-based system of work assignments. And Ionians will balk under the rigid expectations and processes of the Company, which could all reflect poorly on Iona and lead to less Company business for us. It's a potential disaster in the making.

Graham turns to me, his expression equal parts of hope and exhaustion. "I'm hoping you'll agree to put together the team and serve as something of a go-between, so the Ionians don't freak out the OS chief, the OS chief doesn't scare the hell out of the Ionians, and what needs to get done, gets done. Is there any chance of that?" His air is one of entreaty.

I'm a little surprised. This is a high-level assignment, and while I'm well-known on Iona as multitalented and easy to work with, the most responsibility I've fielded here is Pod Leader. Not to mention that I have, for the last eight years, made a concerted effort to stay off the Company's radar altogether.

"Is it appropriate for me to take on such a high-profile assignment?" I ask warily. "It's a bit outside what I normally do."

"I know what you're capable of," he says simply, looking down at the marble tabletop and tracing its veining with a fingertip. "You have the right blend of experience, you know almost everyone here, and they all think highly of you. People will work with you and *for* you. And you know how to talk to Company higher-ups and how to deal with process protocol. This won't be a stretch for you."

He's right, of course. But that doesn't silence the alarm going off in my head. *Too close, too much visibility.* My goal in coming here was to never be at the behest of the Company again and to become as dead to them as they'd tried to make me. If I take this role, my precious anonymity—if it ever really existed—will certainly be shattered.

But it also means I'll have the chance to make sure this investigation goes well, and that the results are unaltered and unfiltered by the Company itself. That could, in the long run, protect Iona and the independence I've come to value so much. That alone could make it worth what is probably only going to amount to a lot of discomfort for a short period of time.

"I have a few questions," I say. "You know I'm still on medical leave."

Graham manages to laugh. "A fact Macha's unlikely to let us forget," he says. "As it turns out, the Security Chief isn't arriving until the end of next week. I spoke to Macha a little while ago just to make sure you could be cleared for this. I assured her you wouldn't have to lift any bodies or attempt to fly any hovergurneys as part of the assignment."

I smile now too, remembering his own heroics, getting not just Pauly but also me, Arden, and himself out of the Warehouse before it exploded.

"I would get to assemble my own team? Any restrictions on that?" I ask.

"None," he says. "And no restrictions on how you manage the process, or interface with Ionians or the Company. That's completely up to you. I just ask you to keep me informed."

"I can do that," I say, and in an instant my decision is made. "Yes, I'll do it."

He lets out a relieved sigh and extends his hand. We shake on this plan, and he relaxes slightly.

"That's an enormous load off my mind," he says. Out of nowhere, he adds, "I wish the pod had made Fanny their leader. She's been here longer than anyone, she knows the entire population, she's easy to get along with. I don't know why they didn't."

"Because no one takes Fanny seriously, least of all Fanny herself," I say. I'm confident Fanny would never have accepted the pod leadership position anyway—that would basically be admitting Pauly was never coming back by stepping into his shoes. "If you need help with pod systems let me know. I have some good ones that work well without much oversight."

Graham lips curve momentarily into a softer expression. "I'm sorry I was so terrible to you that day in Clinical," he says. "The Warehouse accident has affected me more than I expected, and I'm just out of sorts. I've become exceptionally crabby company, no one in my own pod can stand to be around me."

"It's all right," I say, as reassuring as I can manage. "You need time to recover too. We've all been through a lot." We bid each other goodbye in the lobby and I watch as Graham heads down the hall to Pauly's office.

Back at my pod, I start thinking about the investigation team I want to establish. It's a more difficult challenge than I'd anticipated. What qualifications are the right ones? Do we need investigators? Interviewers? Detectives? Scientists? Witnesses? Who?

In the end, I decide I need to work with people I trust. I take Graham at his word that this is all mine to construct. *Fine, then.* The last iteration of my list takes shape, and I'm reviewing it with a sense of satisfaction when I hear Wenda bustling about in our common room. I grab her and plead my case.

She's skeptical at first. "Shouldn't this be a job for safety experts or something?" she asks, twisting her lips into a puzzled quirk.

"I'm not a scientist or a safety expert," I counter. "This is really a public relations moment. The Company is going to make whatever decision they're going to make, regardless—that's just a given. But the way we handle the process, and the way we present ourselves to the Company could have a monumental role in how they see Iona. That's why I want you and your social-scientist perspective on-board."

Wenda looks thoughtful. "I'm still not sure I understand where you're going with this, but I'm happy to help," she says. "It certainly can't hurt."

I look as encouraging as possible, although no one knows better than me how interactions with the Company *can* hurt, deeply and for a long time. "Good," I say, hugging her thankfully. "You're on the team."

The other individuals I hope to recruit I can speak with tomorrow, but one I want to talk to tonight, and he might be a tough sell. This conversation will have to happen in person and include a lot of bribes.

I spend a few minutes digging through the small treasure box on my desk, find what I need, and tuck it into my pocket. I pass through our kitchen and stash some of Hinn's breakfast muffins, freshly made and ready for tomorrow, into my pack. On a whim I add a vacuum flask of hot coffee. Then I grab my jacket and head out through the sandy courtyard, walking briskly toward the square in Iona's fading afternoon light.

16

IT FEELS WEIRD TO walk into Clinical again, even if this time it's by choice and under my own power. Angst rises up in my body as I cross the lobby, and my nerves jitter as I ring for an attendant. I'm not sure if I should be pleased or alarmed when Pepper comes around the corner to respond to the chime, but she greets me with a smile and hears my request. After a quick check of her clinical notes, she gives me a thumbs-up.

"You should probably escort me to the room," I say. "I don't want anybody thinking I'm trying to go somewhere I'm not supposed to be." She rolls her eyes at me at first, but she understands, and together we head to the stairs, where we progress without incident to the third floor. Her headset buzzes and she listens intently, then murmurs into her mic.

"Macha says she trusts you to take it from here," she tells me as we turn onto the hallway not too far from the room I left so happily only yesterday. "He's not scheduled for anything today other than rest and a recheck, so you won't be interrupting anything."

"Thanks," I say, and Pepper waves goodbye and bounces down the stairs. I stand for a moment, anxious in the unnatural quiet of the place. Even a single footstep sounds intrusively loud and discordant here and I find myself tip-toeing toward Arden's room. When I'm a few feet away from the door, however, I hear voices—Arden's, and one other. I stop in my tracks. My first concern is that Pepper was wrong and I'm about to cause a problem, but soon I understand the voice I hear doesn't belong to Macha or anyone on the clinical staff. In fact, there's no one else physically present in Arden's room.

Instead, I'm hearing Arden in a contentious discussion with someone through a holotablet.

"You're not seeing the full picture," he says tersely. "Remember I have a personal relationship ..."

"You *had* a personal relationship," the female voice interrupts him. The speaker is cold, stern, and clearly not used to having her point of view challenged. "You have no real insight here. We know all people are potentially susceptible to corruption by outside forces intent on the destruction of ..."

"I have extensive observation that supports my line of reasoning. Don't tell me I don't have any real insight," Arden snaps. "My reports are on file. It would be to your benefit if you read the damn things. Don't contact me again until you have something of use to say that is not based on raw unfounded speculation. And do keep in mind your chain of command; I can remind you of it if necessary. We're done here."

A few seconds later, the sound of the holotablet smashing into the tile floor erupts from the room. I'm so startled I let out an involuntary yelp. Although Arden might have been preoccupied enough not to hear me, I decide to make myself apparent and pretend I wasn't just eavesdropping at his door. I hurry into his room with as much concern as I can paste over the shocked expression on my face.

He's standing by the window, staring outside with a fierce scowl. The tablet's remains are scattered at his feet.

"Are you okay? What happened? I heard a crash," I say loudly. He spins toward me, initially looking alarmed, but his face softens as he takes me in. "Faith," he says warmly, and opens his arms as he moves a few steps in my direction.

I let him pull me into a hug; I can feel him shaking slightly. The anger may have left his expression, but he's still holding it in his body.

"Are you all right?" I repeat. "What happened to your holo?"

He lets out a sigh, and the tremors begin to subside. "I broke it," he says simply. "I'm okay. Just frustrated."

"Frustrated with what?"

"With being stuck in here, primarily."

That I can certainly relate to, although it doesn't explain the conversation I overheard.

He doesn't elaborate, though. Instead, he hugs me a little tighter and I let him, patting him in what I hope is a comforting manner. I can't even begin to think of how to ask him about what I heard, and it's evident he's not going to volunteer any information. I feel the momentary sting of *déjà vu* but push it to the back of my mind.

"Hey, I brought you food," I say, extricating myself from his arms and setting my pack down on the bed.

"Food? Real food?" he asks. His posture begins to relax, and he shoots me a rakish smile.

"Yes, real food. Wonderful muffins made by Hinn, and fresh coffee." I pull the items out of my pack and arrange them in the center of the bed. We then climb onto opposite ends of the bed and sit facing one another with our legs tucked under us and the food between us, like kids at a sleepover.

"These are amazing," Arden says around a mouthful of muffin. "Hinn made these?"

"Yep. He's taken over as pod chef. It's well-deserved."

"I can't wait to get back. I'm so tired of this place."

"When are you supposed to get out?"

"Macha wants another week, although I'm lobbying for sooner. There was some feedback in my respiratory tests she didn't like the look of."

"That doesn't sound good. Maybe you should listen to her. Breathing is kind of important."

"But Macha isn't worried, she'll tell you so herself. She just wants to make sure everything is solidly normal before I'm discharged given the ... uh ... impact of whatever Pauly was exposed to. She's being extremely conservative."

"Destroy some more equipment. They'll let you out faster."

Arden's lips twist in regret as he looks at the pile of parts that used to be the holotablet.

"She's not going to be happy about that," he mutters. "It was an accident."

"An accident? I wasn't even in the room, and I can tell you threw it at the wall."

"I threw it at the wall by accident."

"Right. You were intending to throw it at the window? Or at the drone, maybe?"

Arden looks defeated.

"All right," he says. "I threw it at the wall on purpose. I was ... worked up. I would be better able to control my emotions if I wasn't stuck in here."

I raise an eyebrow at him. "Can I ask why you were so emotional you threw your holotablet at the wall?"

Arden takes an especially large bite of muffin and chews thoughtfully for many more moments than he actually needs to.

"No," he finally says, wiping crumbs from his lips with his fingertips. "You'll hear about it soon enough."

I throw up my hands. "More secrets," I say.

"Not secrets. Just ... a few things I need to think about how to explain. I promise."

This feels like familiar territory, a place I don't want to find myself in again. I decide to let it drop, but *just for now*.

"Eat, drink," I say instead, gesturing at the remaining scraps of muffin and the thermos. "I have to go soon, and I'm taking anything left with me."

Arden looks at me for what seems like a long time, studying my face, the wheels in his head obviously turning. He eventually reaches across the bed and takes my hand.

"Thank you," he says.

"For muffins?" I quip, chewing my own mouthful.

He squeezes my hand gently. "For everything."

"Don't thank me yet," I warn. "There's more to this than I've let on. Stay sitting down. I have a proposal."

Arden's expression hovers somewhere between excitement, disbelief, and horror once I tell him what I have in mind. "Are you kidding me?" he says.

"Do I look like I'm kidding? Look, I have to put together a team, there's no way around that. And given my ... uh ... experience with the Company, I've decided that what I want is to have a team made up of people I trust. Explicitly. Do you understand why?"

"Gods, yes, I definitely understand why. And I think that's the right way to go, for all the reasons you mentioned."

"Good. So you'll do it, right?" I'm leaning against the wall near the door, watching him. I've been trying to convince him for almost twenty minutes. Just as I expected, he's a tough sell.

He takes a slow turn around the room, winding up at the window again looking out on the Ionian dusk. "You trust me?" he asks, so quietly I almost don't hear him at first.

"Not entirely," I admit, "but it's improving. I may not understand what you're doing here, but at least I think it's unlikely that you'll leave me for dead again."

He turns to me, his face dark. "You thought I left you for dead on Home World?"

"Initially, yes. But you didn't, did you?" I reach into my pocket and pull out my secret weapon—a small card, now dog-eared and smudged with age. On one side, the festive font reading *Congratulations* is only barely perceptible.

I extend my hand and drop the card into his palm. "You didn't leave me for dead. You never left me at all."

A look of wonder crosses his features as he takes the card and turns it over. His handwriting is still clear along the bottom.

"I can't believe you kept this all this time," he murmurs, fingering the card with care as though it's the most precious thing he's ever held.

"I was so miserable when I decided to leave Home World. Then Von brought this, with those wonderful flowers. I knew it meant you were out there, somewhere, thinking of me, and that you thought I'd made the right decision. It's why, even though I came here to start a new life, I could never quite let go of the old one."

Gently, Arden hands the card back to me. "I didn't know if you'd even seen this," he says, "or if you had, what your reaction might be over time. I didn't mean for you to ..." His voice trails off as he looks at me intently.

I turn the small card over a few times, then out of habit kiss it before I put it back into my pocket. "It's time for you to tell me what happened, Arden. Especially if we're going to be taking on the Company again."

He runs a hand through his hair. He looks tired, but there is a hint of a smile on his face. "Do you want to ask questions, or should I just talk?" he asks—another thing the Arden of our youth would have never done.

"Start with the accident," I respond. "Then tell me what happened to you."

"That transpo, barreling down on us ..." Arden shudders briefly. "I tried to get to you, but everything exploded, and it was so horrific. Clinical Aid showed up, and I was barely conscious and pretty banged up, but you were ... oh god you were so hurt, and I didn't know ..."

He stops, his face and voice so stricken he can't continue. I can't look at him reliving all this, and stare at the floor. After a few moments, he gathers himself and continues.

"We were rescued by a Governing Council support team that had been deployed because of my mission abort. You went to Clinical Aid, while I was placed in a private health facility. I begged them to bring you in, but they wouldn't. Eventually I understood if you stayed at Clinical Aid, without any contact from me, the Company would be less likely to see you as complicit in my mission for the Council—maybe not an innocent bystander, but at least not an accomplice."

He cringes saying the words.

"I know how it looked," he says. "I knew you would think I'd abandoned you."

He looks as miserable as I felt back then, waking up without him. We stare at each other silently for an instant.

"Anyway," he resumes, "I kept pushing because I wasn't sure if the Company would go after you again. They at least agreed to assign a local agent to keep an eye on you and act as a sort of bodyguard. That worked out nicely; I understand the two of you became quite good friends."

My eyebrows arch in surprise. "Von? *Von* was a GC bodyguard?"

"Well, a *sort of* bodyguard. Von is exactly what he appears to be—a sweet guy with a great husband and two cute kids. But he's also part of the Council's network."

"All right, all right. You get patched up in a GC facility. Then what?"

Arden laughs hollowly, looking down at his feet. "After you showed me your project, I knew the Company was already a step ahead of me, so there was no more reason to be careful. I went and did the thing you told me not to do."

"Master Control?"

"Yep."

"How?"

"I literally walked in and smashed the place up—took a sledgehammer to it and crushed every control panel and open terminal to bits. I meant to be subtle about it, but you were so horribly injured. You hadn't regained consciousness at that point and I thought ..." His voice breaks and he pauses. "Well. Anyway, I didn't care about being subtle anymore."

"No one tried to stop you?"

"Not a soul. I assumed it was all on camera somewhere and the hammer would come down on me later, so I went back to our pod to wait. I wanted to be close by in case you ... well, I ... I wanted to be close by. I was hoping you would come to before whatever was going to happen to me, happened."

135

He grimaces, and I at last understand the depth of his concern. There's nothing that can make this less horrifying for either of us, so I decide to just cut to the chase.

"Did the Company come after you?" I ask, drawing in a breath that I hope is infused with enough courage to hear the answer. This question has kept me raw for the last eight years.

Arden fidgets with the edge of his shirt, focusing on the movement of his own hands.

"They did," he confirms, not lifting his gaze, "but not in the way you're expecting. They offered me a job."

"A job?" I bark out, utterly dumbfounded. "A *job*? What kind of job?"

"A significant job," he says. "Something that I'm still not at liberty to discuss. But more importantly, there were terms associated with this job. Terms specific to the security of people I loved and wanted to see left unhindered by certain Company pursuits. They understood that would be a particular interest of mine. I had my terms and they had theirs, and in the end we reached an agreement."

"One of your terms was that they would leave me alone?"

"Emphatically yes."

"And one of their terms was you disappearing from Home World and having no further contact with me."

"Again, yes. And without saying a word about it to anyone, although I took advantage of the fact they failed to exclude Von by name. I couldn't tell him everything, for his own protection, but he knew enough to keep you safe, and he had a way to at least attempt to get word to me if necessary."

My brain is reeling. One part of me is wallowing in misery, wailing *how many people lied to me and kept on lying?* Another part is insisting I calm down, focus, and listen. Oddly, I hear Graham's voice sputter, "this isn't about you." I look deep into Arden's face, twisted and strained with almost impossible-to-bear emotion. All these years, I've held my misery close like a precious parcel, but the reality is that I was making that choice, and my freedom to make it came

136

at a price Arden paid. I now know he spent eight years carrying guilt over his decision, anguish over the destruction of our relationship, pain at his helplessness to reconnect or intercede if something went wrong, and the constant fear that, for all the agreements and terms and understandings, the Company would one day simply choose not to honor their part of the bargain and there would be nothing he could do.

"It wasn't what I expected or wanted," he finally says, "but if it was the only way I could ensure your safety, I had no doubt about what I was going to do."

There are still so many unanswered questions between us, but at least the time for recrimination has finally passed, belonging to another life. When I look at him now, I am grateful, I am relieved, I am suspicious, I am annoyed, I am giddy. But despite the parade of conflicting emotions marching through me, all I can think is how right it is that we are here in this odd conundrum together. I throw my arms around him and hold him as tight as I possibly can, and he responds in kind. And although it seems almost ridiculously inadequate, the only thing I can manage to say is, "I've missed you."

He presses his cheek into my hair and whispers, "Me too."

17

It takes a few days to finish pulling together the team I want. In the end, I couldn't be happier with them. It's a mix of people with different skill sets and backgrounds, and none of them bears an excess of good or ill will toward the Company. They'll consider anything we learn honestly and provide what I hope will be useful feedback and information. Despite my trepidations about getting in front of the Company again, I feel sure we have at least a common goal in this case: everyone wants to learn the truth about what happened.

Graham grumbles when I tell him the names of the team members during a private headset chat, and although he offers no comments about them, he doesn't exactly sound pleased with the group's composition. It might only be my imagination, but he seems particularly annoyed when I mention Arden and makes an audible "hmphf" into my ear.

"Any feedback?" I ask in response, but he defers, despite his cranky tone.

"If you believe these people can get the job done, then I'll just have to trust you," he says unconvincingly. "I'm assuming you'll bring on specialists in a flex capacity."

"We don't actually know what our real job is yet," I point out. "And we won't know until we meet with the Security Chief and understand our charge. She'll determine the scope, and I can evolve the team as necessary, depending on what we're expected to do."

"I see." His voice has already shifted to disinterest. "Well, thank you for your effort."

He logs off. The dead air that follows feels warmer than the conversation we just had.

I tap out of Graham's private channel with a sigh and log back into general. I'm still on medical leave, even though I feel perfectly fine and have said as much to Macha, but she will not be moved. At least she no longer attacks me if she finds me listening in; the chatter about ongoing tasks and work getting done is soothing to me, and occasionally I take the opportunity to answer a question or participate in a bit of banter with Fanny or Tommas. Fanny provides gossip, encouragement, and updates about Pauly's condition. Tommas is always good for comic relief, albeit oftentimes unintentionally.

Only seconds after I establish connection with general, Fanny hails me. "I have a rest day today," she says. "Can I come by?" Her voice is tense and anxious; it's obvious something is wrong.

"Of course," I say. "Are you sure you want to come here? We could have lunch in the Star Parlor."

"No, I feel like taking a little walk, so I'll come see you," she says quickly. "I'm ready now. I'll head that way in a few."

"Okay then, see you soon," I respond, but Fanny has already left the general connection.

I feel like taking a little walk? When has Fanny *ever* felt like taking a walk? This clearly isn't an ordinary visit to chat. I'm in the kitchen making tea for us when she arrives on a sand scooter. I hug her and hand her a steaming cup as she comes inside. We step into the quiet common room, and she sits down in one of the overstuffed chairs next to the fireplace. I sit down across from her.

She shakes her head and lets out a loud exhale, staring at the flames with concentration. Her fingers tighten and flex on the cup handle. Her normally-even complexion is stained with patches of pink. Her mouth is set in a firm line, and her jaw is clenched tight.

Fanny isn't anxious. She's furious.

"Tell me what's wrong," I say.

She takes a long sip of the tea, still staring into the fire, and says to me in a voice bordering on the edge of disgust, "He's *taken* Pauly's room."

"What?" I'm completely taken aback. "Who? For what?"

"Graham," she responds in a steely tone, setting her teacup down on the small table next to the chair with a thump. "He moved Pauly's things out of it yesterday and sent them to storage—all of them. He didn't say a word to me or mention it to the rest of the pod. We came in from shift and it was done."

"Why would he do that?" I can understand wanting to encourage everyone to somehow accept what's happened to Pauly with some kind of physical representation, but this seems extreme and counterproductive.

Fanny's teeth are clenched together, and she can barely get out the words.

"He's giving it to the Company Security Chief."

"The Security Chief is staying *here*?" For one knee-jerk reactive moment, I become anxious and afraid. I had assumed the Company would place an enviro into low orbit around Iona as accommodation for the Security Chief, as is standard when their VIPs venture out to other worlds. The enviros provide a level of comfort and convenience that's much closer to what someone from Home World would expect, and far beyond what we can provide, even in specially set-up guest quarters. It never occurred to me the Security Chief would need—or want—to stay on Iona, much less in one of our residential pods. I'm still listening to Fanny, but my mind is spinning question after question in my subconscious.

After eight years, am I still that afraid of the Company?

"It's bad enough that some Company lackey is coming here at all, that we have to be under this kind of scrutiny." Fanny's face contorts as she continues to speak. "But to have them lounging around in Pauly's room ... he just packed up every single thing and sent it to storage, he didn't even ask ..."

The anger breaks and sorrow floods her features. Her eyes fill with tears. She clamps her hand over her mouth, battling her emotions. "He didn't even ask if there was something of Pauly's I wanted to keep with me," she finishes and at last begins to weep. I put down my tea and reach over to wrap my arms around her.

Her body shakes with misery and frustration. "He's making us miserable," she says, between sobs. "I wish he'd never come here."

"Fanny, don't," I say, hugging her tight. I know these tears are more about Pauly than Graham's misstep, but her words highlight the crux of the problem. "Graham hasn't been himself since the accident. That did something to him, and this visit from the Company is causing him a lot of stress. He's reliving everything that went wrong on Bardazel. Taking over Pauly's room like that was ridiculous, but it was just the mistake of someone under a lot of pressure trying to accommodate another demand from the Company. He's your pod leader for now, and don't forget, he's also one of the only people who might be able to help us sort out how to deal with the effects of Blue."

This last statement catches Fanny off-guard, and she sits back, disentangling herself from my embrace. She runs her hand over her face, wiping away the tear-tracks, and her shoulders droop as she looks down at the floor.

"I know you're right," she says, picking up her teacup again and running a finger around its rim. "But I can't help how I feel. This was the last straw."

"There's more?"

Fanny sighs. "Oh, there's a lot more."

The tale she next tells of Graham confirms what I've seen myself. The friendly, easy-going man we welcomed to Iona a few short months ago has transformed into a perpetually irritated loner who speaks only to give an order or answer a direct question—and sometimes not even then.

"He hates being pod leader, you know," I murmur.

"I can well believe it," Fanny says, sighing heavily and staring into her teacup. "I think he hates all of us. And Iona."

"That's not true," I say, shaking my head. "He might not love Iona, but he was adjusting well and seemed to be settling in."

The fire crackles softly in the grate. Fanny presses her lips together tightly for a moment. When she speaks, it is in a low, measured tone.

"Maybe that the old Graham—the one we thought we knew—was all an act to get us to accept him," she says, "and the man we see now is the real Graham Thorn."

I saw for myself how quickly he could flip into his rigid 'Governor' persona when he felt attacked. But I've gotten to know him well enough to gain his trust, and his actions haven't been those of someone who thought little of Iona or of its people.

I reach over and take Fanny's hand. "I'm so confused," she says, looking hard at me. "I know the two of you are friends. I don't mean to suggest your connection with him is all predicated on a lie or that he's fooling you somehow."

"No, it's all right," I tell my friend. "Things have become very confusing for everyone lately." By 'everyone' I mainly mean *me*, but I don't point that out. "What does Tommas have to say? Which man did he know on Bardazel?"

Fanny's lips turn down in irritation. "For someone who can't shut up otherwise, he seems to have precious little to say about Graham," she says. "I can't get him to say anything. I mean, I understand he was very late arriving on Bardazel—he'd only been on-world for six weeks or so when the transfer happened. But he's remarkably opinion-free when it comes to the Governor. He doesn't want to talk about him at all."

In the end, there's little I can say to offset Fanny's concerns.

"I wish I could do something to help," I say, but Fanny waves her hand at me.

"I'm just venting my misery, I know you can't do anything about any of this," she says, her face fallen with despair. "I know he was a big part of saving Pauly's life. He wouldn't have done that if he hated us. A lot has changed in such a short time. It's tough to get my head around it all."

I know what she means. And as if by magic, at that moment my headset buzzes with a private hail. I open the channel and to my surprise hear Macha say, "Someone here has a message for you," immediately followed by Arden, who is so excited he's almost shouting.

"I'm being discharged," he says, his voice bubbling with delight. "Are you at the pod? I'll be home in a couple of hours."

No 'welcome home' party is necessary for Arden. Arden *is* the party, and it starts the instant he comes through the door. Podmates are hugged again and again and complimented fiercely for their bravery, intelligence, beauty, and good health. We're regaled with multiple observations of how much easier it is to eat/drink/sleep/laugh/belch in our presence than in the cold sterile torture that is Clinical. Our common room, already a more pleasant place since my own return, becomes nothing short of celebratory, all day, every day. Arden even compliments the room itself, reflecting on the warmth of the fire, the quality of the light, the perfection of the acoustics, the soothing effect of the colors, décor, and furnishings. His hammock is the most comfortable thing ever devised. The sound of his roommates' snoring is a calming sedative. The echo of the rising chimes across the pod is charmingly energizing. He is delighted by everything.

We're both still on medical leave, so after our podmates head off each day for their work tasks or schooling, we're left in each other's company. I sneak away several days in a row to work on my project, since Arden is still a little weak and needs more rest than I do. But when he's feeling well, we come together to walk, to talk, and to try to make up for eight years of silence and separation. I tell him about my new skill sets in rocketry, maintenance, and automated control design—all things I learned on Iona. He tells me about the skullduggery of transporting dangerous and sometimes contraband materials for the Company and working as a sort of double agent to intercept both Company and Independent transporters who were a little too willing to bend the rules. It's funny to look at the differences side by side. I've spent the last eight years down in the pit alone in the dark, being quiet and steady and as under-the-radar as possible, while Arden has spent them in dramatic, risky, high-profile positions, generally drawing as much attention to himself as possible. "I told you I was a space pirate," he says.

"Tell me how you know Graham," I ask him one afternoon. "It's quite the coincidence that the two of you would wind up on Iona when neither of you ever intended to come here."

For a moment, Arden hesitates. "Well, that's a long story," he says, "and only half of it is mine to tell. The short version is, we worked on the same ship for a few months, and got to know each other pretty well. We stayed in touch for a while, maybe a year. But I eventually lost track of him."

"Was he a space pirate too?" I ask.

Arden laughs aloud. "I have never known a less space-piratey person," he says. "No, our friend Graham is as straight-forward as they come, and a sucker for rules. That's one of the things I like about him. There are a lot of bullshit artists out there. He's the opposite. It can be a blessing, or a curse. It's been both for him at different times in his life, I think."

I consider this carefully for a moment. Maybe Fanny is overreacting, maybe we're all judging Graham too harshly or expecting too much from him. I wonder how being honest to a fault might play out in the coming days with the Company interrogating everyone. But Arden interrupts my contemplation by asking a random question about skiff maintenance, and just like that we're off on another conversational tangent.

He seems so comfortable here, I think to myself. *It's like he was meant to be here.*

I find him a few nights later in our courtyard, sitting on one of the curved benches built into its low wall. He's staring up at Iona's little moons with a small smile on his lips. It's late and our pod has mostly turned in. Hinn is still puttering around in the kitchen, and I can hear the soft sound of Shar's dulcimer, but Iona Town itself is so silent it almost feels like we're completely alone.

"What are you up to now?" I ask from the doorway. He doesn't take his eyes from the sky, but the smile spreads across his face at the sound of my voice. It reminds me of the many evenings we spent on Home World, sitting out in our pod's garden in the dark, just being still together and watching the sky. So much has changed, but so much feels just the same.

"Meteors," he says without looking at me, and pats the smooth plaster-textured bench next to him. "Come sit."

I scoff for a moment. "We don't get meteors here," I say. "This is some kind of trick."

"No trick. Meteors," he insists. "Sit. I'll show you."

I walk across the courtyard and sit beside him. He wraps one arm around my shoulders and angles me against him just so, then points up and to the north, above the ridge that runs behind our pod. I relax against him, letting the warmth of his touch and our familiarity with one another wash over me.

"Look there," he says. "Keep watching."

The sky is clear, and the breeze is light tonight—for Iona, anyway. It's our good fortune that it's out of the south; as I continue to gaze up into the black, I hear the patter of sand blowing against the courtyard wall.

"I don't see any meteors," I say. Arden shushes me.

"You're too impatient," he says. "Give it time. You'll see one any minute."

I smirk. "*I'm* too impatient, says the man who tendered his resignation with a sledgehammer."

He chuckles softly. His arm, now comfortably settled around my shoulders, tightens gently at the mention of our former life together, pulling me a fraction closer. He doesn't look away from the sky as I lean into him, staring up into the darkness above. "That was a matter of efficiency," he says easily. "I like to get every job done as thoroughly as possible."

"You have always been very thorough; I'll give you that."

He lets the double-entendre sink in, and we snort in unison. Suddenly he points upward.

"Look there," he says, a note of triumph in his voice. "See it?"

A flash of light flares over the hills to the north, blazing a sparkling trail through the sky then gradually dying as it falls into the horizon. Almost immediately, another bursts through the darkness and follows a similar path.

"Wow. I've never seen meteors here before," I say.

"Have you looked for them?"

"Oh. Well, no."

"You don't find what you don't look for."

His statement feels serious and heavy, in the context of everything that's happened on Iona. It's true that I trust Arden with my life, but I'm also aware that he's still full of secrets. The mysterious Company job, the contentious conversation I overheard in Clinical ... these things continue to draw my attention like a pebble in my shoe. There are many things I've made a point not to look for when it comes to Arden. In one sense it's none of my business, but in another it could have everything to do with how life on Iona continues to develop. I tell myself I need to stop being afraid of what I might find if I *do* look.

But Arden has taken up the narrative again.

"That's not quite right though, is it?"

"What?" I'm so distracted by my own thoughts, I've lost the thread.

"It's not quite true that we don't find what we don't look for. Sometimes we do, despite ourselves."

I look at him now, questioning. He is still staring up at the sky, but his expression has become philosophical. "Are you talking about yourself?" I ask.

"I am."

"And what is it you found that you weren't looking for?"

"So much," he replies. "Friends. Family. Home."

"On Iona?"

"On Iona."

He looks away from the stars at last and into my eyes. "I thought this was going to be a terrible assignment. A service planet. Warehousing. I never expected to love my life here," he says. "And I never expected ... I could never have guessed ..."

His hand strokes my cheek as his voice trails away and for the first time since his arrival I see some trepidation, nervousness. He doesn't have to finish the sentence. I place my hand over his and turn my face to kiss his palm, then look into his eyes again and say, "Me either. But here we are."

Entranced by the moment, I close my eyes as he lowers his face to mine. I feel the gentle pressure of his lips first on my forehead, then on my cheek. My heart is pounding as he hesitates.

Suddenly, we're interrupted by a blindingly bright flash of light and the scream of engines breaking into Iona's atmosphere. We both startle at the sound and peer upward, blinking, at the massive brightly lit Company transport vehicle carving an arc of light into the night sky as it streaks toward the landing pads.

We disentangle from one another and stand to watch the spectacle. All over Iona Town, headsets are going off, pods are lighting up, and people are hurrying toward the pads in the darkness. With an anxious sigh, Arden folds me into his arms in what I can only describe as a protective gesture.

His tension shows in his posture and breathing. We're again on the same wavelength, sharing an emotional response, but this time it's an unshakable unease compounded by *déjà vu*.

Here we go again, indeed.

"Looks like the Security Chief has arrived," he says quietly. "Time to face the music."

18

THE SECURITY CHIEF'S NAME is Fallon March. I know her by reputation—within the Company she's considered something of a wunderkind. Starting as a mere chemist in Materials Analysis, she progressed rapidly through that division's structure and was soon managing all of Home World's labs. She moved to Operations Security and became Chief in less than a year.

Despite her late-night arrival, March let it be known she intended to address Iona at the crack of dawn, and now bleary-eyed Ionians are attempting to pack into the Preservation Theater. Our population won't fit into this space since the arrival of the former Bardazelians, so there's a fair amount of disorder as people cram in and sit or stand anywhere they can find a spot.

She's only two years older than me, and like me, she grew up on Home World as the child of scientific researchers. I study her, now a top Company official, sitting before us in a crisp burgundy jumpsuit, tapping her long, manicured nails against the tabletop with barely concealed impatience. By contrast, I'm sitting in the back of a dusty, crowded auditorium in mostly clean beige service togs, with grease ingrained into my cuticles and a series of angry red bug bites across my cheek that I'm struggling to remember not to scratch. .

Her presence on the stage is that of an alabaster statue, all white and pale gold except for the jumpsuit and the matching burgundy on her lips. Her assistant, a younger almost matching copy of March except for her pale peach outfit and lipstick, sits on March's right and leans in anxiously from time to time, taking notes on a holotablet. On her left, looking as dour as I've ever seen him, is

Graham. He has a few old-fashioned notecards in his hands, which he occasionally shuffles through. Periodically, he leans toward March and speaks, but there is no indication she's listening to anything he says, and she certainly doesn't bother to respond.

I stare down at my hands and self-consciously rub my sleeve against my cuticles until Arden reaches over and takes my hand, forcing me to stop. We're sitting in the middle of the row far enough back to be out of the primary lighting, working at being relatively inconspicuous despite the steady stream of Ionians who stop to wave at us and make comments about either my "heroism" or Arden's recovery.

Fanny and Wenda are positioned behind the audio console at the foot of the stage. Macha's high-piled jet-black crown of braids is visible over the crowd a few rows away to our right. Holly, Hinn, and Bennid have disappeared in the crowd, despite coming in just behind us. One thing is clear: Iona must be at a near-complete standstill, with almost every adult Ionian in this theater per March's demand. I can't imagine what she'll have to say that will convince us this is anything other than some kind of performance designed to intimidate us with Company power and importance.

Graham is speaking to March again, this time more insistently. She turns to regard him the way an Ionian entomologist might look at yet another sand flea and her expression shifts from impassive to vaguely dissatisfied. Her burgundy lips curve into a frown as she turns away from Graham and proceeds to give her assistant a stream of instructions, which the girl frantically struggles to follow.

"Worst job imaginable," I mutter, gesturing toward the stricken assistant. Arden smirks behind his hand.

"She probably won't last long," he whispers. "Everyone says March is a beast to work for. It's definitely not a job with growth potential."

"Did you run into her during any of your Company assignments?" I ask. Arden has yet to explain what he was doing for the Company, although I know he was a pilot, an enforcer, and later ran what was ostensibly a materials transportation team. Arden shakes his head. "I knew of her, certainly; everyone in the Company did. But this is my first time seeing her in person."

"What do you think?"

"She appears to be very clean," Arden says with a laugh.

"That will change after a couple of days," I say. "I'm sure Pauly's pod isn't any cleaner than ours."

Before Arden can reply, Graham stands and walks to the front of the stage. He looks over at Wenda, who gives him a smile and a thumbs up while Fanny glares at him coldly, then takes a deep breath and begins to speak.

"Thank you everyone for being here," he says in a weary voice. "We'll try to make this fairly quick so you can get on with your day. I want to introduce Fallon March, the Company's Operations Security Chief. As you all know, we suffered a terrible accident in Warehousing that caused some severe injuries and easily could have been much more serious if not for some quick thinking." Graham pauses here and appears to briefly scan the crowd for me, but the moment is so short I can't be certain.

"Quick thinking and *heroics*," whispers Arden. I elbow him sharply.

"Chief March will be conducting an investigation into the accident to help us understand what happened and how we might prevent such accidents in the future," Graham continues. "For that consideration, we owe her and the Company a debt of gratitude. Please help me welcome Company Operations Security Chief Fallon March."

There is an unenthusiastic patter of applause from the crowd as March rises and comes forward. She looks out at the assembly for a beat too long and I realize she is anxious, although her features belie this not at all.

"Good morning," she finally says, in a voice as cool and pale as her features. "I want to echo what Governor Thorn has said. I am here at the behest of the Company, to be sure, but my goal is to help all of you. By understanding and addressing any issues that might have contributed to the accident, we hope to ensure Iona has the highest and best safety standards in the sector, and such a reputation can only lead to good. The Company has long been an enthusiastic and happy customer of this station, with nothing but positive reports, and we relish this opportunity to give back to you in this way."

I can feel the look on my face shifting from incredulity to fury. "Is she kidding?" I hiss to Arden. He squeezes my hand a little more emphatically and whispers back, "Take it easy."

Chief March continues to speak about how delighted she is to be working on this important task, and how pleased she is to have this opportunity to get to know Iona in a deeply personal way, all without looking delighted or pleased in the slightest. She makes some overture about being "one of you", but I'm already so angry I've stopped listening.

"I think we're being set up," I whisper to Arden.

"Then it sounds like you've got some work to do," he whispers back. It dawns on me that I'm the person who will be dealing with her, with this narrative, for the days, weeks, or however long it takes to get to the bottom of what happened. I was prepared for the possibility that the Company might have no real interest in finding out what happened as long as they could credibly cast blame elsewhere, but now it sounds like I'm going to have to wrestle with the specter of Company "help" to overcome a manufactured problem they've helped us "identify."

The address lasts only a few more minutes and concludes with the usual insincere encouragement for Ionians to get involved by offering up any relevant information or concerns to "either Governor Thorn or any member of the newly formed task force."

Finally, March looks expectantly at Graham, who comes forward again to stand next to her, and echoes her closing sentiment. At last, we're dismissed, and hundreds of grumbling Ionians make their way out to their day's work assignments. Arden and I, who are still technically on medical leave, head back to the pod.

"Am I just paranoid, or did that seem insidious?" I ask as we stride across the sand.

"Which part of it?" Arden asks, for once not joking.

"We may have been set up, and by more people than the Company. I mean, *I* was specifically asked to put together this task force."

"Ah. My old friend Governor Thorn."

"Don't call him that. I don't know why *she* kept calling him that. He's not the Governor here."

Arden shrugs. "There were plenty of things in those remarks I found insidious, but that wasn't one of them."

"You don't know..." I start to say, then recall there is actually a lot *I* don't know about Arden *and* Graham. It seems pointless to worry about this now, however. "Maybe I really am just being paranoid," I finish.

"I'd say you're being realistic, based on your experience, but you need to keep as open a mind as possible," Arden says. "We haven't started the investigation yet, although we know part of the narrative she's trying to spin isn't accurate. More concerning to me is that we don't know *why* that's the story they're spinning. Understanding the 'why' may be the most important part of this puzzle."

We turn onto the path toward our pod and walk along in silence. Arden's comment has really made me think. I've always been more of a "yes or no" kind of girl; my early life was a series of clear, obvious decisions. Then I was literally hit by a bus, and I chose a path of making no decisions for a long time, instead letting life wash over me, through me, almost without leaving a mark. Now, it seems nothing is clear or obvious anymore.

As we cross into the courtyard, I turn toward Arden.

"That's it, then," I say. "We'll put the team members on to the specifics of the investigation, if that's what we're charged to do. But you and I will look for the *why*."

For all her haste in getting herself in front of Iona, Fallon March is rather less speedy about meeting with her investigation team. Three full days after our dawn introduction, no word has come down regarding meetings, goals, organization—nothing. I'm not sure if this is due to March's own lack of enthusiasm, Graham's general displeasure with the composition of my team, or the persistent notion I have that the Company has already reached a conclusion and plan of action that requires no actual investigation and no input from us. The latter, of course, is my bet, despite Arden's repeated attempts to dissuade me.

I hear from Fanny that March, ensconced in Pauly's room much to the disgust of the entire pod, has not set about getting to know Ionians in a "deeply personal way" but instead seems to be concentrating on avoiding them as much as possible. The Security Chief spends most of her time hunkered down in Pauly's office at Intake, frequently badgering Graham about record-keeping or historical data. She only returns to the pod at lights out to retreat to Pauly's room without speaking to or interacting with anyone.

Her assistant, who wasn't included on the visit manifest and thus arrived to no planned accommodations, spends one night sleeping in a bed in Clinical and is then packed onto a visiting skiff and shuttled off Iona the next day.

Once day four rolls around, I decide I've had enough. I wake before the rising chimes and scour myself in the shower until I'm almost raw. I wrangle my hair into submission and put on a clean set of service wear with my credentials displayed from a colorful lanyard at my waist. When I look in the mirror, I feel a bit deflated. I still look like myself, although with a little more care applied—my brown hair is twisted up into a relatively neat pile atop my head instead of stuffed under a hat or contained in a messy bun. My skin is clear and fresh-scrubbed but compared with the image of March in her sharp burgundy fashion with her attention-catching burgundy lips and crisp pale blonde bob, I feel like a mouse about to go toe-to-toe with a lioness.

"She'll just underestimate you," I say to my reflection. "It's an advantage."

Fortunately, my reflection doesn't argue. I pop on my headset and set out for Intake. If Fanny's right, March will be there.

When I arrive, Intake is quiet and appears empty, but peering down the hallway I see light from Pauly's office casting a cool white sparkle on the tile floor. As I walk toward his door, March's voice echoes loudly down the hall, terse and irritated. I freeze, in part because I don't want to interrupt, but also because I desperately want to eavesdrop.

"I don't care what you think would make the best presentation," March snaps. "I'm here to do a job, not make friends. That's only going to make it take longer."

A pause. She's listening to a reply I can't hear, which means she's either on headset or using a holotablet set to private mode.

Whatever the second party says chastens her. She listens quietly for nearly a full minute. When she speaks, her response is measured, almost cowed.

"I suppose," she says. "But at least I know he *is* here. I've confirmed that much."

Another pause. "No, I don't believe that's going to be an issue." Her tone becomes more defeated with every word.

Another pause, this one shorter. "Of course. I'll be in touch."

The conversation ends. I hear her sigh and the sound of fingernails drumming against Pauly's marble-topped desk followed by a frustrated expletive. I wait until I feel like I won't be accused of spying, then make it a point to resume my walk toward the office, this time more noisily, and call out "Hello? Chief March?"

The drumming stops immediately, and I hear a desk drawer quickly open and close as March calls out, "Who's there?"

"I'm Faith Feathergrass, I'm hoping we can set up a meeting," I say as I round the corner and step into the doorway. My words freeze in my mouth at what I see.

March is behind Pauly's desk, but she's not sitting down. Instead, she's standing in a defensive crouch, training an impressive and extremely deadly-looking firearm on me.

Instinctively, I throw up both hands, palms facing her, but my anger erodes rationality. "What the hell are you doing?" I shout. "Put that thing down!"

March blinks in obvious confusion. I'm not sure whether it's over the fact I'm clearly not the threat she anticipated or from being given a direct order by a mousey underling in dumpy beige clothes. Either way, she slowly lowers the weapon, and her posture begins to relax. She abandons the defensive crouch in favor of a sort of tense uprightness—an improvement in that she no longer appears prepared to murder me on the spot.

She finally drops the weapon onto the desk unceremoniously and smooths her hair. Her steel blue eyes rake over me in a frank assessment, and her lips twitch in irritation.

"Who are you again?" she asks. Her tone has regained its icy imperiousness.

"I'm your investigation team lead," I say, taking a full step into the office and crossing my arms confrontationally across my chest. "My name—again—is Faith Feathergrass." I look pointedly at the firearm. "Who exactly were you expecting?"

She chews her lip before answering me, still assessing.

"I'm merely trying to guarantee my personal safety," she says. "I never know what kind of reception I'm likely to receive when I visit these backwater planets." Her lips curl in distaste as she gestures around her.

I assume the goal is to insult me, and I am. But it's going to take more than that to diffuse my ire.

"At this point, it seems we might need to be more concerned about *you* than you need to be about *us*," I say, leveling my gaze at her. "You know, you could just keep the door locked."

She makes an exasperated sound. "That would send the wrong message."

"What kind of message do you think *that* sends?" I ask, gesturing at the weapon now lying on the desktop with no more thought given to its disposition than an abandoned scrap of wire.

She mutters something under her breath, but finally sits down with almost regal precision. She opens a drawer and slides the weapon into it.

When she speaks, her voice is steady and devoid of any emotion. "Do have a seat, Ms. Feathergrass, was it?" she says. "And please just get to the point, whatever it might be."

I pull out one of the chairs and sit down gingerly, keeping my eyes locked on her. My own posture mirrors hers—rigid, upright and formal. I'd wanted to get things off on a positive, if not entirely friendly, note, but it seems there's no recovering that now.

"I'm your investigative team lead," I repeat, and wait for some acknowledgement or recognition. There is none. "I was charged with forming the team to assist you in your investigation of the incident at Warehousing?" I prod. This finally rings a bell for her.

"Oh, yes. Governor Thorn mentioned that."

I cringe internally at her use of the honorific, but press on. "*Graham* led me to believe we would be conducting the investigation and reporting to you, so some kind of structure would be useful. Do you plan to give us some kind of charge or process outline? Something to help us understand what you expect from us?"

March lets out another put-upon sigh. "If you're supposed to be investigating, go ahead and investigate," she says tersely. "I'm not doing anything to stop you." Her fingernails begin their annoyed pattern on the desktop again. Her eyebrows are arched in a challenge.

All righty, then. Challenge accepted.

"I'm happy to," I say enthusiastically. "I appreciate you giving us the green light and the resources to determine *exactly* what happened in our Warehousing Unit. That's very generous of the Company, particularly given we've already determined the crate in question was sent to Iona from a Company address. We're quite anxious to discover who within the Company may have been so cavalier as to send a hazardous shipment through without proper labeling and documentation. We *all* want to ensure the guilty parties are held responsible. I suppose that's where you'll come in."

She's completely taken by surprise. Her eyelids flutter a bit as she tries to formulate a response, but I've made my point, so I stand and walk purposefully to the office door.

"I believe we're done here," I say before she can reply. "I'll submit the team report to you once our investigation is complete, and you can add in any measures the Company plans to take to ensure this sort of thing never happens again. We'll then make the report public. I *do* hope we'll be able to wrap this up quickly. Good day, Chief March."

I turn on my heel and walk out the door. As I stride down the hallway, I hear her call out, "Wait!" but I don't stop. If Fallon March wants to have any input or control any part of this investigation, she's going to need to do more than just shout after me. She's going to have to come to me, sans firearm, and give me some answers.

19

WHEN I TELL ARDEN about my dramatic exchange with the Security Chief, he also finds March's behavior peculiar.

"That doesn't sound like her," he says, his eyebrows knitting together. "She has a reputation for being extremely thorough, very prepared, and highly organized. The conversation you had with her suggests she was none of those things."

"Is she also known for being heavily armed?" I'm admittedly still shaken by that aspect of our meeting.

Arden's expression is somber. "I honestly don't know what to make of that," he says. "It's a complex job, but it's not known as a particularly dangerous or high-profile one. Tactical Security, sure—in that case, the whole job is about protective firepower because you don't know what kind of threat you're being sent to mitigate. Operations Security is more about documentation and process-es, contracts, compliance, safety protocols. I've never known of any Operations Security officer who was attacked or threatened, but on the other hand there might be circumstances I'm not aware of. It's really not my area of expertise."

"What *is* your area of expertise?" I ask suddenly. "What do you actually *do*?"

Arden gives me a curious look.

"We talked about this," he says. "Materials transport, pilot, enforcer, space pirate ..."

"We talked about various things you did over the last eight years. But we haven't talked about what you were doing when you left Home World. And we haven't talked about what you're doing here now."

"I'm your Warehousing Leader," Arden says blankly.

"We didn't need a Warehousing Leader. We never had one before. Nothing changed to make us need one. Yet here you are."

"I was assigned this post. That's all I can say."

"You're still working for the Company, aren't you? Still on the payroll?"

"You know perfectly well the Company doesn't control Iona's human resources."

"It doesn't. But this Warehousing position isn't an Ionian position. It's a Company position that just happens to be on Iona, isn't it? If we go down to HR and look at their logs, we'll see Iona's being reimbursed for your expenses by the Company, won't we?"

Arden's response is silence.

It's a painful moment for me, as I'm spun back to that earlier time when Arden nearly destroyed us by keeping everything a secret. Carefully, he takes my hand. "I wish I could tell you everything," he says, his voice low and steady. He looks into my eyes with a pleading expression. "There's more going on here than you imagine. What you see, what you've experienced, is only the tip of a sand dune. I shouldn't even tell you that you're on the right track, although you already know you are. I can't go into more detail now. Hopefully soon, but not now. I hate to do this, but I have to ask you to let me keep this private for now and trust me anyway. Can you, Faith? After all we've been through, and for your own safety?"

I'm moved by the mix of anxiety, sadness, and hope written on his features, but still feeling the niggling irritation of his secrets. So many secrets. And always kept for *my own good*.

I finally say, "You left for my own safety once before, and kept me in the dark for almost a decade. I don't want that happening again. If it comes down to a fight—any kind of fight—this time we fight together. You have to promise me that. And you need to tell me everything, and soon."

At last, his face relaxes. He clasps my hand in both of his in a gesture of solidarity.

"We fight together," he says. "And I *will* tell you everything soon. I swear."

The investigation team meets for the first time that evening. I'm energized, in part because I feel like I won Round One against Fallon March and the Company, and in part because I'm so tired of the enforced inactivity of medical leave I could scream. I'm increasingly buoyed as each member comes into my pod's common room. When everyone is assembled, there are eight people present. Graham, whom I consider a de facto member, was invited as well, but begged off as too busy to attend. At least he sent along with his regrets several bottles of high-quality brew that I'm more than happy to crack open.

I was concerned the atmosphere would be heavy and sad, but my own enthusiasm has proven contagious, and everyone seems invigorated. We start by writing our own three-part charge: to understand the exact cause of the explosion; to pinpoint all responsible mechanisms, parties, and practices; and to issue recommendations for Ionian and Company action as appropriate, whether changes in policies or disciplinary action against individuals or departments found to be at fault.

Our first objective is to determine whether the explosion was accidental or a deliberate act. The natural inclination of Ionians has been to think of this as a terrible accident. But we must admit that other scenarios are possible, especially with what we know about Bardazel's difficult history and the Company's involvement in it, compounded by our own experience with Karloa and Blue, the arrival of Arden, and Graham's rising prominence on Iona, all happening in quick succession.

We plan some initial inquiries and schedule a second meeting two evenings hence, then most everyone heads home to their pods for the night. Even though it's late, a few team members from my own pod, plus Fanny, linger around our communal table sipping brew and nibbling on the remains of some excellent pepper cheese bread Hinn left out for us.

"That's a hell of a task we've set for ourselves," Fanny says, gesturing toward me with her flask.

"I know the answers might be hard to hear, especially for you," I respond sadly. "From your perspective as Pauly's sister, or from Macha's perspective as someone trying to provide care to the injured, it might not matter. The end result is the preoccupying thing. But if Iona was targeted—or if an Ionian was targeted—it's imperative we find out by whom and why."

Fanny scowls, drinks again from her flask, and hands it around the table. "If we find out someone was trying to hurt my brother deliberately, it's definitely going to matter to me because I'll be making that someone pay."

"But who would want to hurt Pauly?" asks Wenda, taking a deep drink from the proffered flask, then passing it back to its owner. "That doesn't make sense."

"No, it doesn't," Arden agrees. "In fact, if we determine this was a malicious act, it's unlikely Pauly was the target. He probably just happened to be in the wrong place at the wrong time."

"Who would be the target, then?" Maybree asks. "Are we looking for someone whose goal was to make Iona look bad?"

"That's a possibility," Arden says, "but I doubt it was a shot against Iona as a whole. To me, the potential targets who make the most sense are Graham Thorn or me."

"What about us makes sense?" The new voice at the doorway is so sudden it makes me jump. Arden is all smiles and stands as Graham comes into the room. The two men clasp hands like the old friends they say they are. Afterwards, Graham bends down with a hug for me and a smile and wave to the others gathered here. His demeanor seems a bit lighter tonight, with a little more of the old Graham on display, although whether genuine or contrived I can't determine. Only Fanny refuses to respond to his greeting and instead slams her flask down on the table as she stands and says, "I'll be going now."

"Oh Fanny, don't go on my account," Graham says, trying to land the comment somewhere between friendly teasing and true entreaty. It's not enough.

"Not at all, I find I'm quite tired," Fanny snarls without any hint of tiredness in her voice. "Good night, friends. Good night, *Governor.*" With that, she stomps out to the courtyard. I can't let her go this way and hurry after her.

"Let me walk you out!" I call, and hurry after her.

"I'm sorry," she says as I catch up with her at the edge of the courtyard. "I can't be around him for longer than five minutes."

"I don't mind if you leave, but we were talking about something important," I point out, "and Graham is part of the team. I don't want to be critical, but you have to stop giving your emotional backlash priority over everything else. It's not helping anyone. It's especially not helping Pauly."

At this point, Fanny's demeanor begins to crack, and she looks back inside the pod, where Graham is having an energetic conversation with Arden. "I don't know why I feel like it's his fault," she says, shaking her head. "I know it's illogical and wrong-headed. I know Graham did nothing to cause this, he didn't come here to replace Pauly, he didn't want to be pod leader or Task Coordinator or have this angry iceberg woman from the Company stay with us. I know that. But I just can't look at him without thinking about what a different place Iona was before the Bardazelians came. It feels like one day Iona was happy, and the next day it was dangerous."

"It's not dangerous," I say, even though I'm not altogether sure about that myself, given my run-in with Fallon March. "Wenda has some thoughts about the future of Iona. She can envision a time soon when people will be proudly proclaiming they're *from* Iona. From here! Can you imagine? Won't that be grand?"

Fanny looks at me with a half-smiling, half-sad expression. "That *will* be grand," she says. "I hope I get to see it. But darling Faith, be careful. Maybe I'm jumping at shadows, but it seems that Iona has become a different place. And I can't shake the feeling it has something to do with *him.*" She looks back toward our common room one more time, then shakes her head as though trying to clear demons from her vision.

She hugs me again and kisses my cheek before climbing aboard her sand scooter and whirring away into the dark.

The somber mood of our exchange is in direct contrast to the energy of the common room that greets me when I return. Arden and Graham, deep into an entertaining story from their "old days" together, have everyone laughing. A few of my podmates who had not yet turned in for the night have joined in as well, and Hinn is clattering around the kitchen getting more snacks for everyone.

There is a feeling of comfort in the air. It's pleasant to see so many people I care about looking relaxed, even if it's just for a moment. I stand in the doorway watching, trying to memorize it all: Arden's laughter, Graham's smile, the way Wenda and Maybree lean into each other and whisper as if passing secrets back and forth, Hinn's cheerful whistle as he works in the kitchen, Shar's sweet voice breaking into song, Darrow teasing Holly and Holly's flirty response.

Each one is so important to me, and someone, somewhere, wants to wreck the beauty I've found here. I won't let that happen. I won't let everything be taken from me again.

20

THE NEXT MORNING, I wake up to a hail from Fallon March.

"I understand I'm supposed to be working with you," she says, sounding only slightly less frosty than she did the previous day. "We can meet later this morning."

I'm glad she can't see the expression on my face.

"Will there be firearms?" I ask.

"No," she says. I hear her fingernails pounding on the desktop in the background.

"In that case, a meeting would be appropriate," I say. "Come to Pod C-1419 within the hour. If you don't have a map, *Graham* can tell you where it is."

I log out of the channel before she can respond. I'm a little concerned I'm being too hard on her, but fortunately the feeling passes quickly.

I spend only a fraction of the next hour getting ready. I'm done with trying to match her level of formality and style. My hair goes into my standard messy bun, my hands look like they always look—mostly clean, but like the hands of a girl who often uses them for difficult dirty work, like wrenching fuel couplings into submission and ripping apart circuit boards. I'm me today. It's more than enough.

Predictably, March arrives late. She's wearing another crisp jumpsuit, this one a tailored linen number in a tasteful cream color that matches her white blonde hair and skin. Her only concession to her surroundings are a pair of enormous round glare-cutting sunglasses, completely unnecessary given Iona's anemic sunlight, and flat sturdy shoes. I imagine her trying to navigate Iona in anything approaching heels and almost laugh aloud.

"This is where you live," she says, coming into our common room and peeling off her sunglasses to look around.

"Yes," I answer. "It's exactly like where you live. For the moment, anyway."

At this, she merely shrugs. "We're meeting in here? There's no special room?"

"We're meeting in here," I confirm. "Have a seat."

She looks around again as if conflicted but sits down at the large communal table.

"Would you like something to drink? Coffee, water?" I ask. Her face registers mild surprise.

"Water, thank you," she says. I step into the kitchen and draw a large pitcher of cool water and grab glasses for both of us.

"Hinn left us some muffins, if you'd like a bite to eat," I say, putting the glasses down on the table and filling them.

"Just water for now," she says, drinking thirstily. "I'm not used to how dry it is here."

"We hear that a lot. I thought I'd never adjust, but I did. It takes a while."

We sit in silence for a moment. Finally, March says, "I suppose we need to get on with it."

"Sure," I say. "You requested the meeting, so let's go with your agenda first."

Her brow creases a bit as she takes another sip of water, then sets the glass down on the table and folds her hands in her lap.

"I had a talk with Gov ... uh ... *Graham*," she says. "He was not terribly pleased with our first interaction."

"Nor was I." I laugh. Instead of diffusing the tension, my humor makes her visibly more irritated. Her hands move to the table in a tight clasp, and she frowns.

"No," she says. "I'm aware."

"And you asked to meet, why?"

"I have some suggestions for parameters to guide your investigation."

I worked for the Company long enough to know what that word actually means. *Parameters* are never a good thing if you're the one they're being placed around.

"You mean you want to set some limitations on the work we plan to do," I say bluntly.

"Well no, not limitations *per se*. Parameters."

"Specific parameters."

"Yes."

"Limitations." I take a long drink from my glass of water, never taking my eyes off her.

"I wouldn't say that. It's important to make sure there is an appropriate focus and the correct methodologies are set."

"In other words, limitations," I interrupt her, setting my glass down on the table sharply. "I know how this goes, Ms. March. Initially you assumed you'd be able to tamp down this investigation by blowing us off, but that didn't work. Then you thought you'd just be uncooperative, but you learned the hard way that we're not going to just go along for that ride either. Now you're worried Graham may have connections above your pay grade, because you know his family owns the Thorn Industry Collective, and they have a reputation for ... well, let's just say they get what they want, when they want it. So your next gambit is to try to control what we do by pretending to help us focus. Am I right?"

March throws up her hands in frustration.

"I'm not here to make you happy," she says, powerfully irritated now. "I'm here to do a job."

"And what job is that, exactly? Because it seems the job we were told you were coming here to do is being done by *us*, but only if we can get around your parameters. Does that sum it up?"

March's mouth draws into a thin, hard line and the fingernails of her right hand begin tapping out a harsh, angry rhythm.

"I don't know what you want from me," she says flatly.

"I want you to *actually* help with the investigation. It's as simple as that."

"What do you mean by 'help'?"

I smile. This is exactly the question I want her to ask.

"I've learned you have access to some records that would be very useful for us to obtain. Don't worry, they aren't classified or anything of that nature. They're just difficult for laypeople to come by. If you could procure that information for us, it would be quite helpful."

March looks at me suspiciously. "What records are you talking about?"

"It just so happens I have a list," I say, picking up my holotablet from the table and tapping a few commands on its screen. A neatly formatted, extremely long document takes shape and hovers in midair between us. I tap it and send it flying to her device with a single touch. "Let's review, shall we?"

We talk for another hour. To be accurate, I talk and March either listens or occasionally makes an annoyed or put-upon grunt. I try to be pleasant but stop well short of friendly, which seems to be the most comfortable approach. By the time she puts on her ridiculous sunglasses and departs, she has agreed to gather most of the information on my lengthy list.

I can't keep the grin off my face as I hail into Arden's private channel. His medical leave has ended and he's doing some Warehouse recordkeeping work in a temporary office at Goods, alongside Graham who was kicked out of Pauly's office when March arrived. When he answers I simply say, "It worked. Let Graham know."

"Oh, good job," he responds with a chuckle. "You'd make a great space pirate."

I laugh out loud. Subterfuge is not usually my thing, but in this case, I'll take it. "I learned from the best," I say.

"You did indeed," Arden says with pride.

I can't believe this plan succeeded. Graham, Arden and I concocted it last night after the rest of the team had gone home and my podmates had succumbed to exhaustion. The basic strategy is simple: create a series of high-level distractions for Fallon March. Just one dramatically-acted conversation with Graham put the plan into motion. In the end, we all proved quite convincing. And Arden's assessment that she was too hyper-responsible to ignore a seriously framed request, and too insecure in her position to risk Graham contacting some of the high-level names he bombed her with, was spot-on.

Truthfully, some of the information on the list I passed to March this morning *will* be quite useful if she manages to deliver it. But for now, we're happy enough to have her out of our way.

Our team meets again that evening and Maybree takes the lead with updates. "The material samples Security collected were sent out to a lab for analysis almost the instant Fallon March arrived, so we may have lost control of those forever, but I at least have a copy of our original report," she says. "I summarized it for everyone, and if you check your holos, you'll find it's been sent for your eyes only."

"Which lab got the samples?" asks Arden. "I might have some pull, depending."

"Unclear," Maybree says with a frown. "There are six labs listed on the outgoing manifest. It might be any of them, or even all of them. We had to follow Company protocol and send the samples to a centralized disbursement center. They would have taken care of the rest."

"Disbursement on Home World?" Arden looks puzzled. "They must have changed protocol, then."

"The center's identified as having a Home World base, but it's located on an orbital rather than on the planet itself," Maybree clarifies. "Safer, apparently. Wouldn't want to accidentally expose all those Home Worlders to some unknown pathogen."

Arden and I exchange looks across the table. Maybree continues consulting the data on her holotablet.

"There wasn't much left of the crate or its contents, so we didn't get many clues from rudimentary inspection," she adds. "Most of the debris was too small and our largest sample remained stuck in Patient Two until Clinical was able to extract and preserve it for us, which took several hours."

We all wince a bit. Wenda wraps an arm around Fanny, who is holding up well but is looking a little ashen just now. Maybree looks stricken and whispers, "Sorry." Fanny waves her off.

"It's all right," she says. "We all know what happened. No sense in trying to make it less awful than it was."

"The one thing we did figure out very quickly was the container that exploded was sent to Iona by the Company, via a Company skiff. But it wasn't from a department or specific individual. It was listed as being from a dummy address that's only used for generic purposes."

At this, something begins gnawing in the back of my mind. "How did you source that information?" I ask. We've all known that the implicated package came from the Company, but this is the first time we've talked about its specific origin.

"We got lucky. The sample that was stuck in, uh, I mean, our largest debris sample, turned out to have a portion of the inventory number imprinted on it. We were able to find a match on the incoming cargo manifest."

"What did they claim was in the crate?" asks Fanny. "Maybe that could give us some clues as to its original sender."

"There's no information on its contents," Maybree replies. "The manifest notes that the 'content details' portion of the shipping tag was left blank."

Arden is reading the Security Team report for himself as she talks and lets out a low whistle. "If this is correct, this thing showed up long before I got here," he says.

"It's correct," Maybree confirms. "Several people working intake at Warehousing remember it coming in and Pauly commenting about the fact it was addressed to 'Warehousing Leader' when Iona didn't have a Warehousing Leader. We know we have the right crate."

"It was addressed TO the Warehousing Leader?" repeats Wenda, wide-eyed. "It sounds like it may have been meant for you after all, Arden."

"If these dates are accurate, I hadn't even been assigned here when this crate arrived, much less when it would have been sent out," Arden says, looking puzzled.

A memory of a day on the pad filters back into my awareness—the skiff pilot and our conversation about the impending arrival of some overemotional former star jockey to take over as Iona's Warehousing Chief.

"You might not have known you were coming here, but someone did," I say, and relate the information the pilot shared with us. "Wenda might be right. What happened to Pauly may have been meant for you."

"But how could anyone assume that this crate would be left alone for this unnamed Warehousing Leader to arrive and open it?" asks Fanny. "If it was meant for Arden, and the sender knew he would be coming here, wouldn't it make more sense if it had been addressed to him by name?"

Addressed to him by name.

I gasp, going cold with sudden recall.

"Faith, what's wrong?" Wenda asks, clutching my right hand. "Are you all right?"

"There's a second crate here," I say, my voice cracking. "There's another crate just like that one, here on Iona. It came in at the same time, on the same skiff."

"What are you talking about?" Arden asks, a note of urgency creeping into his voice.

"I remember it now. There were two crates on that skiff, both from that weird generic Company address, with no details in the contents fields," I recount. "Pauly and I unloaded them and checked them in. One was addressed to 'Iona Warehousing Leader,' no name attached. But the second crate *was* addressed to a specific person by name. It was addressed to *me*."

The room goes silent. Arden reaches over and places his hand on my arm protectively. His eyes are wide with alarm.

I realize I'm shaking.

"Dear gods," whispers Wenda, and I lean into her.

"What happened to it?" Arden asks. He's trying to stay calm, but his voice crackles with anxiety. It reminds me of his tone long ago when he was trying so hard to understand how Transportation could have gone so wrong.

"I sent it to my personal storage and forgot all about it," I say. "I never touched it again. It's still there."

"Does anyone else know about that crate?" he asks gently. "Did you tell anyone else about it, or show it to anyone?"

"Pauly knew about it because we were working the delivery together, but no one else," I say, thinking hard. "He entered it onto the intake manifest, and I sent it to personal storage and that was it."

"Could someone else have learned about it other than from you or Pauly?" Arden asks. I don't know where he's going with this, but clearly his brain is connecting dots. His tone is somewhere between anxiety and barely contained excitement.

I think about this for a moment. "It's on the intake manifest, so I suppose anyone who cared to go through those records one by one could theoretically find it," I say.

"Graham's been complaining about March pestering him for access to all our cargo manifests, both incoming and outgoing," Fanny adds. "Pauly used an audit system that no one else can quite make heads or tails of, so he's having difficulty pulling the exact ones she wants. She's being *very* specific."

"Even if she has the manifests, that was one shipment of a dozen that week and there were hundreds of items that came in," I say. "It wouldn't be obvious to someone just reading through the manifest."

"Unless you knew what to look for," Wenda points out.

"Who would know what to look for? Only Pauly and I knew it was even here."

"The person who sent it would know," Maybree says. "Or someone working for them."

We all trade anxious looks in silence.

Arden breaks the nervous quiet. "Is your storage space secure?" he asks.

I shake my head. "You need generic credentials to get into the warren, but beyond that, no," I say. "I never bothered with additional security."

"Then let's get over there and do something about that," he says.

21

IT DOESN'T MAKE SENSE for the entire team to come along; the specter of eight people traipsing over to the storage warren in the middle of the night might draw more attention than we want, and there's the added possibility that this could take a dangerous turn. Instead, Arden and I set out alone. Maybree will join us after a visit to the Security Office to pick up some potentially useful items.

In case anyone might see our silhouettes in the darkness, we try to look like we're a couple out for a romantic stroll, holding hands as we walk and chatting casually, looking at the stars. Arden offers a running commentary that keeps a smile on my face and some of my anxiety at bay, at least for now.

"Here we are, just two young people out for a little walk, perplexingly late in the evening for that sort of thing, but perhaps reasonable if one is hoping for a romantic tryst," he says in my ear, and I snicker. "All right, maybe not young. Two not-young-but-not-old people enjoying the brisk night air and the astonishing amount of grit that hits your face if you happen to look in the wrong direction. But it's fine. Here on beautiful Iona, the sand tastes like sugar and feels like a soothing ointment in your eyes."

"It is truly a lovely night," I say, wrapping my arm around his waist in continued pantomime. "The constant headwind keeps the bloodbugs at bay. And the natural sand exfoliant gives our skin a youthful glow."

"That's a fact," he says. "I'm often told I don't look a day over eighty, even though I'm only thirty-nine. I credit the Sands of Iona. We could probably bottle this stuff and sell it. All the old high-society Home Worlders would be buying it up by the skiffload."

The comedy routine continues until we reach the storage warren. Despite our dawdling pace, we arrive well ahead of Maybree. I use my credentials to open the door and set the lights to 40 percent, reasoning that dim lighting is less likely to draw attention if anyone else is out and about or looking in our general direction. "Let's wait for Maybree in the share," I suggest, and we walk down the dim central hallway together.

The names on each locker and doorway glow in the pale light. I flinch a little when the name *Karloa Arduval* catches my attention as we pass.

The share space is remarkably neat and clutter-free. Wenda passed the job of managing personal storage and maintaining the share over to Bardazelian podmate Quimby while I was stuck in Clinical, and I'm impressed with his organizational skills. Every box has been emptied out into a series of precisely labeled white bins and the packing debris that littered the floor has been sorted and bundled for recycling. The miniflats are lined up neatly along the far wall. They're all gleaming and look recently cleaned and serviced.

"Wow, this is so much better," I murmur.

"I've only been in here twice," Arden admits. "What was it like before?"

"It was like I was in charge of it," I say wryly. "You remember my house-keeping skills."

"True. But you had many other redeeming qualities."

I toss Arden a sidelong look. He's smirking. "My brilliant mind, my sense of humor, my elegant singing voice?" I ask.

"As I said, many." The smirk is growing. I'm searching desperately for a wicked comeback when I hear the front portal slide open and Maybree's voice shout, "Hello?"

"We're in the share," I call out. The sound of her footsteps and the whir of a hover-flat are amplified as she comes down the hallway toward us.

"I have a lot of equipment," she says, emerging into the share. "Which one is your storage?"

"Number 8 on the left central passage."

"Oh, one of the big ones. That will make it easier."

Arden looks at me quizzically as we start down one of the five hallways radiating out from the share. "Big ones? What have you got in there, the bodies of your enemies?"

I laugh. "Definitely not, I haven't had enough enemies to fill up a cubby. I was working on a project to help me learn the ropes for maintenance and needed the space. I don't have any use for it anymore. I just never downsized."

At the door to Number 8, Maybree waves her credentials in front of the entry panel and the door slides open with a whisper.

Arden shakes his head. "Too easy," he says. "We have to change that."

"We will, right now," says Maybree. She pulls out her holotablet and makes some setting adjustments. "You'll need to confirm this," she says, handing over the holo to me. I enter the necessary information and let it do a quick retina scan. The door chimes pleasantly three times to signify a successful change.

"We've got it set now so that only your credentials will open this door," she says.

"It's a start," says Arden, and Maybree nods. "There are a couple more steps I'd like to implement," she says. "But first, let's take a look at that crate."

Inside, Number 8 is cool, dark, and nearly empty. Our footsteps echo as the three of us enter. I voice-command the lights up to a gentle glow.

"Try closing the door," Maybree suggests, making a few additional adjustments on her holo. The door slides shut without hesitation as soon as I give the command. "Arden, now you try the voice command to open the door."

"Number 8 open," he says. The door slides open again. "Is that intentional?" he asks, peering at the door.

"Yes," says Maybree. "That's what we want. Whenever a door is set so that only one person can open it from the outside, it's important for anyone inside to be able to open it. That way, there's no risk of someone getting trapped."

"Has that happened?" Arden looks at the door again, seeming mildly alarmed.

"No, because the system works," Maybree says with confidence. "Besides, people are in and out of here all the time. Anyone who got stuck would be found in a matter of hours."

"Could we set the door so that Arden can open it from the outside?" I ask. "I'd like to have a failsafe."

"Of course," Maybree says. She makes the adjustments and passes the holo to Arden for his retina scan. The silence of the facility is nearly overwhelming; when the environmental control system cuts on, we all jump.

"Good grief," Arden mutters. "Bring those lights up a little higher. Number 8 close."

The door slides shut with a satisfying thump, and I bring the lights up to 80 percent. It dispels the gloom but highlights the metal and plexi crate sitting conspicuously against the far wall. I feel like I'm lying in bed with a bomb.

We approach it carefully, the only sound the whir of the hover-flat tracking behind Maybree.

"Let's check the data," says Maybree, bringing her holo up and activating the scan. The short, sharp chirp it makes when the data is obtained makes us all jump again. Arden curses and runs his hand through his hair. We can all see the information floating over the crate, but we're still too far away to read it. In almost comical unison, we all take one more big step toward the crate, squinting at the display.

"Bathmats?" Arden reads aloud in a puzzled voice. I can't help but laugh.

"Pauly must have written that in," I say. "He asked me what might be in it, and I had no idea. I said it was probably new bathmats or something. There was originally nothing on the manifest under contents."

"The notation does have Pauly's auth number," says Maybree. "We can safely rule out the possibility that it contains bathmats, right? I mean, it weighs 195 pounds."

We all chuckle, and the tension defuses just a bit.

"It looks exactly like the crate that blew in the Warehouse, if I'm remembering right," Arden says. "But that just means it looks like every Company crate out there. They're all pretty much the same."

"It's similar based on the description, and the sending address is the same generic one we saw on the manifest of the Warehouse crate," says Maybree. "But if the information we have is correct, there are a couple of significant differences. Weight, for example—this one's heavier. The interior lining is listed as a different material, for another. And there appears to be an enviro incorporated into this one, although the settings are so low it's almost nonfunctional."

"And what would the point of that would be?" Arden mutters.

"No idea," says Maybree. "There's a full procedure manual on different types and styles of Company shipping containers and their general uses. That's one of the things we've sent Fallon March after. It might help us sort out what's in there."

"Do they make special crates to contain explosive devices?" I ask, only half-joking.

"They do," Arden says. "But they're supposed to contain any accidental detonation, and that didn't happen in the Warehouse. I think we have to assume it wasn't a malfunction. It was supposed to explode and supposed to do damage."

In my mind I see Bennid, Arden, and Pauly, all battered and bleeding on the Warehouse floor, and shudder.

"Is there any indication of what made the first crate blow?" I ask. "A timing device? Some other environmental factor we should control for?"

"We only have anecdotal evidence," Maybree says, finally taking her eyes off her holo and looking skeptically at the crate in front of us. "Our eyewitnesses suggest the explosion happened after Pauly started actively attempting to open the crate. The electronics appeared to have been damaged and the crate wouldn't open normally, so he was using a prybar to try to get the lid up."

I wince. Everyone knows forcing malfunctioning electronics, especially Company electronics, is not a good idea. They're often double-secured, which basically turns them into booby-traps.

I rub my face with my hands in dismay. "The explosion itself might just have been double-secure doing its job, made particularly problematic by the contents," I say. "Dammit, Pauly, we told you a thousand times. Why was it so important to get into that crate?"

Arden hangs his head. "I guess that would be my fault," he says. "I'm the one who asked Pauly to get it open."

"And the person or entity that sent a crate booby-trapped with an irreversible stasis-causing drug to our facility with no documentation and no way to determine who might open it would be utterly blameless?" I say, scowling at him. "Perspective, please."

"Those double-secures are always highlighted on the manifest," Maybree adds. "Nothing suggested it was double-secured."

"I tried to open it myself, but your report is right—the electronics appeared to be jammed," Arden says, his voice echoing eerily off the bare industrial walls. "Bennid had some questions about something else, so I went to help him, and asked Pauly if he could work on the crate. I didn't expect him to try to pry the lid off."

We look at each other in silence for a moment. "We'll just leave this crate closed for now until we can figure out more about it," Maybree says. "In the meantime, I brought some monitoring devices. They'll take continuous measurements and make sure there aren't any atmospheric changes happening inside that might lead to an explosive state. Once we've ruled out a few things, we should be able to use a resonance scanner on it and produce a visual, but we need to make sure the scan itself won't make it blow."

"We'll have to open it at some point," I say. "It's the best lead we've got."

"And we will, but we'll do it the right way," Maybree says. "If there's an explosive involved, I'm sure we can figure out how to disable it, but that's going to require more time than we have tonight, for sure."

Maybree takes half an hour to set up her monitors and code the system so any of the three of us can read their data remotely. She also puts in place a device that will inform us via headset should anyone else try to communicate electronically with the crate, whether to either open, track, move, or pull any data from it. While Maybree works, Arden and I gather up the small collection of my personal belongings that occupy a corner of the large room and pile them onto another hover-flat, which we then send to Arden's assigned locker. The suspicious crate now has the room all to itself and there's no reason for anyone, not even me, to come inside.

We follow the same pattern departing from the storage warren as when we arrived: Maybree departs first, heading off toward Security, and fifteen minutes later, Arden and I follow.

The breeze has calmed a bit and the temperature dropped significantly. I hug myself and shiver, pulling my thin cotton work shirt tighter around me as we walk. Arden notices and gallantly pulls off his jacket, draping it around my shoulders. It's a goofy old-fashioned gesture, but I'm grateful, nonetheless. I slip my arms into the sleeves and grin.

"Now that's sure to make anyone watching believe we're out on a date," I tease.

Arden reciprocates by draping his arm around my shoulders. He lowers his voice as if telling me a secret.

"How do people hook up here?" he asks, gesturing furtively with his free hand. "Do they actually do it in the storage warrens? There's no privacy whatsoever in the pods, and I'm guessing you can't do anything outside without the literally painful addition of sand."

"Oh, people manage," I say. "Storage warren-trysts aren't unheard of, and believe it or not, the Preservation Theater seems to be a popular spot. And there are a few secret places scattered around that I've heard stories about. You'll have to see the Star Parlor. That's where Graham and I ..." I hear myself and freeze. "Oh, no, I didn't mean ... we didn't ... "

But Arden just laughs. "You and Graham, eh? I wondered. He does look at you that way from time to time. And there seems to be a certain physical familiarity between the two of you."

"No, not like that!" I say, flustered now. "We weren't ... we never ... we only ..."

"Why are you even trying to explain this to me?" Arden interrupts gently, looking at me with a bemused expression. "It's not any of my business. It's perfectly all right if you've been with someone. That's what I would expect, after all this time."

I don't quite know what to say. Of all the responses in all the worlds, this is the most obviously appropriate one. Yet it's the one I least expected.

"I just thought you might be ... upset," I say, knowing it's silly even as it comes out of my mouth.

"I'm completely aware that I *chose* to leave all those years ago—with the best of intentions, and a powerful motivation, but I still made that choice," he responds. "I understood one of the consequences was that you would be with someone else. I didn't love the idea of you moving on and forgetting about me, but I was more interested in making sure you were alive and left completely alone by the Company. I always just hoped that you were happy, whatever that entailed."

There are so many places this conversation could go, so many questions begging to be asked, secrets revealed, declarations made. But the part of my personality that once made Pauly dub me "Carefulina" is far stronger now than the impetuous, impulsive girl who lived in that golden bubble of love with Arden Wilson on Home World and thought her charmed life would last forever. There are other concerns now, more immediate things that must be dealt with, and it doesn't feel right to go chasing the shadows of our personal relationship. Yet some response seems called for. We walk in silence for a moment before I give him an affectionate peck on the cheek and say, "I hoped you were happy too."

Arden's expression is hard to read. I see nostalgia, angst, pleasure, and a tinge of regret all play across his features.

"I'm happy *now*," he says after a thoughtful pause.

I smile at him and say, "Me, too."

The pod is quiet and dark as we return; lights-out happened more than an hour ago and our podmates are all sleeping peacefully. Maybree arrives a few moments after we come into the Common Room. "We'll have some good information by morning, I hope," she says and gives us an encouraging thumbs-up.

"I hope so too," I say, and bidding both Maybree and Arden goodnight, I walk down the hall to my room.

Inside, it's cool and quiet. The window is open a little to let fresh air in. I find the click of the door closing behind me strangely satisfying. I don't bother to turn on any lights. As I stretch out in my hammock, I'm struck by the sound of Iona's sand. It whispers like a low soft song as the grains tumble over one another. If I tilt my head exactly right, it sounds almost like the oceans of Home World dancing along the shore. There's a particular rhythm to the sound coming through my window, and I close my eyes and let myself see the ocean, bright blue and green, fringed by the silky white sand of Home World. Even the sand on Iona is more utilitarian and less flashy—beige and coarse and crunchy underfoot. But it has its own beauty, and I've come to appreciate it more than I ever imagined I might.

I'm just drifting off when I think I hear a soft tap on my door. I sit up.

"Yes? What is it?" I'm convinced I can sense a presence outside in the passageway, but there's no response. "Who's there?" I ask, a bit louder. By the time I get up and open the door to peer out, there is no sign of anyone. The hallway is quiet and unoccupied.

It was just your imagination, I tell myself, but I'm unnerved. I close the door again, then cross the room to close the window. I take a quick look out into the night as I shut it and see two remarkable sights. The first is a shooting star blasting beyond the horizon, in almost the exact same place Arden and I saw meteors the night Fallon March arrived. The second is a human silhouette, barely highlighted

181

by the flash of the falling meteor, speed-walking the ridge behind Residential. As I watch, the figure suddenly disappears in the darkness.

22

WENDA IS SKEPTICAL WHEN I describe the scene to her the next morning at breakfast.

"You're sure you weren't dreaming this?" she asks. "Nobody walks that ridge at night, it's not safe."

"I wasn't dreaming," I say. "I'm on light duty today so I'll have to be on-call, but I'm going up there to see if I can figure out some clues."

"Clues about what?" Arden asks as he walks up behind us, his coffee mug in hand. I find myself reflexively deflecting his inquiry instead of answering it.

"Oh no big deal, I thought I heard something out behind the pod last night," I say, catching Wenda's look as I speak. "I'm going to see if anything is amiss."

"What do you think you heard?" he asks. "Our windows face the same way, and I didn't hear anything. But then, I'm sharing a room with a champion snorer, so I've kind of learned not to hear anything."

"Nothing major. Just some sounds. Something like ..." I'm on the verge of saying the word when a lightbulb goes off and I'm stunned by the realization. I was envisioning the ocean. The sound I was hearing *wasn't* the ocean, of course. But it sounded very much like the ocean because it was so rhythmic and steady. And only one other thing has that particular rhythm.

"Like what?" Arden prompts.

"Like animals prowling around," I invent on the spot. "Something might be trying to get into our food storage."

Wenda's expression is incredulous, but Arden doesn't seem to notice. "Oh," he says absently, already turning away from us and heading for his favorite chair by the fireplace. "Yeah, that could be a problem."

"I'll get it taken care of, though," I say in a voice that's far too loud and entirely unnecessary since he's no longer paying any attention to us at all, instead seating himself across from and starting an intense conversation with Darrow.

Wenda gives me a look and takes me by the elbow, steering me into the empty kitchen.

"What's going on?" she asks, looking at me hard. "Did I just hear you invent a pack of wild animals intent on eating our tomatoes in order to avoid telling the truth to a man you swore to me that you would trust with your life?"

I don't have a comeback for her, or an explanation even for myself.

"That appears to be what happened," I say, wincing.

"You heard somebody at your door, then saw someone up on the ridge and you didn't want to tell Arden about it?"

"Digging," I interject.

"What?"

"Digging. I wasn't lying when I told Arden I heard something. I heard digging last night out behind the pod. Specifically, someone digging with a shovel. I hadn't realized it before, but I'm sure that's what it was."

"And you think this digging is suspect? That Arden is somehow implicated in this digging? Or in the presence outside your room? Or the mysterious ridge-walker?"

"No, not at all. I mean, maybe. I mean, I don't know."

Wenda continues to give me a long level stare until I feel like I've shrunk to approximately three feet in height and have the maturity of a four-year-old. I look at the floor, feeling thoroughly chagrined.

"Well. There's only one thing to do," she says, taking a cup of coffee from the tray Holly is carrying past us and pressing it into my hand. "After breakfast, we're going to go exploring. Just the two of us. And while we look for clues, you're going to tell me what's going on in that head of yours, because I am failing to understand you."

I take a sip of the coffee and look at her guiltily.

"I'm failing to understand me too," I say.

It's mid-morning by the time our podmates clear out, leaving Wenda and me on our own. We start outside just below my window. There's precious little to see. The constant wind and shifting sands means that any evidence of digging is long gone by the time we get around to looking for it.

"Nothing much here," I sigh, squinting up toward the ridge.

"You're sure about what you heard?" Wenda asks.

"Yes. I thought I was dreaming about the ocean, but it was the rhythm of the sound triggering the mental image."

Wenda purses her lips. "It's pretty quiet at night," she says. "Maybe you heard digging further away. Sound can do funny things around here."

I look toward the ridge again.

"Why do I have a feeling I'm about to be invited on a hike?" Wenda mutters. But she's already marching off in the direction of the trail, about 1000 feet behind our pod at the outside edge of Residential. I hurry to catch up to her.

We don't bother to try to hide where we're going. It's not unheard of for Ionians to hike the ridge in the daytime, and we look like any other friends out for a recreational walk. It's a nice day; the wind has slowed and it's calm and temperate. It's not a terribly difficult hike. The path has enough compression to be easier to walk than the sandy flats, and although the initial assent is steep, once we reach the ridge itself, it levels out and becomes an easy stroll.

The trek up to the top of the ridge is steeper than I remember. By the time we reach the crest, I'm panting and Wenda is doing only slightly better.

"Damn medical leave." I wheeze as we stop to catch our breath. "I was in better shape before."

"Of course you were," Wenda replies with a grin. We wait a few more minutes, and once we're feeling relatively normal again, we start following the ridgeline.

"What are we supposed to be looking for?" Wenda asks.

"It could be a couple of things," I say. "The person I saw was a few hundred feet further along the trail, so not very far from where we are now. And they disappeared quickly, as if they had taken a side trail running down the back side of the ridge. So possibly another trail, or evidence that someone left the ridgeline and climbed down on their own."

We walk slowly and quietly at first, studying the terrain. It doesn't take long to work out that there are no side trails anywhere. The far side of the ridge is even steeper than the one I can see from my window and covered in sharp rocks and thorny scrub. As an experiment, Wenda and I try to edge down from the ridgeline at a partial clearing near where I think the mystery person disappeared.

"I can't imagine someone climbing down here at night," Wenda mutters, yanking the hem of her jacket out of the clutches of a thorny shrub. "Between the rocks, the slope, and these damn bushes, I feel like I'm under attack from all directions. And I'm able to see them before I run into them. In the dark, this must be like a mine field."

Looking around, I realize I'm stuck between two sharp rocks and the biggest thorn bush I've ever seen.

"You're totally right and I'm totally wrong," I say as we both struggle to extricate ourselves and make it back to the ridgeline. "Climbing down there makes absolutely no sense."

"Did they fall?" she asks with a snicker. "It's kind of funny, but its's actually a lot more likely than your initial thought. Your mystery person might be clumsy."

"Clumsy and ill-prepared," I say. "I didn't see any lights on them, and one misstep would be all it would take."

"Why would someone come up here without a hand light?" asks Wenda, finally reaching the ridge line and shaking burrs out of her clothing. "That seems really stupid. We all know those little moons aren't bright enough to see by."

"*We* do, but someone who wasn't all that familiar with Iona might not," I say. "A good full moon on Home World, for example, can be almost as bright as a flashlight."

"Bardazel too, apparently," Wenda says. "Maybree talks all the time about how much she misses the Bardazelian moonlight."

My mind is racing as I drag myself back up onto the ridge, taking in the whole of Iona Town below us. Our pod lies closest to where we stand now, its rear-facing windows looking out on the rise. Iona's other residential pods expand out into the distance in a horseshoe shape, snuggling the town's civic buildings in the middle. From here I can see clearly not just our own pod, but half a dozen others. I can also make out the storage warrens off to the west, and in the center of Iona Town I recognize the dramatic peaked roof of the Preservation Theater. The top floor of Clinical sparkles pale blue in the distance beyond it, and at the furthest edge of town, I can see the landing pads. Two silver and white skiffs sit there now, contrasting dramatically with the red-brown cliffs rising just behind them.

Wenda comes to stand beside me. "You can see a lot from here."

"Maybe that's why the mystery person was up here," I propose. "Maybe they were trying to keep an eye on something."

"But what? I mean, you can see the residential pods, and the theater, and storage, but you can't really see what's going on inside. Maybe if someone was outside and you wanted to keep tabs on them."

"Maybe if someone was outside, digging?"

"Oh. Well, wow." Wenda nods appreciatively, looking around, then follows with a more emphatic "Oh *wow*." Suddenly she is scampering and sliding down the sandy near side of the ridge in front of us. She stops about ten feet off the trail above a dense thicket of thorny shrubs. "Do you see this?" she calls back to me.

I almost start laughing. There's a recent, decidedly human-sized deformation in the vegetation, as if a rolling body may have hit it at full speed. Waving like a flag from the bramble is a strip of fabric that was most likely ripped off whatever was being worn by the unfortunate individual who collided with it.

Wenda takes possession of the fabric and stuffs it inside her vest pocket. "There isn't an easy way back up from here," she says, looking around. "It's too sandy to climb. I'm going to just head down this way."

"That's probably what the mystery person did too," I surmise. "Keep your eyes peeled on the way down. I'll meet you back at the pod."

Even though I hurry along the ridgeline back to the trail, Wenda beats me home by several minutes. "It wasn't too hard to stay on my feet, once I knew where I wanted to go," she explains. "There's more sand on that side and fewer rocks, and less scrub. It wasn't exactly a stroll on the beach, but it wasn't as difficult to navigate as the back side."

We head to my room to investigate our find. Wenda hands it over as soon as I shut the door.

"So this is all that's standing between me and accusations of delirium," I say, running the fabric through my fingers. It's about four inches long and an inch wide at its widest point, tapering down to maybe a quarter inch at the base of the tear. It's stitched along one edge and looks like it may have come from a hemline or sleeve. But it's definitely not from one of Iona's standard service outfits—or anything else typical to this planet. It's a fine woven fabric we seldom see here on Iona, and the color is an impressive deep purple.

"It's quite distinctive," Wenda says. "Someone wearing an entire garment made from this would stand out. We should consider that it might not be from clothing at all, but maybe a covering, a bag, or something else. We don't really know what it is."

For now, it's only a piece of cloth that really gives us no indication of who it belongs to or what it came from, but I know it's a clue. I give it one more look before I tuck it into the treasure box on my desk, next to the small card I've kept safely hidden away there for the last eight years.

"At least I know I wasn't hallucinating last night, that's a relief," I say with a smile, but when I turn toward her, Wenda's face is serious.

"You should report this," she says. "Someone skulking around outside our pod in the middle of the night is not normal. It's a weird time right now. They could be planning to do some kind of harm."

I shudder involuntarily but do my best to keep my wits about me. Surely, it's not as risky as Wenda believes.

"Who would I report it to? The Operations Security Chief?" I ask with a sharp, baleful laugh. "She already pulled a weapon on me once before. She's at the top of my suspects list."

"Well, yeah. But to start, I think you should tell Graham," Wenda says.

I feel a bit of illogical ire draw up into me. "He's not in charge here," I mutter, but Wenda isn't having it.

"He's as close to a coordinator as we have right now," she says. "He's helped us in the past, and no matter how Fanny might feel, he's not some spooky bad guy. And he does care."

"I don't know about that," I say, feeling guilty and petulant at the same time.

"He does, and you know it," Wenda contends, "but that's almost beside the point. This is a very strange time on Iona, and this experience of yours is rather dramatic. He'll want to know about this, and he *should* know about it. You need to tell him."

I sigh. "I'll think about it," I say, but I already know the decision is made. "If my choices really are to tell either him or Fallon March, it's not much of a contest."

"You should tell them both."

"What?" I half laugh. But Wenda is dead serious.

"You've said it before, we really don't know *why* she's here," Wenda says. "It's obviously not to investigate the Warehouse accident. We know the Company wouldn't send her here without purpose or just to try to make us all feel better. She's here for a specific reason, and we don't know what that reason is."

"We aren't going to get that from me chatting her up about a mysterious individual doing midnight yardwork outside my window."

"No, but we might get a piece of the puzzle if she has any kind of reaction to it. At this point, that's where we have to start. And who knows, involving her in something like this might get her more engaged. Once she stops seeing us as threatening lowlifes, we might have a chance to make an impression on her that could enhance our standing with the Company. We're going to need all the allies we can get."

Wenda, always presenting the big picture. She's right, as usual.

"All right, you win. I'll pay a visit to Graham and let him weigh in on how to involve the Security Chief," I say. Wenda nods her approval, and I head out into the Ionian afternoon. I feel heavy and anxious. My quiet predictable life on Iona has changed so much in the last few weeks, I would never recognize it were I not in the middle of it. But at the same time, I feel more connected with this little planet, its values, and its people than ever before. If the loss of my anonymity is the price for Iona preserving its independence, it suddenly doesn't seem like too much to pay.

I hail Graham on his private channel first. "Can I talk with you about something in person?" I ask.

He's initially distant and sounds vaguely annoyed. "Can it wait? I'm in the middle of a data run."

"Not this time," I say. "I might be filing a security incident report with Fallon March after I talk to you, and I'd really appreciate your advice."

There's a pause. He seems genuinely surprised.

I can hear ruckus in the background consistent with the usual level of activity at Goods, plus Arden's voice shouting instructions above the din. Graham sighs heavily into his mic. He sounds so tired. I can almost see his drooping shoulders and furrowed brow.

"It's a bit chaotic in here at the moment, but I can meet you at the Theater in about fifteen minutes," he says.

"Perfect," I say, and tap out of the channel. I'm grateful for the change of venue. Arden won't be happy about this either, and dealing with his angst over my safety is something I would prefer to put off until later—maybe much later. This way, I can talk this over with Graham in a reasonably calm manner, and we can strategize how to involve the Company Security Chief. For all the logic of Wenda's argument in favor of it, I'm still not entirely convinced and really want Graham's cool rationality applied, without the typically balls-to-the-wall approach of his temporary officemate.

The Preservation Theater was the first building constructed on Iona, and when more people arrived and it could no longer meet all the needs of the population, new construction spiraled out around it until it became the center of what is now our town square. Although it does house a theater, the name is somewhat of a misnomer. It's really a three-story labyrinth of rooms and passageways that originally served as as shelter, storage, and workspace for the thirty or so pioneers who founded Iona Town.

As Iona grew and settled into its role as an Independent Service Planet, the interior was refashioned to meet a variety of needs ranging from classrooms and meeting spaces to specialized workshops. When Ionians briefly toyed with the idea of a debt-based economy, a few shops sprang up on its lower level. That experiment didn't last very long, but the shops are still here, largely unchanged except for the presence of new-made tables and chairs. The walls remain painted in bright cheerful colors occasionally interrupted by the slightly sad presence of empty shelves.

Each of these rooms also has a door that opens to the outside and floor-to-ceiling windows that look out onto the plaza, although the old acrylic is yellowed and hazed over by grit and years of scratches from Iona's blowing sand. Looking through the distorted panes becomes more like watching a flickering ancient documentary instead of the bustling life of an independent planet.

I like these rooms for their contradictions. I choose one of the smaller spaces for my meeting with Graham. It's painted in bright candy colors and one wall is decorated with a mural of a mermaid swimming in a sparkling sapphire sea, holding a lollipop in her hand. This is the lore and color palette of Home World and nowhere else. I've always wondered who this long-ago artist was. Might it have been a Home Worlder who regretted the decision to come to a little desert planet with no natural external water more significant than a puddle? Or was it someone simply indulging in cheerful nostalgia, sharing a fun bit of their origin story with their new-found family of explorers?

I drop into one of the painfully out-of-context utilitarian chairs and keep watch for Graham through the less scratched of the two windows. Before long, I spot him walking across the square. His expression is flat and dull; he's squinting against a sudden wind gust in a way that amplifies his joyless demeanor. I feel a small pang of sadness that this Graham, so different from the Graham I originally got to know, is the one who is coming to meet with me. I miss that other Graham.

I step out of the door and wave. He sees me and waves back, hurrying his pace across the square.

We retreat into the mermaid room and sit down at the small table. His expression shifts to one of concern. "What happened?" he asks. "What's this security issue about? You seem upset."

"I'm just a bit freaked out," I explain. "Some odd things happened last night. I heard digging outside my window in the middle of the night, and I saw someone up on the ridge behind the pod. There's no reason for anyone to be out there, so I'm worried someone was up to no good."

Graham scowls.

"Did you check out the surroundings this morning?" he asks. "Was anything amiss?"

"Wenda and I had a look around. Any evidence of digging was long gone thanks to Iona's climate. We walked up on the ridge and found some evidence that someone had been there, but we didn't find anything to suggest what they might have been doing. I know it sounds like nothing, but it's so unusual that it's got me concerned."

"It doesn't sound like nothing to me. Is this what you're thinking about reporting to March?"

"Wenda thought it would be a good idea," I say. "Personally, I'm not sure. That's why I wanted to talk to you."

Graham sits back and rubs his face with a sigh.

"I've had to work fairly closely with her over the last few weeks, and she's unlikely to care," he says glumly. "She's focused on some kind of agenda that no one else seems to be able to identify. As you and Arden figured out, she's not really interested in anything or anyone on Iona."

"Wenda's idea was that this might be connected to March somehow. She thought if I reported it as a potential security issue, she might show her hand, or say something that would give us a clue as to what her agenda actually is," I explain. "That would be the gold in this situation."

Graham nods. His eyes are distant and calculating.

"Maybe there's a more subtle way to do that," he says. "Let's make sure our local security people are informed first, though. Let's find Maybree and have a chat with her."

Maybree's workspace in the Security building is essentially a large pile of electronics in varying stages of dissection, decorated with posters and books about her other compelling interest, military and weapons history. She's an almost comical sight, seated behind a semicircular table wearing a piece of headgear that includes a headlamp, a magnifying eyepiece, a set of small tools, and an antistatic cloth dangling from one side. The effect is like some kind of charming young cybernetic one-eyed elf.

Her response to my story is anything but comical, however. She pulls off her headgear and drops it on the workbench in front of her, frowning.

"The digging is weird, but that doesn't worry me as much as someone up on the ridge in the middle of the night," she says. "We've had a couple of other reports about unusual activity up there, and it all seems to dovetail with the Security Chief's arrival. At the very least, it's a safety issue—that area is dangerous at night without high-grade lighting. At worst, there may be something going on that someone wants to keep hidden from everybody, including Local Security. It was worth reporting to me, and I think it's worth reporting to March. It feels tied to Company activity, after all."

"I can't wait to hear what she has to say about that," I mutter.

But the answer, as it would turn out, would be "nothing." Our efforts to hail her yield only silence.

"She doesn't use her headset at all," complains Maybree. "It took days to get her to agree to even have it calibrated to Ionian channels, and the only reason she did it at all was because it's actually one of her own security requirements. I'm the one who had to remind her of that. She couldn't get her head around why she might want to be accessible to anyone here. You'd have thought she was a star and we were just irritating members of her fan club. I've still never seen her wear it."

"We should just walk over to Pauly's office and catch her in person," I suggest, "as long as you're prepared for a potential firefight."

Graham snorts. "She tried to bring that thing into the pod with her," he says. "I wouldn't let her. She didn't like that at all."

"Let's go, then," Maybree says. "Safety in numbers."

We walk the short distance to Intake. Just as during my first encounter with Fallon March, the lobby is empty and quiet, but the lights are on in Pauly's office, creating a sparkling pool of light in the hallway.

"Chief March?" Graham calls out. "We'd like to have a word with you."

We're greeted with silence. The three of us exchange looks and continue moving down the hallway as casually as possible.

"Chief March, are you here?" I say loudly. "No need to try to shoot us." But there's still no response.

"There's a scheduler holo in that office," says Maybree. "If she's not here, maybe we can get an idea of when she might be back."

We continue down the hallway to Pauly's office. As we expected, it's empty.

Maybree accesses the scheduler built into the desk and begins scrolling through data but soon hits a dead end.

"Nothing helpful here," she says. "There are only a few scattered entries, and they seem really random. A lot of them just say 'report' followed by a jumble of letters and initials."

"We should probably just leave it for another time," I say. "She isn't here and we don't seem to have any way to get in touch with her."

"We could go really old-school and leave her a note," suggests Maybree. "At least that way if she comes back to the office, she'll know to reach out to one of us."

"Great idea," I say. "Pauly loved paper so there's bound to be some in this office somewhere."

The first drawer I open has March's hefty firearm in it, which manages to look menacing even without anyone pointing it at me. Graham, looking over my shoulder, scowls his disapproval.

"Why the hell would she have that kind of firepower in her desk drawer?" he says.

"Great," I say. "She wasn't bluffing with this thing, then?"

"If she'd fired it, you wouldn't be standing here," he confirms with a grimace. "In fact, most of this wall wouldn't be standing here."

I close that drawer gingerly. The remaining drawers are all empty except for half-a-dozen packages of stale Snax Energy Cookies and some crumbs.

"No paper," I report, "although I may have discovered the source of Pauly's endless digestive problems."

"Where did he keep his supplies? In here, maybe?" Graham asks, stepping over to a credenza along the far wall and sliding the front panel open. Immediately, something heavy falls out with a thud, followed by an almost musical clatter.

"What the hell?" I hear him exclaim. Maybree and I both turn to look.

Graham is crouching on the floor. Around him are scattered silvery-blue metallic spheres, about the size of my open hand. There must be a dozen of them on the floor, and more threatening to roll out of the bag that contained them, now trailing out of the credenza. Graham is struggling to put the bag to rights, but as Maybree and I come around the desk to help, he shouts, "Stay back, don't touch these! I know what they are!"

We both freeze. "Should we call someone?" I ask, but Graham shakes his head. He's pulled the bag completely out of the credenza and placed it carefully on the floor. I can see that it's more of a wrap, really, like a large shawl tied up into a makeshift carryall. He's gathering the spheres one by one and placing them into its center along with the handful that managed to stay put when the credenza was opened.

"What are they?" asks Maybree. "Explosives?"

"No, they won't explode, but they can break. That would be just as devastating as an explosion. I'll tell you about them as soon as they're secure."

Graham works quickly but carefully, and in a few minutes all the spheres have been rounded up and carefully placed in the wrap. He pulls up the edges and ties it securely. We're all so focused on him that we don't hear hard hurried footsteps approaching until Fallon March bursts through the doorway.

"What are you doing?" she shouts, pointing at Graham. "Leave that alone! Those are my personal effects! Why are you here going through my things? All of you have some explaining to do!"

I'm mesmerized by Graham's reaction. He looks at Fallon March with an expression I've never seen on him, his face darkening and eyes snapping with anger. He makes eye contact with her and holds it, not even blinking, as he stands up and straightens to his imposing full height.

"On the contrary," he says in a voice that underscores his barely restrained fury. "If *these* are your personal effects, I'll need to have you removed from Iona and handed over to law enforcement as soon as possible for possession of a banned and highly dangerous substance. If it turns out you have official authorization to have these objects, you'll be charged with a high crime for not stating it on your incoming manifest and securing it in an appropriate manner. Regardless, you'll be confined to your quarters starting immediately until I get some answers. Maybree, would you please take Chief March back to her room at my pod? Make sure she's chipped and unable to leave the premises. Also, please confiscate that firearm in the top drawer and secure it. I'll pick it up later as evidence."

March's mouth opens and closes as if she's searching for something to say but in the end, she chooses to remain silent. Maybree takes a few seconds to recover from the shock of the scene, then collects the weapon from the desk drawer before stepping in front of March. "Come with me, please," she says, gesturing for March to precede her out into the hallway.

March again looks like she might object, but apparently thinks better of it, and steps through the doorway, with Maybree close behind. She pauses and looks back at Graham with an expression that is half irritation, half disgust. "It's not what you think," she snaps impatiently.

Graham takes a deep breath to steady himself. "I can't imagine what you're doing with these, so that really goes without saying. You'll be formally questioned by an Inquiry Panel tomorrow. I suggest you not waste the intervening time making up some stupid lie about this, because I know exactly what these are, what they're capable of, and more about the rules and regulations governing their handling than you ever could. You *will* want to tell me the truth. Because you're in serious trouble, and I can either potentially help you mitigate it, or make it worse for you. Now go."

He turns his back on her then, looking down pointedly at the threatening package at his feet and then back up at me as Maybree guides March out of the room.

"We have to do something with this," he says, gesturing at the bundle as their footsteps fade away down the hall. "We can't leave it here, and it shouldn't be in any active pod or public space. It needs to be somewhere secure, where people won't disturb it by accident."

My eyebrows go up. "I know just the place," I say. "We have a room in our pod's storage warren that would fit the bill. But you have to tell me, what are those things? Why are they so dangerous?"

"The things themselves aren't dangerous; they're just containers. It's what inside them that's risky," he says, lifting the bundle carefully in his arms. "If this is what I think it is—and I'm certain it is—these spheres contain one of the developmental versions of Blue, one that doesn't have to be consumed to work. Just touch the stuff and the stasis process begins. It was developed on Bardazel, but abandoned early on as too difficult to control. Do you still feel like having it in your storage warren?"

I nod yes. I know I'll want to know more—particularly how he knows so much about this material, and why, if it's so incredibly dangerous, it's been packaged in containers that could break so easily. And of course, he'll have to know more about what's already in that storage room.

As I look at Graham cradling this perilous bundle in his arms, and it sinks in that the fabric of the wrap is a rich, luxurious purple, a material that we almost never see on Iona.

We first go to Goods to procure a hover-flat so Graham doesn't have to carry the bundle clutched to his chest, and then make our way to my pod's storage warren with the flat floating just ahead of us. As we walk, I explain to him what's already in Number 8, and the precautions we've taken to secure it. He takes it all in silently, his expression growing more melancholy with each revelation.

"You weren't planning on telling me this, were you?" he finally says. It's more a statement than a question.

"No," I say. "You haven't been in a good place personally for quite some time now, and it's obvious that you're under a lot of strain. This would have just been one more log on the fire, and we thought we could figure everything out on our own."

It's not a lie, per se. But he sees the subtext anyway, despite my leaving it unsaid.

"You don't trust me," he says. His voice isn't accusatory, just oddly sad.

I sigh. "I don't know," I reply. "Who I trust seems to change every day."

"I understand why you feel that way," he says, "but I'm not your enemy, Faith. Truly, I'm not."

I look at him, his somber expression, his dejected posture. I'm sympathetic, but it's not the time to hold back out of kindness.

"I don't know who you are right now," I say. "It just feels like there's a lot under the surface that you're not telling me, and I learned the hard way that's never good."

He doesn't respond. The way his mouth collapses into a downturned line and the crease that appears between his eyebrows suggest he's weighing his options, which also doesn't fill me with confidence in him.

We complete the walk to the storage warren in silence. Once inside Number 8, I send the hover-flat to the far end of the room, as distant from both the door and the crate as I can get it, and program it to simply descend to the floor and power off rather than going through its usual cargo delivery and return cycle. We don't want to move the spheres any more than we absolutely have to.

Graham walks over to the crate and looks at it solemnly. "Is this it?" he asks. "It looks like a million other Company crates."

"That's the same thing Arden said," I say. "Nothing unusual about it in any respect, at least that we can see from the outside. And as far as he can remember, the crate that exploded in Warehousing was exactly the same."

"How are you going to open it? Are you even going to try?"

"I'm not sure. Maybree wants to do a scan before we even think about opening it. If we decide to open it, we might move it out of here first and into some kind of containment area, just in case the same thing happens."

"Are there places like that on Iona?" Graham asks. "It doesn't really seem in line with the kind of work you do here."

"Not formal constructions like you'd find on Home World," I explain. "There are a lot of big sturdy caves and tunnels in the ridge formations north of town, though, and we have the technology to create barriers to both chemical and human intrusion that would keep it secure long enough to figure out what we're dealing with."

Graham gives the hover-flat with its delicate cargo a long look.

"That's the kind of place those things should be," he says. "Locked up tight where they can't hurt anyone."

We step out of Number 8 into the hallway, and I close and secure the door. I then hail the rest of the team to schedule a meeting at my pod in a few hours. This time, Graham will be there. "Eat with us," I urge in a sudden fit of empathy, but he shakes his head.

"I need to get back to my pod to try to figure out how I'm going to address the Fallon situation," he says. "I'll see you at the meeting, though."

His refusal makes me feel even lower. It must show on my face because as we reach the warren's entry, he pulls me into a spontaneous hug.

"I know there's no point in telling you not to worry, because you're going to anyway. And there's no point in telling you to be strong because you already are," he says. "I'll ask you instead to have confidence. We're going to get this figured out. *I'm* going to get this figured out."

"And I'll ask you not to take it all on as yours alone," I respond. "It's breaking you apart. We can all see it. We need to trust each other more—me included."

He pulls back and looks into my face, his gray eyes luminous in the dying light of Iona's early dusk. "We all have our secrets," he says softly. "Secrets make trust difficult."

I don't really know what secrets Graham is referring to, but my own mind goes immediately to Arden, the mystery conversation, the secret job, the unrevealed details. And I remember then that I have secrets from him; everything that has happened today and last night, none of which I've had the opportunity or inclination to tell him.

Graham is right. We're all keeping secrets from each other on some level, myself not least of all.

"We can change that," I say. "We'll start tonight."

He smiles and squeezes my hand as he releases me from the hug. "You live up to your name," he says. "I hope we all turn out to be worth the faith you have in us. Because really, we're just human beings, and we're all flawed."

"Faith and flaws are not mutually exclusive," I quip, smiling in spite of myself. Graham finally lets out a chuckle and we part, if not entirely friends, then at least feeling a little better about each other.

24

In our few minutes of free time between the evening meal and our team meeting, Maybree shares her report detailing Fallon March's formal arrest and detainment. "Graham wants to interrogate her tomorrow and he thinks you should be part of the Panel," she says. "Good luck getting anything out of her. She's mad as forty stingers and as tight-lipped as a dead drone. She didn't say a word to me after we left Intake."

"What's that about?" asks Arden, craning his neck toward my holo to see what we're discussing. It seems like the perfect opportunity to fill him in on what I saw last night as well as what we discovered today, but I'm not prepared for his response. With each detail he becomes increasingly agitated, and when I describe the scene in Fallon March's office, he can't restrain himself.

"I don't know whether to be more outraged that she had these things or that Graham knew exactly what they were," he says, his exasperation clear. "It means he's handled them before. No one here should be able to say that. Are you sure his response was genuine?"

"What the hell does that mean?" I ask. I had expected Arden to be upset, but not to start interrogating me.

"It seems a bit convenient, don't you think? These deadly things just happen to be in the office, barely hidden, and he just happens to stumble on their hiding place? After all, he was working in that office before March arrived. What if he knew they were there all along?"

"He wouldn't have endangered Maybree and me," I insist. "Suppose one of those things had broken, and we'd all been exposed? You aren't making any sense."

"What if they're not real?"

"What?" I'm incredulous.

"What if the spheres you found don't contain Blue, and Graham just wants you to think they do?" Arden's expression is bordering on angry.

"You're making no sense. First, he's suspiciously knowledgeable about something dangerous, now you theorize that the dangerous thing isn't dangerous at all. Don't you see how ridiculous that is? What would make someone—anyone—go to that level of subterfuge? What could possibly be his motivation for that?" I ask. The pitch of my voice belies my rapidly vanishing calm.

"To make you trust him," Arden responds, leaping out of his seat to pace in front of the fireplace. "He needs to make you believe he's on your side, to get into your good graces, in order to influence you. You don't know what he wants from you."

Before I can speak, Wenda steps in.

"Wait a minute," she says sternly. "There are no 'sides' here. We're all working toward the same thing, which is solving this mystery before anyone else gets hurt."

"I'm contributing theories that haven't been discussed, given this new information," Arden says peevishly. "I'm very concerned about Graham's influence on the integrity of this process."

Wenda huffs at him. "I'm very concerned that you're willing to make up utterly senseless accusations just to avoid your own feelings."

For once in his life, Arden is speechless. He looks from Wenda to me and back again silently for a few seconds, then abruptly says, "I have to take a walk," and leaves the common room through the kitchen. I hear the rear door slam behind him as he strides out into the courtyard.

I look at Wenda, who raises her eyebrows at me and then looks pointedly toward the courtyard. I catch her meaning and go after him.

By the time I reach the door, he's already passed through the courtyard and is a hundred feet beyond its wall. "Arden, wait!" I shout, but he gives no indication that he's heard me and keeps walking.

Something rises up in me, a weird combination of emotions battling for prominence: anger, sadness, disgust, frustration, disappointment, fury. I run after him, sprinting across the sand in the dark, stumbling more than once under the dim Ionian moonlight. But I catch up with him, and when I do, I'm in no mood to make nice.

"Stop walking and turn around, goddammit!" I order. He does, but his face is expressionless. He simply stares at me.

"What are you doing?" I finally ask.

"I don't owe you an explanation," he says, and turns to walk away.

I snap.

"No, you don't owe me an explanation," I spit out, my rage spilling over. "What you owe me is *eight years*. Because you decided *you* knew what was best for me. Because you decided I needed to be protected, I couldn't take care of myself. It was all about me, but somehow you made it all about you. And that's why I lived here for eight years and never connected with anyone else. You're right, Arden. You don't owe me an explanation. I don't even want one. You owe me eight years of my life that your conviction to your own genius basically stole from me. How are you going to repay me? With secrets and half-truths and recriminations? With something that looks like connection until I don't agree with your plan? With jealousy that utterly destroys your objectivity, despite your very adult protestations that you're immune? Because that doesn't quite make up for it, you know?"

He stops in his tracks at this outburst and slowly turns. His face is twisted in anger or anguish, or maybe both. "Really, Faith," he barks. "What do you expect? There's so much going on that you don't understand. And on top of that, I'm only human, there's just so much I can take. Really. What do you want from me?"

I don't even think about the words before they fly out, unconscious, uncontrolled.

"Stop leaving me!" I shout, my voice breaking. "Love me. Tell me everything. Never leave me again."

I immediately clamp my hand over my mouth, but it's too late. The words are out and I can't retrieve them. He stares. The only sound is our breathing and the rustle of the shifting Ionian sand.

He tilts his head toward me, his expression softening.

"Say it again," he says, so softly the words barely carry over the rustle of the sand.

I shake my head, my hand still planted firmly over my mouth.

He takes a step toward me, then another, and another. When we're only inches apart, he reaches out and tenderly moves my hand away from my lips, cradling it against his chest instead. "Say it again," he repeats, his tone gentle. "Faith Feathergrass, what do *you* want from *me*?"

I can barely see his face, because my eyes are brimming with tears.

I let out a sigh and whisper, "Love me. Tell me everything. Never leave me again."

He drops his hands to my waists and pulls me against him, pressing his lips to mine with an explosive urgency. I lose track of everything else as I respond to him, wrapping my arms around his neck and drinking him in, drinking in every second of this embrace, as though it might never happen again. When we finally separate, he keeps me pulled close to him, and whispers into my ear, "I love you. I'll tell you everything tonight—I'll tell everyone. I swear I'll never leave you again, even if you threaten me with Fallon March's firearm." Then we kiss again and again and again, and for the first time in eight years, the constant hitch I've felt in my chest disappears.

By the time we return to the pod, most of the team has assembled. Still in transit are Macha and Graham, who've sent word they're on their way. Fanny's in higher spirits than I've seen in quite some time. Fallon March's arrest appears to have buoyed her spirits and improved her opinion of everything around her.

Wenda gives me a knowing look and smiles her approval as Arden and I walk back into the Common Room hand-in-hand. We sit down beside her at the long table.

"That needed to happen, for both of you," she whispers, and I feel myself blush in response. Fanny, who has been watching with interest, catches my eye and winks at me across the room. But all this focus on me doesn't bother me for once, and I'm strangely content to have everyone around the table apparently know my business long before I was aware of it myself.

A few moments later, Graham and Macha arrive. Arden barely lets Graham sit down before addressing him in front of the entire group.

"Faith told me about your very exciting afternoon," he says, looking at Graham steadily. "I have some things I need to clear up with her, but that also means clearing up some things with you."

Graham doesn't look surprised in the least, but instead simply says, "I thought the appearance of those spheres might bring this all out rather quickly."

"So you *do* know," Arden looks amused. Graham laughs.

"Of course I know," Graham responds. "I do actually enjoy your company, though, for what that's worth."

Now it's Arden's turn to laugh. "That's the second-best thing I've heard today."

The two men pass knowing looks to each other, both smirking. "What a stupid game," says Graham, and Arden nods his agreement.

The rest of us look around the table in utter cluelessness.

"Are we going to be let in on this oh-so-amusing thing or is this a special moment just for the two of you?" Wenda asks pointedly.

The two men look at each other again. "You start," Graham says to Arden. "I'll jump in when it's time."

"All right. If I can get everyone's agreement that this doesn't leave this room, we'll have a little Show and Tell," says Arden. "What do you say?"

Everyone looks confused, but we all nod affirmation.

"Excellent," says Arden. "In that case, we can start here." He reaches into his jacket pocket and takes out two sets of credentials. "This is me as most of you know me," he says, tossing his Iona resident credentials onto the table. "Arden Wilson, former pilot, assigned to be Iona's Warehousing Leader. And that is me, truly. But this is also me."

He tosses the second set of credentials onto the table. This one isn't Iona's distinctive purple and white, but instead a bright green with black lettering and a spattering of golden stars across the top. I can see the Company logo printed across the bottom.

"That's High Defense," Maybree says immediately, staring at him. "That's from the Company's Tactical Security Division."

"Right. I'm a ranking officer in the Company's Tactical Security Division. I have been for years. My specialty is espionage. Faith has already figured out that the Company is continuing to pay me and cover my expenses here on Iona. That's because I came to Iona at the behest of that division, in order to keep an eye on *him*."

Arden gestures toward Graham, who not only seems unconcerned, but even takes a small bow in response to all the gasps in the room.

"Doesn't that bother you?" asks Fanny.

"Goodness, no. He's been surveilling me for years," Graham says casually.

"But I thought you two were friends," I say, looking from one to the other. "Didn't you become friends on some materials delivery mission?"

"We did. We spent a lot of time together and got to know each other very well on that mission, because I was assigned to surveil him," Arden says.

"You see?" Graham adds. "But we actually hit it off, so that made that assignment easy."

"It did," Arden pipes up. "Thank you."

"Most welcome."

"Stop it," I interrupt. "Kill the comedy act, please. I want the actual history. Why was Graham under surveillance?"

"He applied for an important and sensitive leadership position on Bardazel, high up in the Company's structure," Arden explains. "But he had a somewhat, ah, colorful background filled with what I'll just call dramatic behavior. His parents, although both from Home World and Company employees at the time, had expressed some opinions about Operations protocol that made the Company concerned, shall we say, that he might not be right for the job."

"And he passed muster with you?" I ask.

"Not at all," Arden says. "I was 100 percent sure he'd be a pain in the ass and would do all the things they were afraid he'd do if they put him into that position on Bardazel. He's just not a Company kind of guy. So I recommended him."

"I'm confused," says Maybree, speaking for all of us.

"Oh, sorry, I got involved in the storytelling and forgot," Arden says. "There's one more thing."

He pulls from his jacket a holotablet and places it on the table. After a few quick commands, he holds his wrist over the device which scans something embedded in his flesh. The holo finally projects a third credential into the air in front of us. This one is black with silver lettering and a unique logo made of interlocking circles. Maybree gasps.

"Holy crap," she says in a voice tinged with awe. "You're part of the Planetary Equity Alliance."

"What is that?" I ask.

Maybree, the military history buff, answers before Arden can speak.

"They're legendary!" she says enthusiastically. "It's a group of people highly placed within the Company, who joined together when they found evidence of unethical treatment of Independent planets. It started when three planets in the Gordonian Sector claimed Core World status. The Company was ready to employ some insidious tactics against them—things that would have endangered the entire populations of those worlds. The Equity Alliance exposed the Company's plans and convinced the leadership of those planets to work together to resist Company absorption. And it worked! They won and became the first independent network. The Equity Alliance members are very mysterious and their identities are kept secret to prevent retaliation by the Company. And now I'm actually sitting across the table from a member. This is incredible!"

"Oh, I'm not a member," Arden says, arching an eyebrow and proffering a sly smile. "I'm the founder."

Maybree's mouth falls open. A ripple of startled sounds runs through the room. This time even Graham looks surprised.

"You saved all those people," Maybree says. "I'm honored to be in your presence."

"All those people saved themselves," Arden says, waving his hand. "We just helped them prepare for what they had to do. And we were hoping to do the same for Bardazel." He looks at Graham and a flash of sadness crosses his face. "Sorry."

I turn a critical eye on Graham. "Are you part of the Planetary Equity Alliance too?" I ask.

"I am not," he says, "although I have a feeling I'm about to be recruited."

"Then let me explain," Arden says, pointing at him. "Let's get back to the story of what happened on Bardazel."

"There was a mining accident and a cloud of poison gas," I said, remembering one of my first conversations with Graham. "Blue was developed to give them time to get help. Is that not true?"

"It's true in the sense that this is the narrative the Company laid out," Arden confirms. "In reality, there was never any encroaching poison gas cloud on Bardazel. The Company wanted an excuse to expand the development of this stasis-inducing drug and to find ways to test it without drawing the attention of the Governing Council. They chose Bardazel as their laboratory."

"Then the conspiracy theorists were right," Maybree says, her brows knitting together. I've grown so used to her being my podsister that I forget she came to us in the Bardazel transfer.

"There weren't really any conspiracy theorists either," Arden says. "They were, for the most part, people we sent to Bardazel to help with a possible move to become an Independent Core World, or supporters who were already there. Equity Alliance personnel were outed by a mole on Bardazel and were marked for elimination by the Company. The compound and ongoing separation from the rest of the population was a security measure, not just for our people but for the planet at large. We knew what the Company was up to and that these people were at risk. After I heard what the company had instructed Bardazel leadership to do, I knew Graham would try to rescue as many people as he could. He didn't know any of the backstory. He just knew there were people in danger because the Company wanted them silenced, and he wanted to get them to safety. And he almost did it."

Graham rubs his face with his hands. "We were so close," he says, his voice heavy with regret. "Just a couple more days would have made a difference."

"But they all dosed themselves with Blue," I say. "Why would they do that if they weren't the cultish group of conspiracy theorists everyone thought they were? Why would they voluntarily drink ... ah ... oh, shit, no ..."

"Exactly," Arden says, nodding to me. "They *didn't* dose themselves. That's the story the Company put forward to cover its tracks. The people in that compound were exposed to a particularly virulent weaponized form of Blue by an operative, possibly the same person who outed the EA. We haven't been able to determine who that person might have been. We do know they faded into the background on Bardazel after the incident at the compound."

"Which means they came to Iona with the rest of the transferees," Wenda says. I shiver involuntarily and Fanny lets out a low whistle as Graham looks grim.

"Karloa was found at the compound but not dosed. Doesn't that make her a prime suspect?" I ask.

"Karloa is kind of the wrinkle in all this," Arden says. "She's not EA, and she wasn't recruited on Bardazel. Is it possible she's the mole, Graham?"

"That seems unlikely," Graham says. "She showed up on Bardazel as part of the Company expansion team four years ago and was mostly nonpolitical until just recently."

I'm shocked. "I could swear her stat chip said she was an untrained stock clerk. She'd have to have high-level operations experience to be part of an expansion team."

"Yes. She was high-level operations when she arrived. But something happened."

"What do you mean?"

"Initially she seemed competent and quiet. She kept to herself, didn't really interact with anyone or participate in any social activities. So, okay, she's an introvert. But her behavior started to change as the conspiracy theory narrative seemed to gain steam. She became frightened and paranoid. It concerned her coworkers and the people who had to interact with her, so that's when she came to my attention."

"Did she have some kind of mental breakdown?" I ask, remembering how Karloa confronted me on her first morning on Iona.

"I don't know what to call it. She was definitely alarming people, but she was still doing her job. The Company didn't see it as an issue. It's not illegal or costly for someone to be annoying as long as they're productive, so they let it drop and told Bardazel leadership to do the same."

"Somehow she winds up at the Compound just prior to the mass dosing but remains unaffected by it," Arden mutters. "Interesting. She must be involved in some way. It doesn't make sense otherwise."

"We think she witnessed everything that happened, so it's likely she at least knows who the operative is," Graham points out. "She was incredibly traumatized by the time we got to her, and those effects never really faded. She was suffering from delusions and paranoia that we couldn't seem to break, and she seemed convinced that because we were all transferring to Iona, the people here were somehow implicated in what had happened on Bardazel. She was terrified all the transferees were going to be dosed and shipped off to nowhere, never to be seen again. In fact, she seemed to expect it."

Wenda winces. "That explains the weird behavior and the conversations I overheard that first day," she says.

"Why would she go through that and then dose herself anyway?" Fanny asks.

"We aren't sure she *did* dose herself," Macha interjects. "We never found any containers of Blue in her room or on her person. Holly and Hinn found her after she had already collapsed, so we just assumed she disposed of the evidence after taking the dose. But she could have been dosed another way. At the time, we didn't even know that was a possibility."

"She'd have a target on her back if she could potentially identify the operative," I say. "That person would have a lot to gain from having her silenced and perhaps frightening the rest of us in the process."

"There's another thing to consider," Arden adds. "As you say, she was there but was unaffected. It's possible that she might have some kind of natural immunity to the type of Blue that was used. The Company would not want to let that go unexplored, for obvious reasons. She might have been dosed here on Iona to test a new version of Blue."

The room falls silent, stunned expressions on every face. Now I understand the level of overwhelm that consumed both Arden and Graham at times, and I feel it myself, keenly.

"That means there are 200 Equity Alliance personnel—your personnel—in stasis somewhere," I say, measuring my words. Arden looks down at the table for a moment, and I see the sadness and frustration etched on his face.

"I hope there are," he says. "We know they were moved to a medical enviro shortly after the remaining population of Bardazel was transferred here. They were good people; I should have been able to protect them."

"*We* should have been able to protect them," corrects Graham. "If I had known what was at stake, I might have acted sooner."

Arden shoots him a grateful look. "You did what you could," he says. "If you *had* known, you would have been a target yourself and no one would have been saved."

"Let me get this straight. There's an unknown traitor out there who was willing to dose 200 people with Blue so that the Company could achieve its significantly less-that-above-board goals, and that person is on Iona," I say. "And thanks to Fallon March, they potentially have access to a substantial quantity of highly dangerous Blue, as demonstrated by what is now in our storage warren?" Everyone around the table looks anxious. No one says a word.

Suddenly, I'm too exhausted to think.

It must show on my face. "We should break for tonight," Macha says. "Faith's just off medical leave and needs rest."

I start to protest but I'm met with a barrage of objections before I can even speak, so I sit quietly while everyone says their goodbyes. Arden and Graham clasp hands in the doorway. I hear Arden ask, "You in?" and Graham responds, "Of course," as he departs. Finally, it's Wenda, Arden, Fanny, and me left in the Common Room. Fanny and Wenda are beaming at me. Something is clearly up.

"There's a little surprise for you in your room," Fanny says slyly. "We got it for you a while ago, but it wasn't really appropriate until now. We set it up while you were outside talking."

Wenda trades looks with Fanny, then grins at me. "I hope you like it," she says. "It's a temporary measure, but it should be a good start. Go on, off with you."

I eye them both suspiciously as they shoo me toward my room. "Arden, go help her with that," Fanny orders, and Arden joins me as we walk across the small hallway and pull open my door.

Looking inside, I immediately laugh and return to the Common Room to hug my two friends.

"You'll get some good use out of that now, I think," Fanny says, squeezing me tight. "Sleep well. Or, whatever."

Arden is still standing in the hallway, waiting for me. I return, push the door open wide, and clasping his hands, pull him into the room with me.

"Oh," he says, laughing. "I see."

My little beige hammock has disappeared. In its place, lively in stripes of teal and orange and white, hangs a brand new hammock made for two.

Arden studies my face, his eyes sparkling. His lips curl into a mischievous smile. Never taking his eyes off me, he extends his arm and pushes the door firmly shut behind us. Fanny and Wenda's delighted cackles carry down the hallway and out into the night.

AFTER SO MANY YEARS sleeping alone, it's a little confusing waking up next to someone. It takes me a few seconds to remember I'm on Iona in the middle of a crisis instead of Home World shaking off a long, complicated dream. Arden is still asleep, one forearm thrown across his eyes in defense against the pale morning light creeping in through the window. I take a few moments just to watch him as I often did in our other life together. His breathing is deep and steady; occasionally he hiccups or mutters something unintelligible, but for the most part he is peaceful and still. He was the same kind of sleeper on Home World. So much has changed, but so much is just the same.

The rising chimes sound. I try to slip out of the hammock without disturbing him, but he's awake as soon as his brain registers my absence. He sits up, blinking, and rubs his eyes.

"Good morning," I say. "How weird is this?"

"I have to keep reminding myself I'm not hallucinating," he says. "I used to dream this scene almost every night. Usually, we were somewhere more luxurious and somewhat less sandy, but it was always me waking up to you silhouetted against the morning light. Although we weren't always naked. That's an improvement."

His face breaks into a provocative leer that makes me flush. But the chimes are growing louder and the sounds of our pod coming to life echo down the little hallway.

"I'm sorry to infringe on your dream improvement, but it's time to get going," I say. I pick up his pants from the floor where he abandoned them last night and toss them at him with a grin. "I'm sure you have some important space pirate stuff to deal with this morning, in addition to all your crucial data entry and warehouse management duties."

"We both have some important stuff to deal with this morning," he says, swinging his feet to the floor and pulling on his pants. "It's 'Interrogate Fallon March Day.' That's sure to be fun. Where the hell is my shirt?"

I yank Arden's shirt from the corner of my wall mirror and hand it to him. He sniffs it, wrinkles his nose, and tucks it into his waistband rather than putting it on.

"I have to run by my room for a second. I'll meet you in the Common Room, then we'll head over to Graham's."

He crosses the small room in three steps, wraps one arm around my waist, pulls me against him with a dramatic flourish, and plants a solid kiss on my lips.

"Good morning, my love," he says with a wink, then dashes out the door and down the hall.

As he crosses the Common Room to reach the hallway that leads to his room, I hear a chorus of hoots and whistles from our podmates gathered there. When I enter the Common Room just a few minutes later, the hoots and whistles repeat and intensify, and there's even a smattering of applause. I roll my eyes at the attention and can feel myself starting to blush, so I do a theatrically deep curtsey and slip into the kitchen to recover.

The reception in the kitchen is very much the same. The instant Hinn sees me, he makes a loud series of triumphant barks that are no less energetic for the fact that he makes them while delicately stacking fresh breakfast muffins on a tray held aloft by his sister. Maybree contributes a "Yeah, girl," and punches my arm as she pushes past me to get some more coffee. At the center of the kitchen is Wenda. She's not saying a word, but the expression on her face is nothing short of proud.

"I'm dying," I say.

"You're living," she counters with a broad grin. "Was it all right? The hammock, I mean."

It's Wenda's turn to blush, and I let myself enjoy her discomfort for just a second.

"Yes," I say. "It was terrific. And the hammock was fine."

We both dissolve into fits of laughter. We're just coming up for air when Arden strides through the kitchen door wearing a fresh shirt and whistling cheerfully.

"He's *whistling*? That was some good hammock," quips Maybree, who slips back into the Common Room before I can think of a comeback.

All of this appears to sail neatly past Arden's awareness as he comes to stand with Wenda and me. "I grabbed Graham on hail," he says. "He's expecting us after breakfast."

We survive the gauntlet of the Common Room for our morning meal without any major incidents, although the comments, grins, and looks keep coming. Instead of embarrassment, I'm finding the attention pleasant. I know my podmates are happy for me; they understand this was where I was always headed. What other things have they all seen in me that I've yet to see in myself?

On the way to Graham's pod, I drop on my headset and tap into the general channel. I hear the usual buzz about maintenance requests and other tasks that need doing, punctuated by Macha's reminder to us both that Arden and I are supposed to be on light duty for the next few days. When she finishes her reminder by saying, "Try to avoid any unnecessary exertion," Arden gives me a meaningful look with raised eyebrows and we both laugh.

Graham's pod is quiet, with most of his podmates having headed off for their day's duties. We find Graham sitting in the Common Room reading a holotablet. March is nowhere to be seen and apparently remains ensconced in Pauly's room. Maybree told us earlier she was refusing to come out for any reason.

"What's the procedure?" I ask, after we exchange morning pleasantries and decline an offer of more coffee.

"I'm not sure I know," Graham says hesitantly, casting a questioning look at Arden. "This is really more your area of expertise than mine."

"Not mine either, I'm afraid," Arden says. "I just sneak around and watch people, I don't really ask them pointed questions. What's Company protocol?"

"It's hard to sort out," Graham sighs, tossing the holo onto the center of the table. "There's protocol for finding banned or dangerous materials in someone's possession. But since she wasn't caught physically handling the spheres, and wasn't even in the room, those statutes may not apply. It doesn't matter that they were in an office she's been using, since materially it's not her permanently assigned office. There are statutes regarding the standing owner or registered user of a space where controlled materials are found, but that would be Pauly. We know they weren't there because of him."

"Let me see," I say, and Graham slides the holo over to me. I start scanning the regulations, all written in obtuse corporate-speak. It brings back my days as a Company manager on Home World, something I'd rather forget. But I soldier on, looking for anything that might be of use.

"You have grounds to question her," Arden says. "She claimed the materials were hers."

"I just feel like I don't have much to go on beyond that, and she'll know the rule book backwards and forwards," Graham says. "If we start asking questions without a good foundation, she'll probably eviscerate us and this whole exercise will have been for nothing."

"Wait," I say. "She'll know Company protocol. But she doesn't know anything about Ionian protocol. Safe bet?"

Arden and Graham both look at me, curious.

"More than safe bet," Graham says. "Learning anything about Iona clearly has been at the bottom of her priority list, if it was ever on the list at all."

"Then we use Ionian protocol. She's not on Company territory now, Ionian protocol applies."

"That's perfect," Arden says. "What's Ionian protocol in this case?"

I smile conspiratorially. "We're an Independent service planet potentially on the verge of becoming a Core World, so those regulations are in a period of evolution. In other words, they're whatever we need them to be."

Graham lets out a short laugh.

"See?" Arden says to him. "Raw talent. Space pirate in the making. Get Fallon March out here. Let the interrogation begin."

When March emerges, she doesn't look any the worse for wear from her house arrest. Her lacquered nails are still as bright, her hair as perfect and her facial expression just as icy. She literally looks down her nose at me when I invite her to have a seat at the Common Room's table.

"Really, you're just going to ask me questions in here like it's some kind of coffee klatch?" she asks imperiously. "Don't you people have courtrooms and things like that on this planet?"

"We do," I say, making sure my voice is unemotional and steady, "but those are for criminals who are under arraignment. You may get to see them depending on how things go this morning." I indicate again the seat for her at the foot of the table. After glaring at me for a moment, she sits down.

"First, I want to let you know the expectations of our inquiry," I say, taking a seat next to Graham. "You're expected to answer all questions honestly and to the best of your ability. You're expected to acknowledge our explanation of any laws you've broken, and your comprehension of the penalty for those infractions. And you're expected to participate willingly in any recommended sanction, if such is decided upon. Do you understand?"

March looks at me levelly. "You've worked for the Company," she says in a dry, unimpressed tone. "You talk like a management drone."

"And you talk like a bratty six-year-old, but that doesn't make me assume you don't understand what you say," I say to her, unaffected. "Do you understand these expectations?"

She sucks in a breath and opens her mouth to say something else.

"I wouldn't," Graham says quietly. His voice is almost a growl.

She looks from me to Graham again for a moment, then mutters, "Yes, I understand." She follows that with a loud, bored sigh. "Get on with it, please. Ask me your questions. Let's get it over with."

Graham takes over now. "What can you tell us about the spherical objects we found in the office you've been using? Where did you obtain them?"

"Those things aren't mine," March says, smirking. "They must have belonged to the office's previous owner."

"The former owner has been in stasis for a month. We can verify that they were not part of the office's inventoried contents prior to that time," I say.

"Maybe someone else put them there. Maybe he did it," she tilts her head at Arden, who visibly struggles to remain silent. She continues to look him over in frank appraisal. "Have we met?" she asks in a voice just short of a purr. But when Arden answers only with a continued stern and unresponsive stare, she shrugs and looks away. She begins pattering the fingernails of her right hand against the arm of her chair.

"You made a public declaration that the objects were your personal effects and threatened legal action over our handling of them," I remind her. "That means you either lied to us then, or you're lying to us now. Both of which are punishable offenses when dealing with banned materials. With which infraction would you like to be charged? One carries a much more serious penalty than the other."

"You'll do whatever you want, no matter what I say. It's how you do things out here. No respect for the rule of law," March spits out.

"You're the one who's racked up violations not only of Ionian law but of Company policy as well," Arden finally says, in a measured voice. "The protocols we have exist because Iona handles some very delicate operations for the Company—operations that are apparently beyond your security clearance, because you seem shockingly ignorant of them. It's obvious that the Company leadership has a significantly better opinion of this planet than you do."

March sneers at Arden now. "Who are you?" she asks. "One of those Equity Alliance shills?"

"No, I'm a High Defense shill. Commander Arden Wilson, Tactical Security."

March's eyebrows lift in surprise. "You're quite famous in certain circles," she says, "if you really *are* Arden Wilson."

"You want to question my identity? Go ahead. I'll do a live holo with you for your boss. And then you'll be even more famous than I am, but as the biggest idiot who ever wore Company credentials. Let's do that now, shall we?" Arden says, reaching for the holotablet that still sits on the table.

"Fine," March snaps. "It doesn't matter who you are. We don't have to do a live holo for anyone."

I see a curious cloud of anxiety cross March's face. Graham sees it too and reacts.

"What's the problem?" he asks. "You get very jumpy every time someone mentions speaking with your boss. Does she not realize what you're doing here?"

"Of course she does. But she's a very busy woman and she doesn't have time for these petty grievances."

"This isn't a petty grievance," Graham says. "You claimed as your personal effects twenty-seven armed canisters of a weaponized controlled-class substance, colloquially known as 'Blue', which causes dramatic alteration in human function on contact. Both the substance and the delivery mechanism are prohibited from all Worlds, Company and Independent, by Council development decree, as too dangerous to handle near any population. The only place these armed canisters may be loaded or stored is on a military-grade vehicle specially designed for the purpose, on a limited access secure enviro, or by trained personnel at a hazardous materials facility. I don't know if you're fully aware, but a plastic credenza in a public building on a populated planet is not any of those things."

March scoffs. "Obviously those things aren't mine."

"Then why did you say they were?"

"I never said that."

"On the contrary," I interject. "You did in fact say that the things Graham had in his hands were your personal effects. You claimed them. In front of not one, not two, but three witnesses."

March's response is stony silence.

"Well?" I prompt. "What's your story now?"

March scowls and taps her bright red fingernails even more aggressively.

"You're trying to trap me," she says.

"How's that?" I ask.

"You're trying to get me to admit to something."

"What would that be?"

"How would I know? You're the one with the agenda," she shoots back.

"I'm just attempting to sort out what action to recommend to Company Human Resources," I say casually. It's a total bluff, but it works. March blanches, then recovers herself.

"You won't get anywhere with HR," she announces primly. "I have a spotless service record."

"Not anymore," says Arden.

The drumming fingernails abruptly stop. The sudden silence is more unnerving than the automatic weapons fire sound she makes with them. She glares at him, then at me, then leans forward in her chair. When she speaks, her voice has sunken into an angry hiss.

"What are you implying?" she asks.

"I'm not implying anything. I'm telling you that I flagged you this morning as a Tactical security risk," Arden says casually, matching her glare.

Graham blinks back an expression of surprise and my own mouth drops open. Meanwhile, a whole series of emotions parade across March's face, starting with surprise but rapidly proceeding to fury.

"A security risk," she repeats, her eyes travelling around the room, finally landing on Arden with a steely reproach.

"Yes."

"*You* reported me as a security risk." Her voice has lost some of its assurance. Her eyes narrow as she studies Arden carefully.

"It was necessary."

"You can't get away with that. My position ... "

"... is no longer your position," Arden completes the sentence for her. "Eliana Gardette has taken over as Acting Operations Security Chief. You'll be receiving a communique shortly. You would have received it already if you ever wore your headset."

March sighs heavily. Her hands fold into her lap and she looks down at them for a moment, scowling, then returns her icy glare to Arden.

"When do I go home?" she asks. It's a simple question, yet she manages to ask it in a way that makes it charged and insulting.

"You'll be able to return to Home World after we've completed the investigation into what you were doing with this banned substance, which as it happens ties directly into our team investigation of the incident in Warehousing," he says. His voice is calm, but his eyes are dark, sending a clear warning. "In the meantime, you'll be our guest here on Iona. And we'll be happy to host you for as long as necessary."

"You will, however, have to give up that private room," Graham adds with a smile, clearly relishing every word. "I've handed over my duties as pod leader to Fanny MacFarland. That will be her room from this evening on."

We talk to Fallon March for another hour but manage to get nothing useful from her. Despite the shock of losing her position to Arden's skillful end-around and her private room to Graham's decree, her haughty demeanor remains unchanged. And she continues to refuse to answer any questions about her motives or the real nature of her assignment to Iona.

The pod is starting to get busy as its residents return for lunch, so we call a break. Fallon retreats to the courtyard to yell at someone on her holo, while Arden, Graham, and I head into the kitchen to hover over coffee and regroup.

"She's got to give us some answers eventually," Arden says as he fills a cup. "Making her give up the private room was a stroke of genius."

"Genius had nothing to do with it," Graham confesses. "I talked to Fanny about this last night and convinced her to take the reins. After I talked to you this morning, it just made sense to go ahead and make the announcement at breakfast and speed up the timing. Fallon was going to have to move anyway, it just came at the perfect moment."

"Fanny moves into Pauly's room and Fallon gets to share a space with Mila and Alice," I chuckle. "That's sure to be entertaining. I hear Mila snores like a freight train and Alice sings in her sleep."

"And yet it still feels like Mila and Alice are getting the raw end of the deal," Arden says. "I hope for their sakes she comes around soon and tells us what we need to know."

"What if March is telling the truth?" I ask. Arden gives me a look and starts to speak but I hold up my hand to stop him. "She might have been sent here on some kind of mission with only 'need to know' information. It may be that she's got no idea how dangerous those things are."

"Even that wouldn't excuse her from telling us the truth about everything else," Arden says. "We know she's lying about why she was sent here and who sent her. She could have just told us what she was doing here, and that would have made up for almost everything else."

"Maybe after she learned you'd tanked her entire career, she just didn't feel like she had anything else to gain from talking," I say.

"Oh, but I haven't tanked her career. I can clear her and expunge this from her record just as quickly as I flagged her. But it's like working with a mule—she has to make me *want* to clear her," Arden says, grinning.

"There's our next talking point, for sure," Graham says drily.

Maybree comes into the kitchen with a bright red hard acrylic security box in her hand. Inside is March's beastly firearm. "So this hideous thing needs to be somewhere safe, but it can't be in general storage because it's dangerous as crap and I can't keep it locked up at Security because it's March's personal property," she explains. "Which of you interrogator-types gets to deal with it?"

"Give it to me," I say. "I know where this should go."

Arden and Graham continue to strategize. I make my way through the now-bustling common room to the little hallway spur that leads to the Star Parlor lift, carrying the box gingerly in both hands. This should clearly be the responsibility of March's new pod leader, and I'm already several steps into her new room by the time Fanny realizes I'm there.

FANNY IS FLUSHED AND pink from the exertion of moving March's voluminous collection of belongings out of Pauly's room; they're now boxed and stacked in the hallway next to her newly assigned quarters on the opposite side of the Common Room.

Typical Fanny, she laughs when she takes the box from me. "I'll set the lock code and figure out someplace to store this," she says. "I guess I shouldn't just add it to the pile in the hallway, right?" She puts the box down on the single piece of furniture in the room aside from her hammock—an antique wooden roll-top desk that is easily several hundred years old.

"This is beautiful," I say, admiring the way the elegantly carved ivy that decorates its top cascades down the desk's external panels on both sides. "I've never seen anything like it."

"It's Pauly's. I had it pulled out of storage," Fanny explains, running her fingers along one of the dramatic vines. "He loves woodworking—everybody does on Hokka. The planet's one enormous forest, with trees as far as you can see in every direction. Everyone does a little woodworking there. When we came here ..." her voice trails off as she looks out her window at Iona's restless, treeless sand. "Well, he became even more appreciative of fine carving once we got to Iona. It's so dry here, wooden things can last a long time if you keep them away from the sand."

"You're okay with this, right?" I ask. "Running a pod can be a lot."

"I'm okay with it," she says, turning to adjust her hammock as we talk. "Graham can be quite convincing, and he made some good points when we talked about this last night. And I do feel Pauly would want me to step up for our pod. I've been hard on Graham, but I didn't realize how this was affecting him." She lets her voice drift off and loses herself for a moment in uncharacteristic contemplation, but an instant later and just as seamlessly, the Fanny I'm used to returns. "Besides, you're going to help me with the pod when I have questions," she says and winks at me, "But first, you're going to tell me everything you did last night in extensive detail, and I do mean *everything*."

Our laughter is interrupted by a shriek of terror and cries for help coming from the courtyard. Fanny and I run from her room, through the Common Room and kitchen in the direction of the sound. We burst into the pod's courtyard, and I draw a sharp breath: Bennid kneels on the ground, holding in his left hand the dripping remains of a shattered silver sphere. His right arm is around Holly, holding her tight as she gasps and shrieks. She has spatters of the sphere's liquid across her hands and thighs, where her skin has already turned blue. The color is spreading up her forearms and along the hem of the short yellow summer frock she wears.

"Do something!" cries Bennid, turning his head toward us. "Help her, please!"

"Keep everyone back," I tell Fanny, who turns to herd the cluster of arriving onlookers away from the couple. But I don't have a chance to do more than that when a voice behind me shouts, "Get out of the way!" in such an authoritative tone I instinctively step back. I'm stunned to see Fallon March rush past me in a blur of burgundy, physically shoving people out of her path. My first thought is that she's going to use this crisis to escape somehow, but instead she yells, "Someone get me sand, a lot of loose sand!" as she charges across the courtyard to kneel on the ground next to Bennid and Holly.

"Keep breathing," she says to Holly. "Breathe slow. Make yourself calm. You'll be all right, but you *must* stay calm."

Holly is crying, but she listens to March and tries to control her breathing.

"Put that sphere down," March instructs Bennid. "Lower your hand to the ground and let the pieces roll out. Are you cut anywhere?"

"No, no cuts," says Bennid, depositing the shards of the sphere carefully in the sand next to him.

Her eyebrows knit together as she looks Bennid up and down quickly. "Bioequivalent hand?" she says.

"Whole arm," Bennid replies, and March looks visibly relieved for a moment.

"Good," she says in a reassuring tone. "You're going to be okay." Her kind demeanor vanishes in an instant and she looks over her shoulder and shouts, "Where's that fucking sand?"

"Here!" calls Fanny, appearing at the far end of the courtyard with her podmate Mila. The two are struggling to pull one of the pod's planter tubs filled with sand toward the scene.

"Stay here, stay calm," March says to Bennid and Holly, and runs to meet the two women grappling with the tub.

"Keep back," she tells them. "Fanny, give me your jacket."

Fanny peels off her beige jacket quickly and tosses it to March, who zips it up, ties the sleeves together and begins using it as a makeshift sand bucket. Mila, seeing the process, strips off her jacket and does the same, as do several of the onlookers. By the time March runs back to Bennid and Holly, a dozen more people are filling their jackets with sand and others have gone in search of better buckets to replace them. I run to help ferry the containers between the tub and where Fallon has crouched next to the frightened Holly.

"This is going to feel weird," she says to Holly, in a gentle voice I've never heard her use, "but you're going to be okay. Try to relax. I'm going to bury you in this stuff, but you'll still be able to breathe, and you'll be all right. You have to trust me. Okay?"

Holly nods. March rips open Fanny's jacket and dumps sand onto the quivering teenager, starting with the areas contaminated by the liquid and continuing until Holly's hands, abdomen, and upper thighs are covered. "Keep the sand coming!" she shouts, and we all work furiously.

Holly's eyes begin to roll up, but March shakes her. "Stay with me," she says, and the girl gasps a little bit and tries to bring her eyes back to focus. "Your boyfriend is going to move away and you're going to lie back. It's okay. Got me?"

"Y-y-yes," Holly whispers.

"Don't touch her with that left hand," March warns. "Once she's down, get some sand on it and cover up that broken thing, but don't lose track of where it is." Bennid gently lowers Holly to the ground with his right arm, then slips from behind her. I toss him one of the makeshift sand buckets and he dumps its contents onto his contaminated left hand and the remnants of the silver sphere in one smooth motion.

March is continuing to bury Holly as quickly as she can, but I can see traces of blue creeping out from under the sand along Holly's exposed skin. "Can I help?" I ask. "It looks like you need more hands."

March looks at me critically. "Do you know what this stuff is?" she asks.

"Yes," I say. "I'm prepared."

"Start covering, but be careful not to touch it," March responds, and the two of us begin working double-time to cover Holly in the sand.

The next twenty minutes are a blur. Fanny organizes people to continuously fetch tubs full of sand, and still more people to find containers that can be used to ferry the sand to where March and I are working. Holly is beginning to convulse, and her trembling body keeps shaking the sand from her skin, but gradually we make headway. At last, she's almost entirely covered. Fallon leans forward and whispers to her, "We're going to cover your face. Don't worry, you'll still be able to breathe. It may feel scary, but everything is going to be fine. Just close your eyes and remember to breath slowly and stay as still and calm as you can."

With that, she pours sand over Holly's face, completely burying the young woman except for her nose. Several of the assembled people gasp, and March takes a moment to shoot them a disgusted look before leaning down close to the sand at Holly's ear to say, "You're okay. Breathe slowly. Everything will be all right in a little while."

An anxious silence settles over us all. March turns to Bennid and says, "You should be fine now, but you'll probably want to get a new hand just in case. Did you mark where the sphere is buried?"

Bennid, releasing his left hand from its own sandpile, points to the jacket that contained the sand he used. "It's under that."

"Somebody put something on that so it doesn't get moved," March orders, in a voice that's further away from her usual imperiousness than I've ever heard. "But take care and don't smash what's underneath it. Everyone should stay away from here until we have this taken care of."

Fanny, already herding people out of the courtyard, says, "I'll set up a barrier. Macha's been hailed and is on the way. Security is on the way. *Everybody* is on the way."

"What about Holly?" I ask. March looks at me with confusion, and I realize she never even asked Holly's name before jumping in to help her. I indicate the girl's prone form, hidden completely under the sand, and March's eyebrows lift in acknowledgment.

"Holly will be all right, but she needs to stay like this for a little while longer," she says. "She'll need to be monitored. I'll sit with her."

"We can both sit with her," I say. March looks at me carefully for a moment, perhaps unsure of my intentions, so I proffer a slight smile.

She shrugs in response, but the edge of her mouth tilts up into an almost-smile, so I settle in next to her. She leans over to the sand at Holly's ear and says, "Holly, you are going to be fine. Faith and I are going to stay here with you, and we'll uncover you soon. Don't worry. We're here."

March sits up and crosses her legs underneath her, letting out an exhausted breath. She takes the extraordinary action of brushing a small patch of sand from the right knee of her now completely sand-encrusted burgundy slacks.

"That was something," I say. "I don't know what you did or how you knew to do it but thank you."

March's mouth twists in annoyance. "You're nearly all idiots here," she proclaims, in a tone of voice much closer to what I've come to think of as normal for her, but after a slight pause, she adds, "You're welcome."

Over the next half hour the pod becomes increasingly chaotic. Fallon and I continue to sit in the courtyard next to Holly, but she's taken control of the entire situation and barks orders to Security, Clinical, Fanny, and even Graham from her seated position. Arden, after confirming with me that I'm all right, immediately begins an intense discussion with Graham just out of earshot. Fallon watches them with a wry smile.

"I suppose they're trying to decide what to do with me now," she says.

"You saved Holly's life, but this does prove that you lied to us," I say.

She turns and peers at me skeptically.

"I didn't lie," she says. "I answered all of your questions truthfully. *You* didn't ask the right questions."

"Cat's out of the bag now, though." I raise an eyebrow at her. She laughs in a way that suggests she finds the situation anything but funny.

"I suppose it is," she says, turning her head away to look out over the dusk that's beginning to settle on Iona. "I suppose it is."

My attempt at conversation is dead on arrival. All other attempts I make to ask any of the thousand questions screaming through my brain is met with a single syllable response or absolute silence from Fallon March. We sit this way for the next forty-five minutes, during which Fallon studies the horizon or her manicure and I struggle to control my frustration with her.

Finally, Fallon stands and waves Macha over. "You'll want to uncover her now," she instructs, "and take her to Clinical. She'll be unconscious for a few hours, and you might see some residual coloration, but that's expected. The color should dissipate over the next few days. Keep a bucket of sand on hand and massage it into her skin if there's any recurrence. Make sure you're gloved at all times when you're handling her."

231

Macha simply nods and waves over several of the techs who accompanied her to the scene. Together, they glove up and start to work, with Fallon supervising. Once Holly is uncovered and I see for myself that she isn't blue anywhere other than where her skin contacted the chemical directly, I detach myself from the scene and join Arden, Graham, and Fanny on the periphery of the courtyard. I keep watching, however, until Holly's on a hovergurney bound for Clinical, with Bennid following behind on a sand scooter, a red plastic 'hazardous medical waste' bag wrapped around his left arm and hand.

Fallon stays in the thick of the action, giving instructions and directing activities.

"Does your security team have a hazardous materials protocol?" she asks Maybree. "If you do, you need to use it to remove what's under that jacket, along with the jacket and the sand beneath it to a depth of about six inches. And if you don't, you need to invent one immediately. Treat this like the most hazardous thing you can imagine. Because it is."

"On it," Maybree says, and within a few minutes, the security detail descends on the scene like a collection of masked ants.

"We'll want that sphere, don't dispose of it," I call out, and Maybree gives me a thumbs-up. Fallon looks at me like I'm an annoying insect.

"Will this eat through acrylic?" Maybree asks. "Do we need something glasslike instead?"

"Good grief, it's not sulfuric acid," Fallon responds with a huff and an eyeroll. "Put it in anything nonporous."

"She certainly knows a lot about this version of Blue," growls Graham under his breath.

"As do you," Arden says, a tinge of sharpness in his voice. Graham pretends not to have heard him, but I see the tension the remark has caused reflected on his face.

"That turned out to be fortunate, didn't it?" Fanny points out. "Am I wrong to say that not one of us would have had any idea what to do if this had happened without March here, including both of you?"

Arden and Graham look at the ground. Arden seems particularly chagrined. "At least we know that she was lying to us this morning," he says.

"She says she didn't lie," I say.

"But obviously she did," Graham counters.

"Maybe not," I say. "She said we didn't ask her the right questions. I've been thinking about that. We asked her if the spheres were her property and she said no. We asked her what she knew about how they got into the credenza, and she said nothing. We never asked her if she knew what they were, what they contained, or what the impact of breaking one open might be. We never asked her if she knew anything about Blue at all."

Arden and Graham at last have nothing to say.

Fanny hoots. "She outsmarted you," she says. "That's rich. She's still a gigantic flaming asswipe, but I might be starting to like her."

"Oh look, here comes your new best friend now," Graham says drily, looking over Fanny's head. Fallon is rapidly approaching our group, her fists balled and a look of supreme irritation on her face. "Want to stick around and give her a hug?"

"No, no, gotta go run my pod, see you all later," Fanny chirps and slips past Graham to beat a hasty retreat into the pod kitchen.

"What's the story here? Are you in charge, or is she?" Fallon asks, jerking her thumb in the direction of the disappearing Fanny. "Because we need to sort out something else as far as my accommodations."

"Fanny's in charge, but you won't get anywhere with her either. There aren't any other options," Graham says tersely. "You should probably stop whining about sharing. Alice and Mila don't bite."

Fallon studies Graham for a moment, her expression weary.

"Are you really this dense?" she asks. "Did you not see what just happened here?"

233

"You helped Holly, and we're all grateful for that, but it still ... "

"Think big picture, Governor Dirtweed," Fallon interrupts. Graham rolls his eyes at the taunt, but she doesn't acknowledge it. "I'm sure Alice and Mila don't bite, but there's a good chance they might not breathe either if you don't find me more secure accommodations," she continues. "I just drew a skiffload of attention to myself by exhibiting knowledge that certain people we are *both* well aware of may find very alarming, possibly even threatening. How big a target did that put on my back?"

"It's on all of our backs," I say. "Everyone here will know what you did by morning. The target just expanded to include the whole planet."

"They were after you already. I, at least, was somewhat incognito," Fallon protests.

Arden laughs aloud.

"You've been about as incognito as a lander crash," he says. "But I suppose it's all in the interpretation."

"All right, stop," I say. "It's clear we have more to talk about. You give us the information we're looking for and we'll find you a spot somewhere more secure—and possibly more private. Fair?"

Fallon bites her lower lip as she considers my offer.

"I suppose," she finally says. "Let's make this delightful exchange happen as soon as possible, please. And I want my weapon back, also."

"One thing at a time, Fallon," I caution.

She tosses me one last exasperated look, then pushes past me, heading toward the pod. "I'm going to get this filth off me," she says, shaking her hands as if to rid them of imaginary cobwebs. "Find me when you've sorted out your logistics."

"Well. That was something," Graham remarks, watching her stride off. "I have no idea what to make of any of it."

"We aren't going to make any progress standing out here, and Security needs us to leave so they can complete their hazmat protocol," I say. "Let's figure out what we're going to do with her while she's completing her beauty routine."

Between the turmoil with Holly and the approach of evening mealtime, the pod has become crowded and noisy. The Common Room is packed with people. We wind up squeezing into Fanny's room to discuss what to do with Fallon March. There aren't many options available. We can't move her back into Fanny's room, and there's no way the pod can be reshuffled to create a secure space for her. All our other pods are effectively full as well.

The Preservation Theater has rooms that could be made into makeshift accommodation, but the building itself is too out-in-the-open with no security and preparing a secure space will take more time than we have.

We also consider putting her in a room at Clinical, but when hailed with the idea, Macha objects. "If she's potentially going to be in danger, the last place we want her is near vulnerable people who can't protect themselves." It's indeed a valid point.

Soon we all understand there's only one securable, vacant, livable, close-at-hand space that can serve as Fallon's temporary quarters. "That's not going to feel like house arrest," says Fanny glumly. "She'll probably never want to leave." But it's also the only private spot on Iona, so once we're all in agreement, I go in search of our guest while everyone else heads up to the Star Parlor.

I'm intercepted in the Common Room by Tommas. His face is pink with excitement and he's rubbing his hands together like an eager kid in front of a pile of free candy.

"It sounds like it was a very dramatic afternoon!" he says. "Fanny invited me over for dinner, so I only arrived after all the action was over. Is everyone going to be all right?"

"That's the theory," I say. "Time will tell, of course."

"It sounded like it could have been very serious," he says, tugging at his mustache in a contemplative way.

"It certainly could have been. We were fortunate."

He nods and looks at me with wide eyes, waiting for me to say more. When I don't, he fills in the gap himself.

"How lucky that the Security Chief knew that trick with the sand," he says. "Everyone's talking about it. She's not the most agreeable person in the world, but now she's a hero, like it or not."

"Don't be ridiculous. I'm utterly charming," comes a crisp icy voice from behind us. Fallon has emerged from the hallway. She's clean-scrubbed and rosy from the shower and her hair is still a little damp, but somehow, she's maintaining her persona of icy perfection. She's now clad in a more casual forest green pullover and black slacks with a small leather pack slung over her shoulder, but her bearing and the tilt of her head send a message of unassailable authority. Tommas steps back a bit as she approaches, then visibly screws up his nerve and extends his hand.

"Tommas Berinbart," he says. "Pleased to meet you."

Fallon regards the proffered hand for a beat too long, giving its owner the once-over, but then grasps it just after Tommas exhibits profound discomfort under her assessment and starts to withdraw it.

"Hello," she says. She turns to me while still shaking Tommas' hand, as though he's not even there, and asks, "Have things been resolved?"

"Yes, apparently. Come with me. We'll get your things moved after our conversation." I gesture in the direction of the auxiliary hallway that leads past Fanny's room to the lift that goes up to the Star Parlor.

"Good," she says, dropping Tommas' hand without any further acknowledgement of him and walking away. For his part, Tommas simply stares after her, hand still floating in the air, with a puzzled expression on his face.

"Fanny will be down shortly," I tell him. He looks even more confused, then the lights go on and he nods.

"Good, good. Tell her I'll be here," he says. "And tell her I'm glad everything is okay. And I hope she's not in any danger. Or anything. You know."

This statement seems peculiar to me, and I look at Tommas for a moment longer, trying to see any sort of thought process on his features, but they offer nothing out of the ordinary. Tommas is often not the most articulate person in the line-up anyway, so I put it down to anxiety.

Fallon is waiting for me beside the lift and taps the call button as I approach. "He's an odd duck," she says, tilting her head back toward where Tommas is still standing, twiddling his mustache and looking after us.

"I don't know him at all, really," I admit. "Just from what Fanny has told me."

"Fanny!" Fallon's eyebrows go up so high they almost break into her hairline. "That just seems ... unnecessary. I'd have expected more from her."

The silver lift cylinder arrives at our level and we step inside. "She needed the distraction, especially lately," I say. "I'm not sure if you're aware, but ..."

"The Warehouse explosion victim is her brother. Yes, I know."

The cylinder door whispers shut, and the lift automatically begins its assent. In seconds, we're at the top of the cliff and the door opens into the crystalline tunnel that connects it to the Star Parlor. Fallon hangs back to let me step out first, but I gesture for her to go ahead. She does so without hesitation.

"I take it you don't trust me," she says, as we proceed down the tunnel.

"If you were me, would *you* trust you?" I ask. She seems unsurprised by the question and glances over her shoulder at me, a look of amusement on her face.

"You're right, I wouldn't," she says. "But it would be one of the rare times I was wrong."

By the time we step through the entryway, the Star Parlor is nothing short of anarchy. Graham and Arden, standing furthest from the entryway, are having an intense exchange. Arden is doing most of the talking, and his face is flushed with irritation, while Graham's stance, with crossed arms and lifted chin, screams defiance. Fanny is trying to intercede, but with little success. Maybree is hunkered down in a pile of pillows on the floor, calling instructions off a holo into her headset, occasionally looking up at the other three with an expression of distress on her face.

"Can we start?" I say, but I'm ignored. No one even acknowledges me.

I rub my forehead and sigh in exasperation. I'm wondering how I'm going to bring all these individuals together when an ear-splitting whistle erupts from beside me. All conversation halts immediately and every head turns to look in the direction of Fallon March, who is removing her fingers from her lips as though she just consumed a bon-bon. She looks at me, clearly pleased with herself, and gestures toward the now silent group before us.

"Let's start," I say. "Or rather, let's continue but include *all* the participants in whatever the discussion is." I look pointedly at Arden and Graham, both of whom continue to wear hostile expressions and exchange scowls as I speak.

"Yes, let's," echoes Fanny, who begins prodding the two men toward the center of the room while gathering pillows and dropping them into a loosely formed circle. Reluctantly, they respond and eventually everyone present is seated, and Macha, who is still at Clinical with Holly, is patched in via Maybree's holo.

We start with an update on our latest victims' conditions. Macha confirms that, as Fallon predicted, Holly is unconscious but shows no signs of entering stasis. The blue stains on her body where she contacted the substance from the sphere are still visible but have faded dramatically. Bennid's bioequivalent left hand has been removed as a precaution and a new one ordered for him. It should arrive in a day or so.

"Bennid is fine," Macha explains. "His only problem right now is stress. He's worried about Holly, so we're keeping him 'for observation', but that's just so he can be here when she wakes up."

The good news relaxes the entire group. I catch both Arden and Graham smiling as Macha describes Bennid's concern for Holly.

"That's great," I say. "Can Bennid have visitors? We'd like to talk to him about what happened."

"Certainly," Macha confirms. "He'll be expecting you and will probably be grateful for the diversion. But try to get here soon. He does need to rest, as much as he can."

Macha signs off and I look around the room. Fanny sits upright with her legs extended in front of her, looking from person to person with an air of expectation. Arden and Graham, sitting together but leaning slightly away from one another, maintain rigid, almost bristly, postures. Maybree leans back against one wall, buried in electronics, her face almost completely obscured by floating screens. Fallon March, lounging against a pile of pillows with her hands behind her head, is the most relaxed person here.

"What is this place?" she asks. "It's very fancy. It almost feels sophisticated."

No one feels like answering her.

"Let's revisit our line of questioning from this morning," I say. In response, Fallon pushes herself up to a sitting position and looks pointedly at Maybree and Fanny.

"Those two weren't here this morning," she says. "Isn't there some kind of regulation about consistency in interrogation?"

"First, they're both impacted by what we're talking about—Maybree as a Local Security Lead, and Fanny as your Pod Leader," I point out. "Second, this isn't an interrogation. It's more like a friendly chat, in which you are participating voluntarily, as per our earlier agreement."

Fallon looks skeptical. "My accommodations have been sorted? Where are they?"

"You're sitting in them."

A satisfied smile appears on Fallon's face as she looks around the Star Parlor. "Comfortable, private, easily securable—is there only one entrance?"

"There's a sort of escape hatch built into the floor under the rug at the entry-way," Graham explains. "It's only for emergencies and requires an energetic climb down a hanging ladder that deploys when the hatch is opened. It's a *very* long way down."

Fallon peers out across Iona's square. "I can see that. Will my things be brought up? All of them?"

"Personal items only. The rest will stay in our secured storage," Fanny confirms. Fallon looks vaguely displeased, but wisely doesn't complain.

"I need a security detail," she adds.

"I'm activating an electronic barrier at the ground floor lift access and across the walkway just past the door," Maybree explains. "We'll also monitor for attempted breach."

Fallon settles back against the cushions again, and waves one hand in the air, apparently indicating the entirety of what's been discussed. "This is acceptable," she says. "I'll answer your questions if I can."

"Can the sand help our people who are in stasis now?" I ask immediately, holding my breath for the answer.

"No, it's too late for that. The sand halts stasis induction. You need the antidote to reverse the process once it's completed."

All the Ionians in the room exchange astonished looks.

"But there's no antidote," I say carefully.

Fallon rolls her eyes, then narrows them as she glares at each of us, her irritation clear.

"*Of course,* there's an antidote. Are you all blistering idiots here?"

"I was led to believe it was irreversible and that an antidote was on the drawing board but hadn't been formulated yet," Graham says, his eyes darkening.

"The antidote we have is tested and reliable when used with the initial version of the stasis-inducing agent. It's terribly surprising to me that you're ignorant of this. Only a handful of people know, but I would have expected the Bardazellian in the room to be one of them."

Graham's jaw muscles work as he considers Fallon. "No," he says with finality. "I didn't know. I have to question how *you* know for certain that this antidote exists. It seems a bit outside the expertise of Operational Security."

"Oh please. I've known about it for decades," she responds.

"That's not possible," Graham argues. "Blue was only developed a few years ago, and shared with Bardazel because ..."

"... because imminent disaster with toxic gas cloud, blah blah blah. Right, right," Fallon interrupts. "But I know as well as you do, that story was exactly that, a story. This thing you call Blue has been around in one form or another for a long time."

"How do you know that's not just more Company spin?" I ask. "First there's no antidote, then we find out there IS an antidote—what makes you think any of these stories are true?"

"Because I've seen it," Fallon retorts, burrowing further back into the pillows. "My mother invented the chemical compound you call Blue and its antidote, decades ago. And its development continues to this day."

Arden leans forward. "And your mother is?"

"Dr. Janelle Heron."

"*Company Chief Medical Officer* Janelle Heron?" Arden's tone is incredulous.

241

"That's her." Fallon smiles broadly and crosses one leg over the other. She might as well be on a luxurious Home World beach with a cocktail in her hand. "You want the truth? Here it is. I'm here working on behalf of my mother, Operational Security be damned. I imagine she's speaking with your boss at this very moment, Commander Wilson. I'm anticipating the return of my squeaky-clean service record any second now."

Arden's face falls.

"Let's get back to the point," I say. "Could the antidote revive our people who are in stasis now?"

March considers this for a moment.

"It's unlikely," she replies. "The original antidote is kind of a rough entry, but it works, at least for those who consumed the original version of Blue. The transdermal absorption and aerosolized versions are trickier. Those processes and mechanisms are different enough that we're skeptical about the success of the original antidote on those victims because we haven't had the opportunity to evaluate those formulations. I don't have anything that I know for sure would help the people in stasis here. Yet."

"What do you mean yet?"

"I mean I don't have any *yet*."

"You're creating some?"

Fallon lets out a short laugh. "Not exactly. That skiff that's bringing the kid's new hand will have a package for me on it. I should have had some arrive already by different means, but it went missing before I could get my hands on it."

Arden perks up. "So those Sprites were for you," he says. "How many? Five?"

"Seven. Four on the night of my arrival, and three more a couple of nights ago."

"Sprites?" I ask. "What are Sprites?"

"They're like flying cans, if you made a can that was the size of a small car," Maybree says, looking up from her screens. "They're called Sprites because they make a pretty show when they burn through the atmosphere, but they're actually reinforced containers designed to be released into low orbit to plunge to the surface later. The idea is to get materials on the ground without a skiff or a lander. Primarily used for places that are sparsely populated, without any kind of pad facilities. More efficient and less expensive than trying to dry-land a skiff."

"And more clandestine," Fallon adds, sitting upright and leaning toward Arden. "How did you know the Sprites were sent here? I'm very surprised." She's talking to him now like he's a trusted work colleague. It's hard to believe that just this morning, we were all thinking we had Fallon March over a barrel.

"I saw the first ones the night you arrived, and Faith saw one more night before last," Arden says.

In my head, I hear my own voice saying *we don't have meteors here*. How many more things could possibly come to light that Arden has lied to me about? My irritation must show on my face, because I catch Arden eying me with an apologetic expression, but I press on with questioning.

"You say they went missing. How?" I ask.

"The first set was picked up by someone else before I reached the coordinates. I was on my way to retrieve the second set when ..." Here, she falters, and begins fumbling for words. "... when I was distracted by something else. I haven't had a chance to search for them since."

"So all those Sprites contained antidote, even though there are only two people here who've been exposed?"

"Not exactly." Fallon's breezy demeanor disintegrates somewhat, and she begins tapping her fingernails against the maroon floor pillow she's sitting on. "Our mission here—my mother's mission—isn't just focused on the people on Iona who've been exposed. She wants to make sure Blue is never used as a weapon and instead remains a useful medical option, which is why it was created in the first place. But the only way to guarantee that happens is to ensure there are readily-available antidotes for all of the new versions. She's viewing this more as a lab study to develop and test those antidotes, and the only way to do that is to have the new versions of Blue to work with."

"You're saying you had weaponized Blue sent here to Iona, and now it's missing?" Arden snarls. "I can't believe the hubris. What arrogant idiots you all are."

Fallon makes a high-pitched shriek of protest. Her momentary affinity with Arden has ended.

"No one else was supposed to find it, that's why we used such a clandestine delivery method," she says sharply, her eyes flashing. "And as for our hubris, how is anyone going to revive your friends without having the exact thing that put them into stasis to work on? *You're* the arrogant idiot. Weaponized Blue was here long before I arrived. It was here before *you* arrived. It came here with the transferees from Bardazel."

I try hard not to, because it seems an unfair equivalency. But everyone in the room has the same thought, and every head turns to look at Graham Thorn.

The tension in the air escalates to a point of almost being unbearable, and I realize from the smug, disgusted expression Arden throws Graham that this must play a part in what they were arguing about so intensely when Fallon and I first came into the Star Parlor. For his part, Graham might as well be wearing a dark cloud over his head. His eyes are lowered to the floor and his shoulders are slumped. His anguish is palpable.

Arden, meanwhile, is obviously ready to reinvigorate their fight, and the only way we're going to avoid it is if I get him out of the room. And while one part of me would like to just let them have it out, another larger part is too exhausted to put up with any more territorial male bullshit tonight.

"It's getting late," I say. "I don't want to wait to speak with Bennid about this, so I'm heading over to Clinical. Everyone get some rest and we'll come together again tomorrow. Let's plan to meet here. And if anyone has anything they are still not being forthright about, be prepared to share. Everything. Without exception." I look pointedly from Arden to Graham to Fallon.

Fallon flops back onto the pillows again with an exaggerated sigh, but I ignore her and head for the walkway. I hear Fanny tell Fallon to expect her personal kit bag to be delivered shortly and reassure her that the bulk of her belongings are safe in secure storage. This again elicits far less objection than we heard when Fallon was on the verge of having to share a room with two other people. It's then that I remember Tommas.

"I forgot to tell you that your beau is waiting for you," I say with a conspiratorial smile. But Fanny's response is not what I expect. Her annoyance is written on her face when she speaks.

"I told him not to show up here tonight," she says. "Why did he come?"

"He said you invited him to dinner," I say, frankly surprised. "Why would he lie about that? Are you two still involved?"

"Apparently one of us is," she says, wrinkling her forehead in consternation. "I mean, he's amusing, and he certainly came along at the right time, but he's gotten very clingy and I'm not going to have time for it anymore. I've tried to make that clear to him several times, but it never seems to sink in."

"I guess he's smitten with you," I say, but I can tell by Fanny's stern expression that she has reached her limit. It looks like it's not going to be a good night for Tommas.

We approach the lift as a group, but it's small and only three people can fit into it safely. Although I reach it first, Arden glides up behind me and pulls me aside so that Fanny, Graham, and Maybree can enter instead. "I'd like to go talk to Bennid with you, if you don't mind," he says, a touch too loudly that suggests the comment is more for them than for me.

"Of course," I say, not looking at him. I still feel a sharp pang of disappointment over his lie about the Sprites; last night's connection and good feeling seems as if it happened in a distant dream. As the silver cylinder closes and the others begin their descent, he says, "I'm sorry. Please don't be angry with me."

"I'm not angry," I say, studying his face. "I'm not even sad. I'm just tired of it. How many times am I going to have to hear you apologize for lying to me? It seems like it happens every time I think you've finally told me everything. After what we went through on Home World, it's disappointing. Haven't you learned anything in the last eight years?"

He has no response and looks down at the floor, shoving his hands into his pockets. Frankly I'm relieved because I'm tired of hearing the same thing over and over. For now, I want to focus on finding out how Bennid and Holly came to be in possession of one of those spheres, and hang on to the shred of good news that there's hope we may soon be able to revive Pauly and Karloa.

Walking to Clinical in silence, I'm struck as always by the peace of night on Iona. At this hour, our little beige world turns dark purple and periwinkle and has a strange kind of beauty all its own. Most of our people have eaten their dinner and are settled into their pods, playing games in common rooms and courtyards, making music, reading, exercising, meditating. It feels like a sweet, safe cocoon, even though what we've learned from Fallon tonight suggests its anything but.

I cast a quick glance at Arden, walking next to me. The life we shared on Home World was so different, with fractious noise and energy and almost constant movement. I used to love that life. I'm not sure I would like it anymore.

Arden picks up on my expression.

"This world is extraordinary at this time of night," he says. "It's like a beautiful painting of a world, so peaceful, so full of potential, so still." A pause. "Would you ever want to go back to Home World?"

I half-smile, remembering someone else asking a similar question. I also remember my answer, which was true then but is very different now.

"I don't think I would," I say. "Everything I need is here."

"Would you stay here if Iona became a Company planet?"

I'm startled by this question, and that Arden would even ask it. But on the other hand, I'm the one who has been hiding from the Company for eight years while he's been working for them. The mention of them and their machinations simply doesn't shake him the way it does me, despite our shared past suffering at the Company's hands.

"I hope you're not implying that becoming a Company planet is inevitable," I say. "We're on the verge of potentially becoming a Core World. Falling into line

246

under the Company's governance doesn't seem like the right move for anyone except the Company."

Arden is undeterred, and his voice takes on an undercurrent of uneasiness. "Suppose for a moment that something does happen, and Iona becomes a Company planet—not a sector dump, but part of the Company's top tier portfolio. Would you stay here?"

I weigh my answer carefully.

"I have a different emotional relationship to the Company than you do," I say, even though I'm thinking *don't you remember that the Company tried to use me against you and then tried to kill us both?* "I'm not sure I would feel comfortable here if it was under Company control. It would change Iona. It might not be Iona anymore."

"What if it was still Iona but better?" He's hinting at something, but as usual he's less than forthcoming. He has no idea how much this irritates me.

The lights of Clinical glow blue just ahead of us, tinting the sand, and I stop and turn to face him.

"If you know something, you need to tell me now," I say. "Is there a plan by the Company to take over Iona?"

"I wouldn't call it a plan. It's more of an *interest*, from different sectors for different reasons." His gaze shifts from my face to the stars to the sand at his feet. "I know that High Defense believes Iona would be extremely valuable to them, and obviously we've found our why."

Look for the why. I had almost forgotten our charge to ourselves.

It's the sand.

The Company is likely exploring every potential use for Blue, including as a savvy weapon that skirts the Governing Council's anti-genocide laws by simply pausing life rather than extinguishing it outright, with the added "bonus" of potential reversibility. The very guts of our planet renders Blue ineffective, so naturally the Company wants to control it.

And, more than likely, so does everyone else.

Suddenly I understand much better the *why* of what happened on Bardazel. There was no risk of toxic gas exposure, no cult, no social unrest, not even any slowdown in business. The Company lied to Bardazel's citizens and leadership and staged an elaborate theater that displaced hundreds of people so they could close the station and control the sand of that planet—sand so like that of Iona, terrain so like Iona's, that it must have the same effect.

"Bardazel?" I whisper for confirmation, and Arden simply nods.

"Yes," he says. "First Bardazel, and now that interest has spilled over to Iona."

"Did our friend Graham have any role in that?" I ask, and Arden's forehead creases in thought.

"I'm still trying to learn how deep his involvement goes. On Bardazel, he was genuine in what he was trying to do, and he worked very hard to get people out of the compound. I like Graham, and I'm grateful that he seems to be on-board with us here. But something about his story doesn't quite line up. He's generally a straightforward guy, but he does have a dark past and his family is even less forthright. That's why I was assigned to him in the first place."

I feel strange talking about Graham this way, but I resist the urge to say so. I also resist the urge to ask more questions. I can't quite wrap my mind around the existence of a shadowy, sinister Graham compared to the Graham I know now. But I've also had reservations about his motivations, his shifting demeanor, and his changing allegiances. What kind of secrets is he still keeping, despite our heart-to-heart talk at the storage warren just last night?

"Let's focus on Bennid," I finally say, walking again toward the glowing lights of Clinical. "One thing at a time."

Arden laughs cynically. "One thing at a time," he says. "Wouldn't that be nice."

As Macha noted, Bennid turns out to be physically well, albeit clearly rattled and emotionally shaky. He sits tensely in the middle of his bed, torturing the edge of the sheet with the fingers of his natural hand. The technician tells us he won't lie down to sleep and instead has continued to sit, alert and fidgety, listening for any kind of disturbance coming from Holly's room next door.

When I ask him where the sphere came from, he tells a fairly straightforward story.

"Holly found it behind the Theater after school," he says. "She thought it was an egg. We were talking about how to hatch it, and I was holding it up to the sun to try to see through the shell—my grandfather used to do that with sand turtle eggs—and I guess I squeezed it a little too hard with my artificial hand. It broke open and liquid started oozing out. At first Holly was upset because she thought I'd killed her egg, but the liquid was so pretty and not like anything we'd ever seen before—silvery and shiny and all kinds of colors all at once. We knew then that it wasn't an egg, but we didn't know it was dangerous."

His face twists in distress; he blinks back tears.

"And Holly touched the liquid?" I gently finish the narrative for him.

Bennid nods. "She swirled some onto her fingers. And then she said it started to feel funny, so she tried to wipe it off on the hem of her dress. Only it was getting really sticky, and it got on her leg, and then she lost feeling in her hands and started turning blue." He rubs the empty stump of his left bioequivalent arm with his real right hand and hiccups, on the edge of crying. "I'm sorry," he croaks out, turning his head away.

"It's okay, Bennid. There's no way you could have known," I say. "You called for help, you helped keep Holly calm, and you followed Chief March's instructions. You did the right thing." I feel like a hypocrite reassuring this young man; even now, I'm not sure *we* did the right thing by concealing our find in Pauly's old office from the rest of the residents of Iona.

Bennid finally looks at me, his eyes wide. "Is Holly really going to be all right?" he asks. "You aren't just telling me that to keep me from freaking out?"

Arden reaches over and squeezes Bennid's shoulder. "Yes, she's going to be fine," he says. "You'll be able to see her as soon as she wakes up. Macha has promised that you're the first person she'll tell."

Our reassurance seems to calm him a little and he finally relaxes against the pillows at his back.

"Thank you for helping us today," Bennid says to me. "Please tell Chief March we are really, really grateful."

"You're very welcome, and she already knows," I say. "Get some sleep." He nods, but it's clear he won't be falling asleep until he's convinced Holly is out of danger.

We next check on Holly. She still bears a faint blue stain on her hands and thigh, but the creeping coloration that was trying to take over the rest of her body has otherwise receded. Hinn is hunched in the chair next to her bed watching her carefully, a bucket of fresh Iona sand at his feet.

"Her vitals are strong and normal," Macha confirms when she joins us. "She's still not awake, as you can see, but I can't even call her unconscious. Her stats are more like someone who is exhausted and in a deep sleep. If Chief March is correct, she should wake up on her own in a few hours."

Our last stop is the ward that now holds Karloa and Pauly. I haven't seen Pauly except for that brief glimpse the day I broke his quarantine and caused such havoc. Seeing him now is almost as shocking.

He's the same turquoise blue as Karloa. The gashes in his abdomen and head have healed, but he remains armless, and his eyes are still sealed shut. "We'll fit him for bioequivalent arms once we revive him," Macha explains, and I'm grateful for her optimistic phrasing. "His eyes were severely damaged by flying debris in the explosion. His chances of regaining his sight are slim at best."

Karloa is just the same as the last time I saw her. The hovering monitor that was constantly tracking her vitals now sits unused on the shelf at the far side of the ward; instead, she and Pauly are both checked by technicians every four hours.

"I understand her better now, but there are still so many questions," I say to Arden as we descend to the lobby of Clinical. "I keep thinking she's the key to this mystery. We have to find a way to get our hands on that antidote and revive her."

Arden sighs, jamming his hands into his pockets. "Maybe Fallon can help," he says. "Something to hope for, anyway."

I nod, but my mind isn't on what he's saying. A worrying thought, like a rock in my shoe, has captured my attention and won't let it go.

"Holly found that sphere behind the theatre," I say to Arden as we walk out of clinical bound for the pod. "I can't help but wonder if it was planted there on purpose, in a spot where it would be found by someone who had no idea what it was."

Arden's expression darkens and he runs one hand through his hair. "It's certainly possible. If this is part of what Fallon was having delivered in the Sprites, it seems to make sense—the Theater is in a direct line from the Northern Ridge, where the Spites would have landed, and Intake, where you and Graham found them."

"So there could be more, just lying around waiting for someone to break them and fall into stasis. Not a comforting thought."

251

Arden casts a furtive glance around as though scanning for spheres in the darkness. "At least Fallon seems willing to work with us now."

"Yeah. Somehow, still not comforted. I'm getting our Security Team on this."

I hail Maybree. She immediately understands my concern.

"I'll set up an electronic perimeter around the theater tonight and get a team to sweep the area between the ridge and Intake first thing in the morning," she says. "Seems like that would be safest for all of us."

I thank her and barely remember to log off, I'm so lost in my thoughts. Arden is preoccupied too, his eyebrows knit together and forehead creased. I can't imagine what's going on in his brain, but based on our conversation earlier, I'm certain it's coming from a different direction than the things in my brain. That worries me almost as much as the impending threat from Blue.

We complete the walk to Residential in silence. As we reach the edge of the soft golden glow of our courtyard, Arden reaches out and takes my hand. I feel both a smoky relief and a persistent sense of conflict.

I know he loves me, but his love made him lie to me before. I know I love him, but I'm still not sure I completely trust him. There may be more things yet to learn; questions he's dodged or forgotten were asked, answers he's fudged or simply failed to explain. But there is so much more weighing on me now, these personal issues feel like tiny irritations by comparison. I'm already dreading tomorrow.

"Are you all right?" he asks as we walk into the dark common room, the only light the flickering amber of the embers dying in the hearth.

"I'm overwhelmed. Holly's no part of this ridiculous corporate battle for dominance, she's totally innocent, and someone is responsible, but we don't know who. Add to that the fact that everyone could be at risk, but we don't have enough details to protect ourselves. I'm frustrated and furious, but there's no place for that anger to go."

I rub my eyes and sigh. Arden's expression softens.

"Do you want company tonight? Not for, you know, but just ..." His voice drifts off. He reaches up and in a tender gesture, tucks behind my ear a strand of my wild hair that has escaped its bonds. I find myself conflicted again. I want to be my own woman. I want to take care of myself. I want peace and security. I want warmth and comfort and love. But most of all I want to make my own decisions. So, I do.

"Yeah. Company sounds good."

Arden gently takes my hand again and together we walk down the little hallway to my room.

WHEN MORNING COMES, I'M still emotionally raw from the previous day's events. I'm hoping today might prove to be a more normal day—although I have no idea what "normal" might be at this point. At least we have our work assignments to focus on until this evening. The rising chimes haven't yet sounded, but Arden is already up and half-dressed. He greets me with a warm kiss and hot coffee. "I heard a maintenance assignment for you come through General about two minutes ago," he says. "Get cracking."

I watch him buzz around my room getting ready, wondering where his energy comes from. After yesterday, I feel like I've been gut-punched and getting out of the hammock feels like a monumental task.

"When did you move your toothbrush in here?" I ask, and he winks at me in the mirror. "I have accomplices," he says.

I finally pull myself upright and stand, stretching and letting out one last yawn. "Pretty sure of yourself, aren't you?" I say, joining him at the tiny sink. It's crowded with his stuff—cleansers and sunscreen and extra-macho deodorant. I wrap my arms around his waist, and he loops his arm around me in turn. I claim this moment of peace for myself and look at our side-by-side reflection.

The years haven't been too hard on either of us. We both have a few tiny crinkles alongside our eyes. Arden sports worry lines across his forehead, but his smile is as bright and captivating as always. His body is more hard-muscled than it used to be, no longer the lithe form of the 28-year-old engineer I first met on Home World ten years ago but instead the body of a fighter. What else might have changed in the intervening years that may not yet have come to the surface?

He lifts one hand and tangles our hair together. I smile at us in the mirror and he rests his head against mine.

"You're stronger than you used to be," I say. "Space pirate life must be pretty active."

He smiles in return. "We're both stronger." I make a face and flex my dramatically average bicep. He laughs and clarifies, "Stronger on the inside."

By the time the rising chimes sound, we're both dressed and ready. When we enter the Common Room together this morning, there are no salutations or sarcastic cheers, although we do get a warm happy look of acknowledgment from Wenda, who is ferrying food from the kitchen. Hinn stayed overnight at Clinical with his sister, so Wenda is temporarily our chef again. Maybree, coffee in hand, catches me as she heads toward the door to let me know the scan around the theater is in progress. "I'll keep you apprised," she promises.

I drop my headset on and tap in, pinging Maintenance about the request Arden heard come through for me. I'm pleased to hear I'll be taking a damaged skiff and breaking it down to component parts, testing them to determine which work or are repairable, and adding those we can use to our spare parts docket.

This means I'll get to spend most of the day in the peace and quiet of the pit. The pit is always good thinking time for me and based on the revelations of the last couple of days, I have a lot of thinking to do. And there are bound to be lots of extra parts our inventory doesn't need, so it's also a great opportunity for me to finally get enough raw material to complete my project, which is so, so close to done.

As I depart for my assignment, a hail comes in confirming that Holly is awake and appears completely unscathed from her experience, except for the presence of faint blue marks on her thigh and the back of one hand. She'll stay in Clinical one more day for observation, which will dovetail nicely with Bennid's scheduled procedure to attach his new bioequivalent arm.

I look down at my feet crunching over Iona's gritty beige sand, so emphatically unexceptional and normal in appearance. Who else suspects how valuable this little planet's most basic element might be? That value could be a dramatic blessing and speed Iona's progress to Independent Core World status, or it could be a horrific curse, depending on what others might be willing to do to exploit it.

Once I'm in the pit with the broken skiff under my hands, I get into a rhythm and let go of as many of my heavy thoughts as I can. I manage to get almost four hours of peace. Soon after lunch, I'm called to come above and work Materials Intake. Among the cargo is one priority medical delivery, which must be Bennid's new arm. I ping Macha to let her know it's arrived and get it on an autoflat headed to Clinical. The remaining items are unremarkable. Sadly, I note that there is no incoming package addressed to Fallon March. A positive counterpoint is a hail from Maybree, reporting Security's scan of the area around the Preservation Theater found no more spheres, and I feel a moment of relief.

After the unloading is done, I spend a little more time in the pit, organizing my newly acquired goodies—it's a substantial haul, too large for the cart and stash space. I procure an autoflat to carry it off to my primary project area instead. As I watch the flat glide off, I straighten and stretch my muscles, pleasantly sore from my day's physical efforts. I consider heading over to the Star Parlor to try to chat with Fallon before the others assemble, hoping she'll be less dramatic with a smaller audience, but before I can leave the pit, Maybree unexpectedly hails me on my private channel. "Something's happening at the storage warren," she says, barely controlling the anxiety in her voice. "The security system just pinged me. Someone's trying to get into Number 8."

My heart begins to race.

"Let Arden know," I tell her. "I'm on my way." I take a second to grab a couple of choice items from the debris scattered around my feet and run up the ramp to the surface. Within seconds, I'm on a scooter, flying across the sand toward our warren.

It only takes a few minutes to reach the storage warren, but I'm already concerned that I might be too late to catch the potential intruder. I ditch the scooter a few hundred feet from the door—though they're quiet as a whisper, I prefer to make a less dramatic entrance. I hail Maybree on her private channel and ask, "Is it still happening?"

"Likely," she responds. "They've made several attempts, with gaps of a minute or so between each one. The last attempt was about forty-five seconds ago. We're all on the way. ETA about two minutes."

"Keep me informed," I say, pressing myself against the side of the building about forty feet from the door. There's only one way in and out of the storage warren, so if the person attempting to get into my unit is still inside, I'll see them if they try to leave.

No more than half a minute later, Maybree's voice comes over my headset. "Tracking shows someone trying to enter the unit now," she says.

I'm not waiting any longer. The spheres in that unit are too dangerous to be discovered by anyone, much less be allowed to fall into the hands of someone who might know what they are. "Going in," I whisper into the mic, then I pull off my headset and jam it into my pocket. It's in part to prevent distractions, but also to avoid hearing the chorus of objections to my decision that I'm sure are ringing through it at this instant.

I steel my nerves and try to appear at least somewhat casual as I walk to the door and let it read my credentials. The door slides open, and I step inside. The lights are on, but set to a faint glow, just enough to see the outline of the cubbies lining both walls. I walk slowly and quietly to the share, which is also only dimly lit, and pause at the edge of the hallway that leads to Number 8. I carefully peer into the opening. It's too dark to see anything clearly, but I can hear muffled sounds—the soft chirring of electronics and an occasional frustrated mutter. Then, footsteps, slow and casual, moving toward me.

Whoever is here apparently thinks they're still alone. That's going to be the advantage I need.

I pull out of my belt loop the sharp, knife-like segment of piping I snagged from my breakdown and wrap my hand tightly around its blunt end. I then press myself against the wall of the share a few feet from the mouth of the hallway. My heart is pounding like a lander engine on a high-gravity lift-off.

The figure that emerges into the darkened share is preoccupied with some electronics in their hands, muttering quietly to themselves. They walk past my position without ever looking up. I raise my makeshift weapon in front of me and wait until the interloper is in the middle of the share still with their back to me, about 10 feet past my position.

"Stop!" I command. "I have a weapon trained on you. Turn around slowly and keep your hands out in front of you where I can see them. Lights full."

The space is immediately flooded with light. Clearly startled, the person freezes, then with outstretched hands trembling, turns to face me.

"Wha ... what have I done? Don't hurt me," Quimby stutters, his dark eyes wide and terrified.

I almost drop my guard. Quimby is such a familiar face to me by now that I nearly forgot that he, too, was one of the Bardazel transfers. Still, he seems so scared and confused. I keep my weapon in front of me but modulate my voice into something strong but a bit more conversational.

"You were trying to get into Number 8. Why?"

"I heard something. I went to investigate. But the door is malfunctioning and won't let me in, even though I'm the administrator."

"It's not malfunctioning. We changed the permissions. Only certain people can open Number 8 now."

"Oh. I didn't know that." Quimby looks down at the electronics in his hands. "I found this wired into the sensor mechanism in the control console. I thought maybe it was the problem. I can put it back right now if you want."

I peer at the small unit Quimby is holding out to me. It doesn't look familiar.

"Let's wait until Maybree gets here and see what she thinks," I say. At this, Quimby brightens significantly. His reply is cut off, however, by the sound of the warren main door sliding open and Arden shouting my name.

"I'm fine, it's all fine," I call out. "Come back to the share and let's see if we can get this figured out." I tuck my weapon back into my belt loop but keep my eye on Quimby.

Arden literally runs into the room, his eyes wild, followed by Maybree, her stun stick activated in her hand.

Arden looks from me to Quimby, feeling out the situation, and relaxes somewhat. "You went off headset, we couldn't raise you," he says to me.

I shake my head, feeling a bit guilty for worrying them all. "I'm fine. I'm still not sure what's going on here, though."

Arden looks Quimby up and down, his face creased with skepticism. He taps into his headset and says, "Not an *entirely* false alarm, but she's all right. Get here when you can."

Maybree, who has jammed the stun stick back into its holster on her thigh, speaks up next. "Quimby? What the hell?"

"I'm sorry, I guess I did something wrong," Quimby says, gesturing plaintively, his hands still full of tiny electronic parts. "I didn't mean to."

"Oh, forty hells, is that what I think it is?" Maybree reaches out and gingerly takes the electronics from Quimby.

"Probably," Quimby says, clearly relieved to finally have his hands free. "I pulled it out of the console. I thought it was what was keeping me from getting in."

"Oh no." Maybree looks despondent. "You pulled this out of the control console for Number 8? This is terrible."

Quimby nods affirmative. "I can put it back," he offers. Maybree shakes her head.

Before I can ask either of them for clarification, the noise level increases significantly as an entire parade of people enter the warren. In the depths of the hallway, I hear Graham's voice prod, "Come on, speed it up," and Fallon snap back, "Why is it so damn dark in here? Turn up the lights so I can see where I'm going." Fanny's voice chimes in with, "Come on, Fallon, even I can walk faster than you are right now and that's really saying something."

Graham is the first to enter the share. He looks from Quimby to Maybree, and then stares pointedly at the electronics dangling from Maybree's hands.

"What's that?" he asks.

I notice he didn't bother to adjust the lighting nor wait for Fallon, who I still hear swearing and bumping around in the main hallway.

"It's my worst nightmare," sighs Maybree. "All those steps we took to secure entry to Number 8? This circumvents it."

I'm confused. "But then why couldn't Quimby get in?" I ask.

"Because this little guy records access data," she explains, holding up the small device. "In order to activate it, you need a signaler, kind of like a remote. When it gets a signal from the remote, the main unit plays the data it's recorded, and the door thinks it's someone with entry permissions asking to open the door. It shuts off automatically once the task is performed—in this case, once the door is open. When it's not activated, the door operates the way we expect it to."

"Someone's been able to go into Number 8 without detection since the beginning," I say, my stomach sinking.

"Not exactly. The device needs to record data after it's installed. Whoever hooked this up had to wait for someone authorized to open the door again, at which point it would swipe the access data. Gosh, I didn't think to track approved entries," Maybree says, her expression reflecting her dejected spirit.

"I've only opened this door once since we changed the permissions, and that was when we left the spheres here," I say, looking at Graham. "Maybe they haven't had access for very long."

"Let's go back to the beginning, though," Arden says. "Quimby, why were you trying to get into Number 8?"

Quimby, now more relaxed, pushes up his glasses and addresses Arden.

"I came in to organize our new deliveries in the share. I heard a noise down the hallway here, scraping and banging like someone moving something heavy. I thought someone might need some help, so I yelled down the hallway, but nobody answered," he explains. "That was weird, to get no answer at all, so I thought something was wrong. And I started walking toward where the noise came from."

"Did you find anyone? Or figure out what was making the noise?" Arden asks.

"No," Quimby confirms. "I called out again, but still no one answered. That's when I heard a thumping sound and clattering, like maybe a mini had failed and dropped its load. That definitely came from inside Number 8, so I wanted to look inside and make sure everything was okay, but I couldn't get in. I thought it was malfunctioning, so I pulled the console apart and that's when I found that." He gestures at the device now clenched in Maybree's fist.

We all exchange anxious looks.

"We need to make sure nothing is broken in there," Graham says. He's about to shoulder his way through the group to the hallway, but I reach out and stop him.

"You're right, but I have one more question," I say. "Quimby, do you believe there was a person involved in making the noise you heard? Could it have been equipment on auto-adjust?"

He thinks before answering. "I'm not sure," he says. "The scraping and sliding didn't sound random. It sounded like someone was having trouble operating an autoflat. But I haven't seen anyone. And this is the only way out."

"Either there was no one here to begin with, or the person who was making the noise is still here, hiding," Arden says.

Quimby blinks and adjusts his glasses again. "Yeah, I guess so. I didn't hear anybody go through the share or leave the building. But Faith came in and I didn't hear that, so it's possible." His voice trails off.

If only I'd thought to look for evidence of people entering and leaving the building—footprints or scooter tracks in the sand, anything. Those clues, if they ever existed, are long trampled and muddled by the sheer number of people who've come into the building in the last ten minutes.

"We have to check on those spheres, whether there is someone in here or not," Graham says.

I scan the room. Arden, Maybree, Fanny, and even Fallon, who has finally managed to reach the share, are all nodding in agreement.

"Yeah, go," I say, then call out the command, "Lights full, entire sector." Every light in the storage warren comes on, illuminating every corner.

"No place to hide now," mutters Maybree, scowling down the corridor.

"Hold on, Graham, you'll need me to open the door," says Arden, and the two men trot quickly down the length of the hall to Number 8.

"Can you do this safely?" I call out. They exchange looks and Graham tilts his head in an answer that is not an answer.

"It should be all right," Arden responds. "Theoretically, these spheres should contain Blue that only affects you if you touch it, rather than an aerosolized version. We should be okay as long as we don't get any active Blue on our skin."

Before I can object or say anything else, I hear Arden say, "Number 8 open," followed by the soft mechanical swoosh of the door as it slides out of the way. Both men take a step forward. For a heart-stopping second, neither says anything. Then Arden calls out, "Nothing looks broken. I think it's safe to enter. But there's another problem."

I rush down the hall toward the storage unit, followed by Maybree. When I step through the door, I see Graham crouched next to what had been our carefully placed collection of spheres with Arden standing behind him. The miniflat sits askew and has bumped into the wall, as though it had been programmed with destination coordinates by someone who was attempting to drive it blind. Its delicate cargo has shifted off the flat on one side, explaining the noises Quimby heard. But of greater concern is the fact that the bundle is now untied, and the spheres are no longer neatly stacked inside it. Graham's face is ashen as he reports, "There were twenty-seven when we placed them here. Now there are only twenty-four."

"It's worse than that," says Fallon, strolling through the door and crouching beside the autoflat. "When I found them, there were forty."

"When you *found* them?" Graham shouts at Fallon, his eyes blazing. "What do you mean, you *found* them? You had these damn things delivered to you! How many days did you waste pretending you had no idea what they were? How many more people are going to be hurt because of that? What the hell were you thinking, Fallon?"

"Give me a break, you self-righteous ass," Fallon snaps, matching Graham in both intensity and tone. "This isn't what was sent to me. Get real—this was developed on Bardazel. Your people brought this with them when they came here, and you know it. You've always known it. What the hell were *you* thinking?"

30

THE TWO GLARE AT each other as we stare at them in shock; Graham blinks first. He turns his gaze away from Fallon and down at the spheres. He slowly begins stacking them back into a secure configuration, silently working as we all look on. His shoulders droop a bit, and his breathing becomes ragged with emotion.

"I don't want to believe any of my people could have done this," he murmurs, not making eye contact with anyone. "I still can't imagine who is responsible. But Fallon isn't wrong. This particular formulation and delivery mechanism were created on Bardazel as part of an offensive weapons development program."

I gasp. Defensive weaponry is tolerated, but offensive weapons have been illegal by decree of the Governing Council for hundreds of years.

"Specifically, an offensive weapons program that you were running," Arden adds. There is no accusation in his voice, just a simple statement of fact.

"Yes," confirms Graham, "a program that I was running. Until I understood how brutal they intended to be. That's when I started trying to make up for my mistake."

"More explaining," I groan, looking between Arden, Graham, and Fallon. "Maybree, secure that flat and disarm it completely. The rest of you, we're finishing this now."

Everyone looks at me expectantly.

I look at Fallon.

"What?" she barks.

"We're starting with you," I say. "You said you *found* the spheres that were in the credenza."

"Oh, that. Well, yes and no."

Awesome. I sigh heavily, resisting the urge to rub my forehead in exasperation. "Just tell the story and leave out the cat-and-mouse dynamics."

Her mouth twists in aggravation. "I don't know what you want to hear."

"I want to hear the truth. About everything, starting with the spheres. *Everything*," I say firmly. I stare at her until she starts to talk.

"Those specific spheres .... I did find them. But actually, I found someone else with them first."

"Who?" Arden asks, his attention fully shifting to Fallon.

"I don't know."

"Tell the story," I say, as emphatically as I can muster. This woman is giving me a headache. "Start at the beginning."

Fallon harrumphs and crosses her arms over her chest, scowling at each of us in turn, her gaze finally coming to rest on Graham, who raises his eyebrows in expectation.

"All right. You know about the Sprites already. I received information that more were scheduled to drop three nights ago. I came out shortly before they were due to land and was heading for the northern ridge because I didn't want to miss them again."

I gasp. "You were the person I saw on the ridge?"

"I never made it up there. You saw someone on the ridge?" Fallon is suddenly as interested in my story as I am in hers.

"Yes, but go on, finish what you were saying."

"That makes sense," she says, leaning forward. "It has to be the same person."

"Same person for what?" Maybree pipes up. Fallon is about to answer her, but I wave my hand in the air to disrupt her. "Finish what you were saying, then we'll have questions," I say. With each passing minute I'm feeling more irritated and worn.

Fallon blinks for a moment as if trying to reset her brain, which has already gone spiraling off onto a new tangent. It takes a moment, but she finally resumes her tale. She uncrosses her arms and jams her hands into the pockets of her jacket instead.

"Okay. I walked out at about 23:30, and I saw a figure creeping around your pod. I got as close as I could without giving myself away and hid so I could watch them. I realized they had a significant number of those spheres and were placing them in precarious locations where they were likely to be broken accidentally or fall and break on their own."

Fallon pauses to make sure we're all listening. My exhaustion has been replaced by an energizing feeling of absolute dread.

"Clearly this person was up to no good," she continues. "At one point, they appeared to consider tossing spheres through some open pod windows. They seemed particularly interested in a couple on the back side of the pod closest to the ridge."

I glance over at Arden; he's already looking at me. We both have a good idea whose windows those were.

"You already get that I know what these things are and what they're capable of, and I knew I couldn't let this happen. This person had a whole stack of spheres out behind your pod. So I kind of made myself obvious to them—not like I had been *watching* them, because, you know, potentially dangerous psycho with stasis-inducing weaponry. But like I was simply out and about, coming their way, happening upon them accidentally."

"You basically interrupted them," interjects Graham.

"Yes, just like you're interrupting me now," Fallon says imperiously, her eyes glittering at him briefly before she returns to her narrative. "The person fortunately was an enormous coward and ran away when they heard me coming. Just took off and left the stack of spheres. I collected all the ones I could see had been planted and added them to the pile; there were forty in total. I knew I couldn't safely carry them all back to a secure location, so I did the safest thing with them that I could think of."

"You surrounded them with a neutralizing agent," I say. "You buried them in the sand." The picture of that night is coming together quickly in my mind. "You grabbed a shovel from our courtyard, dug as deep as you could, and buried them behind our pod."

"Yes," Fallon says. "I thought they'd be safe there temporarily. I didn't tell anyone about them. But when I came back the next day, they were gone."

"You were seen," I explain. "When I closed my window that night, I saw a figure up on the ridge. That was probably the person you interrupted. My guess is they climbed up there to hide from you but wound up with a perfect vantage point and saw you burying the spheres. Then it was just a matter of retrieving them before you did."

"You had nothing to do with getting them into the credenza in your office?" asks Graham. Fallon shakes her head.

"No. I was as shocked to see them as you were. That must be where this mystery person decided to stash them, for what reason I can't say."

"Why did you claim they were yours?" he presses.

"I didn't know if you understood what they were, or how deadly they were. I was hoping to make you back off and leave them alone so I could deal with them. Of course, now we know they're your little babies, so obviously my concern wasn't warranted." She folds her arms across her chest again, this time with a smug expression and an eyebrow raised in Graham's direction. Graham ignores this dig and clears his throat.

"Can you tell us anything about what this mysterious person looked like?" I ask.

"Not really. It was dark. I already can't see shit in the dark and the moons of this world might as well be nonexistent for all the light they reflect," Fallon says. "The person seemed to be wearing a large, loose overwrap of some kind. I can't say exactly how tall, but in general shorter than Graham and taller than Maybree.

They seemed to have some bulk to them, but again—wearing a big overcoat or something, so it's hard to say."

"Male or female?" Arden asks. Fallon shakes her head.

"I couldn't tell. Kind of a clumsy mover, but that doesn't mean anything. I'm not all that graceful myself."

"Whoever it was, it's probably a reasonable guess that this same person now has the missing spheres," I say.

Graham looks grim. "Sixteen spheres of contact Blue could do a lot of damage, and we have no idea what they might be planning. We have to track them as soon as possible."

"Holly found that sphere behind the Preservation Theater, but our security scan of the area didn't turn up anything more," I say.

"We should do a new scan, given what we've learned tonight, with an expanded search area," Maybree says. "I'll get a team on it tonight; it seems smart to start behind your pod and run through the rest of residential extending all the way to Intake. I think a curfew is warranted as well, to keep anyone from wandering through that area in the dark."

"Makes sense," I say. "Take every precaution you can."

Maybree's reply is interrupted by a strange series of sounds coming from outside. Deep in the storage warren as we are, it's hard to pinpoint exactly what it is, although it makes me think of something I haven't heard since I left Home World: a deep and sonorous rumble, followed by a muffled "whomp." The terrain shakes momentarily. Normally, I'd be expecting a thunderstorm.

But there are no thunderstorms on Iona.

Together we run toward the warren entrance, and find the whole of Iona's population outside, looking toward the far edge of Residential. The night sky is lit by glowing red and orange flames high up on the cliffs and the acrid smell of smoke pervades the air.

Headsets are going off everywhere. Maybree is one of the first to get the call.

Her face is deadly serious as she hurries past us, running toward the spectacle. Without slowing, she turns and shouts over her shoulder, "Get to a pod and stay there, all of you. Someone just set off a bomb in the Star Parlor."

My pod is closest, so the rest of us head there and hunker down to wait. It's not lost on me that had our evening gone according to plan, at least six of us would have been in the Star Parlor at the moment of the explosion. Graham hails Fanny for news of how their podmates are faring. Even though the Star Parlor is accessed through their pod, its position high up on the cliff has limited the destruction. The final verdict is lots of rattled nerves and rattled crockery, but no injuries or major structural damage to the pod.

Iona's Emergency Services quickly gets the fire under control. Maybree hails me on private to let me know Security has blocked off the Star Parlor for further investigation, as the cause of the explosion is not yet clear. "We'll figure out what happened here," she says, her voice steely with determination. "I'm not going to let everybody down twice in one night."

The bad news is all for Fallon March. Of her personal effects, including clothing, toiletries, and holo, almost nothing has survived. At least her research materials were safe in secured storage. And, of course, Fallon now has no place to sleep. "What will you do with me?" she asks, looking genuinely worried. "Am I going to get stuck in a Holding Cell?"

I do some mental gymnastics and come up with a plan on the fly. It requires some shuffling around, but my podmates won't object and it's only temporary. I put my hand out to shake Fallon's and as she gives me a perplexed look, I say, "Welcome to Pod C-1419. I hope you don't mind sharing a room with a lovely teenage girl."

In a little less than an hour, Hinn has moved out of the room he shared with Holly and into the room Arden has shared with Parker the champion snorer. Arden will now bunk with me, and Fallon will be Holly's roommate, something Holly is deliriously excited about when Hinn lets her know. I have no idea how

Fallon feels about the arrangement, but she's not complaining about it at the moment.

Outside, the people of Iona are still on edge, gathering in clusters all over town to stare up at the smoldering remains of the Star Parlor. Graham, anxious to check on his podmates, doesn't wait for the official "all clear" from Security before heading home. Maybree will be tied up with her work team duties for hours. There's nothing else we can do.

Like everyone else, I'm too tense to sleep, so I rummage in our surplus for a few minutes and come up with a change of clothes and some bed and bath linens for Fallon. Her face at the sight of the tan cargo pants, black tee shirt and beige service jacket is a perfect visual representation of the word *disgust*. But she takes the stack of items from me without comment and lets me show her down the hall to her new sleeping quarters.

"You'll have privacy tonight. Holly will be home tomorrow," I explain. "Maybree will set up additional security to make sure you feel safe, and I've set our pod access to credentials only. It should be enough for one night. Almost no one knows you're here, and you're surrounded by people. Try to rest."

She steps across the threshold into the room, taking it in for a few moments before she turns to me. Her face is tired and anxious. "Why are you being so helpful?" she asks. "I realize I'm a total bitch. That's not going to change."

"Life on Iona is collaborative and interdependent by design. We work so closely together and depend so much on one another, it's just our nature to help," I say.

Fallon considers this seriously. "Well, I appreciate that," she says, hefting the stack of clothing and linens onto her hammock, "but it doesn't make these clothes any less ugly."

"And it doesn't make you any less of a bitch, either." The flippant comment flies out of my mouth before I can control myself and I hold my breath, preparing for Fallon's response.

Which is laughter—a rich, musical chiming laugh that is the last thing I expect from her.

"Good one," she says, and closes the door still chuckling.

I enter my room—now our room—to find Arden already stretched out in the hammock. His body posture suggests relaxation, but his face is anything but. Dark circles show beneath his eyes, his mouth is taut, and his brow is furrowed in perpetual worry.

"Tough night," I say, walking in and shutting the door behind me. He rubs his chin and lets out a long weary breath.

"How's Fallon settling in?" he asks. "Is she being a pain in the ass?"

"Surprisingly, not so much. What happened to the Star Parlor shocked her as much as it did the rest of us."

"We were supposed to be there," he says, looking at me levelly. "All of us."

"I know."

"It looks like they might not be coming after only me, or Graham or Fallon. They might be coming after everyone." He doesn't say my name, but the tension in his face conveys clearly that he's remembering Home World, and how the attack on him spilled over into an attack on me.

"It could have been an accident of some kind," I say, "There might not even be a *they*. And if there is, they may want something else. This might just be a way of getting attention."

Arden sits up, swinging his long bare legs over the side of the hammock and putting his feet flat on the floor.

"You don't really believe that." He eyes me critically. His face remains creased with concern.

I sit down in the hammock next to him.

"I guess I'm willing to give myself the chance to believe that it's not what it looks like," I say. "I have to do that for my own sanity. I hope you understand."

He absorbs what I've said for a moment, then leans into me and kicks his feet, sending the hammock into a gentle swing.

"I do," he says. "All the things I've seen in the last eight years have made me suspicious and cynical. It's what kept me alive out there. But when I'm with you,

I want to have your optimism and believe it can all work out. That's the effect you have on me, and I think I'm a better man for it. But I'm not sure it's better for all the rest of us in the long run. Someone needs to stay vigilant."

He shifts back into a prone position in the hammock again and closes his eyes. His face remains alert and tense. When I stretch out beside him and he wraps his arms around me, I can feel the tension in them and hear the elevated rate of his heartbeat.

I remember Fanny saying Iona had become a dangerous place. I didn't believe it then, and I still don't. But things are getting more serious by the second, and we've got to get a break soon or that prophecy might come true.

31

WE DON'T EVEN MAKE it to the rising chimes before there's more ominous news. Arden is barely up and I'm still attempting to snooze when his headset goes off. I hear him murmur, "Oh shit," into the mic before he turns to me.

"Tap in," he says, passing my headset to me. "It's Maybree."

I slip my headset on and join the convo.

"We found four additional spheres last night," Maybree says. "One of my people basically stomped one to bits before he realized it was there. The things were strategically placed around the Star Parlor's emergency exit landing point, and incredibly well-camouflaged, so intentionally set there to do harm rather than left behind by some incompetent weirdo."

I drop my head into my hands for a moment, rubbing my eyes and trying to ignore my fiercely clinching jaw.

"Is your team member all right?" I ask. "Was anyone else exposed?"

"Yeah, he's fine; he was wearing Class Nine safety gear, so the Blue never got on his skin. And he was one of the scanners at the Preservation Theater so he knew exactly what he was looking at when he finally saw it. Thing is, it had some kind of matte coating on it that kept it from reflecting light, but still almost perfectly mirrored the sand surrounding it. I've never seen anything like it. We only found the others by looking for shape variations in the base terrain."

I exhale heavily and drop back against my pillows.

"Thanks, Maybree," I finally say. "I guess we need to let everyone know to be on the lookout for these things."

"Already on it," she responds. "I sent out an alert to all holos a little while ago. It has enough information in it to let people know what to look for and how to respond if they locate a sphere, but I tried to keep it ... I guess less threatening than it could be. I wanted people to take it seriously but not panic."

We log off the call. Arden's face is creased with concern as he looks at me, but he says nothing. He doesn't have to. I know we're both thinking the same thing.

The emergency exit landing point. The exact spot where anyone who survived the explosion and got the escape hatch open would have dropped to the ground. It's easy to envision any of us collapsing into the sand, possibly injured, panicked and horrified, trying to escape the raging fire above, and crushing a sphere without realizing it, maybe not even recognizing what was happening to us until it was too late.

Four spheres.

Arden. Fallon. Graham. Me.

Last night I couldn't sleep longer than a few minutes before the specter of what might lie ahead of us wrenched me awake. After this start to the day, I feel like I might never sleep again.

Arden finishes getting ready, then kisses me gently and departs. I know he can read the anxiety in my eyes, and I see it myself when I finally drag myself to the basin and look in the mirror.

The woman who looks back at me appears almost nothing like me. Her face is tormented, with glazed eyes that seem to be on the verge of tears accented by drooping eyebrows and a severely downturned mouth. I shake my head at myself in disappointment. Just last night I was lecturing Arden about the importance of staying optimistic. With a sigh, I throw a towel over the mirror. I don't know who that girl is. I don't want to look at her anymore.

I'm scheduled to work on pod management duties today, so I gratefully hide out in our room, listening to the sounds of my podmates rising, moving around, eating breakfast. There's no laughter today, no lightness. The atmosphere in the pod is pure tension, the usual air of "we'll figure it out and it will be okay" missing from the tone of conversation. They're concerned after the events of last night and overwhelmed by Maybree's alert this morning. Really, I'm right there with them.

I wait until there's only silence from the common room before I make my entry. But the common room isn't empty. Fallon March sits at the table, drinking coffee and reading something spooling off a borrowed holotablet. Even wearing the generic black tee, tan cargo pants and ill-fitting beige service jacket I handed her last night, she somehow manages to appear crisp and put-together.

"Good morning," I say as I walk in. Fallon doesn't look up right away, and when she does, she isn't smiling.

"There's a crap-ton of lies flying around about what happened here last night," she says. "This is the craziest Company response I've ever seen."

She tosses the holo across the table to me, and it lands in front of me with a thud. It's streaming Fallon's Company communique channel, and message after message either describes or deplores the "actions of a small group of anarchists creating havoc on Iona".

"What the hell is this?" I ask.

"You know what it is; you worked for the Company. What happens if there's social unrest on a planet that plays a very important role in the Company's business plan?"

"They move in to restore order. Temporarily, of course."

"Of course. And what happens when there are no anarchists present as they've been reporting?"

"They make some."

"Does this sound familiar? Have we heard this before?" It's a rhetorical question. We both know the answer.

"Bardazel," I say, my throat dry.

"And who do you think the leading candidates for this group of anarchists on Iona might be?"

"Me. Arden. Graham. Anyone who knows what's happening with Blue, or about the effect of the sand."

"Correct," Fallon affirms with a scowl. "And you can add me. I've been recalled."

"Recalled!" I put the holo down, aghast. "But you just got here!"

"I'm apparently no longer on the right side of the issue. I'm not only being recalled, I'm being sent before the Performance Board." Her lips twist in anger and her eyes flash as she says the words.

The Performance Board only ever means one thing—censure, loss of status, and reassignment, usually to the most painfully inappropriate job available. Although the Company loves to paint it as a second chance to prove one's worth, a destroyed career is usually the *best* thing one can hope for from the Performance Board. At worst, Board rulings can result in something that looks an awful lot like, but of course would never be *called,* forced labor.

"Would your mother be able to intervene?" I ask.

Fallon sighs, leaning forward and placing her head in one hand, while the other begins to tap a pattern on the side of her coffee cup. "She needs to protect the project. If she steps in, it will only draw unwelcome attention and magnify the scrutiny she's already under," she says. "It's too important and has to move forward. She won't be taking a position one way or the other when it comes to me."

"But she's your *mother.*"

"And green is a color. What's your point?"

Oh. Silence drops around us, weighty and dense.

"When do they want you back?" I finally ask.

"Not sure. A couple of weeks, maybe? It depends on how long it takes to go through the adjudication process. I've already let them know I'm exercising my legal right to question the recall and the referral to the Performance Board. So I'm going to fight it, but I'm probably not going to win."

I should never have gotten up today. Things have gone from bad to worse.

"I'm sorry, Fallon," I say.

She arches one perfect eyebrow at me. "For what? It's not like it's your fault."

"No, but I'm sorry all the same."

She shakes her head, a look of bemusement on her face. "You're strange," she says. "I suppose I mean that as a compliment, but you need to be less sensitive. It's going to get you in trouble."

"Sensitive? I nearly shanked poor Quimby last night. That's really sensitive." Suddenly I begin to laugh.

It's the laughter of panic and tension that needs release, of pain and fury and complete exhaustion. But it feels good to laugh, so I don't stop myself.

She stares at me quizzically for a few seconds, but then Fallon's lips curl up into a smile and she starts laughing too.

We spend the morning sharing the space but don't really interact. Fallon continues to monitor her communique channel and occasionally send out terse, expletive-laden responses, and I manage to get our pod shares for food and water adjusted to accommodate our new resident.

Around lunchtime, Hinn brings Holly home from Clinical, and Fallon is put through another round of emotional hugging and grateful gushing, which she bears reasonably well. Afterwards, Holly parks herself at the table next to us like a delighted puppy. When the teen finally bustles into the kitchen to fetch us more coffee, Fallon leans across the table and whispers to me, "Is there anywhere else we can go? I can't take much more adoration."

"Let's get your stuff moved into our warren," I suggest. "You're one of us now, after all."

Fallon's mouth puckers in vague disgust. "I'm definitely dressing the part," she says, looking down at her unremarkable clothes. "God, that burgundy jumpsuit. I'm going to miss that."

I hail Fanny so she can facilitate the transfer, while Fallon lets Holly know we'll be taking our coffee to go. We step out of the pod and into the dim light of Iona's early afternoon. Our eyes are drawn to what's left of the Star Parlor, perched on the cliff face at the far edge of Residential. All that remains is a blackened hulk of twisted support struts and some sharp soot-stained shards of high-impact acrylic that leap up to slice the sky.

"Wow," mutters Fallon. When she lifts her ridiculously unnecessary sunglasses for a better look, her already-pale skin goes a couple of shades paler. I have a feeling she's not thinking about her burgundy jumpsuit any more.

As we walk toward the storage warrens, she tells me about the enzymatic process that makes the sands of Bardazel and Iona halt the stasis kicked off by Blue. "The active ingredient is something native but very rare elsewhere," she says. "We thought for a long time it was only found on Bardazel. That's why that planet was increasingly used for Blue's development. It was considered safer for everyone, because the reversing agent was literally everywhere."

Safer except for the 200 people who were dosed and packed off to storage like surplus parts. The thought makes me wince.

"The ideal, of course, is to create both a modern antidote and an immunity serum that can work no matter which form of Blue we're presented with," Fallon continues. "If all the things I requested from Goods have been delivered, I should be able to formulate a test batch quickly."

I almost do a cartoon-style double-take. "But weren't you waiting for a package to replace the contents of the Sprites you lost?"

Fallon's smile evolves into a smirk. "Well, not exactly," she says. "Not having the samples makes things more complicated and a bit riskier, but not impossible. I've been working on the antidote formulation since I got here, using computer modeling. I made a lot of progress during my house arrest because I didn't have to be running around pretending to be doing something else. That was kind of a godsend, honestly."

I don't know whether to jump for joy or strangle her. I finally opt for something in-between.

"Why in the world would you lie about something like that?" I ask.

Fallon smooths her hands against the sides of her standard-issue cargo pants, somehow magically making them look much nicer than mine. "Truthfully, I wasn't sure which team your friend Graham was on," she says, "and sometimes I'm still not. But I'm confident at least that he's not the person I'm supposed to be tracking, even though he could still be involved in some other way. Oh good, there's Fanny with my things. Excellent."

Before I can ask anything further, she's running across the sand toward the entrance of our storage warren, where Fanny is just arriving with a loaded hover-flat. We enter the warren, and we proceed down one of the radial hallways to Number 4, a large unit on par with Number 8. Several autoflats have already been here and deposited the cargo Fallon ordered from Goods, Security, and Clinical. A makeshift testing lab is beginning to take shape.

Fallon mutters criticisms to herself as she inspects the deliveries. "This is workable," she finally says. "What's the security on this unit?"

"Maybree has already set it so that only your credentials and mine open it," I confirm. "And we now have additional security on the warren's main entry, thanks to our little adventure with Quimby last night. Only pod members can enter, and every entry will be tracked."

Fallon nods approvingly. "Let's get this ready, shall we?"

As we get into a rhythm of unboxing and unpacking, I try to steer our conversation back toward her earlier comment.

"You mentioned you were here to track someone?" I say casually as I pull some high-impact plexi beakers from a box.

"What? Oh right, yes. And Graham is not that someone."

"Who are you tracking?"

A stubborn expression crosses Fallon's face. She doesn't look up from the spectrometer she's calibrating. "That question is more challenging to answer than you might expect."

"Let's change it, then. *Why* are you tracking someone on Iona?"

"It's my job."

I give Fallon an exhausted look, which she returns. Finally, she throws up her hands in surrender and drops her smug expression.

"Oh, all right, fine. It's all supposed to be on a need-to-know basis, but since I'm already considered an outlaw, I won't get into any *more* trouble for telling you," she says. "Soon after I got here, I found data suggesting the container that exploded and injured your friend was sent via a passlink from Bardazel. That means it was shipped to an off-planet holding facility *before* the transferees moved here, then relabeled and sent to Iona once they'd landed. My mother believes it was sent by the same person who managed to steal the Blue on Bardazel and who apparently later dosed Arden's people at the Compound. We're confident that person is on Iona now. But I can't find him."

"What do you mean, can't find him? We did detailed intake for every single person who came over from Bardazel," I say.

"I know, I've seen all your intake data," Fallon confirms. "He most likely came to Bardazel very late, in the last couple of weeks before the mass dosing, and went immediately to the Compound. He appears to have kept a very low profile. He's on the transporter manifest as boarding for Iona with the rest of the population, but that's the last place he shows up. There's no record of his arrival being processed, although no one remained on the transport ship or went anywhere other than Iona from Bardazel."

"You know who he is?"

"I know his name," Fallon says, frowning, "but that's not as useful as you might think. I originally thought Graham was the person pulling the strings here. I'm still not sure he isn't part of the scheme in some way, but I can see that squeaky-clean conscience of his would never let him be the mastermind of something like this, he's just not ruthless enough. Our target definitely had inside assistance from someone, because he wouldn't have been able to get off Bardazel without a full working set of credentials. *Someone* had to help him get those. He left Bardazel as one person but arrived on Iona as someone else. The trail goes cold somewhere in between."

I stare at Fallon meaningfully, waiting. At first, she seems blank to my expectations, then rolls her eyes. "*Fine*," she snaps, her voice crackling with annoyance. "We can't let this get out until I'm certain where he is, because he literally could be *anyone*. The man we're looking for is Kerrit Arduval."

"Arduval!" I blurt out in surprise. "As in Karloa Arduval?"

"Yes, as in Karloa Arduval. He's her older brother."

"How can you *not find him*?" I ask, incredulous. "Even if he's impersonating someone else, other people from Bardazel must know him. Or must at least suspect he's not the person he's pretending to be."

Fallon gives me a long-suffering look like she's about to explain to a toddler yet again why the sky is blue.

"He didn't simply get someone else's credentials, he *played the part*," she says. "He probably lived a double life, both at the Compound and away from it. People on Bardazel who knew him as his assumed identity weren't surprised to see him come to Iona because they'd never known him as anyone else. The only people who can identify him as Kerrit Arduval were at the Compound, and they're all in stasis. Our only chance is his sister. If we can revive her, she can identify him, and we can nail his ass to the proverbial wall."

"Isn't it likely *she* got those credentials for him?" I ask. "Why would she rat him out now?"

"From the records we have, they've had a contentious history and were severely estranged. Perhaps she helped him under duress, or because she believed he sincerely wanted a new life. Or maybe she didn't help him at all. We can't know without asking her."

A switch flips in my mind; I understand Karloa Arduval better than ever before.

"I think she knew what he was up to, both on Bardazel and here," I say, and Fallon stops rattling around with the equipment she's assembling and looks at me in a completely new way. "She might have tried to talk him out of his plan.

And she knew that made her a target after she arrived here. God, now it all makes sense."

"That's an interesting theory," Fallon says. "I hadn't really looked at her behavior here, since she wasn't even on Iona for 24 hours before she got dosed."

"She was in utter fear from the moment she arrived. We thought it was us, but she may actually have been afraid of her brother and what he might do to her and anyone close to her," I explain. "At one point, we thought she was trying to dose the other Bardazelians, because Wenda literally caught her trying to pour something down Hinn's throat."

"What?" Fallon drops the mechanism she's been adjusting with a clatter and crosses the room to me in three strides. "Wenda caught her doing *what*?"

I recount the story Wenda told me: Karloa's strange statements about the food, the store of Bardazelian 'supplements' she claimed to have brought, the liquid she was trying to pour down Hinn's throat. Fallon hangs on every word and literally squeaks when I finish the tale.

"That explains everything!" She's nearly shouting. "Where are those supplies she mentioned? Are they back at the pod?"

"Everything she brought is here in the warren," I say. "What are you so excited about?"

"Show me her stuff."

"That seems like an invasion of privacy," I mutter.

Fallon goes off like a lander marking altitude.

"We. Are. Supposed. To. Be. Dead," she says, glaring at me. "I am asking to see the belongings of a woman who is in full-on stasis because she may have brought with her something that could help us foil the person who *wants* us dead. Her privacy at this point is—*has to be*—secondary."

When I don't immediately respond, she groans and looks up at the ceiling for a beat. When she speaks again, her tone is modulated and calmer, but still urgent.

"My guess is that she wasn't trying to dose Hinn with Blue," she says in a quiet, level voice. "My gut feeling is that it was a chemical cocktail that makes the person who consumes it *immune* to Blue. That's why the mole is so cavalier about handling the spheres; he's immune to what's inside them. Do you not understand how important this is?"

I have the distinct impression that what March really wants to do is grab my head and slam it against the just-assembled lab table between us. Instead, she stands in front of me, her arms limp at her sides, looking into my face with all the calm seriousness she can muster.

I walk to the unit door, and say, "This way."

32

KARLOA'S HEAVY BLACK BACKPACK is sitting exactly where it's been since the day I assigned her a cubby. Because we can't be sure it doesn't contain Blue, I get a hover-flat to collect it and float it down to the share.

Fallon stares at it cautiously, as if rethinking the value of opening it immediately without preliminary inspection.

"We probably shouldn't open this in the public space," she says, mirroring my thoughts.

"Number 8?" I suggest. "That seems to be where we keep all our potentially deadly things these days."

Fallon nods her acquiescence. I tap the coordinates into the hover-flat, and it sails down the appropriate hallway, stopping at the door and waiting for me. The instant I open the door, Maybree pings me on my headset.

"You going into Number 8?" she asks. I confirm that we are, and she audibly sighs with relief.

Once inside, I heave my own sigh of relief when I see everything as we left it the night before. Spheres are still carefully stacked, wrapped in the elegant purple fabric. Hover-flats are all accounted for and lifeless in their assigned positions. On the far side of the room in the shadows sits the crate, conspicuous and silent.

The hover-flat settles and gently deposits Karloa's backpack in front of us. Fallon inspects the sinister-looking black bag for a moment, and we exchange glances. After a deep breath, I reach for its controls.

When I press the blue button in the pack's center, its straps whir to life, dropping the sheath enshrouding the bag and revealing a multitude of side pockets and chambers all stuffed with goods. Another press retracts the flap covering the primary compartment of the pack, leaving it wide open. Fallon and I both lean forward to look inside. The lights of the unit glint off a number of teardrop shaped vials made of crystal acrylic, each containing a sparkling clear liquid.

Gingerly, Fallon lifts out one of the palm-sized vials and holds it up to the light. The liquid creates a prism effect, casting dancing rainbows across her face.

"Bam," she whispers, then casts a sideways glance at me and clarifies, "exactly what I was hoping for."

We empty the central section of the pack carefully. In the end, it contains 48 sealed vials. Each contains perhaps two ounces of clear, slightly viscous liquid.

"If this is what I think it is, one vial would provide immunity for a few months," Fallon explains. "The amount here represents either a short period of immunity for a lot of people, or a lot of immunity for a few people. She had this, yet she's lying in stasis in clinical. I wonder why she didn't consume any herself?"

"We originally believed she dosed herself with Blue in protest," I say. "Maybe she avoided taking this and dosed herself instead to keep anyone from asking her questions about her brother."

"Or to protect herself from him," Fallon suggests. "A kind of preemptive strike."

She's right. Either is possible, depending on how supportive of or afraid of her brother Karloa might have been.

We break down the side pockets of the backpack and find protein bars and food supplements, plus an odd array of items that suggest the bag was put together in a hurry—gloves, scissors, strapping tape, and a small delicate purple spray bottle with a fancy top.

I pull it out and hold it up to the light. "I didn't figure Karloa for the perfume type," I say.

In a flash, Fallon snatches it from my hand.

"That's not perfume," she says. "I'm willing to bet the entire planet that's weaponized Blue. And it's been used. See?"

She points to a faint stain on the glass slightly above the level of the liquid.

My mind is spinning. If Karloa dosed herself with this small pretty bottle, she must have had an accomplice who put the bottle back afterwards. If someone else dosed her, that person got access to the warren and replaced the bottle here. I shudder involuntarily. My reverie of doom is interrupted by Fallon's voice.

"What the flaming dust is this?"

She pulls a small electronic device from one of the pack's side pockets. As she lifts it, my headset erupts with feedback so severe I rip it off my head as fast as I can.

"We should get Maybree over here to take a look at this," I say. "Put it down."

Fallon does, and the feedback subsides instantly. I pull my headset back on and ping Maybree. By the time she joins us, Fallon and I have transferred the vials of immunity serum along with the small spray bottle into Fallon's storage unit. We leave the pack and its mysterious electronic device in Number 8.

Which, as it turns out, isn't mysterious to Maybree at all.

"That's a mat tracker," she says, looking at it nestled in the side pocket. "We don't usually see those in personal effects, but you never know. Some people are super-careful about their stuff."

"It caused holy hell with my headset when Fallon picked it up," I say.

"That means it's transmitting a signal," she says, her brow creasing. "Hang on."

She reaches into the pocket and lifts out the mat tracker. Immediately my headset starts to squeal. I take it off while Maybree picks apart the little device.

"There's no question that it's actively transmitting an alert every time it's disturbed," she says. "But Karloa is in stasis. Who's on the receiving end of the signal?"

I trade glances with Fallon. "My question is, how did it get it in here in the first place?" Fallon says. "When was this pack placed in a cubby?"

I think back. "It would have been the day after she went into stasis," I say. "I put it into storage myself. Before that, it was sitting out in the share with the other Bardazelians' things, but only for a day or so."

"Who can get into the warren? Only podmembers?"

"Only podmembers now. We changed it after the Number 8 debacle. Originally it was podmembers and other storage administrators, who are usually pod leaders."

"Pod leaders like you and who else?" Fallon prods.

"Me, Macha, Pauly when he was able and later ... oh ..." I look at Fallon. Her eyes are sparkling fiercely.

"Graham," I say, feeling my stomach drop.

"But he wouldn't have, would he? That doesn't seem like him," objects Maybree. "He can't be a bad guy. He took such good care of us on Bardazel."

"And he also ran an illegal offensive weapons development program on Bardazel, and lied to us about that for months," I say. "I don't want him to be responsible either, Maybree. But the possibility exists."

The three of us stand silently around the backpack, staring at the mat tracker. Maybree's fallen, sad expression matches my own. Fallon's is more one of triumph.

"I *knew* it," she says, her voice hoarse with excitement. "He's got to be involved in some way."

I'm not so certain. I remember Graham's protestation that he's not my enemy, his genuine alarm at the sight of the spheres in the credenza, his self-condemnation of his role with the Company's clandestine program. And he was nowhere near Karloa when the twins found her, unresponsive and blue, in our pod's Common Room. Logistically, it doesn't make sense.

"I don't think that's right," I say. Fallon looks at me like I must be missing at least half my brain. "It seems a little too convenient, don't you think? Someone *wants* us to believe that Graham is involved. There must be something obvious that we're missing. But I can't quite sort out what."

As I reorganize Karloa's pack, I take a moment to consider each odd, random-seeming item she brought with her. I feel like they're all clues, but we don't understand them. I load the bag onto the autoflat and send it back to Karloa's assigned cubby, leaving the mat tracker on the floor in Number 8.

"We have to try to revive Karloa as soon as possible. No arguments," I tell Fallon as we leave the share. Her face shows her trademark annoyance at being given orders, and she crosses her arms over her chest in a defensive posture, the fingertips of her right hand beating a pattern into the beige fabric of her service jacket. She might not like that I didn't accept her theory of Graham's involvement on its face, but for once, she's not trying to insult her way out of doing what we both understand is imperative.

The next few days are somber and strained in our pod. I question Holly a little more about how she found the sphere and even ask her to think back to the day Karloa collapsed, but she has no new insight to offer. I wander into the room Karloa was first assigned when she arrived, which later became Arden and Parker's room and now belongs to Hinn and Parker, but there are no clues to be found there either. Karloa wasn't on Iona long enough to put any personal belongings into her room—or maybe had known she wasn't going to be around to use them anyway. Fallon spends most of her time at the warren, trying to untangle whatever mysteries the materials we took from Karloa's backpack might hold. I occasionally come across her screaming verbal abuse into her holo at someone about her impending retrieval. When I tell Arden about what we've found that night before bed, I'm saddened when his first conclusion is the same as Fallon's.

"I don't understand why you don't see the connection," he says after my initial objection to his theory. "Are you protecting Graham because of your personal relationship?"

"I'm not protecting him, and we don't have a *personal relationship*, whatever you mean by that," I say with more than a hint of irritation in my voice. "He's a friend. He's trying to help. And even you know that. You like Graham."

"I do like him, but I can't discount any possibility. You don't know what he was like out there."

"I don't know what *you* were like out there," I say, eyeing him levelly. "I'm not completely disregarding the idea that he has something to do with this—you should notice I'm not telling Graham about everything we found in Karloa's backpack. The key to sorting this out is finding a way to revive Karloa. She may be the one who can settle it once and for all."

His mouth draws into a tight line, and he crosses his arms over his chest. "You're right about that," he admits. "But don't be surprised if Graham figures into this somehow in the end. The Thorn Collective is aggressively entrepreneurial. If they somehow got wind of an opportunity like this sand, they'd move to get a foot in the door and exploit it as rapidly as possible. And Graham would be a logical key element."

I study Arden, his rigid body posture, his excessive agitation. "What does any of this have to do with you?"

"Nothing and everything," he responds. "The Company has multiple internal stakeholders, and right now they're all fighting over the fate of this planet. Departments are becoming factionalized; collaboration is breaking down. And this is just the start of what's to come."

"Is the Company splitting apart?" I never imagined, after more than two hundred years of dominance in this system, that the Company might be in danger of dissolution.

"Changing is a better word." His posture softens slightly; I'm not sure if he means what he's saying or just attempting to make it sound less terrifying. "It might lead to dramatic improvements. Many of us on the inside have been working toward that for a long time. But it could also be change for the worse. I believe the former is much more likely than the latter, but with other families and corporate entities getting involved, things have become unpredictable."

It's not the most settling thought to have floating through your mind when you're trying to drift off to sleep. But my unsettled night turns out to be nothing compared to the next morning.

As is his habit, Arden is up before the rising chimes, but he's far from alone this morning. There's a commotion in the common room that almost shakes the walls of our pod. Everyone not already up soon gathers, some still in pajamas and robes, to see what the fuss is about.

It turns out to be directly related to Fallon March. I peer around the edge of our hallway's entrance into the common room just in time to see a holo tablet go flying across the room, followed by a stream of expletives. Sure enough, Fallon stands on the other side of the room, her hands clenched and her face a mask of rage. She's still shrieking, but she's abandoned words and is resorting to banshee-like sounds.

I decide to be the brave one, and step into the room.

"Fallon? What's wrong?" I ask, in the same tone I'd use with a rabid animal. Fallon turns toward me; her face is flushed and her eyes rimmed with red.

"Three days," she barks out, half shouting, half sobbing. "The sonofabitches will be here to get me in three days."

"The recall?" I ask, and she nods, her fists still tightly clenched at her sides. "I thought you were going to fight it."

"I did," she says miserably. "I lost."

Those of us who know what Fallon has been doing in her long hours at the storage warren—Maybree, Wenda, Arden, and I—look at each other. We know what she's thinking. Three days is not going to be enough time.

"Let me see if I can help," says Arden, and Fallon shoots him a look that is by turns sad, appreciative, and irritated. "I know, I know," he responds, "but I might be able to pull enough strings to buy you some more time."

"What about Graham?" I ask, and Arden winces. "His family is powerful. If they're interested, this could be something they might want to see happen as well," I whisper. "Let's use every potential asset now. This might be our last chance."

"You're right," Arden says, sighing. "I'll talk to him, but I don't want to tell him everything."

"Fine," I say. "Just see if there's anything he can do."

I turn back to Fallon. "You can get this done in the time you have," I say. "We'll do anything you need to help move it along."

Fallon finally takes a deep breath and unclenches her fists. "You're right, I need to try," she says. "And sorry, to whoever's holo that was." She drops into her place at our long table, looking uncharacteristically hopeless. She doesn't even protest when Holly, after placing a fresh cup of coffee in front of her, gives her an impromptu hug.

I make her eat some breakfast and grab something quick for myself. Arden disappears back into our room to tap some of his contacts, and Maybree and Wenda make it clear they plan to accompany us to the storage warren. I remember an old adage about how a ship with too many engines can't fly in a straight line. Maybree is finally convinced to go back to her office at Security. Wenda can't be dissuaded, however, so the three of us wind up tramping across the lot toward the storage warrens.

"How much progress have you made?" Wenda asks Fallon.

"Not enough," Fallon says, and for a moment I detect disappointment in the set of her features. "I'm trying to break down the components of the serum we got out of Karloa's pack, but there's something strange about it. It's not consistent from vial to vial—different viscosities, different reactive properties—I don't understand the point of the variations or why there would be so many of them."

"Different immunity serums for different forms of Blue?" I propose, but Fallon shakes her head.

"Not likely," she says. "Immunity only has to prevent the initial action from kicking off. It doesn't make sense."

We credential into the warren. Maybree hails me and says, "Three into the storage warren on your badge," and I confirm. "Number 4 is next," I say, and Maybree responds, "I'll be looking for it."

The change in Number 4 from the day I helped Fallon start her set-up is dramatic. From a single metal table, some crates, and an autoflat full of what looked like random parts, a miniature-but-fully-functioning lab has emerged. In addition to all of the basics, Maybree has managed to scavenge top of the line analyzers and processors. Fallon has all the tools. Now what we need is a little bit of luck to put together the pieces of this puzzle.

We spend a few hours cataloging vials of serum and analysis results, running comparison algorithms, and researching components. Fallon seems buoyed by having permission to boss Wenda and me around, so I don't object. But test after test ends with Fallon frowning at her results.

"Is there a different way to go about what you're doing?" I ask. "Can you start with what you've already developed instead of trying to understand the serums?"

Fallon is lost in thought for a moment. "I initially thought it would be too risky, but I'm at my wits' end," she says. "I'd have to use live Blue, but it feels like the only option left. If I pursue this, you two have to leave. It's just too risky."

"Is there a possibility that it could work?" I ask.

Fallon presses her lips together into a thin line. "It might," she says. "I'll come closer with that than I will with this serum, because I don't know what I'm working with here. If I'm using live Blue, I might be able to guess the components of the serum based on the way they interact."

"Then do it, and we'll get out of here," I say. "But first, we're bringing you a huge tub of sand."

AFTER THE SAND IS delivered as promised, Wenda and I leave Fallon to her work and walk out into the pale Iona sunlight. Once back at the pod, I head into my room and hail Arden. "Any progress?" I ask.

"I'm not sure," he says. "I've called in some favors on the Tactical side to try to make things happen in Fallon's favor, but it's tense in the department already. High Defense seems poised for a takeover, so I'm probably going to be out of a job soon. But since I'm apparently now part of a band of anarchistic space punks causing havoc on Iona, I'm probably out of that job already."

"Then thank the stars you have three jobs," I say, and I hear him chuckle softly. "What about Graham? Did you speak to him?"

"I tried to casually chat him up about the family business and what's going on there, but as usual I can't read him when it comes to that," Arden replies. "He's incredibly circumspect about his relations at home. He did seem concerned about Fallon getting pulled in front of the Board, though, so I hope if there's something he can do, he'll do it."

"Tell him we're counting on him," I say. "We need all the help we can get."

Having been tossed out of Fallon's experiments and with nothing on the work docket for me, I decide to pay a visit to my private project space. My last haul of cast-offs was so rich that it's virtually finishing itself, and I've even been able to make a few upgrades to the original plan. I only need to add a few touches and my project will be complete.

I make my way past the landing pads and up across the bluff to the main entry. When I step inside, I'm almost breathless with excitement. If I can lose myself in this for a few hours, I'll be done. I can't help but smile as I wipe my palms across my tan cargo pants and get to work. I might have one success today, even if I can't tell anyone about it yet.

It's almost dinner time when I finish up and leave my project space for the pod. Halfway home, I get a hail from Maybree. She's so wound up she can barely speak.

"I got a ping from the crate, I'm looking at the data now," she says. "Something's changed. I thought maybe it was an aberration from all the to-do in Number 8 the other night, but there's no way that could have affected it like this."

"What do you mean?" I ask. "Has someone tried to open it?"

"No, no—something is happening *inside* the crate," she says, her exuberance barely contained. "The environmental mix has changed; the CO_2 levels are creeping up. It's so slow it's almost undetectable, but it's consistent."

I'm still not following. "CO_2 in levels high enough to be dangerous?" I ask. "Is it likely to explode?"

"It's not that," Maybree says, her voice crackling with excitement. "It's like something in there is *breathing*. But the oxygen levels are so low that it can't support anything alive for long. I'm bringing the scanner over. I think we should open it as soon as we can."

I hail the rest of my investigation team to let them know what's happening. If what's in this crate is similar to what was in the one Pauly opened, it could be another important break that we desperately need.

Inside the warren I first stop by Number 4. "Fallon," I call, and she opens the door. Her face is ringed in sweat but she's smiling. "Perfect timing," she says. "I'm getting somewhere. But I'm going to need more Blue from Number 8."

"That's where I'm headed," I tell her. "Come on, let's get you what you need."

In Number 8, Fallon selects a sphere from the collection and cradles it against her chest.

"If you get to a stopping point, we're about to open that up," I say, gesturing toward the crate. She looks at it closely now, and her eyebrows arch up in surprise.

"Where did this come from?" she asks.

"Not sure," I respond. "Sender is a generic company address."

"Great flaming stars, that's the second crate," she says. "So that's where it went! Why do you have it?"

"I don't know what you're talking about, but I have it because it was addressed to me by name."

Fallon looks shocked. "The crate that exploded—remember that I told you it came through a passlink from Bardazel? There were two crates on the export statement. This must be the second crate. But addressed to you? Why would it be addressed to you?" Her face reflects her confusion.

"Your guess is as good as mine," I say. "I have no idea who sent it or why, or what it contains. We've been monitoring it, hoping it's not going to explode on its own. But Maybree just pinged me and let me know it appears something inside is producing carbon dioxide. She's on the way with the scanner. Everyone's on the way, in fact."

"CO2? Like ...?" Fallon exhales dramatically.

"Yep. Maybree's words were *it's breathing.*"

She smirks as she begins inspecting the crate. "It does have an enviro attached to it," she says. "But the environmental mix isn't going to support any kind of life very well. Otherwise, it's very similar to the other one."

She taps its lid with one long red fingernail.

"There could be extremely useful material in here. If its contents are also like the one that exploded, that could be very helpful indeed," she says.

"I'm aware. But we could be very dead indeed, if opening it goes the same way," I point out.

Fallon rolls her eyes in exasperation.

"Scan it. Verify that it's not an explosive. That's the easy part. Then get it open," she snaps. "I only have two and a half days left. If there's something in there that I can use, I want it now. Let me know what happens." She stalks away to her space with her sphere of Blue. I'm not sure whether to be happy or disappointed that she appears to be her old self again.

It takes about ten minutes for everyone to assemble in Number 8. Maybree is last to arrive, with Security's most powerful scanner and a collection of other equipment on a hover-flat. She's reviewed the data extensively but sets her holo up on the flat for anyone else who wants to take a look. "We're a go on it," she says confidently. "I'm finding nothing that suggests it has any explosive triggers, mechanisms, or contents."

We all look at each other tensely. "Go ahead with the scan," I say. Within minutes she's set up and is ready to run the crate through an initial survey.

"Anything you know of ever explode from being scanned?" I ask Arden, as he presses in behind me to watch.

"Um, just a few things," he says. He's not smiling as he says it. We both instinctively take a large step back from the crate and scanner.

"It's probably not a bad idea for everyone to go out into the hallway until this process completes," Macha calls, ever the voice of reason.

"Yeah, go ahead, and I'll come out as soon as the scan starts," Maybree says, her enthusiasm momentarily tempered by worry and perhaps the memory of the day that Pauly was hurt. We dutifully herd into the hallway and wait for Maybree to join us. We stand quietly while she tracks the scanner's progress on her holo. The device both creates a visual representation of what is in the crate while also sampling the internal atmosphere for telltale chemical signatures that could indicate a bomb or explosive materials. It takes only a few minutes, and to everyone's relief, completes without incident.

We file back into the room and Maybree pulls up the data on her holo. The visual flickers for a moment, then finally resolves. Floating in the air in front of us is a three-dimensional representation of the container's contents.

Everyone lets out a gasp of astonishment. Macha is the first to speak.

"That appears to be a *person*," she says, blinking.

The scanner has detected no explosive components or caustic agents, so I gingerly approach the crate and use my credentials to begin the opening sequence. After tapping in the right codes, the lid slowly slides back without issue. We all cluster around the crate to have a look.

Inside is a man, knees drawn up toward his chest and hands placed comfortably under his head. He looks to be about fifty, medium height and build, with shoulder-length black hair shot through with silver. He's wearing the standard-issue clothing of Bardazel, along with a woven leather bracelet on one wrist.

He's also a now-familiar shade of turquoise.

Macha calls for a hover gurney to be dispatched immediately.

"Does anybody know him?" I ask. "Graham? Is he one of yours, or just dressed like one of yours?"

Graham shakes his head. "I may have seen him at some point, but I don't recognize him," he says. "Obviously, he's been dosed, but I don't recall seeing him at the Compound either. Arden?"

Arden leans over the crate and studies the man's face. "He's not EA," he says. "I have no idea who he is."

"It's too bad. He looks friendly," Fanny says, a sad tinge in her voice. I know she's thinking of Pauly. But she has a point. Even in stasis, the man's face is relaxed and pleasant, as if he's asleep and having the most wonderful dream.

When the gurney arrives, we help the technicians lift him out of the crate and position him securely. We then search for any hint of his identity. His pockets yield no papers, and no credentials—there isn't even a name on his jacket. The crate is similarly devoid of clues and holds nothing more. His identity is a complete mystery.

"And you don't know him?" Arden asks me. I shake my head no. I know I've never seen him before. "What would make someone send him to you?"

I honestly don't know, and all I can muster is another shake of my head.

"Maybe more psychological warfare?" Wenda suggests.

"This crate arrived early on. We didn't know what Blue was, we'd never seen it, we weren't in any kind of conflict, and the Bardazelian transferees had only been here for a day," I said. "If we'd opened it then, it would have been a mystery, but it wouldn't have meant anything to us."

"Maybe it was about the Bardazelian transferees," Wenda says. "At least some of them knew about Blue and what happened in the Compound. Maybe it was sent to intimidate them. Or make us seem in league with the Company."

"Why not send it to Graham, then?" I ask. "What would be the point of sending it to me?"

"A scare tactic?" Arden proposes. "Or to encourage whoever was in the warehouse to open that crate and create the explosion that set all this off to begin with."

We're all lost in our thoughts of rationale and conspiracy. After Macha departs for Clinical with the mystery man, we close the storage units and leave the warren as a group. Even Fallon comes along—despite her protestations, we convince her that she at least needs to eat. As Maybree and the others chatter with speculation about who the mystery man could possibly be, Fallon casts me a knowing glance. I know who *she* thinks it is—the man whose identity Kerrit Arduval usurped. But why would Arduval take the risk of sending that person to Iona? And how would he settle on me as the recipient?

I'm shaken out of my contemplation by the appearance of Graham at my side.

"I understand Fallon's having difficulties," he says, smiling conspiratorially.

"If what I've heard is right, we all are," I respond. "Congratulations on being promoted to the status of anarchist, although that's probably not great for career advancement overall."

"I've been labeled worse. In fact, I've been labeled worse recently." He looks over my head at Arden walking on my left. Arden doesn't acknowledge the remark, but his eyes narrow and his expression becomes steely.

"At any rate," Graham continues, "I wanted to make sure you knew where my loyalties lie. I'll do whatever I can to preserve this planet and to bring Pauly and

Karloa back. It may not be much, but I'm happy to contribute. You don't even have to ask. And there's no subtext to this. It's simply what I need to do."

His expression is soft, and for a moment I see that lovely man who walked with me under the stars and once kissed me on a pile of pillows in the Star Parlor. I feel a pang—of guilt, of regret, I'm not sure which. It must show on my face, because the same emotions briefly parade across his features before he takes my hand, squeezes it, then trots away to engage Fallon in an animated conversation. Before long the two of them are diverging from the group, and as the rest of us enter the pod courtyard, I see them circle around the building and continue walking, heading for the northern ridge.

Dinner comes and goes without sight of them again. Fanny departs for her pod after the evening meal, and Maybree brings us all up to speed on the latest official Company communiques highlighting the "lawless behavior" of "a handful of reckless individuals who threaten the stability and safety of the population of Iona".

"I'm not included," she says, pouting. "You got mentioned by name."

"I'm sure it's just an oversight," I say. "You're not the only one they missed. They left out Fanny and Wenda, and I have it on good authority that they're reckless individuals too."

"Shhh," Wenda says, sitting down next to Maybree and tucking an arm through hers. "We're flying under the radar."

We all laugh a little, but it sounds a bit forced. We know there may be some serious consequences ahead that we might not even be able to imagine. The Company can be your very best friend, but if it finds it more expedient, it can also be your very worst nightmare.

34

THE NEXT MORNING THE rising chimes have barely begun when I hear Fallon's voice in the common room shouting, "Where are they? Are they up yet?" She doesn't wait for Hinn's answer before running down the hallway and barging into our room.

"Hey," objects Arden, trying to cover himself with whatever items first come to hand, which unfortunately turn out to be a washcloth and one of my fuzzy pink night socks.

Fallon looks him up and down briefly before rolling her eyes dismissively and focusing on me.

"Get dressed as fast as you can and come to the warren," she says. "I've got something to show you." She's almost out the door again when she pops her head back in and says to Arden, "You can come too. Don't wear that, though. Pink's not your color," and disappears.

"Was that a joke?" I ask, astonished. "Did Fallon March just make a joke?"

"Maybe she got laid last night," Arden mutters, dropping the sock on the floor and casting around for some actual clothing. "I don't think they ever came back to the pod."

"I don't know what they were doing up on the ridge, but I'm pretty sure it wasn't *that*," I say. "Although some people might be into sand, sharp rocks, and plants bristling with spikes."

From the Common Room, I hear Fallon shout impatiently, "Hurry up, dammit!"

"Ah, no, my mistake. She clearly didn't get laid," Arden growls. He's managed to get his pants on but is still rubbing sleep out of his eyes with both fists. I toss him a shirt from our closet and pull one on myself. We're in the common room inside of three minutes, but Fallon is pacing the floor as if we'd kept her waiting for hours.

"Let's go," she barks, as soon as she sees us. "I got you a scooter." She runs out and jumps onto one of two scooters poised beside the pod's main entry and is away. We hurry to mount up and follow.

We arrive at the warren and enter Number 4 to find a demonstration set up. A small piece of unidentifiable blue tissue lies in a dish on one of her workstations. She positions us where we have a clear view but aren't standing too close, then opens one of a series of small vials lying next to the dish. She takes two drops of a swirling opalescent liquid from the vial with a dropper and gently applies them to the tissue directly. A small puff of steam rises and gradually the tissue begins to change color. After a minute, it's pink and translucent again. She pokes it with the curved end of her dissection probe. It's soft and flexible, no longer the quality of stone.

She looks up at Arden and me, an expectant look on her face. "Well?" she asks.

"It looks like it works as far as you've gone," Arden says. "But what about on something with complex systems?"

"Keep watching," she says. "I'm not done yet."

She turns to a series of containers behind her, and after a few seconds of rummaging, selects one and places it on the table. When she opens it, we see it contains a small sand lizard common on Iona. The difference is that this lizard's grayish-brown coloration has been changed to a shining turquoise blue.

"You dosed a lizard?" I ask.

"Scientific necessity," she says. "He was a pain in the ass to catch, too. But let me show you what we've got here."

She removes the top of another vial. This time she pours the liquid over the lizard. Again, there is a puff of steam, and his coloration begins to transform.

Although he's soon grayish brown again and moving his head from side to side, something's wrong. He doesn't appear able to get enough equilibrium to stand or walk, and lies on his belly in the tray, panting. His eyes begin to flutter, and his breathing becomes increasingly irregular. I'm preparing myself for his inevitable demise when Fallon intervenes, picking up the lizard in one gloved hand and using the other to squirt several drops of the liquid from a third vial into his mouth and nostrils.

At first, he responds as if he's drowning, shaking his head frantically. His eyes roll back for a second and he stops moving. But an instant later, his eyes snap into focus, and he leaps from her hand onto the table and then to the floor, scurrying off into the pile of containers to hide.

"Oh, that's fantastic!" I cry.

Arden is more skeptical.

"Okay," he says. "Lizard revived. Apparently. But how long does it last? And again, simple systems."

"I'm getting to that, Commander Pink Sock, just hold on," Fallon says. I can almost feel Arden blushing next to me and I hide a smile behind my hand. "I'll answer your questions after the next demo."

This time the container she extracts from the pile contains a mouse, its white fur a dramatic contrast with the turquoise blue of its skin.

"Where did you get a ..." Arden starts to ask but is stopped by the death glare Fallon fixes on him. "Never mind, proceed," he says, waving his hand in the air as if to wave away the question he was about to ask.

Fallon opens three new vials, set apart from the others she's shown us. She pulls some of the liquid from the first vial into a hypodermic needle and carefully injects it into a vein in the distal part of the mouse's tail. Almost immediately the vein grows pale, then slowly becomes a slender pinkish thread, weaving its way into the still-blue body of the mouse.

In a short time, the mouse begins to work its mouth and blink and the blue color of its skin starts to fade. It's still largely immobile, however. The transition is not nearly as dramatic as it was for the tissue, nor as complete as with the lizard, but Fallon is not yet done. She draws up a syringe of the shining fluid in the second vial and carefully squeezes it into the mouse's open mouth, toward the back of its throat, and places another drop into its nostrils. Finally, as the mouse begins to shake its head and make soft squeaks, she droppers liquid from the third vial into its mouth. The mouse swallows, and within ten minutes it's fully pink-skinned, squeaking and nibbling on the edge of the plastic container.

Fallon steps back from the table, one gloved hand on her hip, a smug and delighted expression on her face. "Well?" she says, looking from me to Arden. "And before you talk to me like I'm an idiot, I've done the calculations based on size and weight. There are going to be variables we may not be able to account for, but it will work on people. I'm sure of it."

I have a lot of questions; I'm sure Arden does too. But the moment deserves recognition that goes beyond the things we want to know. As I offer Fallon my most appreciative smile, Arden simply reaches across the lab table and earnestly shakes her hand.

Fallon beams.

"Do you have what you need to make enough of this?" I ask.

She nods. "I pinned down these tests and got almost everything set overnight," she says. "I'll be ready to shift it all over to Clinical in a couple of hours. Macha will hail you when it's time."

Arden and I return to our pod. I'm carrying the container holding the little white mouse, which Fallon pressed into my hands as we left, saying, "Please give him to Holly as a present from me. I'm sorry I'm too busy to do it myself." The mouse seems fully recovered and quite energetic, squeaking and skittering around in the small box as if nothing was ever amiss.

"I hope it's this successful on our people," I say with longing. I know that might be too much to hope for. Myriad things could go wrong; despite multiple computer models run in multiple different scenarios that yield overall positive results, sometimes things end in failure. But there are no other options for testing, and we're out of time. If we want to revive our friends, it needs to happen now. No one else on Iona has the knowledge to direct the administration of these antidotes or has any idea what to do if something goes wrong, and we're all painfully aware that Fallon could be pulled off the planet forever as early as tomorrow.

Holly is beyond delighted with her gift and sets about creating a mouse palace in her room, while Hinn digs through the pantry for mouse-appropriate snacks. "That's going to be the most spoiled mouse on *any* planet," Arden observes. For my money, the mouse has earned all the privileges he's about to receive.

"He's lucky," I say. "Maybe we will be, too."

It's early afternoon by the time I get the hail from Macha. She's very specific about how she wants the work to unfold.

"This is still a highly experimental procedure that may yield unpredictable results," she tells me in a firm, non-negotiable tone. "It's a risky experiment and a clinical learning opportunity, not a viewing party. Fanny will be here for Pauly, and Graham will be here for Karloa. You're the appropriate choice to handle our mystery man, should he revive. This also means you accept the responsibility, as they will, for making possibly life-and-death decisions for him should anything go amiss during the process. Everyone else is welcome to wait downstairs, and we'll keep them informed. Any objection?"

Arden, predictably, wants a front-row seat, but Macha won't hear of it. Eventually he grudgingly agrees to her conditions, although he presses for and is finally granted, permission to stand in the hallway outside the suite as security.

When we walk into Clinical's lobby, we find Tommas escorting a visibly shaking Fanny. Wenda and Maybree stand anxiously next to the glass-walled garden, their hands clutched tightly together. Wenda mouths the words "good luck" to me as Arden and I ascend the stairs.

Pauly, Karloa, and our mystery man have all been moved into a single large surgical suite. Hovering drones track their every bodily function and vital sign, and holo readouts float above each prone figure.

Graham stands near the head of Karloa's bed. His eyes are red rimmed with exhaustion, but when he looks up and sees me in the doorway, he smiles. It's as though he's found—or made—peace with whatever demon has been eating away at him. He acknowledges Arden with a nod as well and a glimmer of respect and friendship passes between the two men. I kiss Arden on the cheek and step through the door, leaving him in the hallway. I then move to my post behind the head of our mystery man.

Fanny is last to arrive, walking up the stairs alone, her face pale and her hands still trembling. As she looks at Pauly, tears glisten in her eyes. Hopeful. Terrified.

"Good," Macha says. "We're all here. We can begin when you're ready, Fallon."

Fallon steps forward then, dressed in standard-issue Clinical green. Her lurid red nails are hidden by gloves, and she's pulled her hair back and tucked it under a surgical headband. Macha stands behind her with four medical techs; more await instructions at the back of the room. One holds a tray of human-sized syringes, needles, and bottles all pre-loaded with the serums we saw her use this morning.

"This is a multi-step process," Fallon explains. "Macha and I will administer the antidote's components three different ways to each patient. Between each round, we will monitor and wait. It won't be an instantaneous reversal, although we should observe some changes very quickly. But a full revival isn't likely for three to four hours. And it may take longer, or not happen at all. I want you all to be prepared."

She looks specifically at Fanny now.

"Pauly is a special case, Fanny," she says. "His injuries mean we have to take a slightly different tact for him in administering the antidote. I don't know how that might change things. But I'm hopeful, and we'll do our best to make things go smoothly." Fanny looks at the floor, takes a deep breath, then looks back into Fallon's eyes and nods.

Fallon looks over at Macha and confirms, "We're ready."

A technician hands Macha a tray containing three hypodermic needles. She takes one, removes the cap, and expresses the air bubbles. She moves from Karloa to the mystery man, administering injections into large veins in their arms.

Pauly's arms are too damaged from the explosion for that to be an option with him. When it's his turn, Macha takes the remaining hypodermic needle and inserts it in his upper chest, slightly below his collarbone and to the right. It's a bit of a struggle to get the hypo through at first, but she's eventually successful. She hands off the tray of hypodermics to a tech, turns to Fallon, and confirms, "First phase completed."

Within five minutes, all three patients' drones start to ping, reporting changes in blood pressure, temperature, heart rate, and respiration. Although small and incremental, they're all trending in the right direction. So far so good. Fallon studies the readouts intensely, taking notes on her holo and constantly scanning the changes.

The technicians monitoring each patient aren't relying only on drones and holo data, however. They actively stroke each patient's face, and occasionally use their fingertips to search for a pulse at the carotid artery. In all three patients, the blue color is beginning to fade.

"We'll decide when they're ready for the next dose based on their progress," Fallon says. "It will be different for each person."

The technician monitoring Karloa is the first to call for Fallon. She looks closely at Karloa's lips, running a finger between them, and gently moves Karloa's jaw from side to side.

"Good," she pronounces. "Just a few more minutes."

It's not long before Pauly's technician signals her. This time, Fallon is more animated. "Macha," she says, after feeling Pauly's jaw, "he's ready."

Macha quickly steps up to Pauly's bedside, syringe in her hand. She's accompanied by another tech who holds a freshly opened bottle of antidote. As Macha fills the syringe, Fallon gently manipulates Pauly's jaw until suddenly his mouth flops open and he takes a loud rasping breath.

Everyone in the room gasps. We all watch intently as Macha depresses the syringe and squirts the liquid into Pauly's mouth, aiming it toward the back of his throat. Fallon reaches over and begins to massage Pauly's neck gently; we see his Adam's apple slide slowly as he swallows once, then twice.

"Atta boy, Pauly," Fallon says softly. A technician hands her a dropper and she places a dozen drops of fluid into each of Pauly's nostrils. He sniffs and makes a small humming sound.

I'm on the verge of tears.

Macha and Fallon now move to Karloa and follow the same process. With each passing minute, her vitals become stronger and closer to normal.

"Right on track," Fallon says to Graham, and the two exchange small smiles.

The technician monitoring our mystery man at last calls for Fallon. She checks him quickly, then waves Macha over for his second dose. He's still much bluer than the other two patients, who are becoming more normal-colored with each passing minute.

Macha examines his vital signs and is satisfied. When he offers up a small burp in response to the antidote trickling down his throat, Fallon pats him on the shoulder and says, "Good man."

There is a longer interval before the final dose is given. Vital signs continue to improve, skin colors return to normal.

Karloa reaches the desired baseline first, and receives her third dose, this version slightly pinker than the one Fallon gave the mouse during her demonstration. The liquid is poured into her mouth from an acrylic cup; she swallows smoothly until the cup is empty and within moments her breathing returns to a normal rate for a healthy person at deep rest. The last of the blue color drains from the base of her nails, and the status monitor on the drone hovering over her shifts to the desired "normal parameters" green.

Graham lets out a long shaky breath. I can almost see the guilt and anguish leave his body, and I realize now that all this time he's felt personally responsible for what happened to Karloa, carrying the weight of both his role in developing the compound that was used against her and as a leader who failed to keep her from harm.

He exchanges looks with Fallon again. This time his expression is grateful and relieved.

Our mystery man progresses slower than the other two patients.

"Are you concerned about him?" I ask Fallon, but she shakes her head. "It's far too early to be worried," she says. "We have a long way to go yet."

I look down at his pleasant face, still slightly blue-tinged, and feel sad for him for a moment. There's no one to cheer for his recovery here, no one to worry. I wish more than anything I knew his name.

Finally, Fallon decrees him ready for his final dose. Once given, his vitals steadily improve. As he draws his first real breath on our planet, I lean over him and whisper, "I'm Faith. Welcome to Iona."

It's another twenty minutes before Pauly is given his third dose. Fallon is not happy with his baseline, but it's close enough. He, too, has no problem drinking down the last drop of antidote, but his vitals do not rebound as smoothly or completely as Karloa's. His heart rate and respiration improve, but his status monitor stays yellow.

Fanny looks disappointed, but Fallon encourages her. "There's still plenty of time, Fanny. He's making good progress."

The patients now need several hours to stabilize before Macha gives them a final cocktail of drugs to bring them back to full awareness. The technicians move the still-unconscious patients back into what has become Clinical's default Blue ward and connect them to a host of drones and monitors. Karloa's recovery remains particularly impressive, while Pauly and mystery man lag.

Despite her protestations, concern is etched on Fallon's face, and she parks herself in a corner with a holo, obsessively reviewing data and occasionally barking out questions to technicians.

Fanny, Graham, and I sit together in the opposite corner of the long room, behind the humming drones that continue to actively track the patients. Macha lets Arden join us. We are all exhausted and hungry to the point that we gratefully accept the auto trays from Clinical's evening meal service that Macha sends our way.

Two hours later, Pauly crashes.

One of the drones monitoring him emits a piercing shriek and begins flashing red. His mouth gapes open as he alternately struggles to draw a breath and goes preternaturally still. Fallon leaps into the middle of the crowd of technicians and starts shouting orders. Macha rushes in seconds later.

"Heart rate abnormal," Macha confirms, checking the screaming drone. "He's jumping from tachycardia to almost stasis levels."

Fanny hides her face and begins to cry.

Fallon swipes at the drone's floating holo display until she finds the 3-D real time image of Pauly's heart. We can see the chambers fluttering and spasming, dramatically out of rhythm. Deep in his left ventricle, there's a large bright blue spot that ebbs and flows with Pauly's gasping.

The two women put their heads together and confer, neither wearing a hopeful expression. A technician brings both a syringe and a hypodermic, which Fallon sets aside.

"We need to speak to Fanny privately," Macha says finally, and my heart drops.

"Please, let them stay," Fanny says, wiping tears from her face with the back of her hand. "I need them to stay."

Macha looks at Graham, Arden, and me, all wearing our heartbreak on our faces, and nods her permission.

"It's not good," Fallon says, speaking mostly to Fanny but addressing all of us. "The antidote hasn't completely purged the Blue from his heart. He won't make it through the revival process."

Fanny's hand covers her mouth, holding back the sobs that are threatening to overtake her entire body.

"Is there anything you can do?" she asks in a whisper.

Macha and Fallon exchange glances. It's Fallon who finally speaks.

"We can put him back into stasis until we figure out why this happened and what we can do about it."

Fanny's eyes widen and she draws a shaky breath. "But we might never be able to revive him."

"But he'll be alive," Fallon says. "At least he'll still be alive. And then we'll have time to try. If he stays like this, he'll be dead within hours, and there will be nothing we can do."

Fanny looks back at us, then at Pauly. With tears streaming down her cheeks unimpeded, she croaks out, "All right. Then that's what we have to do."

"One bonus," says Fallon. "We should be able to give him the awakening cocktail and bring him to consciousness so you can talk to him for a minute, if you like, before we send him back into stasis."

"It won't hurt him to do that?" Fanny asks.

"No, it won't. It will be a very brief time, though, then the Blue will take over."

"Yes, please, I want to speak to my brother."

One of the technicians passes Macha the hypodermic needle and she begins to work on Pauly while Fanny tries to wipe away her tears and get herself under control. Soon, Pauly relaxes, and his heartbeat and respiration begin to slow. Macha squirts the contents of the syringe into Pauly's mouth and gestures for Fanny to come close.

"He won't be able to see you, remember, but he'll feel it if you touch him, and he should be able to talk to you," she says. "He can probably hear you now. Go ahead."

Fanny, still visibly shaking, approaches the bed, and leans down so her mouth is near Pauly's ear. She strokes his cheek with her hand gently.

"Hey, you little rascal," she says. "It's me. I love you. Are you awake?"

A few seconds later, I hear Pauly's voice, fainter and quieter than I ever imagined it could be, say, "Hey, sister. I love you too. Who turned out the lights?"

"Nobody, silly. You're in Clinical and your eyes are covered so they can heal. Your arms are strapped down too, so you might not be able to feel them either. You were in an accident. Do you remember?"

"Accident. Kinda I remember. Everybody okay?"

"Yes, everybody's okay. You've been out for a while, and you'll be going back to sleep in a little bit so you can keep getting better, but I'll be here when you wake up again," Fanny says in a soft light voice, trying to sound conversational and calm despite the tears rolling down her face. "Don't worry about a thing. I'm leading the pod while you're recovering. Graham is filling in as Coordinator. Arden is doing great job with the Warehouse. Faith is keeping Maintenance on its toes."

"All good," Pauly says. His voice has already become noticeably weaker. He pauses several seconds before he speaks again.

"Your boyfriend," he murmurs, "needs to be good to you or he's in trouble with me."

"Don't worry about that either. I broke up with him."

"Good. Didn't like him. Didn't make you happy." Pauly is barely whispering now. Macha, whose eyes have stayed on the drone above Pauly's bed, moves forward and touches Fanny on the arm. Fanny looks up in comprehension, her face stricken with grief.

She plants a soft kiss on her brother's forehead.

"Macha's telling me you're about to go to sleep again. You rest easy, and get well, and remember I love you love you love you forever and to the stars, little brother," she says, her voice breaking as she speaks.

"I love you, Fanny. You always take care of me."

Pauly exhales deeply and the faint tinge of blue creeps up his neck and across his face, sealing him off from us for a second time.

Fanny bursts into inconsolable sobbing. Macha steps forward and wraps her in a hug. I can almost see Fanny as that little girl, holding the hand of her baby brother, waiting for him, walking with him, protecting him. They've laughed and cried together, fought with and for each other, and held each other close for more than half a century. Every other relationship on this planet seems superficial by comparison.

Meanwhile, Graham, Arden, and I are all wiping away tears, and even Fallon hides her face behind her holo for a moment until she can recompose herself.

Technicians reset the drones to track Pauly's stasis vitals. In a matter of hours, a Company skiff will be coming for Fallon, no doubt soon to be followed by a "Security Presence" to help quell the terrible "anarchists". I hope there might be some mercy yet in the Company's approach, as Arden has consistently tried to make me believe, but at this point all I can see is the same mindless apparatus that overtook Home World and resulted in the loss of my community, my home, my lover, my trust, and nearly my life.

After conferring, Fallon and Macha elect to give the other patients more time before waking them up. We leave together as a group, Graham walking with a protective arm around Fanny, who is still weeping softly.

Soon, Graham and Fanny branch off and head toward their pod while Fallon, Arden, and I continue toward ours. That's when Arden says quietly, "A communique came while you were working with the patients, Fallon. The Company transport's at Meridian Station. They'll send a skiff for you after the crew completes its mandatory rest break."

Fallon scowls. "So I have about 36 hours, give or take. Hopefully everyone will be awake and back to normal by then and you won't actually need me here anymore."

"We'll *always* need you here," I say. The comment is spontaneous, but as I say it, I know it's true.

Fallon snorts derisively and starts to respond, but I don't let her.

"I mean it," I say. "Look at yourself. You came here determined to get in and out as quickly as you could. You mistrusted everyone. You were isolated and suspicious. And now you have friends. You went out of your way and risked your career to help people you didn't even know, just because you thought you could.

You're part of us now. You might not want it or need it, but there will always be a place for you on Iona."

I can see Fallon trying to come up with a smart and dismissive comeback. Maybe she's too tired tonight or maybe we've all finally gotten through to her.

As we round the corner and cross into our pod's courtyard, she looks at me and simply says, "Thank you."

We say our goodnights and head off to our rooms. I tumble gratefully into our hammock and fall asleep even before Arden manages to crawl in beside me.

35

Morning arrives far too quickly, and I crawl out of our hammock feeling anything but rested. Arden is already dressed and out of the room. I take my time getting ready, washing my face, brushing my hair. The Company is coming, and my friends are in danger, and a traitor is about to be revealed. Iona could change into something I hardly recognize, as early as this afternoon.

The rest of the pod is bustling about as usual, but the atmosphere is unusually somber. A collection of particularly anxious people cluster together at the end of the table: Fallon, Arden, Maybree, and Wenda. The tension is thick and palpable.

"Tough night last night," Wenda says, slipping her arm around me as I sit down next to her.

"Yeah," I say with a sigh. "What's the plan for today?"

"Macha reports that the patients are doing well," Fallon says. "She's expecting us at Clinical to complete the process and wake them up at around 13:00 hours. Hopefully that will be before the Company jailers arrive to drag me away."

The knot in the pit of my stomach gets bigger and a heavy, uncomfortable silence descends over our group.

Fallon breaks it. "I'm getting ahead of myself and it's not helping," she says. "I'll be right back."

She rises from the table and trots down the hall to her room. When she returns, she's wearing a screaming pink lipstick that could only have come from Holly's stash, and she's carrying a flask not unlike Fanny's, along with five small cylindrical glasses.

314

"I propose a toast," she says, pouring a golden foamy liquid into each glass. She places one in front of each of us and takes the last one for herself. "My mother and father were born on Home World, but my mother's parents are from Gordonia, the newest Independent Core World in our system. Arden's Equity Alliance helped that planet and its entire sector maintain their independence. That makes it an appropriate toast for us on Iona today. This is my grandmother's special Gordonian brew. To Gordonia, and Iona."

"To Gordonia and Iona," we all repeat, lifting our glasses. Fallon throws the shot back in one gulp. Arden and Maybree do the same. I sip it first. It burns pleasantly going down, and the aftertaste is sweet and spicy, with notes of ginger and cardamom.

Next to me, Wenda screws up the nerve to throw all of hers back, coughing and choking a little in its aftermath. I take another sip, then follow suit.

"What was in that brew?" I ask.

"Family recipe," Fallon responds. "Top secret."

It's the last moment of levity we have that morning.

While others go off to their assignments, Fallon and I tackle the depressing subject of what needs to happen with the equipment and samples in Number 4 once she's no longer here.

"I've already sent a step-by-step plan to your holo," she says in a listless voice. "It explains what everything is, and how to maintain it in a viable state. I've spent enough time with Macha so that if you need to reconstitute any of the materials we've been using after I'm gone, she should be able to help. She's got a copy of the plan too."

"What if you don't go back?" I ask.

"What if sand lizards fly?" she responds, not looking up from her holo. "I tried to fight the recall. Arden got Tactical involved. Graham called in a bunch of favors. But they're still coming for me."

"Is it possible to simply refuse to leave with them?"

She looks thoughtful for a moment.

"I heard someone tried that once," she says. "He's dead now."

Alrighty then.

I don't mention it again. Fallon departs for Clinical at 11:00 hours to help prepare the patients for their final dose of antidote. It feels like only a handful of minutes have gone by when Macha hails me at 12:45 to let me know things are on schedule and it's time for my part in the process.

I ping Maybree and Arden to let them know I'm heading to Clinical. Next, I hail Fanny to check in. When she responds, her voice is thin and raw. "Thank you for hailing instead of just showing up," she says, her exhaustion clear. "I don't want company, but I can't seem to get rid of Tommas. He hailed last night after we left Clinical. He just hailed me again to announce he's coming by after lunch to 'make me feel better'. If he was really trying to make me feel better, it might be all right. But he only wants to know about everything that he wasn't part of. I don't have the energy to support some nosy gossip's ego."

This doesn't surprise me; Tommas has always struck me as awkward and grasping. "Didn't you say you broke up with him?"

"I did, but he apparently didn't notice," Fanny says, pausing to blow her nose. "I'm hiding out in my room today. If he knocks on the door, I'm not answering. And I'm not inclined to feel bad about it."

"You have my full support," I say, and log off.

I arrive at exactly 13:00 hours. Fallon and Macha are waiting in the Blue ward, reviewing notes on a holo. Pauly has been moved down the hall to a private room, so only Karloa and the mystery man are here now, both apparently sleeping peacefully. Soft light streams in through the window at the far end of the room, highlighting their faces. It feels so different than it did last night, and for a moment I'm overwhelmed with a powerful sense of optimism.

Fallon looks up when I come to the doorway and waves me inside. She looks serious and drawn except for a fresh coat of vibrant pink lipstick. On Holly, the color looks delicate and sweet, like cotton candy, but on Fallon it reaches a level of powerful in-your-face intensity I would never have expected this shade to achieve.

"Where's Graham?" she asks. "Did he come with you?"

"No. I thought he'd already be here. He must be at his pod."

I tap into his private channel and hail him, but there's no answer.

"He's probably on his way," I say, with more confidence than I feel. It's not like Graham to be out of contact like this.

"I don't want to wait too long," Macha says. "We'll need time to react if there are any problems with the awakening process, and I would prefer to deal with any issues before Fallon has to leave us." Fallon looks glum at the reminder but nods her agreement.

Fifteen minutes pass, and Graham does not appear, nor does he answer our hails. Maybree hasn't seen him; Arden hasn't seen him. I'm concerned, but we don't have time to go looking for him. We need to start.

Without Graham, we need someone to provide a point of focus for Karloa when she awakens. Given how negative my interactions with her were, we decide that Macha will take that role. I'll still stand as point person for the mystery man.

We take our places, with a technician administering the final awakening cocktail to Karloa, while Macha stands next to her bed, leaning over her. Fallon keeps an eye on drone readings and monitors from the other side of the room.

Karloa has no trouble swallowing the cocktail, and within a few seconds her eyelids flutter open, and she draws in a deep breath.

"What happened?" she says softly, her voice faint and hoarse. "Where am I?"

"You're in Clinical on Iona," says Macha, patting Karloa's hand. "You were in stasis. You're going to be fine."

"Oh ... I ... you brought me *out* of stasis?" she whispers.

"Yes, and everyone in this room helped in some way." Macha steps back so Karloa can look around her. When Karloa's eyes fall on me, I hold my breath, but there is only a momentary flinch from her before her eyes drop to the mystery man and her expression changes into one of expansive joy.

"You found him? You brought him out of stasis, too?" she says, in a tone of wonder.

"Yes," I say. "We'll wake him up next."

"Oh! I thought I'd never see him again." Tears are spilling from Karloa's eyes now and she seems to have forgotten anyone else is in the room. "He's all right?"

"Yes, he's fine," Macha says. "You're both perfectly fine and healthy."

"Thank you, thank you so much," Karloa says, looking from Macha to me. "I don't know how you did it but ... such a gift, I can't thank you enough."

"You're very welcome," I say. "I'm glad you know who he is. He didn't have any identification on him when we found him, and I was worried he would be alone here when he woke up. Who is he?"

Karloa's eyes light up as she looks at the face of the mystery man again. "He's my fiancé," she says, beaming with love. "His name is Tommas Berinbart."

MY BODY GOES COLD. Fallon gasps aloud and snaps her holo shut. I do my best to maintain a calm pleasant face for Karloa as I say, "Welcome back, Karloa. Macha will awaken Tommas now, and you two can have some time together. I'll come back later to see how you're doing."

I must be a better actor on the outside than I am on the inside, because Karloa smiles broadly at me and nods her head. Macha steps forward with a cocktail for the real Tommas, and all Karloa's attention goes to her fiancé.

Fallon and I sprint out of the room.

"I know where he is, I know where he is," I say breathlessly. "We have to get over to Fanny's pod. He was going there after lunch."

We run down the stairs and grab two scooters. As we fly across the square, I try desperately to hail Fanny and Graham. No response. I hail Arden on his private channel. "Tommas is the impostor," I tell him. "We're on the way to Fanny's. We can't raise Fanny or Graham."

"On my way," he says. "Be careful."

Fallon and I pull into the pod's courtyard and drop our scooters. It's well past lunch and the pod is quiet. We exchange anxious glances as we creep toward the kitchen entry. It's eerily silent as we step inside, and we pause, listening. The whisper of Iona's sands suddenly seems deafening.

And then we hear a moan.

It's low and oddly muffled, and we can't get a fix on it at first.

"Where?" Fallon mouths to me. I point toward the door to the pod's supply locker, and we both warily take several steps in its direction.

Another moan, still muffled, but slightly louder.

Executive decision time. I push Fallon behind me, slide back the single bar that keeps the locker closed, and throw open the door.

Inside, Graham is lying on the floor. His face is swaddled in a rich purple cloth, and as Fallon and I pull him out of the locker into the kitchen, I notice the edge is torn and frayed.

I prop him up as Fallon removes the fabric from his head. He's only barely conscious. As the last piece falls away, I first see the gash on the back of his head where he was clearly struck with something large and heavy. But my heart almost stops when I see a pattern of blue on his face, starting at his nose and spreading across his features like a wave.

"Don't panic," I say, speaking as much to myself as to Fallon or Graham. "Fallon, hail Macha, get a gurney here. Let's get him out into the courtyard."

We pull Graham through the kitchen and out into the courtyard, as far away from the pod structure as possible. I can't help but be reminded of him pulling Pauly and then me through the smoke-filled warehouse months ago, and I find myself becoming almost impossibly angry.

"Sand?" puzzles Fallon.

I remember the long process we followed with Holly, and although it breaks my heart when I say it, I know my answer is the right one.

"We don't have time," I say. "We have to get inside *now*."

Fallon takes a moment to sprinkle a light dusting of sand across Graham's cheeks, her expression unreadable. Then we both head into the pod at a dead run, slowing only when we reach the middle of the common room.

It's quiet. There's no one here.

"Fanny?" I call. There's no answer, but I hear something—a scraping and thumping, coming from the small hallway that leads to Fanny's room. "Fanny, are you there?"

Fallon and I walk stealthily to the entrance and peer down the hall. At its far end is the blocked lift to the ruined Star Parlor. Halfway down the hall is Fanny's closed door.

"Fanny?" I call again, and we move quietly down the hallway. I lift my hand to knock, but we're startled by a voice from behind us.

"I don't think she's home," the voice says. We spin around to see the person we've thought of all this time as Tommas, standing about twenty feet away, blocking the hallway's exit to the common room. In one hand he holds a metal cannister with a spray nozzle. In the other is a small electronic device, flashing red.

A detonator.

"We know who you are, Arduval," Fallon says. The false Tommas lets out a long, put-upon sigh.

"Looks like you woke up my sister and she gave me up," he says and shrugs. "We have a *complicated* relationship. Although it was so very kind of her to share her credentials with me so I could get into the storage warren. Technically, I suppose, she didn't really share them—I just took them. But she was turning blue, so it wasn't going to be an inconvenience for her."

"Karloa didn't give you up," I say. "We figured it out without her."

"No matter." His eyes glitter. "She preferred that goon she met on Bardazel to me anyway. He was trying to convince her to leave with him. I couldn't let that happen."

"You dosed the real Tommas and assumed his identity. Why complicate things by sending him to Iona?" I ask. "Why send him to *me*?"

He barks out a laugh. "Well, I promised Karloa that I wouldn't separate them. I'm not a complete shit."

"We clearly have different definitions of what makes someone a shit," Fallon interjects.

Arduval rolls his eyes dramatically.

"Fallon, I'm hurt," he says, his voice dripping with sarcasm. "Please don't interrupt me. Faith asked a question. I'd like to answer it."

Fallon raises one eyebrow and gestures dramatically. "Do continue."

He huffs briefly, as if irritated, and resumes his speech.

"I had the crate addressed to you as soon as I found out you were Karloa's pod leader. I thought you would open it right away, you see, and Karloa would get the message that I was watching and not done with her yet. I intended it to be added insurance that she wouldn't give away my plans, and to send a message to Governor Thorn as well. But you didn't do that. So I had to go to Plan B."

"You dosed her," I say.

"I did." He shakes the cannister in his hand. "With something quite similar to this, in fact."

"What's the point of attacking Iona?" Fallon asks abruptly. "Didn't you finish the job you were hired for on Bardazel?"

"Oh, but there was so much more to do," he says, smirking. "Iona is extremely valuable real estate. After I take care of the little detail of turning it into a pariah planet, I'll be in line for some rich rewards from my employer."

"Too bad you won't live long enough to collect them," Arden's voice rings out in the common room. I can't see him, but I know he wouldn't have come to this fight unarmed.

Kerrit Arduval looks toward him and strangely, inexplicably, *smiles.*

"Oh good," he says, licking his lips. "Commander Wilson. Right on time. I would hate for you to miss this. I'd planned for you all to simply die together, but you know, plans change."

I hear Arden shift. Arduval immediately responds, waving the detonator in the air. "I wouldn't do that if I were you, Commander. This device is connected to dozens of spheres of Blue, placed strategically all around this rotten little town. The instant I activate it, they blow, and Blue goes everywhere. Basic math. You get to pick between two dead people or two hundred dead people, give or take."

"Dead people?" Fallon says, her expression hardening. "You've done something to make Blue lethal, then?"

"Mmm yes," Arduval replies, keeping a wary eye on Arden. "Stasis first, followed by death a few days later. We don't have the storage space for all those bodies. You'll be able to experience it firsthand because I'm going to share a little with all three of you. I field tested it a few moments ago on Governor Thorn. It can be delivered in many ways, but my theory is that it will be particularly effective applied to fabric and held to the victim's face."

My stomach flips over. It's bad enough thinking about Graham going into stasis, but at least we know how to deal with that now. But dead, in a matter of days?

"Does your employer know about this 'enhancement'? Because the fact that it *didn't* actually kill people was the entire value of Blue as a weapon," Fallon says. "The Governance Council takes an extremely dim view of genocide for profit. Those rich rewards you're anticipating may not stack up well once whoever hired you figures that out."

Arduval's bravado falters for a moment, but he recovers quickly.

"Fortunately, my employer isn't bound by the directives of the Governance Council," he says with a sneer. Fallon and I exchange glances quickly; we both know what this means—Arduval may not be working for the Company after all.

"Who was stupid enough to pay you to do this?" I ask. I'm furious. I'm not going to let this slime keep playing games with us without giving something up. But Arduval merely smirks and offers no reply.

"You know," he finally says, resuming his bizarre conversational cadence, "this cannister will direct a jet of liquid accurately to a distance of thirty feet. It's a highly accurate spraying mechanism, with hardly any scatter. That's another enhancement I made." He shakes the cannister. Fallon and I involuntarily jump; I reach for her hand, and we back up a dozen more steps, beyond Fanny's door.

"In an enclosed space like, oh, say, a short narrow hallway, you wouldn't need much scatter to be infected yourself," Fallon says. "I'm confident you haven't been able to make any enhancements that violate basic physics."

Arduval shrugs in response. "It's not a problem. Thanks to my sister, I have the advantage of being immune to all forms of Blue."

"We found the serum in her pack," Fallon says. "We've all had some, so we're immune, too. Now what?"

"Now nothing." Arduval says with a smirk. "I knew someone would find those vials eventually. I removed the real immunity serum before we left Bardazel and replaced it with a placebo. The mat tracker let me know the instant you opened her pack, so I was able to time everything perfectly. I'm sorry to tell you, nothing you've consumed has conveyed any immunity at all."

Suddenly, Arduval swings away from us and fires the spray stream into the common room. I hear Arden cry out, and then a thump as he falls to the floor.

"No!" I shout. I'm consumed by fury and anguish, and what I want most in the world right now is to rush forward and slam my fist into Arduval's face, but Fallon catches my arm and pulls me back.

Arduval turns his full attention to us. "I wanted him to see you die, Faith," he says, taking slow steps toward us. "I thought I'd be satisfied with just killing him at first, but then I found you here. Such an instigator, ready to cause even more complications with your probing and planning and heroic deeds. And your past with the Company, and the secrets that only the two of you know ... it was beyond perfect. Alas, with Commander Wilson dying in the common room now, your demise will be somewhat less satisfying. But I at least have the bonus of killing off one of the most imperious arrogant bitches I've ever met along with you, so that will make up for it *a bit*."

"Why thank you, you sweet talker, you," says Fallon drily. "And all this time I had no idea what Fanny saw in you." We take several more steps back, almost to the end of the hallway, as Arduval continues to stalk forward.

"Fanny," Arduval snorts, casting a sidelong glance at her door. "That was really taking one for the team. But it was the only way to insert myself somewhere I could track everyone crucial to my plan. I suppose Fanny might have grown on me over time. But alas, it was not to be. Just more collateral damage, like her brother and that kid who lost his arm, and his irritating chirpy girlfriend. I do owe you a debt, Fallon, for proving my employer's theory about the sands of Iona. That little adventure with the girl did not go as I'd intended, but in the end, it saved me a lot of time. And everyone's preoccupation with it made it much easier for me to plant explosives in the belongings you were having dragged up to the Star Parlor. If only you'd stayed on task, I could have taken out the lot of you in one go. It would have been so much more efficient. "

"Sorry to have inconvenienced you," growls Fallon.

My headset suddenly crackles to life, and I hear a commotion. Then Graham—*Graham?*—says, "Keep him talking, Faith. We're moving in."

"What did you expect to gain by sending that crate that exploded on Pauly?" I ask, frowning. "What was the point of injuring *him?*"

Arduval rolls his eyes again and throws me an impassive look. "That was meant for Graham Thorn. I had envisioned him rushing to open that Warehouse crate as soon as you discovered Tommas. It was designed to do exactly what it did, you see." As he speaks, Arduval is raising both hands, holding the detonator high in one hand while carefully aiming the sprayer at us. "But that idiot brother of Fanny's got to it first. One more change in plans. Enough questions now, children. It doesn't matter. It all ends for Iona and for you, right now."

Suddenly a thunderous roar and blaze of light erupts from our left, followed by a deluge of disintegrated plexi, dirt, and metal raining down on us.

Fallon and I crouch low and cover our heads. As the last bit of plexi falls to the floor, I see the very little that remains of Kerrit Arduval, still holding the spray cannister and detonator, covered with the very little that remains of the wall between Fanny's room and the hallway. Through the floating haze of dust sparkling in the sun from her bedroom window, I see Fanny, her back braced against Pauly's rolltop desk, a fiercely determined look on her face and Fallon's freshly fired weapon in her hands.

37

Shouting and the sound of people running toward us fills the Common Room. Within seconds, Graham and Maybree appear at the end of the hallway. "Are you all right?" Graham calls out, as Fallon and I slowly stand amid the rubble. I look at Fallon, whose expression could not be more smug. She surveys the vaguely disgusting remains of Kerrit Arduval and her lips curve up in satisfaction.

"We're fabulous," she says, straightening herself and smoothing her hair with one hand, as though it's not full of dust and plastic particles. "But I think fake Tommas just got the point that Fanny doesn't want to see him anymore."

Graham is picking his way through the debris, working his way toward us. I'm relieved to see only a faint blue spatter across his nose, like an old tattoo, instead of the rapidly spreading bright turquoise I expected.

Maybree gestures to me. "Come out here," she says. "Arden needs you."

Graham reaches out one hand and helps me climb through the destruction until I reach the part of the hallway that still has its structural integrity.

My heart leaps when I see Arden, not dead but sitting upright on the floor, rubbing his face and cursing energetically. There is a pale blue pattern like an old cobweb stretching from his right eye to his temple and up into his hairline on the right side of his forehead. Macha is kneeling beside him, but when she sees me emerge from the hallway, she stands and steps back with an encouraging smile.

I run to him and collapse at his side, throwing my arms around him and feeling the terror I've been holding in reserve bubble up to the surface.

"Sonofabitch got me right in the eye," Arden mutters.

"I thought you were dead! Why aren't you dead?" I shriek nonsensically, gasping with relief. Inexplicably, I then punch him hard in the arm.

"Ow!" he objects, grabbing his bicep where my fist landed. "Should I apologize for not being dead?"

I'm laughing and crying at the same time. He looks into my eyes and tucks another wild strand of my hair behind my ear.

"I thought you were dead too," he says. "For a second, I thought we all were. How did Fallon get her weapon back?"

"She didn't," I say. "It was Fanny."

"There are a lot of heroes here today," Macha says, as Maybree emerges from the hallway, carefully carrying the detonator and the spray cannister. She's followed by Graham and Fallon, both of whom have their arms around Fanny to steady her as she walks. Her expression is vacant and it's clear that she's in shock. They ease her to the floor next to Arden and me, and I immediately hug her tight.

"You saved us all," I say. She shakes her head.

"No, no ... it's just ... I saw Tommas come into the pod, and I thought he was here to pester me with more questions, so I hid in my room. Then I heard him attack Graham in the common room, and I was so scared ... I remembered Fallon's weapon was still in the desk, and ... I couldn't let him kill you, I couldn't let him say those things about Pauly ..."

Her voice breaks and she begins to sob.

"It's all right, Fanny," I say quietly. "He was an awful person. Worse than you know. He was never who he pretended to be."

Macha insists on diagnostics for all of us, although they reveal nothing terribly wrong beyond stress, exhaustion, and a few bruises and scrapes. Even Arden and Graham, whom I took for dead based on Arduval's claims, check out fine, although both seem to have acquired a permanent faint tattoo where the Blue initially hit them.

Fanny is rattled but unharmed, and gratefully accepts sedation and a room next door to Pauly's. The rest of us huddle in a conference room on the third floor, overlooking the little desert garden.

"Am I the only person confused that Arden and Graham aren't dead?" I ask.

Macha smiles. "I hear you've all had a dose of immunity serum, and it appears to work."

Fallon huffs in indignation and mutters, "Of course it works."

"When did anybody get a dose of immunity serum?" Now I'm deeply confused.

"I got some a couple of nights ago. I was a test case," Graham offers.

"He didn't drop dead, so the rest of us got a dose this morning," Fallon says.

Of course. I hear Fallon's voice over breakfast, saying *this is my grandmother's special Gordonian brew.*

"But Arduval said he replaced the immunity serum in Karloa's pack with something else, how did you …"

Fallon interrupts me.

"I knew that wasn't genuine immunity serum the instant I started working with it. Fortunately, I was able to get my hands on the real thing."

A conspiratorial smile passes between Graham and Fallon.

"The missing Sprites?" I ask. "Graham had them, all this time?"

"I had some of them," he admits. "Arduval got three. But I got the first four."

"And you didn't let us know this exactly *why*?"

"When I saw what the Sprites contained, I was worried," he says. "I didn't know who was expecting it or what they might do with it. I didn't want anyone to know I had them before I got that figured out. Once Fallon told us they were intended for her and it turned out she needed them to complete the antidote, I had to sort out my next move."

Graham looks down at his hands contemplatively. "I shouldn't have even had to think about it. My family's enterprise has been interested in Blue since I started working with it on Bardazel, and this could have been a tremendous boost for their plans. But it was obvious that returning them to Fallon was the right thing to do."

"That night you two went up on the ridge," I say. "You went to where Graham had hidden the Sprites."

"Yes," Fallon confirms. "That was the last piece of the puzzle I needed. Otherwise, I couldn't have gotten everything ready before my time here was up."

Everyone goes quiet at her words, considering the fact of Fallon's impending removal.

"That's the other thing," Arden says quietly. "The skiff's been cleared to leave Meridian Station. They'll be here tomorrow."

"Terrific," she mutters. "I guess it's time to pack."

The next morning, I'm awakened by the vibration of my headset. When I drop it on and tap in, it's Maybree. I can tell by her voice that she's exhausted, but at least she has good news.

"Two things. Thing one, we found and neutralized all the spheres that were attached to Arduval's detonator," she reports. "It took a little reverse engineering and some luck, but we did it. If we go by Fallon's last count as our benchmark, all the spheres are accounted for. So that's good as long as her math is correct. Sending out a reminder to all holos today to be on the lookout for anything suspicious, though, just in case."

"Great work, Maybree. That's a huge relief."

"Thanks. But now for the less-great part, Thing Two. Fallon's not wearing a headset, as usual, so someone needs to tell her the skiff is in range. They've kept their flight plan dark so I can't pinpoint the exact moment of arrival, but it appears they'll touch down within the next hour."

"Who's aboard?"

"The pilot's name is Nam. The Company rep is listed as a Dr. Ardea. I can't find any information about them on the stream, not even a profile. It's got to be an alias."

Maybree signs off. I jab Arden in the ribs and wake him. "Do you know a Dr. Ardea in the Company hierarchy?" I ask. He blinks for a moment, rubbing sleep from his eyes, then murmurs, "No. What's this about?"

"That's who's on the skiff. Maybree can't find any information about them. Would the Company send someone out under an alias?"

"Sure, if the person is high-profile. It's a tactical security protocol."

"We're about to start screwing around with a Company official who is high-profile enough to travel incognito?"

Arden sits up in our hammock and stretches. Only the pitch of his shoulders and the set of his mouth show he's feeling the same tension I am.

"Sounds about right," he says flatly.

I sigh. "All righty then," I mutter. "Let the games begin."

At least they won't catch us unaware. Even though we can't be certain when they'll arrive, cold skiff landings aren't uncommon on this planet. We would be prepared under normal circumstances. We'll be prepared today.

In the common room, Fallon sits at the far end of the table, glued to a holotablet. As I walk in, she looks up, her eyes wide, biting her lower lip. She already knows what I'm about to say.

"They're in range," I confirm.

Her jaw clenches and her expression shifts to pure frustration, but she doesn't comment. Instead, she drops her attention back to the holo. "The stream is insane today," she says.

"Do I want to know what kind of stuff is coming up?"

"Probably not." Fallon scowls. "Just more drek about the terrible lawless troublemakers causing problems for the good and gentle people of Iona. There's a lot of friendly chatter about Kerrit Arduval."

I nearly drop my cup. "Why?"

"Here. Take a look." Fallon flips the stream up into the air in front of us. I see a photo of a young, slender Arduval I barely recognize. He's outfitted in coveralls and standing in front of a docking port. The picture must be at least twenty years old. The accompanying description doesn't identify him by name or as an attacker, but instead captions him as a resident, recently relocated from Bardazel, who died in the disruptions on Iona.

"That's rich," I mutter. "He died trying to kill us all."

All three of us know what's going on here. It's the Company's favorite tactic: control the narrative. If the true narrative doesn't support your position, invent one that does and popularize it until it seems more credible than the truth.

"We can't let them do this," I say. "We have to get the story of what really happened out there."

"We might be about to get some help with that," Arden says, taking a large bite of his breakfast and chewing casually. I stare at him hard, but he never looks up from his plate.

Fallon reaches over and slaps the fork out of his hand.

"Tell us what you mean, you blistering jackass," she snaps. "Really, Faith, I don't know how you put up with this."

Arden has the good sense to look apologetic.

"I can't say more because I'm not sure yet. But I *think* there might be some help on the skiff coming in from the Company," he says.

As if cued by his words, we hear the rumble of a skiff passing low overhead, descending toward our landing pads. Fallon lets out a long sigh, and I hear the request for Incoming support go out on the general channel.

The next voice over the channel is Arden's, an odd stereo effect since he's sitting next to me. "Wilson, Feathergrass, and Thorn responding to Pad Arrivals in five. Divest cargo at site, pending instructions. Security consult requested prior to disembark."

"On it," Maybree's voice comes through my headset.

Arden rises from his seat. "Let's go," he says.

331

"What's this about? You never work Pad Arrivals. You, me, and Graham? What are you up to?"

"We're dangerous anarchists, remember?" Arden says. "Obviously we should be the ones to welcome the Company to poor troubled Iona. Come along, you'll see." He looks at Fallon. "Especially you. Come on, you too."

Fallon huffs as she stands, her expression resolute. "Fine. Let's get this over with."

By the time we reach the pad, the skiff's cargo has been removed to a hover-flat and floats a short distance away. I punch into its console the coordinates for the Preservation Theater, where Wenda is busy creating a temporary home for Fanny, Karloa, and Tommas, as well as our overnight guests. The volume of cargo looks suspicious to me; it's a lot for two people who are just here to grab a recalcitrant employee and depart. I try to catch Arden's eye, but he's very carefully not looking in my direction.

Graham waves to us from the control shack. "Finishing enviroscans now," he says.

"Certifying clear to disembark," Arden responds with a thumbs-up. In a few moments, the skiff's underbelly slowly drops open and two people appear at the top of the narrow ramp.

The first to stride down it is a young man with tawny skin and jet-black hair. He wears a pilot's uniform with Company insignia in the Tactical Division's distinctive colors. He's crackling with energy and alertness.

He immediately approaches Arden and offers a formal salute, which Arden returns before pulling him into a bear hug.

"Euc, it's good to see you," he says. The younger man laughs. "Same, Sir," he responds.

Arden turns to the rest of us, his arm still around the pilot's shoulders.

"This is Lieutenant Euclid Nam, one of the best pilots in Tactical, and one of the Company's most trusted fliers. He also happens to be a valuable member of the Equity Alliance. Euc often gets chosen for tricky diplomatic missions, so it wasn't terribly hard to pull the strings that got him this assignment."

Before I can wipe the astonished expression off my face, the second figure moves down the ramp with a smooth, powerful walk. Strong blue eyes peer out over the edge of a complement of sand-resistant head and neck gear, all very finely made. As the individual stops in front of us, I'm struck by both their height and upright perfect posture. This is someone who must be highly placed within the Company and has the power and confidence to make a truly formidable enemy. But as the coverings are unwound, I'm amazed to see a face that could almost belong to someone I know, if she were perhaps twenty-five years older.

"Mom?" gasps Fallon.

"Surprise," says Arden wryly.

Chief Medical Officer Janelle Heron pulls off the last of her elaborate headwear and smiles at her daughter.

"Hello, everyone," she says, her voice rich and sonorous. "Fallon, dear. I told the Managing Director that, as your mother, I would be able to ensure you returned promptly and caused no trouble. Of course, you've never listened to me a day in your life, but let's get the official business out of the way. I'm charged with ordering you return to Home World with us immediately, where you will go before the Performance Board like a good girl and accept the severe consequences for your terrible anarchistic anti-Company actions. Will you?"

Fallon lifts her chin, eyes glittering, a hint of a smirk tugging at the corners of her mouth. "Absolutely not," she says.

Her mother smiles again. "I thought as much. Insurrection it is, then. Lieutenant, if you would be so good as to let our handlers know we are unable to secure Ms. March and will be returning shortly."

Lieutenant Nam nods curtly, and steps away from the group, pulling out a holo and messaging someone on a private channel. Dr. Heron holds out her arms and steps forward to fold her daughter into a massive hug, which Fallon winces through.

"Returning shortly?" asks Fallon, finally disentangling herself from her mother's arms. "You're going back? But I could really use your help with ..."

"Those were our instructions," Dr. Heron interrupts. Her tone is nothing short of amused as she continues. "Of course, I understand maintenance issues often occur on little modular boats like this. Easy to build, easy to break, as they say. Really, anything could happen." Her gaze shifts between Arden and Euclid Nam, who has completed his call and rejoined us. Both men wear deadpan expressions.

Graham leans out of the control shack and says, "Ten minutes."

"Excellent," says Arden. "Everyone, follow me." He leads us well away from the pad back toward the Square. I see Graham leave the control shack and enter the belly of the skiff. A few minutes later, he exits the skiff and catches up with us.

"Not long now," he says.

"What are we waiting for?" I ask.

The question is barely out of my mouth when I hear popping and sizzling coming from the skiff. Its support struts suddenly disintegrate, and the craft drops heavily to the ground, crushing the still-extended ramp underneath. A few seconds later, a soft contained "whoomph" sound tells me that something inside its cockpit has burst into flames. Its viewports cloud over with smoke, and the acrid smells of burning plexi and electronics fill the air.

"Mechanical difficulties," Lt. Nam says impassively. "Most unfortunate. I believe our return will be delayed."

"Surprise again," Arden says, this time with more enthusiasm. "Let's all get a drink, shall we? And get our guests settled in? Maintenance will want to look at that craft, although really ... looks like scrap to me."

38

"You knew this was happening all along?" I ask as we cross the sands to the Preservation Theater. "And you couldn't be bothered to tell me?"

"Not exactly," he says, his expression shadowing and becoming more circumspect. I know from our years together that this is a sign he's processing an unanticipated result. "I got Euc in the control seat early on; he was already in line for the assignment and an obvious choice from the Company's standpoint, so that was an easy sell. But I couldn't find a way to influence which Company rep made the trip. Initially, we heard it was going to be the new head of Operational Security. Dr. Heron was very vocal about not wanting to get involved. I didn't know she was aboard until she came off the skiff. Although when you asked about Dr. Ardea this morning, that made me hopeful."

"You said you didn't know a Dr. Ardea."

"I don't. But I do know that *ardea* is a historical genus designation for the bird known colloquially as a heron."

I'm so stunned I have to remind myself to keep walking.

"An ideal time to mention that would have been this morning when I asked you," I say, trying hard to keep my voice even.

Arden blinks. "I guess," he says. "But I wasn't sure, and ..."

It's the same argument. *Again.* I rub my temples in frustration.

"When are you going to stop this?" I ask, my irritation bubbling over. "You need to tell me what's going on while it's happening, not afterwards. I worry that there's a potential sucker punch coming I'll never see, just because you decided to keep me in the dark. I have to be able to protect myself, Arden, and I can't if I don't know what's going on. And don't you dare say I should just let you protect me. I'll punch you right here."

Arden's response is part laugh, part choking sound. "Okay," he sputters as we mount the steps and walk into the cool dark of the Theater. "I guess I'll work on that."

The space Wenda has created in the Theater's row of old shopfronts is nothing short of magical. Hammocks hang neatly in the smaller shop spaces; privacy curtains cover the age-marked plexi that looks out on the square. The lollipop mermaid smiles at us from the wall of the newly designated common room. Food and drink are laid out on a long communal table at its center and the fireplace glows invitingly. Near the fireplace are a smattering of upholstered chairs and piles of soft floor pillows. The remaining former retail shelves now hold flickering votive candles and smartly folded paper birds.

Across from me, Wenda and Maybree settle together into a comfy pillow-pile like nesting doves. Fallon and her mother chat near the fireplace, each unconsciously mirroring the other's physical posture and facial expressions. Arden continues his energetic reunion with Lt. Nam. Graham settles into a seat near Fallon and her mother. Fanny joins us as well, and plops down onto a pillow next to me, briefly resting her head on my shoulder before pulling out her ubiquitous flask and offering it to Maybree.

Maybree is so focused on her holo she doesn't even notice. Wenda repeatedly elbows her in the side until she finally looks up from her device.

"Sorry," she mutters, accepting the flask and throwing back a shot, then handing it to Wenda. "I got caught up in the stream."

"Anything new?" I ask.

"Not on the general stream, it's still the same old same old about violent insurrectionists blah-blah-blah. Sorry, Wenda, you're still not making the cut. I know it's a dream of yours. You'll just have to try harder."

Wenda snickers.

"But there's something that just came through on the Company stream," Maybree continues. "I don't speak Corporate Jerk-ese, so I'm not sure what it means, but if you Company types could take a look …?"

Maybree flips the display into the air and the communique materializes above us, ominously blocking my view of half the room. The genial hum of conversation is replaced by anxious silence.

Lt. Nam is the first to speak.

"The Company has petitioned the Governing Council for Transactional Jurisdiction of Iona," he says. "They're claiming their personnel and property are at imminent risk and are asking the Council to let them take over until the threat has been neutralized."

"Gosh, are we going to need a defensive force?" Maybree asks, her eyebrows arching upward. "I mean, we have a security team, but I don't think thirty-five people with stun sticks will be much of a match if the Company sends out a Tactical Squadron."

"They can't send out a Tactical Squadron without approval from the Governing Council," Lt. Nam responds, "and the Council would never authorize it. But they *will* seriously consider an application like this. If the Council decides the Company's claims are legitimate, they'll next look to see if the Company might otherwise financially benefit from the arrangement—if there's an emolument entailed, so to speak. If not, Transactional Jurisdiction is likely to be granted. There will be hearings and information gathering to get through, of course, but if things go their way, the Company could be running Iona in a couple of weeks without ever firing a shot."

Arden nods. "That's how they like to do things. Killing is messy and makes people emotional. Legal acrobatics are neat and just as effective."

"But there's clearly an enormous financial incentive," I object. "We know that they want to control the sand. It's an obvious conflict of interest."

"*We* know that, but with Arduval dead and no traceable connection between him and the Company, we don't have any proof," Arden says. "The Company will argue that Blue was never intended to be a weapon, and with Graham painted as part of the 'insurrection,' his testimony will be easily discounted. We can work with Transactional Jurisdiction. There are rules about what they can and can't do here, and those rules will be enforced by the Governing Council. If we play it right, we might be able to turn this into a win for Iona."

I roll my eyes hard. "When has the Company ever cared about the rules?"

"Exactly!" adds Wenda. "There's nothing that the Company can do for Iona that wouldn't be better if we did it ourselves. We *must* maintain control of our own destiny. I can't believe you're saying that!"

"The Company has incredible resources," Dr. Heron chimes in. "Consider what a planet like this could do with those resources. And Transactional Jurisdiction is temporary. Why not try to figure out how to take advantage of it rather than expend what little energy you have fighting it?"

"Mom, please! You know as well as I do that Transactional Jurisdiction is nearly always a steppingstone to a full-blown takeover. What if people here don't want to take that risk?" Fallon interjects.

"It doesn't sound like they have much of a choice, dear. Things are what they are."

Suddenly the entire room is embroiled in clashing opinions and vigorous protestation.

I almost have to shout to regain control.

"We have proof that the Company has a vested interest in the sand. At least, I know where we can get it," I say, loudly enough that every person goes quiet and turns toward me. "The same thing happened on Bardazel. Right?"

Heads nod agreement.

"There are 200 people—your people, Arden, Company people—who know for a fact what Kerrit Arduval did on Bardazel, and why he did it. They're the link to the ulterior motive. Once the Governing Council hears from them, there's no way they'll grant this petition."

"Except they're all in stasis and we don't know where they are," Graham says.

"If we can find them, we know how to bring them out of stasis. Once revived, they can provide testimony to the Governing Council. And Arden, you have an idea of where they are, right?"

Arden eyes me cautiously. "They were initially sent to an enviro in orbit around Bardazel. We have intel that suggests they were moved back to the planet after the remaining refugees settled on Iona."

"We find them, revive them, and there's our proof," I say. "And once revived, those people will make up the numbers we need to petition the Governing Council to make Iona a Core World."

"Core Worlds can't be subjected to Transactional Jurisdiction," Graham adds. "That's genius."

"It's a wonderful thought, but we have no way to get to those people," Arden says. "While the Governing Council considers the Company's petition, all craft aside from its own are prohibited from landing here. The only skiff on the planet right now is fried on the landing pad and will take weeks to repair, if it can be repaired at all. So, we're basically stuck."

My turn.

"Come with me," I say, standing up and gesturing for everyone else to do the same. "I have something to show you."

I lead them out of the Theater in an impromptu parade, across the Square and up the small path that runs behind the landing pads. We're a funny sight, eight very different people traipsing around the cliff to the back of the ridge on this obscure, nearly hidden route. I can hear murmurs of curiosity behind me. No one has any idea what to expect.

Arden can't stand being in the dark, of course. He jogs to the head of the group and falls in beside me.

"Where are we going, Faith?" he asks. "What's this about?"

"We're going to see my pet project," I say. "It's all finished and ready to go."

"That's great and I'm proud of you, but we were in the middle of a very serious discussion, so I just don't know if this is the right time to ..."

I take great pleasure in interrupting him.

"Well, we're here now so might as well, right?"

We round the final bend and step into a massive natural cavern in the rock. There, gleaming even in our weak sunlight, is the project I've invested my heart and soul and thousands of hours into over the last several years.

"Lights," I say, and the ring of recessed lights I installed along the edge of the cavern come to life.

Arden stares.

"Surprise," I say.

Everyone walks forward slowly, as though they think what's in front of them might be an illusion. But when Arden puts his hand on the shiny white flank of my carefully constructed skiff, poised on its struts and ready for launch, a smile breaks across his face and his anxiety is replaced by a look of pure admiration. He chuckles aloud as he spots her name, painted in careful script across her nose.

"*Gabriella*," he reads aloud his eyes sparkling with amusement.

I'm delighted he remembers.

"She can be a little bumpy," I explain.

"You built a skiff," he says, tapping his knuckles against her hull.

"Re-built. It came in as salvage a few years after I arrived. Most of the interior and electronic components needed to be redone from scratch, though, so yeah, you could say I built a skiff. Its insides, anyway."

"Will it fly?"

"It will."

I look at each person now walking around my project and I'm not sure what I'm most proud of—this beautiful machine, or this beautiful community. Iona will be an Independent Core World one day. I'll do everything in my power to make sure that happens.

"Let's get back to the Theater," I say. "We have a rescue mission to plan."

39

EPILOGUE

OVER THE COURSE OF the next two days, Wenda starts work on the application to change Iona's status to Independent Core World, Dr. Heron and Lt. Nam keep pestering the Company for intel, and finally, Arden, Fallon, and I board my skiff for the nine-hour spaceflight to Bardazel. I'm excited and confident. This is going to be what saves Iona, what makes its future as a self-governing Independent Core World, what makes up for everything we all suffered at the hands of the Company. My anxiety and self-doubt fade away and are replaced by something that feels like pure relief as I guide my ship through the blackness of space.

It doesn't last.

We drop into orbit around Bardazel with Arden working the commscanner. "I'm not picking up the presence of the enviro," he says, checking and re-checking the display. "I'm getting too much atmospheric interference when I try to scan the surface."

The Bardazelian atmosphere is not what I was expecting. The planet's completely obscured by thick hot clouds, full of reflective particulate matter. Graham's told me multiple times how similar Iona and Bardazel are, but this is nothing like the slightly gritty atmosphere of the planet I now consider my home.

"Those clouds are really dense. It's odd Graham didn't mention this beforehand," Fallon says.

Arden mutters a disdainful, "Hm."

"I'm taking her in," I say. "I'll get us low so we can get a better view."

I fly down slowly. When we pierce the final cloud layer, we're a scant 250 meters above Bardazel's surface, and everyone aboard gasps at the scene.

Not only is there no enviro parked on the small planet, every structure and trace of settlement has been wiped away. The loose sandy ground that made Bardazel an ideal testing ground for Blue has been replaced by bare black rock stretching out in all directions, as far as can be seen. The only sand left on Bardazel now hangs in its atmosphere, blocking out the light of its sun.

The attacker is gone, but Iona is far from safe. Faith won't give up, but wrenching Iona from the Company's grasp may mean leaving behind everything—and everyone—she loves behind to risk it all on one last desperate plan. *Beyond This Dark Horizon*, the surprising conclusion to the Iona Duology, is available NOW!

- Read the first two chapters of *Beyond This Dark Horizon* **free!**
  https://BookHip.com/TDWALRR

- Buy *Beyond This Dark Horizon* from your favorite platform:
  https://books2read.com/u/3yAwXn

- Buy signed print copies and duology bundles directly from the author!
  https://emarierobertsonauthor.square.site/

- Subscribe to my newsletter, *Unreliable Narrator,* for progress updates,
  free fiction, and the occasional rant or cat picture:
  https://e-marie-robertson-author.kit.com/32a7431e0

Want to stay connected?

USE THIS QR CODE for all my links in one place: website, newsletter subscription, FREE Patreon, social media, ongoing promos, events and more!

*Find clickable links to all
my socials in one place!*

ACKNOWLEDGEMENTS

To say "it took a village" is a wild understatement; writing a novel is difficult enough, and dragging it through multiple edits and across the self-publishing process is something else again. And while many people played a role, a few played a key role, and I want to recognize them here.

First, my Discord writing group, especially the original Fab Four: Tracey Canole, Marc DeGeorge, Michelle A. Darnell, and J. Logan C. Rice. You read my work, you listened to my rants, you talked me off ledges, and you encouraged me to do more. You're the best and I'm so thankful for you.

I might never have figured out the twists, turns, and depths of indie publishing without the remarkable and generous Sarra Cannon. Sarra, you have been an invaluable example, support, and friend, and I'm so grateful to know you.

I might never have figured out the business and productivity side of writing without Amber McCue (who introduced me to Sarra, back in the day). Amber, you are a constant source of inspiration and encouragement, and I appreciate you so much.

I might never have figured out life without the ongoing sisterhood of the **YWLC**. Ladies, you know who you are ;)

Thank you to Evelyn Fasio for her encouragement and cheerleading from the very first version of this book, and to Lisa Lee of Lisa Lee Editing, for such stellar and speedy work!

I wouldn't have gotten through this at all without my wonderful husband, John Sams. I can't come up with enough words to adequately thank you, so I'll just tell everyone to never underestimate what the unconditional love of the right person can do in your life—no matter how long it takes you to find that right person. Thank you, honey, for everything.

Lastly, I want to acknowledge someone who's no longer with us—my friend John Bumgarner. Fifty or so years ago, I ran into him in the Bartow Public Library, reading a science fiction novel. I hadn't read *any* science fiction at that point, and he wrote down several recommendations for me. I took one of those books home, and a lifelong obsession began. Thanks for that, John Bum. I would that you were still here.

So many people helped me drag this book to its final form. From agents and editors who offered feedback, to fellow writers and old friends who offered encouragement, if you touched this manuscript please know how grateful I am for your contributions.

About the Author

E. Marie Robertson began her writing career in the 3rd grade by penning an epic that involved a ghost, a cave, and a magical ham sandwich. While perhaps less epic, her current collection of works in progress include science fiction, fantasy, alternate historical, and romantic comedy.

She produces an aspirationally-monthly newsletter, *Unreliable Narrator*, and hosts an even more sporadically-produced podcast for writers, *Read Write Geek*. When not working, writing, or podcasting (or worrying about working, writing, or podcasting), you'll find her reading, creating artwork, or making fun things out of paper. She currently lives in upstate South Carolina with her husband and their cats; they all dream of moving somewhere less humid.

Sign up to receive *Unreliable Narrator*, plus bonus fiction and sneak peeks, on her website at www.emarierobertson.com

www.ingramcontent.com/pod-product-compliance
Lightning Source LLC
Chambersburg PA
CBHW070332030726
47505CB00004B/1169